Frank Lee Benedict

Mr. Vaughan's Heir

A Novel

Frank Lee Benedict

Mr. Vaughan's Heir
A Novel

ISBN/EAN: 9783337349110

Printed in Europe, USA, Canada, Australia, Japan

Cover: Foto ©Andreas Hilbeck / pixelio.de

More available books at **www.hansebooks.com**

MR. VAUGHAN'S HEIR.

A Novel.

By FRANK LEE BENEDICT,

AUTHOR OF

"MY DAUGHTER ELINOR," "MISS VAN KORTLAND," "MISS DOROTHY'S CHARGE,"
"JOHN WORTHINGTON'S NAME," &c., &c.

NEW YORK:

HARPER & BROTHERS, PUBLISHERS,

FRANKLIN SQUARE.

1875.

Frank Lee Benedict's Novels.

MY DAUGHTER ELINOR. 8vo, Paper, $1 00 ; Cloth, $1 50.
Destined to attain a wide popularity.—*N. Y. Evening Post.*

MISS VAN KORTLAND. 8vo, Paper, $1 00 ; Cloth, $1 50.
Bright, lively, entertaining.—*N. Y. Tribune.*

MISS DOROTHY'S CHARGE. 8vo, Paper, $1 00 ; Cloth, $1 50.
The brightness, freshness, grace, and good feeling of the whole story.—*Standard*, London.

JOHN WORTHINGTON'S NAME. 8vo, Paper, $1 00 ; Cloth, $1 ~
Of all our American novelists, he is undoubtedly the most accomplished, the most vivacious, the most dram~
the most natural.—*Christian Intelligencer.*

MR. VAUGHAN'S HEIR. 8vo, Paper, $1 00 ; Cloth, $1 50.

PUBLISHED BY HARPER & BROTHERS, NEW YORK.

☞ HARPER & BROTHERS *will send either of the above works by mail, postage prepaid, to any part of the United States, on receipt of the price.*

Dedication.

———

To J. T. HART.

Dear Friend,

I dedicate to you this book, written in Florence during the past autumn made so pleasant to me by your companionship. It will reach you at the time when the work to which you have devoted ten years approaches completion. The .rt-lovers and art-students of our day have already pronounced their verdict thereupon, so that I only repeat what has been said and written scores of times when I express the certainty that, once chiseled into marble perfection, it will be acknowledged, not only by our own generation, but by all time to come, that the sculptor has equaled the genius as well as the patience of the old Greek masters.

FRANK LEE BENEDICT.

St. Dalmas di Tenda, Italy, 1874.

MR. VAUGHAN'S HEIR.

CHAPTER I.

LA MALADÈYRE.

It was a gorgeous September afternoon. The steamboat neared Lausanne, on its way up from Geneva to Villeneuve, and at length the far-famed lake began to redeem the promise held out by its reputation. Elizabeth Crauford sat on the deck, talked with her father, watched the people, and kept to herself a certain sense of disappointment which had been growing from Geneva to Ouchy. But once beyond the pretty little watering-place, with gloomy Lausanne frowning on the height above, the whole scene changed. The hills towered into mountains; in the far distance Mont Blanc showed like a pinnacle of yellow flame. Here the real beauty of the lake commences, increasing constantly, till, within the sight of Vevay and Clarens, its full perfection is reached, deserving to be raved over and to have poetry written about it even in this scoffing, materialistic age.

The sun was setting as they gained Vevay. Behind stretched a lofty mountain range, glorious with rainbow tints. In front rose the mighty Dent-du-Midi, with its eternal crown of snow, the Jamin peak and lesser crags guarding the head of the lake like giant sentinels. Another landing—a village which is in reality a bourg of Vevay, though taking a name from some picturesque ruins near the water.

"Perhaps it would have been better to leave the boat here," Mr. Cranford said; then, with characteristic vacillation, added immediately, "But we may as well go on to Clarens; La Maladèyre is nearer there, in fact."

Elizabeth was too well accustomed to unexpected propositions and their withdrawal on the part of her father, whether in regard to journeys or other matters, to pay much attention. She was gazing up and down the lake—watching the magic light—taking in every feature of the beautiful panorama. But she did not forget to answer. Mr. Crauford always waited for a reply to his suggestions. As a rule, the response, whatever it might be, did not exactly please him; but one of some sort must be given. So now Elizabeth said dutifully—

"Yes, papa."

Mr. Crauford neither noticed nor heard. He leaned over the railing, and looked earnestly out toward the left bank, close to which the boat ran. He had not seen the spot since he and his wife came here during their wedding journey. Mrs. Crauford had been dead many a day, and her widowed spouse was past fifty; still he liked to indulge in romance of a lachrymose and uncomfortable nature. He had determined to bring his daughter to visit the place in which he had been so happy, or thought he had, though he and his bride had quarreled a good deal on the banks of the famous Lake Leman, after the habit of newly married people, wherever they may chance to wander. He wanted to spend a month in the very house in which he and his lost angel had dwelt, and, writing to secure it, found himself obliged to pay a high price for the indulgence of his fancy. It was probable that he would be wretched, and would render his daughter, his faithful Gervais, and every body about him, as miserable as he well could.

There is no companion more to be dreaded on a journey than a man doing romance, unless it be one who means to write poetry about the marvelous scenes; they both invariably scold and find fault from morning to night.

Presently the boat passed a point of land jutting out into the lake, covered with trees, two great weeping-willows and three tall poplars conspicuous among them. Mr. Crauford pointed to the roof of a house visible amid the greenery, and spoke for the first time in many minutes.

"That is La Maladèyre, my dear."

Elizabeth looked and tried to feel sentimental, and to fancy her father and mother there in their youth; but the fitting poetic sadness refused to make itself felt—it never will when one tries to call it up. Somehow, her vagrant fancy would only picture her living parent in a hideous red and yellow dressing-gown, which he donned in the seclusion of his chamber, and her mother taking physic out of a large spoon. She had enough pleasanter recollections of that dead mother, but they refused to keep her company now.

The Clarens landing was reached; beyond lay Verney, Terretêt, and the Castle of Chillon; a little further sweep of water, then the vast mountains closed in the scene. It was almost dusk, but Elizabeth could perceive that Clarens was as unlike the Clarens of Rousseau as could well be imagined.

"It is not far down," Mr. Crauford said, as he and his daughter stood comfortably watching Gervais and Margot struggle with porters over the luggage. "We might walk; but we can easily get a carriage," he added, before she could agree to his first proposition.

Gervais learned that the road along the lake was undergoing repairs; it would be wise to take another which wound among the hills from Montreux to Veray. Six times Mr. Crauford changed his mind, but Gervais ordered the coachman to go on to the upper road. He had not wavered in his determination, "though he let his master talk," as he expressed himself later to Margot. It was a pretty route, among trees and sheltered farm-houses, a spick-and-span new castle standing where the *bosquet de Julie* used to wave. From thence a rapid descent between the chestnut-trees, a sharp turn, an arch under the railway to traverse, then the lake road and the pretty *campagne* Mr. Crauford had pointed out to his daughter.

The carriage passed through the iron gates, just within which stood a picturesque chalet, rolled on a short distance, and drew up before the entrance to the villa. A square, rather gloomy house, much older than it looked, but pleasant and comfortable within—though, after the fashion of Swiss dwellings, the best room in it was taken up by the kitchen. There was a pretty salon, a library beyond, both looking toward the chalet; on the other side of the hall a dining-room, with a view of the lake and the Dent-du-Midi. Above-stairs a sleeping-chamber and dressing-room for Elizabeth; next that a large apartment for her father, and a glorious outlook from the windows.

They had dined early at Geneva. Mr. Crauford met one of his numerous and sudden neuralgic headaches at the house-door (they were always lying in wait for him in the most unexpected places), so he retired at once to his chamber, thinking himself saddened by memories of the past; in reality, very cross and fretful, scolding Gervais as long as that patient adherent would stay to listen.

Elizabeth escaped from the house, and the hospitable propositions of its good-natured mistress, promising to have some tea later, and went out to survey the spot which was to be her home for a few weeks. In front, a narrow lawn, thick with chestnut and pine trees; to the right the chalet; at the left a tangle of shrubbery, a little vineyard, and an *espalier*, where the great Duchess pears grew rich and golden, clumps of rose-bushes and laurustinus, two vine-covered arbors, then a winding path to the back of the dwelling. A broad sweep of greensward, dotted with noble trees, sloped down to the massive stone wall, against which the waves beat and moaned with a force that made one feel as if upon the sea-shore. In one place the land jut-

ted out in a point; the basin thus formed made a harbor for a sail-boat, and had a bit of outer wall to protect it. Beyond the landing-steps rose one of the grand old willows; at the extremity of the point towered a poplar, its trunk encircled by a bench.

The moon was coming up, tinging the snow-crown of the Dent-du-Midi, and casting a broad line of golden radiance across the waters. Away stretched the beautiful lake; far in the distance streaks of daylight yet lingered; great masses of white clouds sailed slowly up the sky; the air was soft and warm, as if the sheltered valley had been deep in Italy.

Then Elizabeth walked back to look at the chalet—a long building, standing upon a declivity which brought the ground-floor of the front part on a level with the upper story of the back. A wide gallery ran along the side, roofed by the overhanging eaves; at the back was a flight of stairs. A home beneath the building (of course) for the cows, and a paved space between the chalet and villa, with a fountain sending its jet into a huge stone basin, which served as a drinking-place for the cattle and a convenience for the wife of the *fermier*—established in some rooms next the cow-house—to wash her clothes, Swiss fashion, in cold water.

There were lights in the upper room of the chalet; a young girl was pacing up and down the long gallery, humming snatches of French songs. Elizabeth stopped under the shadow of the trees to look at her, but it was too dark to distinguish more than a tall, slight figure wrapped in a loose white mantle. Presently, through one of the open windows, came a peevish voice, calling in French—

"It is that thou art resolved to take cold, I suppose? Come in, I entreat thee, my child."

"It is not cold in the least," replied the clear young tones; "and I do not wish to come in. Thou art disagreeable, mamma, and Monsieur La Tour is disagreeable likewise. I prefer the gallery and my own society."

Expostulations from the peevish voice, entreaties from elderly masculine tones; but the girl turned impatiently and resumed her march. Elizabeth walked away, smiling at the brief dialogue, and entered the house.

While she drank her tea, Madame Bocher informed her that the apartment in the chalet was occupied by a lady and her daughter. The name was L'Estrange. The mother was a valid—here for her health. She would not here or any where long. Well, we must all die. Mademoiselle Nathalie was to marry Monsieur La Tour. He was a little elderly man with a wig, and Mademoiselle laughed at him a great deal. She was a blithe young thing, was Mademoiselle. Madame was *dévote*, *bigote* even—natural enough, since she must die soon. But she was odd—very odd! However, Madame

Bocher was not one to gossip, and the lady paid her bills regularly, and Monsieur le Curé came several times a week from Vevay to visit her. Of course, under other circumstances Madame might wish to be rid of her lodger—nothing hurt a house like having a death happen in it—but Madame's lease of villa and chalet would expire in the spring, and who could be cruel enough to turn out the poor invalid when she had a fancy to stay?

"I hear a carriage," Elizabeth said at last, more to interrupt Madame's torrent of talk than because there was any thing extraordinary in the sounds she mentioned.

"It is Monsieur La Tour driving away: he stops at the Hôtel du Lac, the grand hotel by the landing near Vevay," Madame explained.

Elizabeth went into the salon; from its windows she could look into a couple of rooms in the front part of the chalet. She saw the young girl who had been walking in the gallery. She had her window open; the moon lighted her face—a pretty, girlish face. A window of the salon was open too. At some noise Elizabeth made she looked up, and waved her hand gayly.

"Good-evening," she said in English, with scarcely a trace of foreign accent. "We are neighbors, you see; I have been expecting you all day. Ciel, how could you bear to come to this awful place? Mamma will be in bed in a few minutes; then I am going down to the lake; don't you want to come? Your papa is in his room with a headache, Madame Bocher told me. She tells more in less time than any body that ever lived, except me. But I've given you no chance! Don't speak; meet me under the great willow. I want to hear your voice suddenly; then I shall know if we are to be friends or enemies—do one another good or harm."

She was gone, and Elizabeth stood quite confused by this sudden and rapid outburst of talk, delivered half in English, half in French. But it did not weary her as Madame Bocher's monologue had done. There was something bright and piquant, more in the way the words were spoken than in any merit they themselves possessed, which caused Elizabeth hastily to decide that the stranger would prove a pleasant companion.

She went dutifully up-stairs to inquire after ther, but neuralgia and memory had been uch for him. He could only kiss her y, grumble a little about Gervais, and his head on his pillow. So there was nothg to prevent Elizabeth's accepting the French irl's tryst by the lake. Margot met her in the all, and insisted on wrapping a shawl about her. Elizabeth submitted, because that was the quickest way to get her liberty. As she passed the great tree which spread its branches out over the lake, and sighed softly to the whispers of the waves, she caught sight of a white-cloaked figure on the bench by the poplar beyond. She remembered the French girl's odd words. Like most young people, Elizabeth was fond now and then of yielding to superstitious follies.

"Here I am—is it for good or evil?" she called suddenly.

The girl sprang to her feet with a sharp cry—started back as if with some wild intention of running away—then moved forward a few steps, looked full in Elizabeth's face, cried out again, tried to laugh, and ended, to Elizabeth's great discomfiture, by bursting into a flood of hysterical weeping.

"I frightened you; I beg your pardon. I oughtn't to have come up so quietly," she said in French.

"No, no, it is not that; it is not that! I was waiting for you; but it is for no good! I shall do you mischief; I know I shall do you mischief."

Elizabeth began to laugh.

"We will not allow the old Breton superstition so much weight," said she. "I dare say you are tired to-night."

"Yes, mamma was so wearisome, and Monsieur La Tour was worse," returned the other, beginning to laugh also. "What a goose I am! You see it rained yesterday, and I could not get out; and to-day mamma was suffering, and needed me—or thought she did!"

"Stopping in the house has made you nervous and excitable," added Elizabeth, kindly.

"Yes, that is it," returned the other; but she still gazed earnestly at her new acquaintance, and shivered as if the air had grown chill. "Why, there is nobody to introduce us," she continued, merrily. "Well, I am Nathalie L'Estrange."

"And I am Elizabeth Crauford."

"Yes, I know; Madame has told me; your papa was here long ago." She laughed again. "I beg your pardon, but it seems so droll! Now I am sure that twenty years hence I shall not go hunting up the places where Monsieur La Tour and I spend our honeymoon. I am to marry Monsieur La Tour; of course Madame has told you?"

"Oh, yes," said Elizabeth, not knowing what to say, and wondering if she ought to add some sort of good wish or other polite nothing.

"Very soon, too," continued Nathalie, "and he wears a wig! Mon Dieu! in the convent I always said I would die before I would do that; but, after all, it is not worth while to die for such a trifle—now is it?"

Elizabeth agreed that it was not—all the same, the idea of the wig made her shudder.

"I am just nineteen," said Nathalie. "How old are you?"

"About twenty."

"You are an American. So was my papa,

for all he had a French name; but I never saw him. You must not speak of him to mamma. I have lived all my life in a convent. I only came out to be married. Are you going to marry?"

"I don't know what may happen to me in the future," replied Elizabeth, smiling at the other's childishness; "but I entertain no such intentions at present."

"They say American girls choose their own husbands," pursued Nathalie. "Well, I am sure I would not have chosen Monsieur La Tour. But I dare say he will do tolerably well, and I have no *dot*, so mamma thinks I am very fortunate. The *corbeille* will come next week; she says there will be lovely things in it. But how have you lived, and where?"

"We were in Europe a good while when I was little. I was born here," Elizabeth said. "At last we went back to America, and lived in the country. When papa and I were left alone, he grew weary of that, and we crossed the ocean again. This time we have been here four years —sometimes in England, but mostly in Italy."

"And I only know that horrid convent," sighed Nathalie. "Mamma sent me there when I was a tiny thing. It's in Paris—the Rue Picpus—where the grave of La Fayette is, in the cemetery back, down beyond the alley of lindens."

"Oh, I know it," rejoined Miss Crauford. "Such a still, pretty place!"

"A horrible place," said Nathalie; "what the English girls call a beast of a place. But I used to rave over La Fayette, because I was half American, and put on great airs."

"I remember the beautiful linden-tree alley so well, and the bee-hives, and the old lame gardener, and the sisters in their white dresses—"

But Nathalie cut Miss Crauford's reminiscences short.

"You make me shudder! I see it all again, and old Sister Ursule, who used to tyrannize over us. Bless me, any thing is better than that—even to marry Monsieur La Tour."

Love and marriage were sacred subjects to Elizabeth—inseparable, too—vague, visionary subjects, which looked very far off, very beautiful, very solemn. It hurt her somehow to hear her companion speak like that. Yet she had lived in the world enough to know that such talk and ideas as Nathalie evidently cherished were not uncommon among her sex.

The French girl had turned abruptly away. She sprang on the low wall that bordered the lawn like a parapet, and walked up and down in silence, while Elizabeth sat and watched her. A slight, frail creature, almost giving the idea of delicate health, but the form so wonderfully pliant that it appeared more slender than it really was; lovely violet eyes, quantities of golden hair, and a mouth whose smiles were at once childlike and coquettish—sometimes fairly cruel.

Of course all these details were not visible to Miss Crauford in the uncertain light, but the description may as well be set down here.

She seemed a creature whose nature was not yet half awake, which perhaps lacked force ever to develop into real strength, though so capricious that she would appear to have half-a-dozen natures as the years went on. A girl who, with a stronger organization, mental and physical, might have grown into something dangerous as a tigress and cruel as death, sparing neither herself nor others in her reckless course. But the feline instincts would probably never get beyond the kitten stage. She might do mischief enough, but it would be from caprice and vanity, not hardened wickedness.

She darted off the wall as suddenly as she had mounted it, and came back to Miss Crauford.

"I shall love you very much," said she. "Haven't you a pet name—a nickname, as you say in English?"

"Papa calls me Queenie," replied Elizabeth, smiling as one would at the forwardness of a spoiled child.

"How delightful! I shall call you so too— may I, Queenie?"

"Oh, yes, if you like."

"*Reine!* That is better yet. You look like a real queen—so stately and—Oh, dear, do you believe you are prettier than I?"

"No," said Elizabeth, honestly. She greatly undervalued her own pale, grand beauty, and thought Nathalie's piquant face a thousand times more attractive.

"Well, I am glad of it. I might have hated you if you had been!"

"Just for that?"

"Of course! Why, there are only two things to make one woman hate another—if she's more beautiful, or a man comes between."

Miss Crauford looked contemptuous.

"Both odd reasons," said she.

"Oh, you evidently know nothing about life, though you have lived in the world," returned Nathalie, sagely. "But ah, my presentiment; I had forgotten that!"

"Then let it go," laughed Elizabeth.

"So I will! At all events, it is not now I shall hurt you, and we can keep out of each other's way hereafter. *Ay de mi!* (What a lovely Spanish girl we had in the convent!) It's an old world, anyhow. Hark, there's old Susanne calling me. She will wake mamma if I don't go in, and then I shall get a dreadful lecture. Good-night, Queenie—good-night, *ma reine.*"

Away she ran, and Elizabeth followed in her sober, dignified fashion. So their first meeting ended; but, unimportant as it seemed, the time was to come when Elizabeth Crauford would look back across the lapse of years, and shudder to remember Nathalie's childish mirth and frightened warning.

CHAPTER II.

A CALIFORNIA COURT-ROOM.

THERE is a certain excitement apparent in Moysterville this morning. The town always possesses life and animation enough, but it shows something more now.

A crowd fills the street leading to the court-house; groups at shop-doors discourse eagerly; a subdued, fiery indignation is apparent on all faces, causing one to think of days gone by, when Moysterville bore a less pretentious name, and presented a very different aspect. Those were days when it boded ill for any offender whose crimes or misdemeanors had roused that look of indignant determination, and brought a crowd toward Shippey's "liquoring-place" on the confines of the village.

Shippey's place had for some reason been elevated to the dignity of serving as court-room, and there stood in convenient proximity—just a little back toward the ravine—an old oak-tree, a gnarled, knotted oak which had suffered from wind and storm in its babyhood, and grown up with humps on its trunk; and its branches, misshapen, and many of them dead, stretched down like gigantic hands in search of prey. The old tree found prey enough at a period when even peaceable, God-fearing citizens were forced to admit that Judge Lynch's was the only law on which they could depend to save their homes and their town from ruin.

But those days are long gone. Shippey's is not—the oak is not—Lock-jaw Corner is not. Here is Moysterville now, broad-streeted, gas-lighted, boasting handsome shops, hotels, theatres, and a fashionable quarter. The town no more remembers the time when it bore the ugly appellation I have set down than a butterfly does its season of being a grub. A fine, flourishing place is Moysterville; a very old town (for California), and a rich one—small wonder, when it stands within the shadow of the mountains whose hearts are gold, with a broad river to help its commerce, and railways which connect it with San Francisco and Sacramento.

But this morning Moysterville, as I said, has a certain repressed indignation about it which reminds more than one of Lock-jaw Corner and Shippey's, and the old oak that used to be called "Luck's End." The truth is, of late Moysterville has been very much annoyed by sundry attempts at garroting, not to mention outbreaks at the gambling-houses and rows in the streets. Now Moysterville has put all these annoyances to the score of a party of "roughs" from San Francisco, though there has been no possibility of fastening the crimes upon them. But only a few nights since a woman was arrested for stealing some valuable jewels from a man stopping at the hotel where she lodged. Moysterville believes that at her trial there will creep out disclosures which may serve to criminate the rest of the band; for it is a foregone conclusion in the mind of Moysterville that the woman was in league with the San Francisco desperadoes. It chanced that court week began forty-eight hours after this woman's arrest, and now, on the third day since its opening, she is to have her trial.

So there is a throng in the street, and a dense crowd in the court-room, waiting with what patience it may until several unimportant cases are disposed of, and Milady is brought into public consideration.

Every body knows that name for her, and no other. During several seasons there was a noted drinking-house in a bad quarter of San Francisco which bore for sign "Milady's," and this woman ruled over the den and the gambling-tables up the tortuous back stairs where the police so often stumbled. Milady disappeared from her familiar haunts one fine day, and nobody thought about her until it became known that she was the person accused of stealing the diamonds, and that she made her entry into Moysterville at the same time as the gamblers and the garroting attempts, and other disturbances of the public peace by which the town had been of late afflicted.

There is another cause of interest afforded by the coming trial, which affects even the elegant portion of the community who dwell amid the grandeur of the court end. The principal witness against Milady will be Darrell Vaughan, who has just come into possession of a large fortune by his uncle's death. Though Darrell Vaughan is not a resident of Moysterville, and was never here until a short time before his relative's decease, every body knows about him, and the court end has a natural interest in his affairs.

Moysterville considers it a most fortunate thing that old Mr. Vaughan died here, and that his nephew came to catch his last sigh and inherit his fortune, because it has been through the young man's assistance that Milady was entrapped. Pious people call it a "providential circumstance," and even those who are not pious feel a sense of obligation toward Darrell Vaughan, since they hope that in the course of Milady's trial there may come out damning evidence against those men who have so lightly disregarded Moysterville's power.

The last trifling case ends—there is a sudden hush in the court. Even judge and jury look with undisguised interest toward the door, through which a brace of constables lead, or rather force, a veiled woman, who obstinately hangs back, and is not to be induced to take her proper position by any gentle means.

The preliminaries are gone through; the woman sits crouched on the bench where she was placed, huddled together in an odd fashion, which somehow suggests a wild animal about to spring. But she never stirs; does not even move her hands, which lie crossed in her lap—small white hands, too, though disfigured by sundry scratches and red marks, the result of the struggle wherein she indulged when the officers arrested her. She is ordered to put up her veil, but she pays no attention. A constable draws the lace off her head—she wears no bonnet. His quick movement brings away the comb which confines her hair, and that falls in heavy, dark masses down her back, unkempt and ill arranged, but beautiful hair still. Her face is visible now—a face which is young, though without a trace of youth in it, which must once have been marvelously lovely; not so many years ago either, for Milady is not over twenty-five. The complexion is fair yet; the mouth, sullen and hard as it is, possesses a certain feminine softness; the low, broad forehead is smooth and white. It is an utterly reckless, hopeless, apathetic face—a face that tells of degradation and sin and evil courses, of womanly instincts grown fiendish, and womanly gifts employed only as additional aids in an awful life.

She wears a rusty black-silk gown, somewhat frayed and rent; an old shawl drawn over this; but the ladies from the court end of town notice that the faded garment is of Indian cashmere—a relic, probably, of days when sin brought pleasanter wages than it has done of late. It is evident that she has made no effort to arrange her attire before coming into court. She looks tumbled, soiled — a mere wreck of what was once beauty and grace; yet there is an odd pathetic shadow of the old fascination left about her still.

Suddenly Milady raises her eyes; she has not before so much as stirred finger or eyelash—has not appeared even conscious where she was since the constables pushed her down upon the bench. But Milady looks up now. Her great brown eyes wander slowly about the court-room; there is a dull film over them—a film through which they blaze with sombre fire. It is plain that she sees nothing in that long, slow gaze she bestows upon the throng—nothing whatever. They are like the eyes of a dead person, yet as if the dead person had been consumed to the last by a fever so horrible that the flame and heat are not burned out, though death has mastered all the rest.

Now, if possible, the attention of the crowd is more closely riveted upon her, for certain questions are being put by the grave servant of the law. Her name is asked. She does not seem to know that she is addressed. The lids have fallen over those heavy eyes. She sits as motionless as ever. An impatient constable near—for from first to last they have guarded the woman with unusual care—touches her shoulder, and in a whisper bids her speak.

"What is your name?"

The great eyes are lifted again so quickly that their blaze startles the very judge in his chair and the jury on their bench.

"Milady," says she, in a hoarse voice.

It is suggested to her that this is no name whatever. At the little preliminary examination on the occasion of her arrest she was hopelessly obstinate. There is nothing to be gained by this; it will be much wiser to answer civilly. Now she does indeed look hopelessly obstinate. The mouth shuts as if the delicate jaw were framed of iron; the whole face grows so much more hard, dull, and dogged that the spectators wonder they could have thought it all those before.

The hope in the minds of judge, lawyers, and the rest is that this woman may be induced to turn State's evidence against the men whom every body believes her accomplices—men who are more than suspected of having been engaged in the great Sacramento robbery a few months previous. Hence, before the district attorney begins his statement of the case, this somewhat informal questioning has been attempted. Certain hints of what is desired of her are thrown out—they can not be new; she has heard such several times during the past days—but she made no sign of comprehending then, and she makes none now.

"What is your age?" is the next question, tried in a mild tone, as if by way of holding a little amicable conversation.

Then comes a quick answer, in the form of an interrogatory though, and not at all what could have been expected; it is—

"How old is your sister?"

A subdued titter goes through the room. Judge, jury, and lawyers are furious. Constables would like to believe that a knot of men suspected of belonging to the band of desperadoes have been guilty of this infraction of order, but the men are stolid and serious.

There is one more question attempted—

"Will you tell your name and birthplace?"

Milady, roused into life, bends forward in her seat, clasps the railing in front of her so tightly that the muscles stand out on her lithe, dangerous-looking hands; her eyes blaze so fiercely for an instant that the film over them is quite dispelled.

"You go to hell!" she exclaims, with a ferocious candor which under any circumstances would do much toward settling her case in advance with both judge and jury.

Nobody laughs now. There is something fairly melodramatic and awful about the woman, in spite of the coarse speech. She lets her hands fall from the railing; sinks slowly back in her seat, her body and limbs huddled together in that strange attitude so like a wild animal crouched ready to spring; and the lids droop again over the fiery eyes.

The prosecuting attorney begins his speech; he explains the charge; he goes on grandiloquently to state how he is prepared to prove by competent witnesses the woman's positive guilt. Yet even here he is mindful of that wish in all hearts to persuade the creature into revelations which shall bring to justice more dangerous criminals than herself. She listens for the first time; looks toward him in a perplexed, absorbed way; lifts her hand, and astounds all listeners by her sharp, hoarse voice.

"I wouldn't waste my breath, old fogy! Milady I am — game to the last. Now push on with your caravan."

The prosecuting attorney brings his speech to a hasty conclusion; Milady has made a climax which renders any efforts at eloquence on his part utterly futile.

The first witness comes forward. He is only a waiter at the hotel. His evidence is not important; though every body listens attentively to what he has to say—every body except Milady—she evidently has lost interest in the proceedings. Another witness—not much more exciting. Milady is still absent, dull, vacant, looking as if partially stupefied by the influence of some powerful drug.

Darrell Vaughan is called; straightway he emerges from a nook where he has been ensconced to avoid attention—a tall, handsome young man—and takes his place in the witness-box. Milady has not stirred at the utterance of his name; seems unconscious of his proximity. She does not look up while the oath is administered, but his voice answering the first question brings her out of her stupor.

Again she leans forward in her seat—the eyes of the accused and the witness meet and look full into each other. If it were not a folly, one might say that the calm, steady gaze of the witness holds a strange menace and warning. One might say that Milady feels it too, for she drops again into her former attitude, only her eyes never leave the witness's face; there is no fire left in them now—they are quite dead and cold.

I have no intention of carrying you through a chapter of such details as you might read in the columns of a police newspaper. The evidence against Milady was conclusive, and I shall give it in a few words. Darrell Vaughan had gone in the dusk of evening to call upon Mr. Carstoe, an agent for the Moysterville property lately come into the young man's possession. Mr. Carstoe lived at a second-rate hotel; he was to set out the next morning for San Francisco with these diamonds, which he had taken in payment of a debt. There were two studs, a ring, and a quantity of unset stones—a rare and valuable emerald among them; the market value of the whole perhaps reaching thirteen thousand dollars. Their loss will be ruin to Mr. Carstoe. He went through a long, tedious suit to get them from a former partner in business, who had cheated him in their affairs, destroyed his prospects, and yet kept himself secure from the law for years.

Mr. Carstoe had taken the jewels out of the bank, intending to start by the next morning's early train. Vaughan was with him when he went on his errand.

The two stood on the outer steps of the house, and talked about the diamonds, Vaughan being of opinion that Mr. Carstoe would do better to send the gems to New York than to sell them in San Francisco. They had held a long and animated discussion when they became aware that the woman called Milady was standing just behind them in the hall. The bank was in an upper story; the lower floor held shops, offices, and, in a court at the back, an establishment where money was lent upon tangible securities.

The two gentlemen stepped aside to let the woman pass; they both saw her face distinctly. Whether she had just come up or had remained listening to their conversation neither knew, nor did either, it appeared, think about the matter at the time.

On the evening of this day Vaughan went to the hotel where Mr. Carstoe lodged; he had asked that gentleman to carry a parcel for him to a friend in San Francisco. The waiter believed that Mr. Carstoe was in his room, so Vaughan walked on up the two flights of stairs which led to No. 45. No. 45 was a room down a narrow, dark passage off the broad corridor traversing the house. A woman—it was Milady —came swiftly out of this passage, and passed Mr. Vaughan without seeing him, as he stood in the shadow, uncertain whether he had taken the right turning.

Mr. Carstoe was not in his chamber; the door was locked. Vaughan waited for a little in the corridor, thinking Mr. Carstoe might appear. At last he went down stairs again, and confided his packet to the waiter, with instructions that it should be given to Mr. Carstoe. Vaughan went home. Before the evening was over Mr. Carstoe came to tell him that the diamonds had been stolen. It had immediately occurred to him that he and Vaughan had been passed by Milady on the bank steps. The suspicion in his mind was of course rendered a certainty by Vaughan's having seen Milady come out of the passage which led to room No. 45.

The two went at once before a magistrate, and procured without difficulty a warrant for the woman's arrest. When they reached the hotel, in company with the officer, the waiter — the same to whom Vaughan had confided the packet

—told them that Milady had not left the house. She was, indeed, found in her apartment in a deep, lethargic sleep, from which it was difficult to rouse her. Her dress was open, and fastening the band of her chemise was a diamond stud, which Mr. Carstoe recognized as his property. But no trace of the other jewels appeared. In the bottom of Milady's trunk was discovered a skeleton-key done up in a package of rags. Probably this key was to have been thrown into the river, but, oppressed by drink or opium, the woman had lain down to sleep first. The general theory was that a confederate had taken the diamonds away at once, that from some freak of feminine vanity she had retained the button which completed the chain of evidence against her.

Like a mad woman Milady fought, and the faces of the officer and the waiter, called in to assist, were tattooed as curiously as those of South Sea Islanders before she was secured. She refused to walk; she yelled like a wild beast in the street; in the end she had been tied hand and foot, thrown upon a dray, and conveyed to jail.

Mr. Carstoe was not a vindictive man: many persons thought he showed great weakness in the matter, a culpable pity for the woman, but he could not avoid pursuing the case. Darrell Vaughan was firm, though very kind to Milady. He actually visited her cell, and promised, for Mr. Carstoe, that the proceedings should be dropped if she would disclose the names of her confederates.

Until Vaughan undertook this merciful errand Milady had raged up and down her narrow quarters like a bedlamite, beating herself against the barred window and the iron door; but from that time till she appeared in the court-room to undergo her trial she remained perfectly quiet —apathetic even.

Mr. Vaughan made no discoveries; he represented Milady as never so much as speaking to or looking at him during the half-hour he stood pleading with her. But from that moment she became composed—sleeping a good deal, or, if not sleeping, lying for hours on her truckle-bed with her eyes half shut. The jailor knew that she was under the influence of some drug, but though they searched her and the cell, nothing was found, nor did it seem that she wished to kill herself—probably it was an old habit to deaden her senses in this way.

There had been such firm belief that she could give information which would lead to the tracking of the Sacramento thieves that many efforts were made during the days she lay in jail before her trial. A clergyman went to see her; a noted female philanthropist paid her a visit; both interviews taking place after Darrell Vaughan's generous effort to save her—an effort which was considered at the court end of town a feat more noble than that of any handsome Paladin of old. Neither clergyman nor philanthropist was more successful than Mr. Vaughan. During the clergyman's eloquent exhortation Milady uttered but one remark—she repeated that with such sullen persistency, and it was in itself so absurd and irrelevant, that the good man could only suppose her brain disordered by the drugs she had taken.

"Twice ten are twenty—he said so—twice ten are twenty."

The virgin philanthropist was quickly driven from the field in disgust. She had requested the keeper to stand at the door during her interview, in order that there might be a witness of her fervid eloquence. Milady sat crouched on a bench when the servant of Vesta and all good works entered; it was one of Milady's utterly dead hours. At length she interrupted the philanthropist by a question—a question which convinced that lady of the creature's utter depravity, and the uselessness of trying to aid her, though there was neither sneer nor mockery in Milady's voice; an odd tremulousness crossed her features, and her glazed eyes softened for the first and last time, as if they had tears under them.

"Have you got a baby?" she asked.

The philanthropist was convulsed with rage, the keeper outside nearly suffocated himself in an attempt to stifle his laughter, but Milady only stared straight before her, with the same shadow of softening in her stony face.

The daughter of Duty was gone; the keeper locked the cell and followed her. As he closed the grating, he saw Milady look wildly about, raise her arms high above her head, and fall or throw herself heavily upon the floor; but he had no time to waste over her performances. Let her bang about and bruise her body if she liked, she could do herself no real harm.

So the trial has come on and ended. The jury has no need to leave the box. The verdict requires brief deliberation—guilty, of course. Yet when it does come, few people can be quite unmoved; many ladies shiver and weep, and Darrell Vaughan looks pale and worn, and leans his head wearily on his hand. But Milady is utterly untouched; she does not appear to have heard; her head is bent, and under the shadow of her forehead those dull eyes always watch Darrell Vaughan. His glance never left her while giving his evidence; it has held her firmly ever since he finished and seated himself almost in front of her.

Then the judge's hard little speech, and the judge's sentence. Milady is to have ten years in the penitentiary!

She hears that—she rises—she is looking still at Darrell Vaughan, not at the judge—her voice is audible.

"Ten years. Oh, my God! ten years!"

If it were not a folly, one might say that

Vaughan's firm lips frame the words also, "Ten years—ten years," while his eyes never move from hers.

A stir, a rustle among the audience, promptly repressed by the constables. Hush, the judge is speaking again. Ten years in the penitentiary for Milady! At the end of that time there will follow a new case, if in the mean while Milady has not come to her senses enough to give the evidence which they are morally certain she possesses in regard to the Sacramento robbery—a new case which the judge promises her shall add yet ten more years to her term of imprisonment. He does not explain, but most people have heard something of this other business during the last few days. Stories have spread that Milady had attempted to steal documents and bonds from old Mr. Vaughan's house just after his death. So, altogether, this affair of Milady's creates great excitement, because it is felt and believed that she is only an instrument in the hands of those abandoned men whom she so obstinately refuses to betray.

"Ten years, and again ten; you will no more escape the iron hand of Justice then than you have done now."

She hears the judge's words—she is on her feet—her apathy or stupor quite gone. She writhes to and fro—her hands work up and down. Only that it is a foolish thought, one might say she is like a person partially magnetized, trying to break the spell as she turns and twists and strives to move her eyes from Vaughan's. Then at last her voice rings out, sharp and discordant. She has half flung herself over the railing. Her eyes, mad with newly awakened agony, seek judge and jury.

"Oh, my God! gentlemen, ten years! I can't go to prison for ten years," cries the suddenly distracted creature. "I can't go—what will become of the child?"

Let us hope there are hearts to which that cry strikes home; lost, fallen as she is, let us hope it! Let us believe that even the judge has a struggle to say so sternly—

"You should have thought of that before."

"Ten years! Oh, my God! I can't! Ten years! Oh! the child!"

Milady has dropped on her knees now, still clinging to the railing. Her dilated eyes have wandered from judge and jury—wandered back to Vaughan's face. Perhaps she does not see him; perhaps she is only blindly gazing about for some trace of pity, some hopeless hope of help.

"Ten years! Oh, my God! gentlemen, I can't! Oh! the child, the child!"

There are tears now from women, and men too. No change could have been more sudden or more unexpected to the spectators themselves than this which has come over them.

Milady is still on her knees, swaying to and fro, smiting her breast with her hands, her great, tearless eyes uplifted, and again her voice rings out in that frantic wail—

"Ten years! Oh, my God! I can't! Oh! the child, the child!"

The constables approach; she pushes them off; she fights like a maddened animal; her long hair floats out like a torn, bright banner in her struggles. Women cover their faces. Strong men turn away unnerved. Always Darrell Vaughan leans back in his seat, pale, weary, watching still.

"Ten years! Oh, my God! the child!"

Still that agonized cry—a horrible moan now. The officers have seized her, bound her hands. She is lifted from the dock and carried away; but to the last that cry rings back—a low groan only, but piercing as a shriek—

"Ten years! Oh, my God! the child!"

The court adjourns, and the crowd spring up eager to get out. They had come for a sensation, but this closing scene has been more than they bargained for. Milady goes back to jail as a temporary residence before repairing to her quarters in the penitentiary. People go off to their employments, to drinking-places, and those from the court end return home to dinner, for the September day is drawing to a close when the throng gets into the street.

Great piles of gorgeous red and yellow clouds have gathered in the west and cast a lurid light over the mountain-tops, which rise frowningly above the town, strike the river with their fiery tints, and turn it into a sea of flame.

The court-house and the jail stand near the water, an open space in front. As Milady is hurried from one to the other, she too catches sight of the bright sunset. If the constables were weak, imaginative men, they might wonder what thoughts are roused in her mind by the sudden glory which she may perhaps not see again for years. But the constables are staid, sensible fellows, bent on their duty—that of getting Milady as speedily as possible into her cell before her demons again attack her; and Milady only gives one groan, half of misery, half of sullen defiance, and allows herself to be led on.

CHAPTER III.

AFTER THE TRIAL.

THE comfortable carriage in which old Mr. Vaughan, deceased, used to take his airings during the months he had for some years annually spent at Moysterville, drives up to the court-house. Young Mr. Vaughan comes out surrounded by a group of the principal personages of the town, who delight to do him honor. There are the mayor and the judge, and several lawyers and merchants with marriageable daughters, and they are all exceedingly friendly with young Mr. Vaughan. But he looks tired and pale still, and gets away as soon as he can, though he has something pleasant and fitting to say to each of the prosperous gentlemen, and he says it with a grace and cordiality which are fascinating indeed.

Then he takes the arm of Mr. Carstoe, who has stood modestly aside, as befits his humbler station, and walks on toward his carriage. But Mr. Carstoe receives greetings, too, from the great men, somewhat patronizing, no doubt; but, in his way, Mr. Carstoe is a person who deserves and gains respect.

"You will come and dine with me," Darrell Vaughan observes, as the sleek, fat horses trot off in a decorous fashion. "What a set of tiresome idiots those fellows are! Now that is a dangerous freedom of speech, Carstoe—but you are a safe man; one can say what one likes to you."

Mr. Carstoe smiles grimly, yet it is evident he appreciates the compliment; that the smile looks grim is the fault of his features, not his will. He is thin, weedy, anxious looking, with a stoop in his back and a melancholy crack in his voice, but the face possesses energy, and truthfulness into the bargain. The world has not dealt kindly with Mr. Carstoe. He came to California long years before, when other men coined gold whichever way they turned, but somehow misfortune always stood between him and the wealth he was just ready to touch. Since his partner ruined him he has subsided into a small lawyer and agent for other people's property, and is a man to be trusted, else he would never have been admitted, as all Moysterville knows he was, to the confidence of the late Mr. Vaughan, as suspicious and restless a gentleman as could easily be found even among those unfortunates of the earth—old men with goodly fortunes which they must soon forsake.

The carriage crosses the bridge, rolls down the principal street, gay with shops and showy hotels, and makes its way up the hill toward the quarter of the town where fashion dwells. Very elegant houses there are here, filled with gorgeous furniture and Parisian luxuries; and dinners and balls are given in them, and life is so dull and stereotyped that one wonders these dwellers in a new land are content to accept it.

On the outskirts of this little star of avenues and streets stands the commodious villa erected by Mr. Vaughan several years since, when the physicians recommended the climate of California as likely to invigorate his failing health. A fine place, with a broad lawn, and grand old trees spared in the destruction of the noble grove which once towered here. Within there is comfort and elegance, for in his quiet fashion Mr. Vaughan had liked to enjoy the wealth heaped up by his own exertions.

The carriage stops before the entrance; the last rays of the setting sun touch Darrell's forehead as he descends, and with his usual courtesy offers an arm to his elderly companion.

"It has grown chilly," Darrell says, and shivers.

As he speaks, at the other end of the city the door of a prison cell has shut; a turnkey has brought Milady her supper, and locked her in alone for the night—alone with her ghosts and her remorse, if she is haunted by such—alone with the miserable plaint which still at intervals breaks from her white lips—the wail whose fierce agony startled judge and jury, witnesses and court, not long since in the court-room— "My child! Oh, God! my child!"

The great doors of the villa have closed upon Vaughan and his guest. The host leads the way to the library, where the gas-lamps are already lighted, and a log of odorous Californian wood blazes on the hearth. It is too early in the season for the nights to be very cool, but old Mr. Vaughan liked a fire at most times, and the housekeeper has ordered it to be lighted from habit.

"We shall have dinner in twenty minutes, they say," observed Darrell. "Let's try a little sherry while we are waiting."

The wine is brought. Mr. Carstoe contents himself with a few sips, but Darrell drains two glasses of the bright, golden cordial in rapid succession—drinks another as hastily when Mr. Carstoe stands by the fire with his back toward him.

Mr. Carstoe's meditations are naturally not of the brightest. This recent loss is scarcely calculated to raise his spirits. But life has been too hard for him to be greatly astonished or cast down by any new trouble.

"It is just what I might have expected would happen," he has said to Vaughan more than once during the past few days. "That money—for the diamonds were as good as money—would have started me afresh in the world. I meant to buy up those loose lands about Mumford's Hollow, and in two years I should have been a rich man."

Probably he is going over a train of similar thought now, perhaps contrasting his companion's position with his own, as he knocks the toe of his boot against the low fender, glances about the handsomely appointed room, and says moodily—

"And there are people who don't believe in luck: why, if you're not born with it, life is about as easy as climbing up a wall without any chinks between the stones."

Vaughan laughs at the odd comparison, but it is neither a hard nor an unsympathizing laugh.

"It is never too late for luck to turn," he replies, coming up to the fire. "You're a good fellow, Carstoe, and I've taken an immense fancy to you. I know my uncle liked you."

"Well, I never knew any body's liking to do me any great amount of good," observes Mr. Carstoe, candidly. "Still, I own I am glad to have it; and I can say for your late uncle that, though he was a difficult man, he paid well, and did justice to one's attempts to do one's work."

"And as far as that last goes, you shall find his nephew resembles him," says Darrell, holding out his hand. "I've not said much—words are poor things—but I'm deucedly cut up about your misfortune, and— Ah, here's Tony to announce dinner; well, we'll feed first and talk it over afterward."

They dine exceedingly well, and Vaughan presses many varieties of generous wines upon his guest. By the time the meal is over and they sit alone near the fire again, with their cigars lighted, Mr. Carstoe is much more cheerful and talkative than usual. He has reasons beyond the effects of claret and champagne for this change. Darrell Vaughan has offered him the agency of all the Californian property, from the unopened mining tracts to the lands in several growing towns—offered not only a generous salary, but percentages so large that a new career, the certainty of a moderate fortune, presents itself suddenly to the eyes of the world-buffeted man. They talk a great deal about the business; they talk of the late uncle, whose memory Mr. Carstoe holds in affectionate reverence. They speak, too, of another matter connected with the will, and of the person whom it affects. This is Launcelot Cromlin, Darrell's cousin. When a boy he had been a favorite with his uncle. Five years previous, a youth of one-and-twenty at the time, Launce Cromlin fell under the suspicion of a terrible deed. Mr. Vaughan had been spending the summer in Vermont on account of his health. His two nephews had visited him there in turn. Early in the autumn Launce was going to Europe to pursue his art studies. When the young man's birthday arrived, Mr. Vaughan sent him a check for fifteen hundred dollars. It was months before the old gentleman saw this check again; when it came back the amount had been altered to fifteen thousand dollars, and on the back was an indorsement signed by Cromlin, making the check payable to the bearer.

Launce was in Europe. Mr. Vaughan made inquiries of the bank-teller, but not in a way to excite suspicion. The teller was positive that Mr. Cromlin had presented the draft in person. He recollected Cromlin saying he had been out of town, and expected to send the paper by a friend to be cashed, but had himself returned.

Mr. Vaughan was a secretive, proud man—terribly suspicious too; for he had suffered much from the treachery of several persons whom he had best loved. He kept the discovery from every body but Darrell, whom he liked, though this nephew had never been so dear to him as Launce. Apparently Launce had hoped the indorsement would persuade his uncle that the check had passed through other hands, thus relieving him from suspicion.

In his brief letter to Cromlin, Mr. Vaughan did not even state the reasons which led him to disown and fairly curse the youth he had loved so tenderly. Epistles came from Launce; they were returned unopened. Darrell naturally paid no attention to the appeals which his cousin addressed to him, begging to be told what had caused this change in his uncle.

Partly on account of his health, partly because familiar haunts had grown hateful in his grief and increased misanthropy, Mr. Vaughan went to California, where he owned an extensive property. He divided his time between San Francisco and Moysterville, only once revisiting the Atlantic States about a year before his death.

Some two weeks previous to Mr. Vaughan's decease, a lawyer friend in New York, to whom during that last visit the old man had communicated the secret, sent him a statement of facts, which, though they did not clear up the mystery, were proofs to Mr. Vaughan that Cromlin had been the victim of fraud and treachery. For weeks before and after the presentation of the check Launce had lain in bed helpless from a fracture of the right arm. Besides this, it had been recently discovered that a systematic series of thefts had been long carried on by the teller and cashier of the bank. Both men were since fugitives from justice, and it was probable that the teller, at least, had had a share in the crime until now ascribed to Cromlin.

Launce had never returned to America. He had lived upon the limited income inherited from his father and pursued his art studies. After those first efforts at reconciliation the haughty family spirit had risen, and he attempted nothing further. He and Darrell had met once in Europe, but Darrell gave him no clew to the cause of their uncle's conduct, though he promised to tell their relative how honorable and straightforward Launce's life was, and do his best to end the estrangement.

When the news came which convinced Mr. Vaughan he had wronged his nephew, he wrote to his lawyer friend in New York, inclosing a letter to be forwarded to Launce. There must be some means of discovering the young man's European address, and he begged piteously that his friend would act with the utmost dispatch; he wanted to see his boy again. But all the lawyer could discover was the name of a London House to whom letters were forwarded by Launce's bankers in New York. So Mr. Sandford sent the epistle to them, and wrote to Mr. Vaughan that he had done so, proposing to dispatch an agent to Europe in search of Cromlin, but when his response reached California Mr. Vaughan was dead.

After the old gentleman became convinced of Launce's innocence, he told the whole story to Mr. Carstoe, bitterly lamenting the injury he had done his boy. Mr. Carstoe was aware that the fortune had been left to Darrell, with the exception of a small bequest (provisional in a certain way), which even in his wrath he could not forbear allotting his former favorite. But from his conversation, Carstoe supposed that on the receipt of this news he had changed his will, and divided his wealth equally between his nephews. He knew that on the very day the tidings came, Mr. Vaughan was closeted for hours with his lawyer, John Smith. The next day but one Mr. Smith was sent for again, and this time it was to add a codicil to the will, and that codicil Vaughan read to Mr. Carstoe after he and the housekeeper had witnessed it, and the lawyer was gone. It was an odd, romantic codicil enough, but in keeping with Mr. Vaughan's peculiar character and theories; and, indeed, that night, talking to Carstoe more freely than he had ever before done, he told him enough of his own past to account for the whim.

After Mr. Vaughan's death, to the law-agent's astonishment, the original will was found, with the codicil attached. Mr. Carstoe was utterly confounded. The only solution to the mystery seemed that Edgar Vaughan had composed the codicil when his feelings changed toward Cromlin, but that he had put off, as men so often do, the alteration in his testament until too late. Darrell inherited the fortune, with the exception of ten thousand dollars bequeathed to Launce. Darrell was to pay the whole amount to his cousin if he found the young man behaving well; if not, he was to retain the principal, and pay an annual interest counted at ten per cent. But even this interest was to be withheld for five years if Darrell became convinced that Cromlin would only squander it in dissipation. So to-night the conversation between the two men gets round to Launce Cromlin, and the strange stipulation in the codicil concerning a certain portion of the property.

"Your cousin is an artist, I think," Mr. Carstoe says.

"He dreams of being one," replies Darrell, with a shrug; "whether he will ever do more than dream is doubtful. I saw him about two years since in Europe—an agreeable fellow—clever, too; but I am afraid not a man to trust."

"Indeed! And did you talk over that affair? It seems so odd, since he was innocent, that he never tried to clear himself."

"I knew nothing about the matter then; my uncle never told me a word till he chose to think he had proofs that Launce was not guilty."

Mr. Carstoe wonders how he could have been so mistaken; he thought Mr. Vaughan had told him that Darrell knew all from the first.

"Well," he says, "when the poor fellow gets our letters he will be glad to know that the affair was cleared up before his uncle's death."

"Glad to know that my uncle was convinced," amends Darrell; "real proofs of Launce's innocence he never had."

"But you have no doubt?"

"I can't tell; I want to like Launce; I mean I want to believe in him—like him I do. Now about the will itself. You believe that my uncle meant to make another?"

"Yes, as I told you," Mr. Carstoe replies, firmly.

"I shall act," says Darrell, "as I think my uncle would like to have me. To divide the fortune equally would not be fair, for the foundation of a good deal of it was laid by my father."

This is news also to Mr. Carstoe, but he can not doubt the fact.

"You will behave rightly, I am sure," he answers.

"The ten thousand dollars he will have at once," pursues Darrell. "If I find him steady, hard-working, trying to atone for past errors, I will make that sum a hundred thousand. More than that I know my uncle would not have done."

Mr. Carstoe feels, and says truly, that under the circumstances few men would do so much. The declaration might sound less generous if he were acquainted with Launcelot Cromlin; he would then be aware that there is not a possibility of Launce's listening to such an offer.

"He has still another opportunity," continues Darrell, with a smile. "If he succeeds in winning Miss Elizabeth Crauford's favor, he will inherit the two hundred and fifty thousand dollars of Eastern bonds and stocks that the codicil awards to whichever of us two may gain her favor."

"It was a romantic sort of thing for a business man to hatch," Carstoe replies; "but Mr. Vaughan was very odd. He had once cared for the young lady's mother. He talked freely with me during that last fortnight, though I had always thought him a very secretive, silent man; but you often notice these changes toward the end. He read me the codicil after Smith had gone, and talked a great deal about Launce Cromlin—about his own past too."

"Yes," from Darrell.

Mr. Carstoe had given every one of these details weeks ago, on the night of Darrell's arrival, while Mr. Vaughan was still alive, but Darrell has a certain pleasure in hearing them again.

"How odd that he should have outlived Smith, after all. He was so frail and miserable, and Smith looked such a tower of strength. I remember Mr. Vaughan's saying to him in his caustic way, 'You look so disgustingly well and strong, Smith, it's fairly insulting.'"

Mr. Carstoe rubs his hands together, and shakes his head.

"And poor Smith was killed the very day of my uncle's paralytic stroke," says Darrell.

"The very day! Thrown from his horse, and picked up with his neck broken," returns Mr. Carstoe, opening his hands wide and bringing them together again with energy. "It is odd how we go—very odd."

"Yes," once more—an assent this time.

"I had gone away two days before on business," pursues Mr. Carstoe, in a low voice. "When I got back, Smith was dead and your poor uncle little better." He sits silent for a while, then speaks again, to get rid of this mournful train of thought. "You will see your cousin in New York?"

"If he is there I shall."

"Oh, he'll come as soon as our letters reach him. I lost no time, as you directed, in writing about the legacy and the codicil. If he is in Europe, those bankers whose address you gave me will forward the letters at once."

"Naturally," replies Darrell.

"And about your own chance. You don't mean to let your cousin take it by default?" asks Mr. Carstoe, slyly.

"I shall never sell myself for money," returns Vaughan, quietly. "I never saw Miss Crauford. I should be certain to dislike her. Let Master Launce win her and the fortune, if he can."

"If neither succeed, the whole goes to a charity," pursues Mr. Carstoe; "to a charity," moving his finger slowly, as if reading the conditions of the codicil in the embers.

"Better, perhaps, for the young lady and Launce Cromlin too."

"Then you put yourself quite out of the question?"

"I don't like that mixing up of romance and business. I told you I should be sure to hate her," replies Vaughan.

Tony brings in coffee and curaçoa and kirschwasser. Darrell makes his guest taste both liquids. He always likes to feel his power, no matter how trifling the thing in which it is shown. He has pleasure in forcing his abstemious companion slightly to muddle himself; he enjoys seeing that the steadiest person has his weaknesses. Mr. Carstoe is a wonderfully temperate man for California, but a little excess is excusable to-night. Since the loss of the diamonds he has thought himself on the verge of ruin, until Vaughan's generous proposals at dinner cleared the way to comfort and a competency. It is not surprising that he should be pleased and excited enough to forget somewhat his customary prudence under his host's persuasions. He is by no means intoxicated; his brain is quickened, his thoughts come rapidly, he feels in a talkative mood, and very happy—that is all. He has not forgotten the business either; he begins discussing what wonders can be done with the mining

tract and the "town lots" in the new villages, but Vaughan does not want to talk business.

"Time enough while we are going down to San Francisco to arrange these affairs," he says. "Besides, I shall stay there for a few days."

"I shall come back as soon as I have attended to your matters there," Mr. Carstoe replies. "But one thing—about this house—what do you mean to do with it?"

"Sell it when there is a chance; in the mean time you can look about for a good tenant or purchaser."

"Then you'll not live in California?"

"I!" He utters the monosyllable in a tone of disdainful surprise, but changes his voice as he adds—"No; I may go abroad for a time, but New York is my home."

"And you have already made a start in politics; think of having been a Congressman at your age!" exclaims Mr. Carstoe, in an admiring tone. He looks at the handsome, elegant fellow who, still under thirty, has wealth and honors in his grasp, and wonders why human destinies differ so. He remembers when he too was young, and had hopes and aspirations; but they have been dead so many years now that even their ghosts have almost ceased to haunt him.

Darrell Vaughan is one of those men who could drink a whole dinner-party under the table without showing signs of being affected by his potations. To-night he has an unusual craving for stimulants—a desire for companionship too. He keeps Mr. Carstoe until very late. He orders materials for hot punch, and will not spare his guest. Such murderous hospitality is too common in California for Mr. Carstoe to be surprised, but he can not resist Vaughan's entreaties as he is in the habit of doing those of other men. This young fellow has a rare gift of fascination about him, to which Mr. Carstoe yields as readily as do most people. Brief as their acquaintance is, Vaughan has assumed a complete ascendency over him; yet the lawyer is not an impressionable person.

Darrell talks in his turn, brilliantly, dashingly, in terse, quick periods, which show talent, careful thought and study too, easily and naturally as he converses. He enjoys drawing out his visitor. Mr. Carstoe is no ordinary business-hack; there are all sorts of odd corners and quaint ideas in that mind long accustomed to the depressing influence of business drudgery. Vaughan brings these forth successfully; he hears about the old hopes and struggles; old loves and disappointments too; and is interested, even while he feels a certain contempt for this man who had the making of so much in his disposition, and yet has never succeeded in raising his life beyond a dull, commonplace failure. Of politics, of professions they talk—of women too; for Vaughan, who must always study somebody, is curious to know what creeds or ideas are in the man's brain. But this last discussion brings to Mr. Carstoe's mind the events of the day—events from which Darrell has hitherto kept the conversation aloof.

Mr. Carstoe shudders. He knows that it was right the woman should suffer the consequences of her guilt, be shut up beyond the possibility of continuing her evil career; but to be forced to bring the charge, to follow up the process, has been the hardest task he ever undertook. Lost, abandoned as the woman is, he has pitied her from the first. Nothing but necessity, the sense that it is right and just, has carried him through.

"I hope such a thing will never happen to me again," he says suddenly. "But I could not act otherwise—I could not."

"You are somewhat excited still," Vaughan replies coldly. "You could not condone crime; we have gone over all that often enough."

"Yes," sighs Mr. Carstoe. Then a pause, after which he adds—"There is some mystery under it all that we shall never understand. Mrs. Simpson says she did come twice to see your uncle—was with him when he had the fit."

Vaughan is lighting a fresh cigar; when he has succeeded, he puffs out a graceful column of smoke, and says quietly—

"No doubt there was an intention to make some great haul like that at Sacramento. People here had better take care. Milady was probably only an instrument in the hands of those men. It might not have been legal, but they'd much better have kept her from trial on condition that she exposed the whole."

"It was your telling the judge of catching her about the house after your uncle's death which got her so long a punishment."

"Perhaps; it was my duty though," replies Darrell. "Ten years! Ten years is a long time, Carstoe!"

Mr. Carstoe assents in a troubled way to this self-evident proposition.

"Especially when one must pass them in prison," adds Vaughan.

Again Mr. Carstoe shivers as he answers. He could almost think there is a harsh, triumphant ring in the young man's voice; but when he looks up, Darrell is leaning his head on his hand and gazing wearily into the fire. From first to last he has been very kind, and shown a humane interest in the poor wretch. Mr. Carstoe feels a pang of self-reproach that he can for an instant have fancied there is any thing hard or cruel about his engaging companion.

Vaughan drinks more punch, and Mr. Carstoe with difficulty escapes imbibing another glass, which he feels would upset him entirely. He looks at his watch, pleads the lateness of the hour, and suggests the propriety of a sober business-man getting home and to bed without delay.

"Nonsense," says Vaughan, "you can't go back to-night. I'd have the trap out, only the servants would hate me forever. You must stop here. I told Mrs. Simpson to get a bed ready."

Mr. Carstoe is quite overcome by this last touch of friendly attention. He feels that Darrell Vaughan is a man to work for, stand by, die for if need be! Punch and gratitude render Mr. Carstoe fairly heroic in his sentiments.

"They've given you the room next mine," pursues the host, finishing his glass. "This house is a gloomy old barrack at the best. I'm glad of society."

He moves impatiently, and stirs the embers into a flame. It occurs to Mr. Carstoe that, in spite of his energy and vitality, this young Vaughan is a very nervous man—any great strain now or sharp illness would tell terribly on him. Darrell begins laughing and jesting again, and the guest forgets his thought. He has not seen his companion so gay before; Vaughan has been greatly affected by his uncle's death, and during the first days did nothing but lament his own dilatoriness in not coming before. Those self-reproaches have placed him on a high pinnacle in the minds of the dignitaries of Moysterville. They do not believe them deserved; but have given him great credit therefor. Old Mr. Vaughan was a reticent, moody man, who liked to be alone; even the nephew whom he loved could not intrude upon him unasked. Darrell has made this known too; but he has reproached himself all the same, and Moysterville admires him, and will long talk of his behavior—so fitting, "so sweetly melancholy," the ladies at the court end pronounce it, and other people say the same.

Vaughan himself shows his visitor up-stairs; bids him not take pains to be quiet, because he likes to know there is some living thing near besides the rats, and is amusing and agreeable to the last. He is in his own room at length; but, instead of going to bed, he throws himself on a sofa, and lies staring at the shaded light. His lips move occasionally, and if there is any spirit listener bending over him unseen, these are the words that ghostly visitant must catch—"Ten years—ten years."

Sometimes there is the hard ring of triumph, which for an instant surprised Mr. Carstoe in his voice; sometimes a weariness and unrest; but he says the words over and over.

Then he rises; goes to a dressing-case, unlocks it, and takes out a tiny box—a box that holds a quantity of greenish pills. He swallows three of these, and, since sleep will not come, sits down at his writing-table while waiting for the hasheesh to do its work of bringing up a pleasant vision.

He turns over certain papers, among them a letter from his uncle to Robert Crauford—a letter in which are detailed the conditions of that odd codicil. Whichever of his nephews wins the hand of his old friend's daughter will claim the two hundred and fifty thousand dollars exempted from the rest of his fortune.

The letter to apprise Launce Cromlin of this bequest is on its way to New York, but as Launce is terribly careless in the matter of addresses, it is likely to lie a long time unclaimed.

Vaughan still sits at the table, but the potion has begun its work. The walls expand; the room stretches into space. Bright tints and colors float about; his physical frame seems to lose its density, and to drift up—up toward the radiant gleams. Sounds of music are in his ears. He knows what is coming—that glorious vision of an Eastern scene—palm-trees—desert sands—enchanted cities in the distance—golden rivers—amber skies—heavenly shapes. He keeps full possession of his identity; he has learned so to graduate the dose that he can do this—knows what amount will serve to make his speech eloquent, bring glowing visions or passing forgetfulness, as he lists. To-night he wants the vision, and it is near; the stately music always announces its approach. Suddenly there is a jar, a break—a discord in the grand diapason. The vision floats slowly up, and fills the immeasurable space; but, horrible, it is only the hot court-room, the eager crowd, the crouching form of Milady, that present themselves. It is the first time the spell has ever failed; he is sufficiently conscious to struggle, to separate reality from the dream.

He thrusts the papers into the drawer, closes the desk, flings off his coat, and lies down on the bed. The music recommences—slowly, stately—crash after crash of golden harmony. Great ivory doors swing wide—he is entering the charmed realm. He can not move now—can not lift a finger; he must drift on. But he sees that dwarfish gnomes guard the portals instead of the radiant forms he knows as well as the faces of his most familiar friends. The Eastern scene is there—the palms, the desert, the enchanted city. But side by side, jumbled with the vision in inextricable confusion, yet apart from it—a sort of shadow, though full of awful reality—the court-room, the crouching figure, and the mighty orchestra, from organ tones to voice of flute, only wails and echoes that dismal cry—"The child! oh, God, the child!"

Always bound hand and foot; no more able to stir than if his frame had been of marble. Still the vision sweeps on, beauty and its dreadful shadow side by side. Out of the farther past troop shapes and memories. Faces and voices which perhaps he has not seen or heard for years—loves and hates so fierce that it would be hard to tell which were the most cruel.

But whatever he sees or hears, always there comes back at last the court-room, the crowd, and Milady crouching there, while her white lips repeat in mockery the pet name of other days—

the name to which she has clung in her fall and degradation, perhaps only in scorn and bitterness of her own self, but clinging to it still.

What else does he behold? Always the palm-trees and the broad plains with their magic light, but they serve merely as the theatre upon which this drama of recollection plays itself out.

Does he see himself arrived in Moysterville? Does he listen again to the frightened servants' account of the paralysis which struck his uncle only the day before, after receiving a visit from a stranger—a woman? The two incidents are not, in the minds of the speakers, connected with the illness; but they relate them as people, in such a season of alarm, laboriously go over the slightest events that immediately precede the disaster. Does he hear Mr. Carstoe's voice, with its piteous croak—like a constant lament over life's disappointments—relating, also on the evening of his arrival, the affair of the codicil; telling him of the lawyer's death; uncertain of the contents of the will, but positive as to the codicil?

Does he see himself, two nights later, in the library, secretly searching among the papers? Does he read again the revelations which caused so horrible a shock to the old man that his enfeebled frame could not support the blow? Is he back in the room on the night his uncle died, seeking to destroy those terrible records?

Does he see suddenly the haggard face of Milady rise like a menacing ghost? Does he despise her threats, and let her go? Does he wait until a few more days have seen the old man laid in his grave, to find the strong arm of the law relieving him of this wretched woman who has dared to threaten him in her madness? Does he see himself visiting her in prison, overwhelming her by the one plea that could move her? Does he hear her frantic appeal—"The child! the child?" Does he go over again the bestowal upon her of the drug which, long ago, she learned to crave—the drug which keeps her in a state of semi-idiocy up to the very hour of the trial—with a vague fear of him controlling her always and sealing her lips, though her stupefied mind can scarcely realize why, until when all is over, and the dreadful sentence pronounced, memory and consciousness break forth anew in that passionate moan—"The child! the child!"

Yes, he sees it all, lives it all over, and suffers—he who, in his normal state, has so slight capability of suffering. He writhes and moans, but can not break the spell. Then a great darkness gathers: he sinks down—down. The Eastern plain is a sea of blood. Towers and palm-trees are fiery fountains afar off; he in the dark; and he falls, falls, slowly, slowly down an awful height—down a terrible eternity into a dull, dead insensibility, which holds no thought, no perception.

But the morrow's sun has risen. Two days come and go. Mr. Carstoe and Vaughan are speeding toward San Francisco. Only a brief waiting there, and he is on the great steamer bound homeward, and, once arrived at the great Atlantic sea-port, another steamer bears him away to the Old World, and his face is full of life and hope, and the past is as dead for him as if it had never existed.

CHAPTER IV.

IN THE GALLERY.

MONSIEUR LA TOUR had come to pay a morning visit to his affianced: it was not his habit to appear until the afternoon, but he was obliged to go down to Geneva to-day, and Nathalie, seized by one of her sudden caprices, had ordered him, on the previous night, to bring her a bouquet of flowers before his departure.

So Monsieur appeared at the chalet at ten o'clock. Madame L'Estrange was not yet visible, but old Susanne played propriety during the interview, Madame L'Estrange being fully alive to the indecorum of a young lady's receiving her affianced husband alone. The coachman had begged permission to drive on to Clarens while Monsieur paid his visit, promising faithfully to be back in time to meet the boat.

Nathalie proved so teazing and capricious that the little elderly gentleman spent an unquiet half-hour. Old Susanne was cross this morning, and with reason, for in the middle of the night Madame had been attacked with one of her nervous spasms, and insisted on Susanne's saying a score of long prayers, and then, relapsing from piety into worldliness, kept her till near daylight discussing mundane matters. So Susanne, feeling at war with the human race in general, suddenly announced that it was almost time for the boat, and informed Monsieur, with malicious satisfaction, that the carriage had not returned.

"You will have to walk to the landing," said Nathalie, when a consultation of watches and clocks proved that Susanne was correct, as well as ill-natured, in her remark.

"But that faithless *cocher*—where is he?" moaned Monsieur, with the theatrical gestures and appearance of utter despair which, like the rest of his countrymen, he displayed on every possible occasion. "He is a fiend—the son of a demon! My business is most important! I desire to go by the boat—the train invariably causes my head to ache, and he knows it—the accursed wretch knows it well."

"That may be; but if Monsieur waits any longer he will not get the boat, that is certain," pronounced Susanne, with the easy familiarity of a French domestic.

Nathalie clapped her hands and laughed, and Monsieur La Tour looked at her over his spectacles with mild reproach.

"Mademoiselle can be amused at my perplexity!" quavered he.

"Oh, no, Monsieur; I was only remembering that not to reach the boat would give me the pleasure of your society," returned Nathalie, uttering the polite falsehood with all a woman's—a Frenchwoman's—glibness.

"I am touched; I am overwhelmed!" cried Monsieur; for Nathalie did not treat him often enough to pretty speeches for them to lose their effect. "But, *mon amie*, I am forced to go to Geneva to-day. I have made certain business arrangements; I desire to purchase—but it is needless to weary you with explanations."

"Then if Monsieur wishes to go by the eleven o'clock boat, he must be off," chanted Susanne, monotonously. Susanne was sleepy, and wanted him gone, that she might secure a little doze before it was time to dress her mistress.

"We shall walk a little way with you," Nathalie said. "Come, Susanne. You like an early promenade, Susanne; you know you do."

Susanne made a dissatisfied grimace; but, as refusal was out of the question, she scorned to offer any observation whatever.

The three set off, and were seen by Elizabeth Crauford, who had left the house to enjoy the delicious morning. Not far below the villa grounds was a steep hill overhanging the road, walled and terraced to the top, with vines growing on the terraces. The hill made part of a private property; but Elizabeth had walked up a side road which gave admittance thereto, and a courteous gardener had permitted her to enter. She had strolled on to the brow of the hill, and seated herself in a summer-house which commanded a lovely view.

Along came her acquaintance of the previous evening; of course the natty, carefully dressed little man by her side was Monsieur La Tour. Elizabeth regarded him with a natural womanly interest. He had taken off his hat for an instant, and she could see his wig distinctly. She turned, with as natural a thrill of girlish sympathy, to look at Nathalie walking by his side, overtopping him somewhat, lithe and graceful, her hair shining like gold in the sun, and her face brightened by its most mischievous smile.

They were just under the hill now—Elizabeth had to lean forward to see them. Up scuttled Susanne, her tall Breton cap wavering to and fro in her haste, like a miniature tower shaking in the wind.

"The boat!" she shrieked; "the boat!"

"Just heaven, all is lost!" groaned Monsieur. Then a tableau. Susanne a statue of reproach and self-satisfaction; Monsieur with one hand clutching the wig which he did not dare to pull, his spectacles raised to the heaven he had invoked; Nathalie with her head averted, but her countenance brimful of mischief and enjoyment, plainly visible to Elizabeth. A person unacquainted with French manners might have supposed, from the melodramatic attitudes of Monsieur and the old woman, that some terrible catastrophe had occurred, but Miss Crauford felt certain the case deserved no very profound sympathy.

"If Monsieur runs, but runs very fast," suggested Susanne, suddenly bursting into speech— "the boat is only at Clarens, I heard the whistle—Monsieur might catch it yet at the lower landing."

"Ah, do try," cried Nathalie. "You know the motion of the train always makes you ill, *mon ami.*"

"I shall try," sighed Monsieur. "*Au revoir, chère* Nathalie; *au revoir.*"

"Yes, yes, but do not stop to kiss my hand; *vite, vite,*" pleaded Nathalie.

Monsieur still hesitated; he had no fancy for displaying his powers of rapid locomotion to that audience.

"The whistle!" cried Susanne.

"And your head—the train will make you ill!" from Nathalie.

Away bounded poor Monsieur, as an elderly gazelle might bound; his coat-tails flew out like twin banners of distress, his wig bobbed up and down, and threatened to desert him utterly. Elizabeth Crauford leaned back in her seat and laughed silently; Susanne watched with a face divided between amusement and ill-temper; and Nathalie clapped her hands and danced.

Monsieur's style of racing was peculiar; those elderly gazelle bounds seemed more like ineffectual efforts to leap up an imaginary height than well-directed attempts to reach a goal lying far down the smooth, curving road. Full five minutes of that gazelle business ensued, yet Monsieur was not a hundred yards away. Another scream from Susanne—

"The boat! the boat!"

A burst of laughter from Nathalie, echoed by sounds of merriment from Miss Crauford's retreat, a groan from Monsieur, and a cessation of the mad bounds. He stood for a few instants watching the boat as she swept down the bay-like curve, then walked slowly back, wiping his forehead with his handkerchief, speechless between annoyance and exhaustion.

"You must wait till to-morrow," was Nathalie's first remark.

"I have business—I shall go to-day," returned Monsieur; and though his voice sounded like the expiring wheeze of a broken bellows, the words expressed a firm resolve to do his duty, though he perished in the attempt.

"There is a train at half-past eleven," chanted Susanne, in her shrill tones.

"We will walk to the station with you," Nathalie said.

"You are very good—always," sighed Monsieur, displaying a spirit of forgiveness which ought to have overwhelmed the naughty sprite with remorse, but produced no effect whatever.

"Madame will want me," put in Susanne crossly, her last hope of getting a half-hour's peaceful slumber destroyed by this cruel proposal on Nathalie's part.

"Mamma will not rise till noon; she never does," said the girl. "Susanne, I suspect you of some dark design! There must be a man in the case, or you would not be so insane to get back to the house."

"For shame, Mademoiselle—before Monsieur!" grumbled Susanne, yet secretly pleased at the idea that such notions could still be imputed to her. "What will Monsieur think?"

"Monsieur will think whatever I bid him," cried Nathalie. "Is it not so, *mon ami?* Poor dear! how warm he is—ah! it is too bad!"

She seized his handkerchief, and actually wiped his forehead. Monsieur was so overcome by her goodness that he could only gasp.

"Bah, it smells of snuff!" exclaimed Nathalie, suddenly thrusting the handkerchief into his hand. "*Allons!* It is fortunate this train stops at Burier."

Burier was a little station just back of the hill where Elizabeth Crauford sat, only a few minutes' walk from the high-road. Nathalie danced along by Monsieur's side, and Susanne followed in grim silence; but her faded lips moved, and it was evident from the expression of her countenance that she was not calling down blessings on the heads of her mistress and her mistress's betrothed husband.

"I forgot"—Monsieur stopped short as he spoke, and once more despair darkened his heated countenance—"I have not my paletot and my *sac de voyage*—both in the carriage. Ah, that fiendish man!"

"Well, there he comes now," called Susanne, who seemed the goddess of discovery in person this morning.

Sure enough, now that it was too late, the carriage appeared up the road, and halted before the side gates which were close to the chalet.

"Fiend with a donkey's head," shouted Susanne, "can you not come on then? Are you blind as well as an idiot that you do not see us standing here?"

Her shrill voice rang out like a cracked trumpet, and, as the coachman urged forward his steed, her tones changed to withering sarcasm. "Ah, yes, now that it is too late thou canst come; thou canst be in great haste; thou canst beat thy poor horse! *Hé!* Lout, fiend, seventh son of seven times seven brigands, come on then—come!"

She danced up and down in the road, and shook her fists and her cap, until a horse unaccustomed to living among people of her country would have dashed off in a fright; but neither horse nor driver paid the slightest attention to the dramatic burst whereby she somewhat relieved her long pent-up ill-humor. As he neared the group, the coachman lifted his hat, and explained, in his slow, Swiss fashion, that the delay had not been owing to any fault of his. Monsieur could see that he had another horse. Would Monsieur just observe that?

"Stolen, no doubt; thief! assassin!" shouted Susanne.

"Susanne, I will have you drowned in the lake if you do not remain quiet," observed her young mistress, calmly.

"But she is right; the man's conduct is unpardonable," cried Monsieur, glaring at the guilty wretch through his spectacles as ferociously as his kindly eyes could manage.

"Let him explain," ordered Nathalie, animated by a not unusual spirit of contradiction. "Tell us what detained you, my good man."

The coachman announced his conviction that Mademoiselle was an angel. There was a fiendish chuckle from Susanne; but whether intended to express anger at the guilty wretch's presumption, or scorn of the young lady's claims to the title he had bestowed upon her, did not appear.

"Indeed, Mademoiselle, it was not my fault. I set out in ample time. I had accomplished half the distance, when my stupid brute of a horse stumbled, and lamed himself. I had to tie him to a gate, and go back to Clarens for another."

If ever a sound from human throat—half a snort, half a laugh—expressed utter incredulity and contempt, it was the sound wherewith Susanne greeted this explanation. But she had no time to speak; Monsieur quickly interposed, and, so weary that he only asked to get where he could sit down and rest, said, with touching resignation—

"Well, well; give me the paletot and the sac de voyage. I go by train."

"I can take Monsieur and the lady to the station."

"No, no—it is only three steps," interrupted Nathalie.

"Hé! a step is a step, and my legs are fifty years old. I shall be driven," cried Susanne, indignant that the coachman had not included her in his proffer. She mounted nimbly into the carriage, and sat up as erect as if her spinal column had been a steel bar. "Go on, then," she exclaimed, in grim triumph; "and if my neck is broken by your stupidity, it shall cost you dear, if I have to bring the case before every court in Switzerland, should there be such a thing as justice in this accursed land. Go on!"

The Swiss gave her one glare from under his bushy eyebrows; but she looked so warlike, so bristling with a desire for battle, that he did not venture upon a syllable in reply. Susanne spared him neither taunt nor gibe as the horse toiled up the steep little hill, and Nathalie and Monsieur followed.

The carriage stopped at the station: Susanne descended, paletot and sack in hand; descended in silence, for she was at the end of her breath, if not of her eloquence.

"Hé!" called the coachman, suddenly taking advantage of her condition. "Devil—she-devil —daughter of the fiend! A witch—a wrinkled witch—hé, hé."

He lashed his horse into a gallop, and dashed off. Susanne dropped the bag; recovered from her first stupor; made a movement as if to pursue the retreating wretch; but the vehicle disappeared, and she passed on into the station with a face which would have caused a sphinx to laugh.

The train steamed up, and cut short Monsieur's pathetic little adieus. A frantic guard, who looked as if he had been born in a hurry and had been in a hurry ever since, bundled the elderly gentleman into a compartment with irreverent haste, and shouted the signal for departure. Monsieur, gallant to the last, struggled up from the recumbent posture into which the guard's violence had forced him, tried to lean out of the window to wave a last farewell, knocked his head against the door, lost his hat, nearly lost his wig, and fell back with a groan: it was a morning of disasters.

As Nathalie and Susanne descended the steps of the station, Miss Crauford was just coming down the road.

"I am so glad to see you," cried Nathalie, running toward her. "Are you tired? Would you like a long walk? I have the whole day to myself. Monsieur has gone to Geneva. Oh, he nearly lost his wig at the last! If you had seen it! But will you come? Please do! I have been so lonely here—so anxious for your arrival! Now do not be stiff and stony, like an English girl—let us be friends at once."

"With all my heart," said Elizabeth, holding out her hand.

"Oh, the pretty hand!" cried Nathalie, looking at the ungloved fingers with naïve admiration. "Nothing so pretty as an American hand. Mine is well, because it is half American; but yours is perfect. Only look, Susanne."

Susanne was dropping courtesies, her face radiant with smiles. She had heard that the newcomers were very grand people, and Susanne turned into a model of decorum and respect at once. Still she retained possession of her senses. Susanne hated long rambles, and had no mind to be dragged off on one of her mistress's wild expeditions, even in the society of the rich American.

"Dear Mademoiselle," she whispered, "I am

desolated; but, Madame—I must return to the house. That sweet, suffering angel will require me."

"How vexatious!" cried Nathalie. "Mamma would be shocked at our going alone; and it is a shame to lose such a beautiful day."

"We might go to the house and find my maid, if some sort of protection is an absolute necessity," suggested Elizabeth, good-naturedly. Nathalie looked so pretty and childish that she could not bear to have her disappointed.

Susanne volubly pronounced this a most admirable suggestion. Mademoiselle was full of goodness and resources! It was a grief to her, Susanne, not to be able to accompany the young ladies; but her duty, her duty!

"Susanne," retorted Nathalie, "do you remember my explaining to you the other day what an English word meant?"

"Ah, yes; ze hoomboog!" cried Susanne, proud to show her accomplishments before the stranger.

"Just so," said Nathalie; "and that is what you are, a humbug—the hugest one in existence."

She took Elizabeth's arm, and walked on. Susanne was crest-fallen for a few moments; but by the time they reached the gates she recovered her power of speech.

"Mademoiselle loves her joke," she said, apparently addressing nobody in particular. "Mademoiselle laughs at her Susanne; but she knows her worth and her fidelity notwithstanding."

All the while the old sycophant was wondering if some scheme could not be devised which should oust the young American's maid from her present enviable position, and transfer it to that embodiment of worth and fidelity christened Susanne.

While Nathalie ran into the chalet to obtain her mother's consent, Miss Crauford entered the villa. Her father was up and dressed; but he was still neuralgic and sentimental, and though he talked a good deal of poetry about the scenery, was quite willing that Elizabeth should begin making its acquaintance without the necessity of exertion on his part.

"Be sure you admire the view from the Montreux church," he said; "it was your dear mother's favorite spot. Ah, well! I must not try too much at first. I am not strong, and each haunt here is so full of memories. And there's a young lady at the chalet—L'Estrange—very good name—is to marry a Monsieur La Tour. Hum! ha!—I once knew a La Tour. Yes; go by all means. In general I do not approve of intimacies with strangers; but it seems these people are quite safe. Madame Bocher tells me they are most respectable. Yes, exactly—"

And his speech driveled into nothingness, after his habit. He seldom brought his halting remarks to an end; they just faded away in ejaculations; an irritating, indolent fashion, which made one long to shake a little energy into him.

Mr. Crauford had been a valetudinarian for the last ten years—a sore trial to himself and every body about him. The worst of it was that he could write verses, and this caused him to believe himself a poet. He never had gone beyond publishing a few stray rhymes in some newspapers, but he believed himself a genius, kept back from toil and fame by ill-health. His genius served as an excuse for all sorts of ill-humors and selfishness. But he was not a bad man at bottom, only a weak one, and fortunately for his daughter's peace, her influence over him was very great.

Elizabeth had expected demur on his part as to allowing her to make acquaintance with the French girl, until by some means every particular in regard to her and her mother had been got at. Mr. Crauford was given to suspicion of strangers—a man very severe too in his judgments of his acquaintances. Mr. Crauford could tolerate neither slip nor stumble. He was as unmerciful as certain elderly women; so very unmerciful that ill-natured people sometimes wondered, as such persons do in regard to those female censors, whether somewhere in his youth there had not been peccadilloes or worse to cover up. Naturally, Elizabeth thought nothing of the kind. She did not even admit to herself, what at the bottom her clear-judging mind must have known, that in the present instance her father yielded just because it was a personal convenience. Elizabeth loved her father, and hid his selfishness from her sight, concealing it under pretty names and generous excuses; and it spoke well for her character that she did so.

Having given his consent cheerfully, his next speech was to urge the propriety of her remaining at home. But Elizabeth was too thoroughly accustomed to such change and vacillation on his part to feel surprise, and too determined to preserve her illusions in regard to her father for either amusement or contempt. It was just a habit of papa's—invalids always fell into certain odd ways—people possessing the poetic temperament especially. Elizabeth, with all her desire to elevate her parent on a lofty pedestal, could not persuade herself that he was a poet; but to attribute the poetic temperament to him made a very satisfactory and well-sounding excuse for his vagaries.

They had luncheon together in an upper room, which Mr. Crauford decided to appropriate as a study. Wherever he went he must have a study: it served at least as a place in which to smoke and doze comfortably. Madame Bocher wondered why they could not take all their meals in the dining-room, and informed Gervais that "if they went on this way they would find plenty of

extra-service in the month's bill." Gervais had
the luncheon-tray in his own hands, and being a
humorist after his fashion, was so tickled by the
idea of Madame's expecting to be paid for service rendered to Mr. Crauford by Mr. Crauford's
domestic, that he nearly dropped dishes and
plates in his silent laughter.

Three separate times during the repast Mr.
Crauford was of the opinion that he would send
for a carriage and accompany the young ladies;
twice that Elizabeth had better remain at home.
But these were trifling changes.

"You see I want a walk, papa," Elizabeth
said, patiently. "You must have a carriage
come as usual each day; you must not give up
your drive, and I shall go with you. But I must
have my walks too, and ride donkeys. Mademoiselle L'Estrange says one can get such jolly,
obstinate little donkeys up at Montreux."

"The very thing. Well, I would advise you
to-day to get donkeys, and go to the château of
Rochelle." Exactly in the opposite direction to
that decided on by the girls. "What do you
say to going out on the lake in a boat?" This
last suggestion, delivered with airy cheerfulness,
as if Elizabeth had been at a loss how to amuse
herself, and he had hit on this proposal in his
fatherly care.

"Certainly, papa, if you would like to go."

"My child!" in horror, "when you know I
hate a sail-boat! Ah, me! young people are so
heedless. Your dear mamma would never have
forgotten that I detest a sail-boat. Indeed, I
wonder you can ever wish to get into one;
they're never safe. Elizabeth, we might go
down in the train to Vevay, and see what we
find in the way of horses and carriages to take
by the month."

"Yes, papa."

"On the whole, Elizabeth, I suppose I am
better off in the house; my neuralgia is very
troublesome."

A tap at the door. Margot, Miss Crauford's
maid, to say that Mademoiselle L'Estrange was
waiting.

"Go, by all means, my love! Don't mind
me; I shall get on very well," sighed Mr. Crauford.

He was anxious to be left alone, in order that
he might indulge in more smoking and a longer
nap than was reasonable; but the poetic temperament led him to veil this desire even from
his own eyes under the pleasing shape of self-
abnegation. Elizabeth understood the truth as
well as he, but she blinded herself too, and really
felt pangs of reproach, as if she had been a hardened sinner pursuing her own gratification at the
expense of her father's comfort.

As she reached the porch in front of the villa
she saw Nathalie pacing up and down the gravel
walk which ran before the house and chalet.

"I thought you would never come," cried the
French girl, hurrying forward to meet her new
friend. "Mamma has been so tiresome; her
head aches, and that makes her horribly pious.
She says she wishes she had made a nun of me,
instead of bringing me out of the convent to be
married. I do think elderly people are dreadful; do not you?"

It was plain that Mademoiselle Nathalie made
slight attempt to keep up illusions where *her*
parent was concerned. Miss Crauford did not
approve of this speech, so she returned no answer whatever. Nathalie gave her graceful head
a toss and walked on; but as they reached the
gate she stopped short and confronted her companion, looking rebellious and heated, though
her eyes danced with mischief in spite of her
evident irritation.

"If you mean to be English and awful, I shall
remain at home," said she.

"But I do not mean to be either."

"*À la bonne heure!*" cried Nathalie. "Then
have the goodness not to look shocked at my foolish speeches. If I can not say whatever comes
into my head, I shall not talk with you."

Elizabeth laughed; the girl was so arch and
childlike that one could neither take offense nor
think her rude.

"You look very handsome when you laugh,"
observed Nathalie; "you had better indulge in
the exercise whenever you can, for your mouth
is a little sad and stern."

"Never mind my mouth."

"Pardon, one ought always to mind pretty
things."

"In the mean time the morning is passing;
we shall have no walk," suggested Elizabeth.
"Where is Margot?"

That eminently respectable female appeared at
the door of the chalet, where she had been indulging in a little gossip with Susanne. They
had formed acquaintance already; and as Susanne was too old to receive the least notice
from Gervais, Margot felt in her heart a nascent
friendship for her countrywoman. Could she
have gained the slightest clew to the wild thought
which had this morning crossed Susanne's brain
as to the possibility of exchanging her present
service for that occupied by Mademoiselle Margot, the fiery Burgundian would have throttled
the wily Breton on the door-step. Fortunately
for the general harmony, no suspicion troubled
Margot's mind, and the two parted amicably,
and with as many mutual compliments as could
have been devised by their betters.

Susanne watched the two take the road which
struck across the hills directly in front of the
gates, and wished rather enviously that she were
not elderly and stout and very lazy. Then she
went through the dark passage, with two bedrooms on one side, and a little salon at the end.
From here, the only means of admittance to the
rest of the habitable part of the chalet was by

the long outer gallery, the front portion of the interior being occupied by great *pressoirs* and casks, where later the wine would be made. Two more bedrooms opened on the gallery; then came glass-doors which led into a large, comfortable salon. Beyond was a dining-room, a back passage connecting with all these chambers, a kitchen opposite the *salle à manger*, and another covered gallery at the back, which overlooked the Vevay road and the route among the hills.

Susanne heard her mistress's voice from the bedroom, and immediately burst into a cheerful flood of song. Her notes were a little sharp and cracked, but she sang with a will.

"Are you never coming? Am I never to be dressed?" called the peevish accents.

Susanne was traversing the salon by this time; she checked her music. "*Dieu!*" cried she; "if I did not think Madame was having a little repose after her chocolate."

"Come here this instant," ordered Madame.

"*Moulin qui dort, qui dort,*" chanted Susanne, as she reached the passage into which her mistress's bedroom opened. "The young ladies are off," she said, gayly. "Does Madame desire to get up and be dressed?"

"You are a wicked woman," cried the fretful voice from the bed.

Susanne stood in the doorway and shrugged her shoulders. "Madame has her nerves," she murmured.

"I have nothing of the sort," contradicted Madame. "I am thinking about my soul, and yours, and every body's. No one ever tried so hard to make their salvation as I do. I have said twenty *paternosters* this morning, and have gone through the Litany of St. Barbara without missing a line."

"Then I am sure Madame ought to be comfortable: she has done enough for one day," returned Susanne, soothingly.

"I have never done enough, and I am so tired," moaned Madame.

"I shall give Madame her drops," said Susanne.

She bustled about and prepared the potion; it was to be administered in curaçoa, and Susanne made the dose of liqueur very strong. It told favorably and immediately upon the weak, emaciated woman. She sat up among her pillows, twisted the curls of her still luxuriant hair about her lean fingers, and said more cheerfully—

"I think I will put on the new *robe de chambre* with the pink trimmings, Susanne, and the head-dress to match; perhaps Monsieur le Curé will kindly look in before night."

"Good," thought Susanne, "at least she is away from her prayers and her salvation for a little! Of course one must think about such things when one is as near one's end as Madame, but that is no reason for wearying those

in health. It is my firm belief that Madame will not more than last through the autumn," pursued Susanne in her meditations, while getting out the new gown with the pink trimmings. "She might as well not tumble and spoil her prettiest clothes by lying about in them. But, bah, Madame was always selfishness incarnate —she never thinks of me, in spite of my devotion. As for dying—well, I thought the same last year that I do now, and here she is yet; that woman is made of iron."

Madame in bed, with a cap concealing her hair and all the lines showing in her worn features, was a very different-looking object from Madame carefully dressed, with a little rouge dropped into her sunken cheeks, and her spirits elevated by the tonic and the curaçoa. She had been a wonderfully handsome woman, and her great flashing eyes were yet beautiful, though unnaturally bright. She suffered a great deal of pain, which she bore philosophically enough. She was slowly dying of some internal disease, but she had been so long about it, that, like Susanne, she had her doubts whether she might not live as long as other people after all. She was horribly afraid of death; she tried very hard to make her salvation, as she expressed it, but it was tiresome work. Madame had lived a gay life, and she hankered still after her old pleasures; and sometimes the old fiery spirit came up, and she fairly cursed in the midst of her prayers, in a sort of desperate rage at having lost her youth, her beauty, and the health which had rendered both gifts enjoyable. She liked to bemoan her past sins to her spiritual director. She really thought she did it from contrition and remorse, but in reality there was a satisfaction in living over those memories, even while she smote her breast and grew frightened lest the errors should drag her down to hell in spite of her prayers and her penances.

"I find myself wonderfully well to-day," she observed to Susanne. "I wish Monsieur La Tour had not gone to Geneva. But it is a comfort to be rid of Nathalie; she is so full of spirits, so well and strong, that child!"

Susanne smiled secretly. She was very shrewd, this godless, hard-headed old woman. There were days when Madame fairly hated Nathalie for her beauty, and her youth, and her health, though she loved her daughter in her own way —sometimes in a rather tigress sort of way. Susanne understood every one of her mistress's weaknesses, and amused her monotonous life by studying them, quite unconscious that she was a kind of heathen philosopher in her fashion.

"Susanne," said Madame, "I think if I were well wrapped up I might sit in the gallery. I can't walk about the grounds to-day; I had a little pain in the night, and it leaves my legs weak."

Susanne moved out a low easy-chair, enveloped her mistress in a great shawl, and established the invalid comfortably. The sun was warm and bright; the birds sang in the walnut-trees; the waters lapped musically against the shore. Madame could look down the lake where the light lay golden and beautiful. But Madame had never cared much for Nature; the dullest street in Paris would have been more lovely in her eyes than the grandest landscape. Only the express commands of her physician kept her in this quiet spot. Life had lost all interest; she was fearfully bored; she suffered martyrdom from physical pain; still Madame clung to the existence she hated, and was even content to bury herself in this stupid Swiss valley, since in so doing lay her one hope of putting off that last solitary journey she dreaded.

"I think I might read a little," she said, as Susanne stood watching her with a cynical face, amused to see how natural it was to Madame to pose and put herself in a graceful attitude, although there was no one to see—no man, that is; women had never any importance in Madame's creed. "There is a new book under my pillow, Susanne; I hid it for fear Nathalie should find it."

Susanne went in search of the volume, and returned with it in her hand—a novel—an autobiography of a Parisian gallant, whose revelations were enough to make one's hair stand on end.

"I said the whole Litany of St. Barbara," murmured Madame; "I might indulge myself, I think. Remind me to go over the Offerings of St. Joseph before dinner, Susanne."

Some sound from below roused Madame; she raised herself among her pillows and glanced through the railings. Mr. Crauford had strolled out of the villa and approached the chalet. He was standing on the lawn now, speaking with the *fermier*. Madame's eyes—those sunken, feverishly bright eyes—were as sharp as an eagle's, and Madame possessed a memory which neither illness nor time had touched.

Mr. Crauford's face was turned full toward her as he stood; Madame looked curiously down, looked more closely; a puzzled expression crossed her features, and was succeeded by a great trouble. She caught hold of the balustrade with both hands to steady herself, for a nervous trembling began to shake her whole frame.

Presently Mr. Crauford walked slowly on, and was lost to sight among the trees. Madame fell back in her chair; her eyes closed; her breath came in quick, convulsive gasps. After a while Susanne, busy in the farther room, heard her mistress's voice in the sharp, broken tone which denoted one of her attacks of pain. She hurried out, and found Madame leaning weak and helpless against her cushions, a ghastly gray pallor overspreading her countenance—a pallor rendered the more dreadful from its contrast to the painted spots in her hollow cheeks. Susanne had sometimes seen her look like this when awakening suddenly from a bad dream, or when a fear of death came over her.

"Madame is suffering," she said, kindly enough. "Is it the old pain?"

The woman made a motion that she wished to go in-doors. Susanne wheeled her chair through the open window into the salon. Madame was no great weight nowadays.

Susanne went off in search of restorative medicines, moving rapidly, and speaking good-naturedly, though she did think it selfish of the invalid to cause her so much trouble.

"She looks very odd," was Susanne's secret comment, as she worked over her. "Each attack seems to get worse. Any body else would soon go to bits; but there, Madame was born with a constitution like a horse; she is iron, no less!"

Madame lay down on the sofa for some time; gradually the trembling ceased, the face lost its drawn expression. Susanne knew the *crise* had passed.

"It was only fatigue," Madame said, after a while; "I am better now."

"Shall I bring Madame a soup?" Susanne asked, wondering, as she often did, at the fortitude with which the woman fought against these attacks.

"No; I could not take it yet; I will have some more drops presently." She lay quiet again for a little. Susanne thought she was dropping into a doze, but she half opened her eyes, and asked, "What did you say was the name of the new people in the villa? English people, I think Nathalie told me they were."

Susanne was accustomed to such efforts on Madame's part to distract her mind when suffering.

"They are Americans," the old woman answered, quite ready to converse, if her mistress was able to listen; "though I can see no difference between the two; they all talk the same impossible jargon."

"Americans!" repeated Madame, in a low tone.

"Yes, Mademoiselle says America is very far off—oh, farther than Sicily, even."

"I dare say," returned Madame, absently, who, in her character of Frenchwoman, was probably almost as ignorant of geography as Susanne.

"When people live so far away, I wonder they are not content to keep at home," pursued Susanne. "Not that one has any thing to say against them. The father is rather tiresome with his fancies, Madame Bocher says; but the demoiselle is as sweet a lady as one could wish to see. She is fond of our little Nathalie, too."

"Ah!" said Madame. She had her head

turned away; there was a very peculiar expression in her face; she looked as if trying to make herself believe that she had been disturbed by some accidental resemblance when she saw the stranger standing below her balcony. Twice her lips parted to ask a question; twice she checked the words, afraid that the answer would only confirm the truth of what she was endeavoring to regard as a fancy of her own.

In the mean while Susanne ran on volubly in her account of the strangers. She was interested even in the strength of their coffee, knew exactly how many pairs of stockings the young lady carried among her possessions—Margot had given the information—and the number was almost incredible to Susanne.

"Ah," said Madame again, without having heard a syllable of the monologue. "And their name is Lisbet, is it not?"

"No, no; that is the name of the demoiselle, or some outlandish name like it. How is it one says the other—*le nom de famille?* Wait—I have it—Monsieur—oh, those accursed English names! Ah, Monsieur Crau-ford," panted Susanne, with great difficulty.

As Madame asked the question, she raised her head from the pillow, awaiting the answer with an eagerness which escaped her companion. Once more a hollow groan startled the Breton. Madame had fallen back on the sofa, and fainted completely away.

CHAPTER V.
MONSIEUR'S RETURN.

MONSIEUR LA TOUR certainly deserved a warm welcome on his return from what he would have called "*son petit voyage,*" for not only had he found leisure to purchase an exceedingly pretty bracelet to clasp on his betrothed's arm, but Madame L'Estrange and Susanne were both remembered. Monsieur displayed a happy tact, too, where Madame was concerned. He brought her some illuminated legends of a favorite saint, which gratified her superstitious attempts to be what she termed religious; and he added a quantity of carved boxes and other articles for her toilet-table, lest her worldly mood should chance to be uppermost on his arrival, and cause her to regard the legends and their pictures with secret disfavor.

Madame was charmed; she examined the fancifully shaped bottles of rare scent, the porcelain ornaments twisted into heathen gods, with the glee of an old baby; and Susanne was almost equally delighted. Then a pain seized Madame in her back. She ordered the pretty vanities to be put out of sight, and began her Jeremiades and frightened prayers; but there Susanne could not follow her—she could stand in no need of either herself while her health was so perfect as at present.

"Tell Nathalie to take Monsieur out on the lawn, Susanne," said Madame, dolefully. "Oh, my back! Oh, my sins! I am the most wretched woman alive! I have no peace here, and I shall have none hereafter, and I try so hard! I wanted a taste of *confitures* yesterday, and I would not touch them just by way of penance, and I save and save from my annuity in order to leave something to the Convent of the Sacré Cœur. The Superior is almost a saint; she promised to have prayers said for me, and only to think, Susanne, she was once a sinner like the worst of us. Yes, indeed, she was put into that very convent by her family to quiet a horrible *esclandre*, and now she is at the head, and would rather than not live on pulse and lentils the whole year. I do not think people deserve half so much credit when they can make their salvation so easily! Here she is a saint nearly, and will escape purgatory, and I—oh, Susanne! dear Susanne! send for the Curé; I am worse—I die; send for the Curé, I implore thee!"

"To the devil with the Curé," was exactly what Susanne thought. "The poor silly soul is frightened enough now. She shall have a draught, hot and strong, to steady her nerves, and then she will forget about purgatory for a little while. Really, the best she can do is to die as soon as Mademoiselle is married, for this becomes of a tedium that is insupportable; it is too much to be tortured here and scorched hereafter also."

Down by the lake Nathalie and Monsieur encountered Elizabeth Crauford; and Elizabeth liked him for his quaint, old-fashioned manners, and long compliments which sounded like speeches out of a last-century's romance. She felt vexed with Nathalie for laughing at him, but Monsieur did not seem greatly to mind, and looked at her over his spectacles with beaming admiration. He was so little, so dainty in his dress, so marvelous in his bows, that it might have been difficult for this irreverent youthful generation not to smile at his antiquated elegancies; but Elizabeth read goodness and probity in every line of his face—a certain strength of will and determination, too—and she conceived a respect for him accordingly.

After a while Mr. Crauford came out to sun himself for a space, and the four spent a very pleasant afternoon, and Nathalie yawned less than she was in the habit of doing during her affianced's visits.

Mr. Crauford and Monsieur discovered that they had been slightly acquainted some ten years ago in Paris, and felt now—as acquaintances meeting in a very quiet spot are apt to—as if they had been old friends.

"They will play piquet and talk together,"

thought Nathalie. "What a mercy! How droll they both are! I should like to tie their coat-tails together, and hear them go *crac* when they tried to get up! It is very tiresome, to be sure. I would rather be married; then I should get to Paris, at least! I am sure I shall turn wrinkled and gray if I do not soon find some excitement. How can Elizabeth listen so patiently to their prosing? I am half afraid of her, but I do love her already, and I wish she had not come."

Elizabeth was listening with more than patience—she was interested in the conversation. Her father talked very well when he forgot himself—his fancied ailments and his poetical temperament; and if Monsieur was a little heavy and stilted in his speech, every thing he said displayed good sense and culture. Elizabeth was more inclined than ever to think Nathalie ungrateful. The girl needed exactly such a guardian and protector as she would find in Monsieur. He would keep her from follies, and perhaps teach her the Latin grammar. One must excuse Elizabeth, for as yet she had no perception of what love really meant — not the very slightest breath had stirred her heart in its maiden slumber. It was plain that Monsieur adored the willful girl, and to Elizabeth it seemed only fitting that she should love him in return, just from gratitude.

Monsieur had lived to be fifty without falling in love; he had property enough not to need any young woman's *dot*, nor would this usual reason for marriage among his countrymen have influenced him. His mother had lived until within the last few years, and that gentle lady ruled him all her life. He had vegetated calmly in his provincial town; going occasionally to Paris for a change; had attended to his duties as proprietor; had sometimes been mayor and once préfet, and had grown elderly almost without perceiving it.

Less than a twelvemonth ago he had gone one day, while in Paris, to visit a distant relative, the Superior of the convent in which Nathalie had been a pupil from childhood. While Monsieur sat conversing with the old lady, who liked an occasional gossip about the outer world, Nathalie entered the room to ask some favor of the worthy head of the establishment. Monsieur was dazed by the radiant vision. Monsieur turned into an antique Romeo at once, and nobody could have been more astonished than he at the transformation.

Monsieur was very attentive to his relative during his stay in the capital, and contrived to see Nathalie several times. Inquiries in regard to her family were less favorable than could have been wished. There were very odd stories connected with the youth of Madame L'Estrange —nothing distinct to be got at—so pass those stories over as Monsieur did. Madame had married an American, had lived with him in It-

aly, had held a certain position among a tolerably respectable world. Soon after the birth of her child her husband had separated from her. There was gossip, but the actual reasons were never known. Madame at this time had a small property left her by a relative: she took that and the relative's name. Only a few years later she fell into ill-health. Long since she had retired into complete seclusion and been forgotten.

Monsieur was alone; Monsieur was in love; so, in spite of these discouraging circumstances, he sought Madame L'Estrange and told his story. He did not do this without reflection. He would have put Nathalie from his heart if he could, but that being impossible, his obstinacy helped him to disregard the scruples which prudence suggested. The fact of Madame's change of name must prevent the quiet people, among whom Monsieur La Tour's wife would live, from connecting her in any way with the old scandals in regard to her parent. Nathalie was sent for to Dijon, where her mother was staying. She saw Monsieur twice; then she accompanied her mother to Switzerland. Monsieur arranged his affairs, and that done, came on to claim his bride, for long engagements are never in favor among his countrymen. The *corbeille* would arrive next week, the marriage would take place very soon after. In the mean time Monsieur sunned himself in such smiles as Nathalie could be induced to bestow, and was too loyal and honest ever to admit in his soul the slightest suspicion that he had been either hasty or unwise.

There the four sat and talked pleasantly in the soft golden light, while the waves sang, and the breeze whispered of the Italian plains across which it had blown. Nathalie threw aside her listlessness, because Elizabeth was attracting attention, and set herself to the task of fascinating the two elderly gentlemen—a task in which she succeeded without difficulty.

It did not occur to Elizabeth to be jealous of her success; she enjoyed the creature's gay chatter as much as either of their companions, and Nathalie saw that.

"How different she is from me," mused the girl; "now I should have hated her if I had not succeeded in attracting their attention from her. Ah, well; one's character is one's character; it is useless to struggle against it."

Mr. Crauford brought her away from her doubtful philosophy by observing, "I trust we shall soon have the pleasure of making your mother's acquaintance, Mademoiselle."

The conversation was carried on wholly in French, because Monsieur La Tour, Gaul-like, was beautifully ignorant of any language except his own. As soon as he attempted a labored or complimentary speech, Mr. Crauford's accent was so very marked that Nathalie had much ado not to mimic it. She was only deterred by the fear of offending Elizabeth, and her momentary struggle between her impulse and her dread kept her silent till Monsieur La Tour, thinking that he understood the cause of her hesitation, hastened to add—

"The poor Madame is so terrible a sufferer! Nothing could gratify her more, I am convinced, than to share in the enjoyment which is just now permitted to Mademoiselle and myself." Here he bowed, first to Elizabeth, then to her father, by way of emphasizing his words. "But her nerves are in a sad state. She would gladly have come out to-day—an attack of pain prevented—made it necessary even for us both to leave her."

"I know how to sympathize with illness," returned Mr. Craufurd, in a martyr-like voice.

"Each is worse than the other," thought Nathalie. "Oh, I certainly would tie their coat-tails together if it were not for Elizabeth!" Then aloud, "Poor mamma; it is dreadful! And I am such a selfish little monster. I get away always when she is suffering from her attacks."

"Dear Mademoiselle, only because you can not aid. If there were any thing you could do, you would remain," said Monsieur, fearful that her careless speech might produce an unpleasant effect on the strangers.

"Please, do not try to make me out good," cried Nathalie, "else I shall disgrace myself and horrify you all immediately."

Monsieur was shocked; he never could accustom himself to Nathalie's conversation. He was relieved when Mr. Craufurd and Elizabeth laughed heartily.

"Ah," thought Monsieur, "it must be the *esprit Américain;* they seem to comprehend her. A wild, rebellious nation those Americans. I am glad that little Nathalie is at least half French."

At length Mr. Craufurd proposed a game of chess. A table was brought out under the walnut-trees, and the two gentlemen soon became so absorbed in their occupation that the girls wandered away unnoticed to the edge of the lake.

"Now, let us talk," said Nathalie, as they sat down beneath the great willow. "We've not even Margot to bother us, so we need not confine ourselves to English. When I feel wicked, I prefer to speak French; and to-day I feel wicked."

"Do you mean cross—fractious?"

"No, no; wicked! Don't you understand? As my countrywoman felt when she said she could enjoy cold water if only it were a sin to drink it. Now you look shocked—are you?"

"Puzzled rather, I think," replied Elizabeth.

"I fancy you could not comprehend the feeling I want to express," said Nathalie, complacently. "To be sure it is all theory with me yet, but then my theories are immense."

"In regard to what?"

"Every thing! Life—marriage—freedom!" cried Nathalie, her eyes shining, and the beautiful rose tints deepening in her cheeks.

"No," said Elizabeth austerely; "I do not comprehend you."

"You look horrified again," exclaimed Nathalie gayly. "You disapprove of what I said. I forget each instant that we are strangers; but, bah! friendship does not count by time—either one is fond of a person or one is not. When I fall in love, I mean it to be at a look—a glance —how do you say?—first sight."

"Please to remember that you were just speaking of your marriage," retorted Miss Craufurd, austerely.

"*Qu'est-ce que ça fait ? L'un n'empêche pas l'autre,*" cried Nathalie, with a merry laugh. "As if a woman were expected to love her own husband—bah, how tame!"

Elizabeth was accustomed to such sentiments in French novels, and certain English ones, but a little startled at hearing them so calmly enunciated by this childish-looking creature, yet somewhat curious, too, to hear how far she would go in her borrowed theories.

"Are you more horrified than ever?" continued Nathalie, not trusting herself to the cold Saxon accents again.

"I think you are talking great nonsense," returned Elizabeth.

"Not nonsense at all!" exclaimed the other. "It is a truth—a solemn truth, if you will. Is it our fault? We young girls are dragged out like slaves in a market. Some wretched old Mohammedan intimates to our parents that he will take us with such and such a *dot*—the matter is arranged. 'Mademoiselle,' says the parent, 'behold your husband!' This is the first the girl has heard of the business. What can she do? She is given to him—disgusting!"

Her eyes flashed, her cheeks blazed. Elizabeth would have sympathized with her more deeply only that she felt convinced the girl was talking out of a novel, not expressing any deep personal dread or conviction.

"Do I not know?" pursued Nathalie. "It was thus with me. Monsieur La Tour was presented—not on trial, not that I might try and learn to like him, but as my affianced husband. Do you not consider that awful?"

"What did you do?" asked Elizabeth, rather Jesuitically.

"Do? I? Ah, well, just for the time I was so busy admiring a beautiful diamond ring he gave me—this is it—that I did not think much. I had always been insane to possess a diamond ring—Marie de Courcelles had one in the convent, and was so proud!"

She caught Elizabeth's somewhat cynical smile, and stopped.

"I wept bitterly enough when he was gone," she continued, after a pause; "but was I not powerless? Then opposition made mamma so ill that I dared not let her see my misery."

"Are you so very unhappy now?" asked Elizabeth.

"Oh, no; I do not much mind," replied Nathalie, laughing. "One must marry—as well Monsieur La Tour as another. Only he thinks to bury me alive in that dull provincial town. I say nothing; but he will see. Mamma says, once married I can do what I please with him; on that account an elderly husband is much more *commode* than a young one."

"You want to live in Paris, I suppose?"

"Of course; could one exist elsewhere? I mean to have a salon—be a power—gather the lights of the literary world about me. I do not care much for women, but there are a few I will have. I have arranged it all."

"If Monsieur La Tour consent!"

"If he do not—" she began, in a hard voice, which scarcely sounded like hers, then laughed, and added carelessly—"*Alors, tant pis pour lui !* But never mind him. Do you know the works of—"

She ran glibly over certain names which I will not set down—names that were only such to Elizabeth.

"It is not possible you have read those books?" she exclaimed.

"What a child you are! I have read every thing! We had a club in the convent; most of our books came through Blanche de Savigny's cousin—an angel, a god! He and Blanche adore one another; but Blanche is to marry a duke, an uglier man than Monsieur La Tour. But she will not give up her cousin, she is quite determined on that."

"You mean—"

"I mean just what I said! It is plain that you know nothing. They tell me American girls have odd ideas; that once married, they settle down patiently into a humdrum life—*si bête !* Blanche's aunt told her—"

"I do not wish to hear such talk," interrupted Elizabeth.

"Ah, do not be prudish, else I shall hate you. But it is no matter. I could not explain what Blanche said, for I did not understand myself, but she did. I never met a girl so wise as Blanche," and Nathalie gave a sigh expressive of admiration for Blanche's wisdom and regret at her own ignorance. "But she is an impassioned nature, and I am snow, Blanche says. She says if I run away from my husband, or make an *esclandre*, it will be just from pity for some one—"

"What a horrible creature she must be—a monster!" broke in Elizabeth, with indignant energy. "If she were still in the convent, I would write to the Superior, and tell her to be careful that girl did not teach others such things as she has you."

Nathalie shrugged her shoulders, and hummed a few bars of a gay song.

"Eh, if you go about setting trifles to rights," said she, "you will lose all power of seeing and fighting against great evils—it makes one small! A grain more or less of wickedness is not of much consequence."

"I don't think we should agree with or even understand each other's ideas on these subjects," returned Miss Cranford coldly.

"Possibly not," assented Nathalie, with complacency. "It requires a good deal of thought and study to see clearly from my stand-point. You may blame Blanche as much as you like, but I owe her a great deal. She is not a genius herself, but she makes others conscious of their genius."

Elizabeth burst out laughing. Nathalie looked first vexed, then scornful of her companion's lack of comprehension, then suddenly joined in the merriment.

"I forget you did not know I was a genius," said she; "but I am, all the same."

Elizabeth bowed mockingly. Nathalie turned away her head and remained silent for an unprecedented length of time, in her companion's brief knowledge of her. When Miss Cranford spoke, she started, and said reproachfully—

"You brought me out of a dream—such an odd dream!"

"You dream altogether too much," chided Elizabeth.

"Would you know your destiny if you could?" demanded Nathalie. "I have been thinking such strange things—seeing them, I mean. I am sure it was a vision. Give me your hand, Queenie."

"Only be quick about it, Sibyl," she said, playfully.

Nathalie peered earnestly into the white palm which Elizabeth extended.

"You will have great suffering," she said, slowly. "I see the lines—here and here—ah, poor Queenie! Oh! I had forgotten—my presentiment! I hope the trouble will not come through me! Go away—go away—do not ever come near me again!"

She flung Elizabeth's hand from her and started to her feet. She had grown very pale, and her sensitive features worked painfully.

"How childish you are!" Miss Cranford exclaimed, with a certain compassionate scorn in her voice.

"It is not childish! I dreamed about it last night—I remember now! I wish I had never seen you—never!"

Elizabeth could not decide whether the girl were fond of melodrama, or had read doubtful novels until her brain was a little disturbed. Still Nathalie's character presented a study so new to her limited experience that she felt wonderfully attracted even by her follies.

"Suppose we go in," she observed, in a matter-of-fact tone; "that will be more sensible than trying to frighten ourselves with fanciful ideas and superstitions."

"You reject my warning—you refuse to believe!" cried Nathalie. "So much the worse for both—so much the worse!"

Her face darkened; she stood staring straight before her, trembling, shuddering, as if some weird phantasmagoria unfolded itself to her gaze.

"Nathalie!" exclaimed Miss Crauford, a little alarmed.

The girl sank back on the bench, and covered her face with her hands, shivering and gasping still. Presently she began to laugh in a rather hysterical fashion.

"It is gone!" she said, looking up again. "I do not know what I saw—something dreadful—but it is gone. Blanche always vowed I was a medium or a mesmerist: I am very odd, I know. Do not mind—let us talk of other things."

"I do not mind in the least," retorted Elizabeth, determined to be severely practical, by way of bringing the other out of these heroics.

"You laugh—you jest!" cried Nathalie, in an irritated voice. "But let the matter go. I will do you no harm—I am determined that I will not." Then, after an instant, she added in a complacent tone—"But I suppose I shall be a very wicked woman all the same—oh, very wicked."

"I never heard a girl talk such nonsense in my life," returned Miss Crauford, horrified in earnest now. "You will end in a lunatic asylum if you do not stop living dramatics and a hash of sentiment and transcendentalism."

"Ah, I have read Kant," exclaimed Nathalie. "I have read Comte too. I am a Socialist—oh, a Socialist acharné! My first book will be a Socialistic romance; my second, Blanche's biography; my third—"

Elizabeth was laughing so heartily by this time that Nathalie left her third work unnamed, and joined in the merriment with childish glee.

"It is true, though," she persisted. "You think I am a goose; but I shall write books—many of them."

"Oh, your being a goose would not prevent that," interrupted Miss Crauford in sarcastic parenthesis.

"But let me tell you about my third novel."

"No; those two are quite enough. The idea of Mademoiselle Blanche's biography is overpowering."

"You do not appreciate me, Elizabeth!" sighed Nathalie, with a resignation that was exceedingly comical.

"You must pity my inability," laughed Miss Crauford.

But further words were checked by loud repetitions of Nathalie's name.

"It is Susanne," said the girl, starting up.

"And Monsieur La Tour," added Elizabeth. "What can be the matter?"

Both were frightened, and hurried toward the chalet from whence the summons proceeded. Nathalie flew on into the house; Elizabeth found her father rubbing his left arm, regarding the chess-table which had been upset, and looking at once alarmed and indignant. He could give slight explanation. They had reached the most exciting point of their game; suddenly Monsieur had observed that Madame L'Estrange was coming out on the gallery. Mr. Crauford turned to look—heard a dreadful shriek—saw a female figure totter back. Monsieur had knocked the table over, and hurt Mr. Crauford's neuralgic arm. That crazy old servant had rushed out screaming—Monsieur had screamed, and that was all Mr. Crauford could tell, only that he was much offended by the whole performance. If Madame L'Estrange wished to faint, she ought to choose her seasons better, and not interrupt his game of chess, and cause him to be deafened by an insane noise, not to mention the serious injury to his arm. It was very inconsiderate, to say the least, and disgustingly French.

CHAPTER VI.

AN UNEXPECTED DELAY.

THE next days were pleasant ones at La Maladèyre. Such excursions as could be made in carriages were not objected to either by Mr. Crauford or Monsieur, and Nathalie was kept in high spirits by the unusual excitement.

The Frenchman wished to present his old acquaintance to Madame, but Madame put him off each morning with new excuses, and he at last settled down upon the conviction that it was a pain to her to see strangers now she had lost the beauty and gayety which she never ceased lamenting even in the midst of her loudest renunciation of the vanities of this mundane sphere. Neither Mr. Crauford nor Elizabeth perceived any thing surprising in Madame's refusal; indeed, it was only a delay always—a pleasure deferred. She was constantly hoping to be well enough to receive Monsieur La Tour's friend, and he and Nathalie were daily the bearers of elaborately civil messages both to father and daughter. In truth, poor Madame was almost wholly confined to her rooms. The motion of a carriage was insupportable—a Bath-chair her detestation. Once in a while she could walk about the lawn supported by her future son-in-law and Susanne; but delicacy kept the Craufords from intruding at such times.

Elizabeth was at length permitted to see her. Madame was feeling unusually strong one afternoon, had caused herself to be arrayed in a becoming toilet, and hearing from Susanne that Miss Crauford was in the salon with Nathalie, she sent for them both to her own parlor at the back of the chalet.

It was a spectacle Elizabeth did not soon forget. She wondered that Nathalie and Monsieur could become enough accustomed to it not to mind. Madame sat up among her bright draperies to receive the young American, her grizzled hair carefully dressed, her attitude theatrically graceful, pouring out a torrent of pretty speeches, playing with the rings that decorated her bony fingers, smiling, nodding, talking trivialities one instant and quoting scraps from doleful sermons the next. Altogether she was such a bundle of awful contrasts and incongruities that Elizabeth felt as if she were undergoing an interview with a skeleton galvanized into a spasmodic semblance of life, rendered more painful by the effort to hide its ghastliness under paint and fanciful decorations.

The curtains were drawn, and the room so dark that, entering from the brightness of the sunny gallery, Elizabeth could at first distinguish nothing whatever.

"Why, mamma," called Nathalie impatiently, "we shall break our necks—it is a dungeon! Why has that foolish Susanne shut you up like this? Where are you, Susanne?"

"Of course it is the fault of Susanne—blame her; every thing is always the fault of Susanne," grumbled that worthy female from her corner, for Susanne had no idea of obeying the advice of St. Peter, which urges us to suffer wrong in silence.

"Chut!" said Madame. "Our visitor will think she has got into a mad-house instead of a dull invalid-room. Come here, Nathalie, and bring Mademoiselle. This is a great, great pleasure—"

"Now, mamma," interrupted Nathalie, "do not talk about seeing her, because it is utterly impossible to see any body in this gloom." ·

But as Elizabeth's eyes became accustomed to the obscurity, she could perceive the emaciated shape propped up among the pillows, and was almost startled for an instant. Somehow in the shadows, Madame, with her rouge, her scarlet shawls, and her skeleton head, was more appalling than she would have been in the broad light of day. Nathalie, perhaps, noticed this too; she pushed back one of the curtains in spite of a rapid expostulation from her mother.

"At least Mademoiselle will not think we have designs on her life," she said. "Besides, that was an awful light, or darkness rather; it made us all look as if we had been dead a week."

"Be still, child, be still," cried Madame. "Do not use such dreadful language."

By this time Elizabeth had reached the sofa. Madame was extending that bony hand which it required an effort to touch, and Madame's great sunken eyes were looking curiously at her; uncomfortable eyes to have fixed upon one, their fire seemed so out of keeping with the thin, ghastly face.

"Dear Mademoiselle, it is so good of you to come to me—so very good," Madame said over and over, still retaining her hand, and glaring at her with that attempt at a smile which was more like a spasm than any thing else. "I love the Americans—they have always been a mania of mine: is it not so, Nathalie, my child?"

"I can not tell, mamma; I have not known you all your life," returned Nathalie, who was in one of her impossible moods.

"She is half American, that bad girl," laughed Madame, "though I am sure her naughtiness is entirely French. But you are standing, dear Mademoiselle. I entreat you not to stand—I implore!"

Madame was as earnest and beseeching as if she had been begging her visitor to step out of the fire or away from a precipice, but Elizabeth was accustomed to these little exaggerations of tone and words among the Gallic race.

Susanne sat upright in her corner, knitting as if her daily bread depended upon her industry, for Susanne was in an ill-humor to-day, and at such times always knitted violently. Nathalie leaned on the window-sill, and peered out between the half-closed shutters, and wished the world would come to an end—for no particular reason that she knew; but Nathalie's spirits went up and down as irregularly and irrationally as a barometer that is out of order. Elizabeth remained by the sofa, and endured as best she might the feverish glare of Madame's eyes, and followed as well as she could the rapid changes of Madame's conversation.

"You can not think how you remind me of—" Madame uttered this beginning in the midst of talk about Nathalie's marriage, and checked herself as abruptly as she had commenced.

"Of whom does she remind you, mamma?" asked Nathalie, who had looked back just in time to catch the broken sentence.

"I can not tell—you know it always tires me to think," returned Madame, peevishly. She resumed the explanation of Nathalie's prospects, and Nathalie took refuge in the window again.

"It is bad enough to be married," she thought, "without living it all over forty times each day in advance."

Madame asked Elizabeth a great many questions—about her age, her life, her father; but Madame's tact caused them to sound like inquiries dictated by profound interest and budding affection instead of vulgar curiosity.

"You have been so kind to my spoiled infant yonder, and she has talked of you so much, that I seem to know you well already," said Madame. "You see I find I have grown fond of you in advance."

Elizabeth turned her eyes away to avoid the spasmodic smile, and thanked Madame for her graciousness.

"Finding Mademoiselle Nathalie here has been a great pleasure to me," she said.

"You are good to say so, adorable!" cried Madame. "Nathalie is a dear creature, but so spoiled—a child—a baby! She has lived all her life in a convent, and knows no more of the real world than an infant."

From the corner where Susanne sat knitting, like a grim representation of Industry, came a low, sardonic chuckle.

"Are you coughing—have you taken cold, Susanne?" demanded Madame, in a voice of awful politeness and interest.

"I choked—I think I swallowed a bit of yarn," replied Susanne, unhesitatingly and very crossly.

"Susanne is laughing at the idea of my innocence and ignorance—I don't wonder," observed Nathalie, putting her head into the room again.

"Fie, for shame, beloved!" exclaimed Madame anxiously. "What will Mees Crauford think?" Madame spoke in French, but she thought that "Mees" was a neat bit of English—it was her only one.

"She knows me pretty well by this time," laughed Nathalie. "Besides, Susanne can not deny that was what she laughed at."

"I said I choked, Mademoiselle," retorted Susanne stoutly.

"I know you *said* so!"

"And I never tell lies," added Susanne. "I beg that Mademoiselle will not quarrel with me; I am busy."

"Very well," said Nathalie; "I only wanted to settle the question of my babyish innocence."

"A mere baby!" repeated Madame.

Once more a bit of yarn got in Susanne's throat, else she chuckled.

"Susanne," said her mistress, "you have a cold assuredly; I shall give you some of those drops."

Susanne rose, made a neat roll of her knitting, and laid it on a table.

"Farewell, Madame and Mademoiselles," said she.

"Where go you?" demanded Madame.

"To drown myself," quoth Susanne, calmly. "I told Madame that if she ever again insisted on my taking those drops I should drown myself—the time has come."

"Go get some of mamma's curaçoa instead," said Nathalie. "You like curaçoa, Elizabeth? I am a baby, but I would intoxicate myself with it every day if mamma gave me the opportunity."

First Madame laughed at all the nonsense; then a pain seized her, and she grew grave.

"I am a dying woman, Mees Crauford!" she exclaimed, so suddenly, and with such despairing

emphasis, that Elizabeth's first thought was some vague one of rushing for the doctor. "I have done with the world—I ought not even to laugh! I try to make my salvation; I said at least fifteen Hail Marys last night each time I awoke. Ah, it is dreary work making one's salvation; but you know nothing about that yet—you are young and strong."

She looked at Elizabeth with an envious glare in her eyes—she often looked at Nathalie like that. There were moments when it was not easy for Madame to avoid hating any body who still retained those blessings she had lost—health and youth.

"They ought not to be severe on me, they ought not," she muttered. "I try so hard—Monsieur le Curé says I try."

"Taste of the curaçoa, mamma," urged Nathalie, bringing her a tiny glass of the grateful cordial. "Is it not good, Elizabeth? Monsieur La Tour gets it for mamma; he is useful in his way, is Monsieur."

"He is an angel!" exclaimed Madame, with as much energy as if no thought of purgatorial pains had ever tormented her. "Mees Crauford, is not this child a fortunate one?"

"I like Monsieur La Tour exceedingly," Elizabeth replied. "He is so kind and gentle, it would be impossible not to like him."

"You hear, little difficult?" cried Madame.

"Yes, mamma, I hear," returned Nathalie, sipping her curaçoa contentedly. "But just ask Mademoiselle how she would like to marry this epitome of all the virtues."

"Mademoiselle could have no thought of the kind in regard to a man who is affianced," said Madame with dignity.

"That comes of my being a baby—you see I know no better," observed Nathalie.

"You are incorrigible!" laughed her mother. "Where is Susanne?"

"Drinking curaçoa behind the dining-room door," replied Nathalie, promptly.

Susanne put in her head with an indignant squeak.

"I never so much as smelled of the cork," cried she, wiping her lips as she spoke. "I know I shall drown myself one day. I can not bear such constant injustice from Mademoiselle."

"I shall never try that mode when my time for suicide arrives," said Nathalie. "Which way should you choose, Elizabeth? Now, Blanche always declared—"

"Do not talk of such horrid things," moaned Madame. "I do not know what possesses you and Susanne to-day! The doctor says I am to have cheerful conversation."

It seemed to both her daughter and servant that Miss Crauford's visit made Madame unusually nervous and excitable; still she would not let the young lady go.

"It is so great a pleasure to me to see you,"

she said several times, and always Elizabeth fancied that Madame looked as if she would have liked to bite her. "One evening, perhaps, I shall be well enough to receive you all—Monsieur Crauford likewise. I think I am stronger than last week. Do you not think I am stronger, Susanne?"

"Not a doubt of it," Susanne replied to the inquiry uttered with piteous eagerness. "Madame is very much stronger; I said so only yesterday."

Nathalie sat down by the sofa, and passed her arm about her mother. There was more tenderness in face and gesture than Elizabeth had yet seen her exhibit.

"I have not been a bad parent to you; I have not," cried Madame.

"No, no; a dear little mamma—there, there!" replied Nathalie, stroking her hair, as one might endeavor to quiet a child.

The little scene touched Elizabeth, but it only lasted a moment. Madame gave one or two dry sobs; an expression made up of terror and remorse crossed her face; then she was first to get away from the softened mood.

"We are wearying Mademoiselle," she said.

"You can not think that," Elizabeth replied earnestly, and Madame could see that the sympathetic tears had gathered in her eyes.

Madame looked touched, then irritated; but she was altogether so odd and changeable that Elizabeth would not have been surprised at any vagary.

"Mademoiselle has a tender heart," she sneered. Nathalie raised her head at the altered tone. Madame added, with sudden sweetness, "Love our new friend well, Nathalie; hers is a rare nature."

Nathalie turned and gave Elizabeth a laughing embrace, glad to escape from the seriousness which had oppressed her for a little. There was a strange light in Madame's eyes as she watched the two; then as quickly she made a sign of the cross. Madame knew she had been thinking wicked things, and she was too near death to allow herself that privilege.

"Monsieur le Curé is coming up the road," called Susanne from the dining-room.

"Ah, put away the curaçoa, and give me the Offerings of St. Joseph," cried Madame to her daughter.

"But the Curé likes curaçoa," said Nathalie; "and he admitted the last time he was here that he thought St. Joseph's meditations very gloomy ones."

"So he did," assented Madame, relieved; then in a changed voice—"But no matter! It is the Curé's business to console me; I need consolation! Give me St. Joseph! He shall have no curaçoa unless he console me—not a drop."

"I am going out to walk with Miss Crauford," said Nathalie.

"Yes — go," said Madame. "Adieu, dear Mees, thanks a thousand times for this visit! Ah, you are like—"

She had taken Elizabeth's hand; she dropped it suddenly with a glance of aversion.

"Like whom, mamma?" persisted Nathalie.

"I can not remember—I forget every thing," replied Madame, querulously. "Do not tease me, child! Adieu, dear Mees; you are an angel of goodness, I am sure. Ah, I am a miserable woman; broken down, old, dying! Where is Monsieur le Curé? Why does he not come to console me? That is his business. I gave a hundred francs to his new church, and I am poor; if he does not do his duty, it is he who will go to purgatory. Susanne, Susanne, take away this red shawl, and bring me the blue one. Monsieur le Curé likes blue. Quick!—how slow you are!"

The two girls passed out through the dining-room, and went down the flight of stairs which was the usual mode of egress from this part of the chalet. They met the Curé panting up the steep staircase—a jolly, fat man, who ought to have made a very comfortable and indulgent confessor. He stopped to pay them both a quantity of florid compliments, and to inquire after Mr. Crauford and Monsieur La Tour, who were having a quiet game of chess in the villa.

"A pair of rosebuds!" cried the Curé, before his question could be answered.

"Elizabeth's papa and Monsieur La Tour?" asked Nathalie, saucily.

"You are a little witch," said the Curé, beaming. "I go to see the dear mamma; is she tolerably comfortable to-day?"

"Oh, yes; but please persuade her not to be doleful," sighed Nathalie. "She does nothing but repent, and I am sure she is very good. If you console her a great deal she will give you some curaçoa—I am certain she will; and it is very nice too."

The Curé laughed heartily, and went his way.

"Well, well," he thought, "it would be pleasanter if one's duty lay more among the young and happy than the dying; but I hope they set it all right for us somewhere: I trust they do."

The Curé stopped on the balcony, took a pinch of snuff, and glanced up at the sky. He was a large-hearted, easy-going man, and liked to keep his theology as mild as his conscience would permit. I am afraid the Curé would have abolished purgatory altogether, if it had been in his power, and made every body happy in this world and the next. He was careful, however, to guard such unorthodox fancies in the secrecy of his soul, and was sometimes shocked at his own wickedness in indulging in wishes of that nature.

His visit cheered Madame, but in spite of it she awoke in the middle of the night from a bad dream, and was very ill. She wanted the Curé and doctor sent for at once, convinced that both body and soul were in a bad way; but Susanne paid no attention, aware that neither authority could be of the least use. She was prepared with the necessary remedies for those crises, and did not even disturb Nathalie, certain that the girl would only terrify her mother by her fright.

Frictions with liniment, and repeated doses of the drops and curaçoa, at last produced their effect.

"It is over for this time," Madame said wearily. "I do not seem to get any weaker. I should think I may last a long time yet."

"There is no doubt of it, I believe," returned Susanne, rather grimly. It was this power of endurance, this inability on the part of Madame's physical frame to wear out, which aggravated the old woman: she thought people ought to die or get well.

"*Eh bien*," thought the Breton, when her mistress at last fell asleep from sheer exhaustion, "if all this does not count in my favor in this world and the next, Monsieur La Tour is a brute, and the blessed saints are no better!"

It was only three or four days later that Madame and her proposed son-in-law received a severe shock. Monsieur appeared one morning at the chalet earlier than his wont. Elizabeth chanced to be in the grounds as he drove up, and perceived that he looked sorely disturbed and annoyed, though he tripped down from the carriage with his usual alertness, and treated her to his customary eloquent and elaborate greetings. Monsieur always reminded Elizabeth of a cross between a legal gentleman and an old beau of the *ancien régime*, with a plain wig in place of a powdered one. But though one might smile at his quaint courtesies, Monsieur was never ridiculous, and Elizabeth respected him highly.

It was not very long before Nathalie came flying out of the chalet, and joined Elizabeth as she walked down the path toward the lake. Nathalie's eyes were dancing, and her face lighted up with animation and excitement.

"I saw you from the window," said she. "I am out of breath. I ran away fast, fast, for fear mamma should stop me. What do you think has happened?"

"I have not the slightest idea. Get back your breath and tell me," replied Elizabeth, tranquilly.

"Figure to yourself, my dear—it will not be soon—it is put off—unavoidably put off!"

"It? What?"

"I am to have a whole month, perhaps six weeks," continued Nathalie in triumph. "Do you not understand? The marriage, of course. Fancy—only fancy it!"

They had reached the poplar-tree by this time. Elizabeth sat down on the bench which encircled it, and looked grave and reproachful.

"Monsieur is obliged to go into Belgium," pursued Nathalie, on whom the glance was utterly wasted. "A relative of his is dying—a horrible old maid, who hated every body and whom every body hated. I am sure if she had lived she would have made us a visit, and I never could have borne that."

"Your sympathy must be a sweet and soothing thing to Monsieur La Tour," observed Elizabeth, sarcastically.

"Oh, I do not think he wants sympathy on account of that dreadful old woman; but he has to go away. She wants him, and she has money; it is his by right, but she has harpies of relations on her mother's side who might steal it."

"I think he would go in any case if she wished it," Elizabeth said.

"Oh, I dare say; but it would be silly. She lives near Brussels. He must go at once, so there is no time for the marriage; indeed, it would not be decent under the circumstances, and so I said; neither he nor mamma could deny it."

"Oh no! Your regard for the proprieties is most edifying!"

"You are vexed; you sneer! But I shall have at least a month—more, probably. Only think of it, my beautiful!"

"Suppose he saw you at this moment, and heard you!"

"I can not help it! I said several decorous things; then I ran away for fear I should laugh. It was so funny to see mamma's face and his, and they both wept a little. I had my handkerchief at my eyes. I was supposed to weep also."

"I think you are very ungrateful to him," returned Elizabeth. "I saw Monsieur when he drove up; he looked distressed and troubled."

"No doubt—it was his duty; he could do no less," pronounced Nathalie, complacently. "But do not scold. What walks we will have! what donkey rides! Oh, my dear, remember I shall have the bliss of Monsieur's society all my life—all his life, I mean—while I shall only have you for a few weeks! Kiss me this instant, and look pleased; at least you need not kiss me, there is always something so tame about one girl embracing another; but say you are glad."

"Personally, yes; but that is selfish, and I am sorry for poor Monsieur," said Elizabeth.

"Well, I do not know," observed Nathalie, meditatively. "I have an idea that he is to be congratulated, if he could only think so; it is a reprieve. My dear, Monsieur La Tour does not seem to me eminently fitted for a wild-beast tamer; and I do assure you, in confidence, that I fear he is undertaking a whole menagerie."

"And I think all this talk about yourself is nonsense," said Elizabeth. "But if it were not, I fancy you will find Monsieur La Tour a much more determined man than you suppose him."

"Then we shall quarrel horribly. At least that will afford a little variety," returned Nathalie, yawning. "Well, I must go back now. I only ran out to tell you while he and mamma wore off the first edge of their despair. See, I shall look decorously grieved. Will not this answer?"

She drew her face down in such a caricatured assumption of melancholy that Elizabeth could not help laughing, though, when Nathalie danced off, she was obliged to think, as she had so often done since their first meeting, that there was much to disapprove of in the girl. But severe as Elizabeth was inclined to be in her judgments, somehow she pitied Nathalie more than she blamed her. What could be expected of any creature with a mother like Madame? And Elizabeth shuddered with abhorrence and disgust. Then she felt heartily contrite; but be as sorry as she would for the physical sufferings, there was something loathsome to her in the remembrance of that skeleton face, with its rouged spots and the frizzed curls adding to its ghastliness.

There was not much time for Madame and Monsieur to yield to their anguish, for it was necessary that he should set out the next morning on his journey. Indeed, after her first paroxysm of distress, Madame remembered that the death of this relative would give a sensible increase to Monsieur's fortune, and she was not sufficiently weaned from this world and its vanities to despise that. She sighed to think that it was not likely that she could live long enough to have much enjoyment of the money, and she felt a fierce resentment rise in her soul as she glanced at Monsieur—so upright, so strong, with such hues of health on his cheery face. He was older than she; what business had he to look so well, and seem likely to live for the next twenty years to enjoy his fortune? Then she waxed penitent, and tried to think that Paradise must be a pleasant place—perhaps even pleasanter than Paris! But then Madame knew Paris, and she was not acquainted with the other blessed abode. Ah! why could she not be allowed to seek the one she liked! It was all very well for people to go to Heaven who were not contented here; but, for Madame's part, give her decent health and enough money, and she would not grumble at being forgotten by death, even though her youth, her beloved youth, was gone forever.

Of course Monsieur spent the afternoon and evening with his betrothed, and Nathalie encouraged herself to win Elizabeth's admiration for her discreet behavior, by remembering that she would have the next day and many next days free from Monsieur's society. As Madame's invalid state did not permit of late dinners, Monsieur and Nathalie dined at the villa, by Mr. Cranford's invitation. They had a very pleasant meal; Monsieur tried his best to be cheerful, though it touched Elizabeth to see how his mouth would quiver and his eyes turn pathet-

ically upon Nathalie, as the girl laughed and chattered, champagne-glass in hand; for Nathalie had a great appreciation of good things in the way of table enjoyments.

Then Nathalie and Monsieur had to return to Madame, and Elizabeth spent the evening playing chess—which she hated—with her father, and wondering how Nathalie could prove so utterly regardless of the great love lavished upon her.

"It is so beautiful to be loved," thought Elizabeth. "A woman ought to be proud of a good man's affection; and the contentment and rest would be so much sweeter than all that excitement and passion novels are so full of."

Which wisdom showed the complete ignorance wherein Miss Cranford had lived, so far as emotions of that nature were concerned.

Madame dreaded greatly this delay. She was morbidly anxious for the marriage to take place; but to dwell upon the money Monsieur was going to claim did soothe her somewhat at the parting, and afterward even more.

Still it was a miserable business, viewed in its best light, and Madame and Monsieur were very wretched. Nathalie remained as lachrymose as she could, though her gravity was often sorely tried to see how odd her mother looked as her tears spotted her paint, and what grimaces Monsieur made in his efforts not to weep also. Besides, Susanne, not to be deceived by any shallow pretense, passed in and out of the room on frequent errands, and upon each occasion favored Nathalie with such glances of stern reproof, such scornful consciousness of the girl's hypocrisy, that Nathalie would have given the world for somebody to enjoy the whole comedy with her.

CHAPTER VII.
"LA CHAUDERON."

ALMOST four weeks went by, and very pleasant ones they were to Elizabeth. Mr. Cranford was in an uncommonly placid mood, the duration of which was of such length that it astonished his daughter, though she did not put the matter in this brutal fashion. It was a bettering of papa's health, longer freedom than usual from nervous pains, and similar reasons, or well-sounding names rather, such as Elizabeth always insisted on finding for her parent's caprices. He even worried himself and her less than ordinary by his indecision upon affairs in general, great or small, from the important doubt if coffee or chocolate would best agree with his "system" of a morning, up to debates whether the newly invested funds should be drawn out and established in some other quarter.

He discovered two or three acquaintances staying at Vevay, several more up at the hotel

"Lord Byron," between the Castle of Chillon and Villeneuve. He could give occasional dinners, and indulge now and then in a game of whist in the evening. He had a poem in his mind—not that he was writing one, nor ever would or could—but he believed each night that he should commence so doing the next day. He not infrequently stumbled on a few rhymes, which he repeated to Elizabeth or his guests as "extracts from the work that would be *the* labor of his life," with an emphasis on the article as if he had been from early youth busy with grand mental tasks whereof this was to prove the crowning glory.

The weather was gorgeous. The beautiful region grew more and more into Elizabeth's heart. She had admired it at first, but she had learned to love it.

Mr. Crauford sometimes recited little poetical quotations about scenery. He offered these with such a conscious manner, such an air of condescension and proprietorship, that few people were bold enough to suppose them not original, even if an effort of memory could have traced them to their source. But in spite of these proofs of genius and taste for the beautiful, Mr. Cranford had slight fancy for going in search of it, especially when the road led up steep hills. In consequence, Elizabeth and Nathalie made a great many excursions together, guarded by Gervais or Margot, sometimes, to the latter's contentment, by the pair in company. And there were such quantities of lovely places to visit, it is a shame that the attempt to describe them would only sound like a page torn out of a guide-book. The old château of Blonay was within walking distance, so were numerous picturesque hamlets perched on the hill-sides. Then there were jaunts in a stout *char;* climbs up the rocks of Naze, which command a wonderful view of the Savoyard and Bernese Alps and a glimpse of Mont Blanc; a journey to the Col de Jamin, a wild, frowning pass, with the needle-like cliff towering above: every where one turned new routes delightful to follow, new scenes more charming than those discovered hitherto.

There was a little boat at the villa landing which Elizabeth could row, and, though Nathalie was at first given to slight fears, she overcame them, and the two were very fond of drifting about the lake on the warm afternoons, when Mr. Crauford did not see fit to grow nervous and keep them at home.

Then, too, Madame was capricious, and not unseldom prohibited Nathalie's seeking her new favorite. Madame had her days of liking Miss Crauford also, and would even sometimes beg the favor of a visit; but she generally turned sulky or fretful before Elizabeth had been five minutes in the room, and almost forgot her thin varnish of French politeness under the force of some secret irritation. Of course, Miss Crauford bore her moods patiently; she knew how terribly the poor woman suffered. She could not so easily pass over the capriciousness with which Nathalie was treated; she could see that it had a bad effect upon the girl, who certainly possessed faults enough already.

The days flew by. The vintage came and passed. This was a disappointment to both girls. They had looked forward to witnessing a scene at once poetical, picturesque, and bucolic, and had talked in advance of the pretty sight it would be to watch the stalwart youths and sun-browned maidens gather the amber clusters of grapes, poising the rustic baskets on their heads, singing quaint songs in their free, musical young voices.

The reality of which picture was that dirty old men and ancient crones, hideous of aspect, collected the grapes in ugly wooden buckets, crushed the fruit with heavy sticks to make the buckets hold the more, and after that the masses were put under a huge black *pressoir* to be squeezed, and both men and women were drunk day and night—alas for romance!

Between that cruel disillusion and her mother's increasing fretfulness, Nathalie began to lose patience.

"I wish Monsieur would come back," she said often. "He is little and he is ugly, and he wears à wig, but at least he is always good-natured, and mamma is so tiresome with her temper."

"Remember how long she has been ill," Elizabeth said one day when Nathalie had come in to see her, indignant and annoyed.

"My dear, I never attempt to blind myself to facts," returned Nathalie, with a cynicism that was painful. "Illness has nothing to do with the matter. Mamma was always the most tyrannical and capricious woman in the world, and her temper was always fiendish. I recollect that as a child, though I was not much with her—I was in the way."

"Nathalie!"

"I was in the way, I assure you. Did I not just say I never made to myself illusions? She put me in a convent for her own convenience—she kept me there for the same reason till I was grown up—she took me out because it suits her that I should marry."

"Do you not suppose what seemed best for you had something to do with her resolves?" asked Elizabeth.

"I will suppose so if you like. I should have been sent just the same in any case. Now, do not make me out worse than I am. I bear tolerably well with her caprices, you must admit."

"Yes, in general."

"Ah, well, one is not perfect—even mamma, though she is trying to make her salvation."

Nathalie was so accustomed to regard her

mother as an invalid, and knew so little of illness, that she was not anxious about her—no proof of hard-heartedness in her case. Indeed, it seemed an even chance whether Madame's strength might not hold out till she had exhausted the patience and health of all surrounding her.

"I do bear with her," pursued Nathalie, "because she is ailing. If she were well, we should have one battle royal that would prove to her I meant to be mistress, and I should probably be forced to box her ears."

"Nathalie!" in a tone of horror.

"I should infallibly and without doubt box her ears," amended Nathalie, as usual goaded on to fresh extravagances of language by this note of disapproval. "I boxed Susanne's ears the other day; she thought I was mad, and has been very docile ever since."

"Nathalie!"—disapprobation that was almost disgust now mingling with the horror.

"What will you? I told you long since I was a whole menagerie," returned Nathalie, shrugging her shoulders. She rose and looked at herself in the glass—they were in the salon of the villa—and continued pensively, "I look so sweet and amiable, too—it is odd! After all, I am not ill-tempered; I mean that I neither scold nor fret—all I want is my own way! I must have that; I was born to have it, I suppose, else the instinct would not be so strong in me."

Elizabeth had learned the uselessness of expostulation or other attempt to set right Nathalie's peculiar ideas.

"Have you had a letter from Monsieur this week?" she asked, by way of changing the conversation.

"Yes, this morning. But, bah! his letters always vex me—half to mamma, directed to her, read by her first; it is odious! Such a marriage as mine has little enough romance; they would be wise to leave me at liberty to weave a few shreds about it. But no, they are blind, blind!"

She walked up and down the room, stamped her feet, inveighed against French customs and the peculiar idiocy displayed by her betrothed and her mother; and Elizabeth let her alone, aware by experience that she would soon rave herself into calmness. Presently she sat down again and began to laugh: Elizabeth looked so perfectly unmoved that she could not avoid coming out of her heroics.

"I really believe if you did not act like a wet blanket on me they would drive me into something desperate by their folly," she said.

"Folly which exists in your imagination," returned Elizabeth. "You would like to get up a grief for yourself, and you have no materials. You have told me twenty times you had no objection to marry Monsieur La Tour."

"Just so," said Nathalie; "but sometimes the prosaic look of the whole thing drives me wild."

"Bah! you always want an excitement of some sort."

"So I do. You know me very well; but you like me?"

"Oh yes, I like you; shall we go out? Papa is busy in his room with letters—he did not want my help, he said; odd, too, now I come to think of it, for I am usually his amanuensis."

"I never mean to be useful," said Nathalie; "it is a mistake! Monsieur La Tour will find that all the sacrifices must come from him."

"What a selfish, petty life you will lead!"

"You think it? Ah, well, at least I shall be helping Monsieur to win the way to Heaven—you know it is sacrifice does it," laughed the incorrigible girl.

Elizabeth went up-stairs to see her father before going out, and found him still occupied. He looked flurried and worried, but, as he declared there was nothing the matter, she concluded that he was only oppressed by a sudden afflatus of his genius. Sometimes, when waiting to be delivered of a few verses, the agonies of labor were extreme. If he had not possessed a dictionary of rhymes to serve as a sort of mental midwife, there is no knowing what misfortune might have happened; even with that aid, the struggles more frequently ended in doleful abortions than any completed effort.

Down by the fountain between the villa and chalet the girls met Margot, of whom they were in search. They met Susanne too, and Susanne and the Burgundian were both in a towering passion. Susanne had threatened to drown her opponent in the basin, and the two were displaying an invention in the matter of bad names which only French tongues could have shown. A seven-headed monster, and each head that of a donkey, was the mildest term of opprobrium Susanne lavished upon her foe, and the Burgundian replied by cruel taunts in regard to her enemy's age. It seemed difficult for either to tell what the quarrel had arisen about; but Gervais was standing at a discreet distance, wearing an expression of such modest merit that the young ladies felt certain his fascinations were at the bottom of the disturbance.

Fortunately, both women stood sufficiently in awe of Miss Crauford for her presence to bring the dispute to a close and postpone the proposed drowning of Margot.

"I wish you had stayed in the house," whispered Nathalie; "they would not stop just for me, and I dare say the noise might have amused me. Proof of a vulgar taste, is it not?—but true all the same."

Miss Crauford requested Margot to follow without delay, and to have the goodness to check her sobs, which had burst forth with appalling vehemence at sight of her mistress.

"It was no fault of mine," she began.

"I have not said that it was," replied Elizabeth.

"She goaded me; she maddened me with her vile language. Mademoiselle must not blame me," cried Susanne.

"I have not told you that I did," returned Miss Cranford. "I have only to say that I would advise you both to end the quarrel at once, and to be careful that I hear of no future one."

They could neither of them have told why they stood in awe of her, since she never scolded; yet they both did. Perhaps it was her very composure which caused them to feel that some awful threat lurked under her cold reproof. Susanne passed meekly into the chalet; Margot dried her eyes in haste, and followed the young ladies without as much as a gurgle in her throat.

"I can not think how you manage it," sighed Nathalie; "I am so fond of making people do as I say, yet I never succeed half so well as you, who seem to care nothing about it."

They took the hill-road to Clarens, and walked on past the pretty cemetery which overlooks the village and lake. No more tranquil place of rest could be imagined. Weeping willows drooped over the grassy graves, melancholy cypresses stood up like funeral urns. Strangers from all lands slept there under the blue sky. Beneath them stretched the long, narrow valley, the lake spread out, a sea of molten amber, in the far distance, where sky and water seemed to meet, a golden-pink haze floated like a curtain, fairly dazzling the eyes with its splendor. Vineyards dotted the hill-sides; picturesque villages were scattered here and there, some close to the lake, others clinging to the mountain; beyond was the mighty sweep of snow-crowned cliffs that guard the road toward the Simplon.

The two girls went their way at length, talking more gravely for a while than they had before done. But Nathalie soon recovered her gay spirits. She gave reminiscences of her convent life, possessing the enviable faculty of making the events and people she described stand out living and real; and her mixture of fun and cynicism was very droll. The pair had few tastes or ideas in common, still they enjoyed each other's society. Both were enthusiastic in their way, each secretly contemptuous of her companion's subjects of enthusiasm, but eager to hear about them all the same. Elizabeth Cranford had not lived much with girls of her own age. By nature and habit she was reticent, yet she always found herself talking to Nathalie with a freedom at which she wondered. Perhaps some feeling that the creature needed a missionary to point out the beautiful and true animated Miss Cranford to a certain extent; but, independent of that, there was a charm about Nathalie which she could not resist; she might disapprove, still she loved her.

They went on through Montreux, and turned down the precipitous hill toward Terretêt and the lake, to where the Castle of Chillon rose close to the water's edge. They were fond of going there, though the castle was always a disappointment, in spite of romance and Lord Byron. The exterior looked more like a great whitish-gray farm-house than a château, and the dungeon Nathalie pronounced too dry, and light, and comfortable. But, though Elizabeth did not care about Lord Byron, she liked to dream of Bonnivard and his struggles for freedom; while Nathalie called that view prosaic, and preferred Byron's imaginary hero and the poet's name cut by his own hand in one of the columns.

At least the château boasted a drawbridge, a turret, some high-walled courts; and there was a dismal den which had been the chamber of an ancient Duke of Savoy, and next it a room, with a single window, giving a lovely view over the lake, where his duchess, perhaps, used to sit centuries ago and look across the waters, and think ... doleful thing was a ducal existence, while ... snored in the outer apartment after the ... of the chase.

"A duchess who only had one window to her bedroom!" cried Nathalie. "Marrying Monsieur La Tour is not so bad as that."

"You so often find states of life which might be worse, that I wonder you complain so much," said Elizabeth. "Admit once for all that—supposing such a thing possible—and you would be very sorry if your engagement were broken off."

"So I should," said Nathalie. "But, then, I am not satisfied. Ah! if one could only be a duchess now!"

"With a bedroom like this?"

"Nonsense!"

"My dear, we are neither of us very old nor very wise, but we do know, or we ought, that the woman who has a heart offered her like that of Monsieur La Tour's has won a prize."

"No doubt; but what I want is twenty prizes, not one."

"Well," said Elizabeth, "I only hope Monsieur will make you live in some quiet place where you can not get into mischief."

"I would get into mischief if he shut me up in a box!" cried Nathalie. "At least one could put an advertisement in the newspapers—'Wanted, by a handsome young woman, whom an old husband guards like an ogre, a speedy and amusing chance to disgrace herself.' Something of that sort would bring answers."

They left the château, mounted the hill again, and reached the gray stone church—the last building on the mountain road. It hangs suspended midway along a mighty cliff—a frowning mass of rocks towers above—just space for the highway, the church, and a terrace; then the hill sweeps down almost in a precipice toward the lake. A marvelous spot that terrace for watching sunsets and dreaming dreams!

They seated themselves on one of the rustic benches arranged under the low, sturdy trees; and even Nathalie was silent for a time. The bell up in the gray tower was ringing slowly; the rooks circled about, and answered its chime with their hoarse ejaculations. A bird, perched on a window-sill of the church, sang as if he would sing his very soul out; the breeze stole softly past; the magical view brightened, and grew glorious each instant as the colors of the approaching sunset began to gain strength and brightness. The mountain range that shut in the lake miles and miles below was a long line of rose-colored flame; the nearer cliffs had their summits bathed in gorgeous tints, while awful shadows began to wrap their sides, and spread far out over the waters, till in the centre of the lake the sunset hues struck broad and full, dazzling the eye with their radiance.

"I like to come here," said that provoking Nathalie, suddenly, "because there is occasionally a man to look at me."

There were plenty of people scattered among the different villages, but few whom Nathalie called interesting. There were flocks of heavy Germans who came for the cure, and were to be met on all the roads with *cabas* of grapes, busy devouring their ten pounds per diem. There were quiet English families who could not afford to go any where else, and seemed occupied in wearing out their old clothes; one woman in particular appeared in a succession of faded ball-dresses, whose colors made Nathalie sea-sick; quantities of bustling Americans, who came because they must rush into every nook and corner; but genuine young men—handsome, stylish fellows—were so scarce that Nathalie often declared she feared the race must be nearly extinct. She followed up her first remark by a speech of this nature.

"Luckily, the race is nothing to you any longer," said Elizabeth, inclined to be severe at this disturbing of her reverie.

"Is it not?" demanded Nathalie. "Let me get within reach of a dozen or two, and you shall see, and Monsieur La Tour also."

"You might prove less irresistible to them than you fancy," returned Elizabeth; "your vanity is excessive."

Nathalie laughed, not in the least nettled.

"You really do me good, in spite of myself," she said. "I believe I should turn out a very decent woman if I could always have you near me."

Presently along came a troop of Germans, all with noses like sausages, all eating grapes, and making a terrific noise about it. Nathalie vowed that she could not endure their society.

"I should hate a view into heaven in such company," she said with her usual vehemence. "We might go on to the village, and back to the Chauderon; we have never been there but once."

In trifles it was easier to yield to Nathalie for the sake of peace, so Miss Crauford complied with her whim.

Back of Montreux is a great caldron-shaped gap in the mountains, torn out ages ago by some mighty convulsion of Nature. In the centre a white cascade leaps and foams down the rocks —a mad torrent when swollen by spring rains and melting snows, but diminished in volume, lovely rather than grand, at that time of year. The path by which one descended the cliff was precipitous enough. Margot begged piteously to be left at the top.

"I am afraid," she whimpered; "I dreamed twice last week of breaking my neck by a fall in just such a place."

"Did it hurt?" asked Nathalie.

"Ah! do not laugh, Mademoiselle. I can not go—I can not."

"Wait for us here," returned Elizabeth. "No one wishes you to do what frightens you."

As soon as she found herself safe from the expedition, of course the Burgundian proceeded to find a lie wherewith to cover up her cowardice.

"It is not that I have fear, Mesdemoiselles," she said with dignity, "but I possess an aged mother dependent upon my exertions. I have no right to risk a valuable life."

"Only a mother?" asked Nathalie.

"Four little brothers and sisters, one a lame boy, and a brother-in-law who is paralytic," said the Burgundian glibly, putting her handkerchief to her eyes.

"The lame boy and the paralytic have appeared since the last time she told the story," whispered Nathalie to her friend. "I always thought our Breton the hugest story-teller in the world till I saw your Burgundian."

They left her seated on a flat rock, tranquilly munching a cake, and forgetful already of her suffering family in the pages of a cheap *feuilleton*, fuller of wonderful incidents than any imagination save that of a Frenchman could have conceived.

At the bottom of the immense ravine a rustic bridge spanned the stream, just below the cascade. On the other side a path as arduous and difficult as that by which the two girls had descended led up among higher cliffs, where dark pine trees cast gloomy shadows about.

The cascade talked so loudly that Nathalie's voice was drowned, and she relinquished in despair any effort to converse, feeling that she rather hated the noisy thing, as she had just been ready to propound some wonderful theory which had struck her, and which she believed startlingly original.

Elizabeth stood on the bridge and enjoyed the lovely scene to her full content for a time. Suddenly it occurred to her strange that Nathalie had left her so long in peace. She looked about; her companion had disappeared. Elizabeth crossed the bridge and gained the opposite bank, caught the flutter of a dress, and heard Nathalie's voice, half in merriment, half in terror. That creature could no more keep out of mischief than could a kitten. She had gone down to dip her hands in the water, had slipped on the spray-wet turf, and entangled her skirts about the branch of a fallen tree so that she could not extricate herself.

Elizabeth hastened to her rescue. How it came about neither could ever tell; but after getting Nathalie free, and helping her part way up the bank, Elizabeth slipped and fell, knocking her head with such force that she lay senseless. Nathalie shrieked, and became utterly helpless and insane at once. Fortunately a gentleman, who had been higher up among the hills, heard and saw what had happened as he came down toward the bridge.

It was the work of only a few minutes for him to raise the prostrate girl, carry her to the bridge, and assure the frightened Nathalie that her friend was not hurt. In spite of Nathalie's alarm, she had eyes to see that he was a tall, fine-looking man, and young—an artist, too, judging from the sketch-box slung over his shoulder. But the stranger did not notice her—he was studying the face of the girl he held in his arms. Launce Cromlin was a painter, and this face like the ideal he had been searching for for years. But he had no leisure for such thoughts—every moment was precious. He had only reached Montreux a few hours before; the long-delayed letters, informing him of old Mr. Vaughan's illness and desire for his immediate return, were awaiting his arrival. There would be no train until toward evening. He had gone up the mountain with his sketch-box to pass the time, had lingered longer than he ought, and was hurrying toward the village, afraid of missing the train, when stopped by Nathalie's frantic cries.

The fainting girl was not hurt, he was sure of that. He had no time to waste in absurd, romantic fancies.

"She is coming to herself," he said. "Mademoiselle, you will think me a brute; I can not stop—I must catch the train; I am going to a dying relative. Stay here, and I will send you help; no, better, I'll carry your friend up the hill."

It was not an easy task to carry a well-grown young woman up that ascent, but Cromlin did it. Elizabeth was conscious now, though she dared not stir, for a very prosaic reason—she had turned horribly sick. She could not open her eyes; she knew she was placed on a bench; heard Nathalie's voice and that of the stranger, but could only cover her face, and whisper to Nathalie to send the man away.

"She is better," Nathalie said. "Thanks, a thousand times. Ah! here is Margot, Mademoiselle Crauford's maid. We shall do very well now. Don't wait, please; you need not send any body. If you see a carriage, you might order it to wait for us at the turn. We must drive back to the Maladèyre. Thanks, again. Good-bye."

Cromlin would have given a great deal for one more look at that pale, beautiful countenance, but it was carefully hidden. He comprehended that for some reason the ladies were anxious he should take himself off. Indeed, he had not a moment to lose; his best exertions would barely bring him in to the station—away down near the lake—in time. A few more hurried words, and off he dashed.

That night as Nathalie sat in her own room, thinking over the incident, she said many times to herself—

"That is not the man; there will no harm come to her through me where he is concerned. Yet he is to be something to her; such things do not happen for nothing."

The mishap was to be kept a profound secret from Mr. Crauford, lest he should prohibit any future excursions. The girls hired a carriage and drove home, and Elizabeth was quit of her accident with only a headache.

Launce Cromlin had found time to ask questions at the station in regard to the inhabitants of La Maladèyre.

He knew that Robert Crauford was an old friend of his uncle's. Mr. Vaughan had formerly talked much to Launce of Mrs. Crauford, of this very young lady he had just aided—a child in those days, never seen by Mr. Vaughan since her babyhood.

And Launce, borne swiftly away through the dusk of evening, was thinking it odd that he should have been thrown momentarily into the presence of this girl, for he had known from his own mother of Mr. Vaughan's youthful love and disappointment.

That face haunted him like the realization of a long-cherished dream; and often during his rapid journey, and the sea-voyage which succeeded, he marveled when and where he should meet it again.

CHAPTER VIII.

FACE TO FACE.

MR. CRAUFORD had not passed an agreeable night. Having taken very little exercise during the day on account of a fancied bise, which he was certain would give him neuralgia, he naturally did not sleep soundly, and was beset by bad dreams. He had no idea that he could blame himself for the restlessness: he regarded it as entirely the result of his delicate health and nervous organization.

Daylight came, and he was disturbed by the groans and expostulations of an unfortunate swine that the farmer and his man were dragging away to sacrifice. The Mosaic outcast did not go forth to martyrdom with any attempt at calmness or dignity. His yells were actually heart-rending. This tumult startled Mr. Crauford from the only peaceful doze he had encountered since going to bed. When the voice of the victim died in the distance, he fell asleep again, and dreamed of seeing a pig with a nightcap on, who addressed him in the words of the elder Hamlet, "I am thy father's ghost!" Mr. Crauford awoke in disgust. Nothing so thoroughly vexed him as to have unromantic dreams. It hurt his vanity to think that even in slumber his poetic nature could be visited by commonplace fancies.

So he rose in a mood to suffer, and to make life uncomfortable to those about, as is the privilege of poets. Elizabeth paid him a visit, and was full of sympathy for his complaints, to which she would have been obliged to listen all day, instead of going out on that ramble with Nathalie, had not a fortunate occurrence — whereof she was in ignorance — made her father anxious to be left alone.

The postman brought a letter for Mr. Crauford—an American letter. On opening the envelope, he found the closely written sheet marked private.

The mystery was quite delightful to him; he fairly forgot the neuralgic pain at the back of his left ear, and the second line he had been vainly seeking as a continuation to what he believed a poem.

The letter, which he read with great interest —for any thing approaching romance was agreeable to Mr. Crauford, as it is to most people, however stoutly they may deny the charge— came from Darrell Vaughan. It detailed the facts of his uncle's illness and death, the fortune which had devolved upon himself, and the odd, unbusiness-like council appended to the will: I should say, the story of the codicil with a difference. Darrell Vaughan made no mention of Launce Cromlin. The dead man had decreed that his nephew should inherit the additional two hundred and fifty thousand dollars on condition that he succeeded in obtaining Elizabeth Crauford's hand.

"You will see," wrote Darrell, "from the foregoing, why I have asked you to keep this letter a secret for the present. If your daughter knew of this strange codicil, it might either prejudice her against me or cause a certain embarrassment between us. You will perhaps smile at my romantic folly when I tell you that my heart has gone out toward a woman I have never seen. Yet it is true. Before my uncle's death I·had been shown by a mutual friend your daughter's portrait and several letters from her.

I had contemplated a journey to Europe with but one object—that of seeing her.

"Among my uncle's papers I have found a letter for you, and one also for your daughter. I do not inclose these, because I shall soon hope to hand them to you personally; and I can not bear to risk their possible loss by post. Every line penned by that dear hand seems sacred to me.

"There are other trifling details which his letter will explain, and which can wait until I place it in your keeping. I have stated the one fact of importance, that he desires his nephew to have the great happiness, if possible, of winning your daughter.

"Although we have never met, I believe you may know something in regard to me and my brief past, such as it is. I have tried not to waste my youth, have endeavored to make such talents as I possess useful to my kind. That you could for an instant suppose me unduly influenced by this money part of the question, I feel, from what I know of your character, to be impossible. I am a richer man now than is necessary for the gratification of such quiet tastes as mine. That the romance and uncommonness of the codicil appeal to me, I shall not deny, nor do I believe you will smile at the folly which leads me to fancy my previously seeing the portrait and those letters an omen that my uncle's wish was to be my fate."

There was a good deal more, written in a manner which appealed powerfully to Mr. Crauford, as the writer of the epistle had been certain it would do. Mr. Crauford was much excited by this news, and in a state of delightful misery. I can think of nothing except this paradox which will exactly express what his feelings were. It was difficult for him to avoid calling his daughter at once and telling her the whole story; yet he enjoyed so thoroughly the importance of his secret that he would not have done this for the world. There mingled, too, other emotions, which touched upon old jealousies and pains. Mr. Vaughan had loved the woman who became Robert Crauford's wife. Mr. Crauford had always been haunted by the idea that pique influenced Laura Marlow in her acceptance of his hand. Still she proved a faithful wife. The one storm which arose and threatened their peace grew out of his faults. That was a period upon which Mr. Crauford did not like to look back. His conscience had grown tender since he became a victim to dyspepsia, and there were certain episodes, before and after his marriage, whereon he never dwelt if he could avoid it. He was never so severe upon the frailties of others as when something chanced to rouse those troublesome recollections. Perhaps he thought repentance and remorse left him at liberty to judge his neighbors with unsparing rigor. Perhaps in some way it was a relief to inveigh against folly or vice—a proof to his own mind that he abhorred it. I do not mean to say that Mr. Cranford had ever been a very bad man, that is, led a reckless, disreputable life. In the height and heyday of his youth he had not been guilty of any beyond what society terms venial sins, and readily pardons in youths possessing money and position. In fact, his record was quite as clean as that of nine men out of ten—yours, my virtuous clergyman! yours, my decorous judge! It spoke in his favor that he could still feel remorse when old memories came up. I wish he had not been so severe on other people; but I notice that peculiarity in most persons whose consciences are somewhat uneasy over their own past.

Mr. Cranford was thinking, too, of his wife this morning, and that outbreak on her part, so different from her ordinary cold, quiet manner —the one cause for an outbreak he had given. He was thinking, also, how he used to be haunted by a fear that she had been fonder of Edgar Vaughan than of him. Their married lives had not brought them into contact with the man, but the idea was ever a sore place in Mr. Cranford's mind. He had fretted and scolded a good deal over trifles all his days; and whenever he worried his wife by so doing, and she grew silent and proud, he used to fancy she was contrasting him in her thoughts with the man whose love she had rejected. This fear did not induce him to cure his faults. He was weak, so he only pitied himself, and felt it hard indeed that any foolish fancy, any girlish predilection, should stand between him and the woman he loved. After a while the sight of the letter on his table brought him out of his uncomfortable reverie. He wrote to Darrell a pleasant, friendly answer—he was rather good at epistolary efforts. He should be happy to see Mr. Vaughan and make his acquaintance. In the mean time he agreed with Darrell it was better no communication should prepare Elizabeth for the purpose contained in his coming. Should Mr. Vaughan's business detain him in London as long as he expected, he would overtake them in Pisa. If he could leave sooner, he would find them in Clarens, where they might still remain for several weeks. Darrell's communication came from America; but he was to sail soon, and had given an address in London, to which he begged Mr. Cranford to write, so that he might have the reply on his arrival.

The answer finished, the hypochondriac decided to go out, feeling quite upset by the unusual excitement of the morning. It occurred to him that, perhaps, the young ladies had not yet departed on their ramble; he would propose joining them in a drive instead. Before this thought struck him, he had sent Gervais to post his letter. Of course, now he forgot that, and summoned Gervais with his customary impatience—a stranger would have supposed him in danger of a fit, or the house on fire, at least. But Madame Bocher, who replied to the bell and his frantic voice, was too thoroughly Swiss to be hurried or flurried. She reminded him that Gervais was absent. He proceeded to fret a little, in a feeble way. He might fret, for any thing Madame cared. Did she know if Miss Cranford and the other young lady had gone yet? Madame knew nothing about the matter, but she wanted to get back to her kitchen; and, as Mr. Cranford said he thought of driving out if they had not departed, she promptly answered that she believed they were still in the chalet, in the little salon where Mademoiselle and Elizabeth often sat.

Mr. Cranford tied up his neck—he could not move from one room to another without this precaution, bronchitis being one of his pet bugbears, though he never had a sore throat in his life—and proceeded in search of the pair. The entrance to this salon was on the opposite side of the chalet from Madame's apartments, separated from them, as I have said, by a long gallery. Mr. Cranford had been in here on several occasions with Elizabeth. He did not waste time knocking at the outer door of the house, for a vestibule and a dark passage stretched between it and Nathalie's salon, and the girls could not have heard him if he had pounded till doomsday. There was a bell, to be sure, but to ring that was useless too. It rang down in the wine-cellar— what for, nobody save the Swiss architect or a madman could have imagined; but there it was. Susanne had decided it must be to frighten the rats; and when they made too much noise at their revels under the floor, she used to rush out and pull the bell vigorously. Then one could hear the rats scamper in all directions, like ladies caught unprepared to receive visitors, and warned by the tinkle to make their escape.

Mr. Cranford moved forward, stumbled through the dark passage, and reached the salon. He rapped, and fancied that he heard somebody bid him enter. He pushed open the door, and as he did so a voice said—

"Why did you knock there, Susanne? You startled me."

Mr. Cranford stopped short in considerable embarrassment. The window looking toward the villa had its shutters closed, the other window looked onto the gallery, so that the room was very shadowy indeed. Mr. Cranford descried a figure extended on a sofa; neither his daughter nor Nathalie was visible. He was not quick in thought in general, but he perceived that he must have intruded on Madame L'Estrange. He had not dreamed of disturbing her. Nathalie had often remarked in his presence that her mother detested this room, and never set foot in it. No man's brain was less fertile in expedients than Mr. Crauford's. Whether to stay and apologize or slip silently out he could not decide. But he had little space for meditation; the voice spoke again—

"What are you doing, Susanne? Help me up—I shall not stay here—I hate this room—why did I come?"

The demon of change, or some other imp equally ill-natured, had prompted Madame's visit this day of all the days in the year. She was especially restless and suffering, had fasted and repeated choice bits from St. Joseph's Offerings until she was utterly miserable. Susanne persuaded her to try the fresh air of the gallery for a while; and at last she wandered into Nathalie's salon, and lay down there for the first time during all these weeks she had lived in the chalet.

Mr. Crauford was exceedingly confused and annoyed at his own blunder. There he stood, helplessly holding the door-knob in his hand. Madame L'Estrange turned her head, and perceived him. She started up in astonishment and nervous terror. The sofa was close to the window; the dim light fell full upon her face; Mr. Crauford saw it distinctly, recognized it too in spite of the alteration and ravages years and illness had worked on its beauty.

He remained speechless, staring at her, and Madame stared at him, with her presence of mind as utterly astray as his own. She was dressed in a loose gown of some sombre material made with a capuchin, which she had drawn partially over her head; her hair uncurled, her cheeks without paint, her wasted countenance more ghastly than ever from excitement.

"Nina—Madame Tracy!" exclaimed Mr. Crauford at last, looking like a man who has seen a ghost.

"Yes; Nina," she answered, shivering. "Do not speak that other name."

Then Mr. Crauford's face darkened with sudden anger, and his voice changed to a querulous accent as he tried—

"What are you doing here?"

Madame sat erect; the fire flashed into her great eyes; the old spirit roused itself, and gave her a momentary strength.

"I suppose I may sit in my own house, Robert Crauford," retorted she. "I think it is for me to ask what you are doing here. I did not send for you, I believe."

"Could I dream of meeting you? Could I suppose they kept you here? No one told me you lived with these people—how dared they keep it a secret?" pursued he, wrathfully and in stammering haste.

"Where else should I live?" demanded she.

"What are they to you?—what—"

"He was always dull, this Robert Crauford," interrupted she, with a scornful laugh. "Can you not understand?—I am Madame L'Estrange."

"It is not your name! What do you mean by going about under an assumed name?" he exclaimed.

"It is my name, and has been for years," replied Madame, growing suddenly composed before his agitation. "If you wish to know how I came by it, I can tell you. Long ago a relative left me some money, and I took his name; I had a right. Left me money; do you hear, Robert Crauford? You never knew nor cared whether I had starved to death or not."

"And you have been living here—you have dared to receive my daughter, to let her know your girl—to—"

He was so angry that he could not continue. He grasped the door for support, and his words died in a gasp.

"Not too fast," cried Madame, in the same sullen, defiant way. "Your daughter sought me, forced herself on me, as you have done, Robert Crauford. As for my girl, she is an angel; say one word against her if you dare!"

She looked such a fury that he was reminded of days and scenes which lay half a life back. He had been afraid of her temper then; he was frightened now in spite of his anger.

"Could I dream of its being you?" said he. "To think of my daughter having set foot in your house!"

"I should not hurt her; I am trying to be good; I have tried so long and so hard," whined Madame. Then her voice changed from its lachrymose tone to one of bitter irony. "Oh, these men! They may be as wicked as they please, and set up for saints when they will; but we, poor women, that they fool and ruin—we must not venture to lift our heads from the mud where they have flung us. Bah! You are all alike. I never knew a man who was not a coward—Gerald Tracy was; but you—you are the greatest coward I ever met."

A sharp spasm of pain seized her; she pressed her hand to her side; a hollow cough choked her passionate speech; her strength forsook her, and she leaned back panting for breath. Mr. Crauford was a bad-tempered, unforgiving man, but not inhuman. He saw how ill she was—dying perhaps; his anger yielded a little. This Nina de Favolles had done him a great deal of harm. When he was in Paris, a very young man, she had just reached the acme of her infamous career. She would have ruined him had he not discovered in time that her love was a feint—that as soon as his money failed he would be flung aside and laughed at for his idiocy. He saw no more of her until several years after, when he was in Italy with his wife. Before then, the woman had fascinated the young American, Tracy, and he had actually married her, knowing nothing of her antecedents. Nathalie was a year old when the truth came out. The unfortunate husband lost his life in a duel with a man as worthless as the woman on whose account he fought. Previous to that, Madame had tried to regain her old ascendency over Robert Crauford, and failed. By way of having revenge, she wrote him letters, and managed that they should fall into the hands of his wife—letters which revealed the old intimacy, and implied that it had been begun anew.

This was the cause of the outbreak of which I spoke. Crauford had been at length able to convince Laura that, in the present instance, he was blameless, and a peace was patched up, but he knew that, to her dying day, his wife never forgot the knowledge of his past which she had thus gained.

It was not surprising that, of all human beings, he believed this Nina the worst—that the bare recollection of her after these years could make him shudder. And now actually, to be face to face with her again—to know that his daughter had been in her company, held her hand, was friendly with her child!—this woman, who had almost wrecked his youth, who had nearly lost him the wife he loved. Certainly one would require to get nearer perfection than humanity often does to support such a catastrophe with any show of patience.

"How can you be so hard on me?" cried Madame. "See what a wreck I am! I have been a changed woman for years. Ask my Curé here—ask my Curé at Dijon. I am dying slowly; I suffer horribly; I am trying to make my salvation. Oh, it is cruel to force yourself on me, and to say wicked things, and to look at me like that!"

"I do not wish to be hard on you; it is not for me to judge," Mr. Crauford said, falteringly. Then he remembered Elizabeth, and his voice grew more stern. "You ought not to have let my daughter come here. I blame you for that."

"It was not for me; I have only seen her a few times. Nathalie is so fond of her," pleaded Madame. "Nathalie is good; she has lived always in a convent. She knows nothing. I changed my name to L'Estrange while she was a little thing. She is to marry Monsieur La Tour."

"Good Lord!" cried Mr. Crauford, struck by a sudden thought. "Does he know—does—"

"Oh, he is a kind man," broke in Madame. "He is not like you, ready to crush my poor child for her mother's faults. And I was not so bad; there were many worse. I often repented, and once I gave a diamond bracelet on hearing a charity sermon. Let my child alone. I am dying. She will be Madame La Tour, and live a quiet, respected life."

"I have no wish to interfere. I will not have my daughter meet her, that is all," said Mr. Crauford.

"What are you going to do?" cried Madame in terror.

"I shall go away—"

"Ah! I wish you would," interrupted Madame, with a sigh of relief. "I have never felt easy since I heard you were here. I tell you I am trying to make my salvation. I do not like to meet people that remind me of the past. I fast and pray. I try so hard, and I am afraid—afraid!"

She flung up her arms, and her voice rose almost to a shriek. Mr. Crauford only asked to get out of the room; his nerves would not stand any further shocks.

"We can none of us do more than repent," said he, rather clumsily, after searching in vain for some consolatory words.

"No, the Curé says that, and I repent—I do. Look at me; could I wish to be wicked? My youth is gone, my beauty is gone. Oh, I was so beautiful! And now I am dying. Why could I not have been left to get very old, and grow accustomed to the idea of the next world? I have money enough to live on, and I could have been quite comfortable. To be sure it is tiresome leading a good life, but one would get used to it. Oh me, oh me!"

"I—I must go," stammered Mr. Crauford.

"Go, then," returned Madame, violently. "I hate all men. I despise you. I wish I had ruined you outright. What business have you to look well and strong when I am dying?"

Her sudden fury rendered him more nervous, but he could not even then endure hearing that he looked vigorous.

"My health is wretched," he said; "I am a great sufferer."

"You are a hypochondriac. Monsieur La Tour told me," retorted Madame. "You are rich and lazy; so you indulge in little illnesses by way of occupation."

Mr. Crauford felt more convinced than ever that the woman was a fiend. He doubted whether any amount of penitence could help her.

"Are you going?" asked Madame, as he moved toward the door.

"Yes," he answered, peevishly. "The idea of my having strayed here!"

"Come back. I'll tell you something first! You are rich, and prosperous, and well. Why should you not bear part of the burden that oppresses me? Come back, I say!"

She was so fierce in voice and aspect that he involuntarily yielded to the potent will which had once ruled him so entirely. Madame clutched his arm with her bony fingers, bent toward him till her hot, feverish breath made him shudder. She whispered a few words in his ear, then pushed him roughly away.

"Now go and try your hand at repenting!" she exclaimed. "There is something for you to bear as well as me."

Mr. Crauford looked pale and alarmed. Some broken words fell from his lips. First Madame

D

laughed, then a new spasm of physical pain and mental trouble seized her.

"I try to repent—I do try!" she moaned. "I am haunted by ghosts, and all my prayers will not quiet them. But others are more to blame than I. Nobody taught me, nobody told me! My own mother made me what I am—what I was—for I am changed, I am. Oh, go away; let me alone. I want the Curé—the doctor; perhaps I am dying already. Oh, my soul! Oh, my poor soul! Oh, I can not—"

Mr. Crauford heard Susanne's voice and step on the gallery, and fled.

When Elizabeth came home she found her father in a state of great agitation, and learned that they were to start for Italy the next day. He was obliged at length to tell her that he had seen Madame L'Estrange, and recognized her as a woman whom it was not proper for her to approach.

"You are unjust to visit her faults, whatever they may have been, on Nathalie; she is not to blame," Elizabeth said.

"That woman once came near killing your mother. I can not tell you the story. The daughter will do you some harm too. I'll not have you near her."

This was all the explanation she could gain. It brought Nathalie's superstitious fancy to Elizabeth's mind; but she was not given to yielding to such follies.

"I am ill—I need change—I insist on starting at once."

Her father took refuge in this plaint, and there was no more to be said.

"It is so sudden, so sudden," sobbed Nathalie, when Elizabeth carried her the news. "And mamma is ill. Ah, me! these have been such happy weeks! Good-bye, darling—good-bye! And I shall never see you again; I am not even to write to you. There is something wrong, I know, by the way your father behaves, and mamma will tell me nothing—only shiver and moan, and rave against you both."

Happy weeks, but they were over.

"At least," thought Nathalie, when she had cried herself ill and blind—"at least I can do her no harm. She is gone, and I shall never see her any more; and I loved her so—my Queenie, my beautiful Elizabeth!"

CHAPTER IX.

NATHALIE'S HERO.

NATHALIE spent several very lonely, miserable days after Elizabeth Crauford's hasty departure; and when Nathalie set about being wretched she threw her whole soul into the business, just as she did when pleasure, or any other excitement, actuated her.

She used to sit by the lake and moan that she could not endure this dull existence, and watch the waves and think about suicide, and wonder if Monsieur La Tour would never come and take her away. His image looked absolutely agreeable to her during this dead season; and she wrote him letters two days in succession, which made his elderly heart thrill with delight. But Monsieur could not leave his post—his relative still lingered and would not hear of his going. Monsieur was in love, but then he was nearly sixty, and at that age Romeo does not willfully throw away the chance of inheriting a hundred thousand francs. But I do Monsieur a little injustice: he would have stayed if there had been no money in the question. The old maid begged so piteously for his presence that he could not have found the heart to leave her.

Madame L'Estrange suffered terribly, and her mental anxieties added to her pain. She was haunted by the dread that something would prevent the marriage, and she scolded Nathalie and raved at Susanne, and prayed and begged their pardons, and rushed from one scene to another so rapidly that even a very good person could not much have blamed the young girl for getting away from her whenever she could, or Susanne for thinking it would be far better if Madame were safe in the next world, and they repeating masses for the repose of her soul.

At least Nathalie had a great deal of time to herself, though it was a sorry business to go wandering about among the haunts where she and Elizabeth had spent so many happy hours. There was an old woman, some relation of the *fermier*, who was glad to earn a few sous by playing sheep-dog for Nathalie's benefit. But Nathalie usually found her some commodious resting-place, and gave her chestnuts and bonbons to eat, while she strolled on alone. The old woman's chatter and slow steps annoyed her, though she hated solitude too. It was November, the nuts were all gathered, many of the trees had lost their leaves—even the poplars wore a golden crown, which showed that they must soon suffer like their companions—only the weeping willows were as fresh and luxuriant as ever, and would remain so until the ensuing month. But late in the season as it was, the days were balmy and bright; one could still sit for hours in the open air. The little valley was so sheltered that a nook in the south of Italy would not have been warmer or more sunny. Roses still bloomed in the gardens, and the autumn flowers were out in full beauty. Each day the grand old mountains grew more stately and seemed to increase in height. Often the snow fell at night, and the morning would find them wrapped half-way down their sides in a white mantle that looked as if studded with jewels. Just across the lake, in the Savoy country, the snow sometimes swept to the water's edge, but not a flake fell in the Montreux valley, and fires, except of an evening, were not to be thought of.

The glory of the landscape increased; the sunset tints and changes waxed more gorgeous and wonderful; the soft haze that lay over the scene of an afternoon, and the morning halo on the mountains, were enough to drive one wild from sheer excess of beauty. But it was a sad time to Nathalie, nor did she love Nature enough to study and admire it alone. She could weave romances, and dream exciting visions, and her fancy and imagination were quick and creative; but she did not like solitude, and would rather have looked out on the Boulevards than down from the heights of the Rhigi.

One day, straight into the midst of her restlessness, her desire for change and excitement, her longing for adventure, her hash of transcendental and socialistic theories, came Darrell Vaughan, and the danger which any one who had studied Nathalie's character must have dreaded rushed upon her without the slightest warning.

This was the way it befell. It chanced that Darrell's banker in Paris was the man who had charge of Madame L'Estrange's matters, and managed for her the bonds and shares which made up her competency. Vaughan had known this banker formerly in America, and he chose to be very civil during the time Darrell made in Paris—a period which the young gentleman lengthened beyond his original intention, as young gentlemen will a stay in the fascinating city.

Vaughan never told his private affairs to any body; but mentioning to the banker that he was going to Clarens, that personage ventured to burden him with some documents for Madame L'Estrange, aware that the lady, Frenchwoman like, would be grateful to him for sparing her the expense of the postage on the heavy papers. The banker's daughter had been a companion of Nathalie's at the convent, and showed Vaughan a marvelous photograph of the girl, a picture which brought out her peculiar beauty in its highest perfection. Of Madame L'Estrange the banker only knew that she was the relative and inheritor of an old acquaintance of his; he had assumed the care of her business on that account, never connecting her in any way with the woman whose celebrity had once been something to make sober people shudder.

Before Darrell left Paris he learned that he must go on to Pisa to find the Craufords, but he did not alter his intention of passing by Geneva and Clarens, informing himself that it would not be too late to cross comfortably over the Simplon into Italy, and having no mind to lose a glimpse of the beautiful lake because the people he meant to join had seen fit to change their plans. This was his second visit to Europe, and portions of Switzerland he knew well, though not the Lake of Geneva region.

So it happened that one bright afternoon Nathalie, sitting to rest on the steps of the chalet after a walk, suddenly became conscious that a very handsome man was standing at a little distance contemplating her. Look and manner were both a compliment, in spite of the rudeness: he seemed to have stopped short to stare literally because he could not help it. He came on now, and Nathalie rose; and he said, in very fair French—

"I beg a thousand pardons; it is Mademoiselle L'Estrange, I am sure. I am Darrell Vaughan."

"Ah, yes," said Nathalie, with one of her quick, beautiful blushes, that came from excitement, not shyness. "Monsieur Guyon wrote mamma you had been good enough to take charge of a package. She will be so much obliged! Please come in. I shall see if mamma is well enough to thank you. I fear—"

She led him through the dark passage into the little salon, and sped off down the gallery to her mother's apartments. Madame would have been glad of the opportunity to see a stranger, but she really was not able. She tried to sit up and think she might be dressed and rouged, but a whole night of pain had left her so weak and nervous that the bare effort to raise herself was such misery that she began to cry.

"It is always so," she moaned. "I am not allowed the least pleasure—it is hard! I shall not pray to St. Joseph any more; he is no use whatever. I shall tell the Curé to choose me somebody else! *O mon Dieu! mon Dieu!*"

But she sent Nathalie to the guest. Of course Susanne must go to play propriety; and Madame lay back among her pillows and wept, and upbraided St. Joseph for his cruelty in not finding her a brief strength sufficient to receive a male visitor.

"Mamma is so sorry; she is suffering dreadfully to-day. She hopes that you will come soon again," Nathalie said, as she appeared anew at the door of the salon, with Susanne peeping over her shoulder—that worthy creature as much excited as her betters over the arrival of a handsome gentleman.

Nathalie spoke in English; she did not expect to say nor hear any thing to which Susanne might not listen—still it was a pleasure to speak a language unintelligible to the inquisitive old creature.

"How beautifully you speak English," Vaughan said.

"I ought—I one half your countrywoman," returned she, proudly.

Darrell knew this as well as she. Perhaps there were not three persons in all Switzerland acquainted with the old life and former name of Madame L'Estrange. But Darrell had met at Vevay on the previous night a man who told him enough to make him feel that he could adopt toward the daughter a manner different from what he would have ventured on under other circumstances; and to Nathalie, with her head full of novels, the most exaggerated language, even to an avowal of love during their first interview, would have appeared perfectly natural.

"I am sorry Madame can not see me," he went on. "Must I go away at once?"

His face grew so eager—his voice so pleading! "No, no," laughed Nathalie. "One does not have visitors often enough in this dull place to be willing to lose them."

"And I have looked forward for days to this pleasure," he said. "Do you think one must take weeks and weeks to grow acquainted? Mademoiselle, I met your old friend, Marie Guyon; she showed me your picture. I ought not to say so, but it was that picture brought me to Clarens. Are you angry?"

Nathalie was a good deal fluttered, but she enjoyed the scene, and was quite ready to take her part. She answered gayly; she could treat his words as idle badinage, but they moved her nevertheless, and he, watching the sensitive face, could see that.

Susanne sat upright in her chair under the shadow of her cap-tower, and stared at the two. She would have given her ears to know what they were talking about, and had three minds to risk a hint to her young lady that she ought to speak French.

They talked of her school-life, of Marie Guyon; they strayed away to other topics; and Vaughan, with his usual quickness to read and understand others, was soon as well able to tell what subjects would interest her, what an impossible hash of sentiment, romance, and false theories there was in her mind, as if he had known her for months.

Nathalie spoke of her newly acquired friend who had recently gone from her. Did Mr. Vaughan know the Cranfords? No, Mr. Vaughan did not. He wondered if the two young women were in correspondence—he must discover. It did not require much artful questioning to draw Nathalie out, for her heart was full of this subject. Mr. Vaughan had been sitting there some time; they had talked themselves far past the beginning of an acquaintance—conversation that was new to Nathalie, which possessed a keen fascination, because it was like the talk in the books Blanche de Savigny's cousin used to procure for them to read.

That dragon and guard of the proprieties and youthful virtue, tightly-laced Susanne, had gone fast asleep in her chair after the fatigues of her mistress's bad night. She sat upright as ever, but her cap-tower had tilted a little to one side, her hands were crossed in her lap, and faint murmurs, like the distant hum of bees, proceeded from her parted lips. Darrell called Nathalie's attention to this. They both laughed, then went out on the gallery, and sat down, perhaps good-naturedly desirous not to disturb the woman's slumbers; for Nathalie mentioned the tiresome watch, and was in a mood to do justice to Susanne's merits in general.

"But you were telling me about this friend of yours," Vaughan said.

"Ah, yes—I loved her so—she is very beautiful, and so wise and good! I tried to hate her for that, but I could not. And I shall not see her any more—we do not even write letters. Is it not sad?"

"But why?"

"Indeed I do not know—I think Elizabeth does not either. Only just at the last, Mr. Cranford—such a stupid old man, with a horrid nose—found out—well, mamma did not explain, so I could hardly understand. But it seems he and my papa were enemies, and mamma and Mr. Cranford were both shocked to find they had been living near one another, and that their daughters were intimate."

"A little hard for you and Miss—Cranford, is it not?—to visit old quarrels on you," said Darrell.

"Yes; but we shall not see each other any more," sighed Nathalie. "It was best; I know it was," she added, rather to herself than him; for she was thinking of her superstitious presentiment. "It was all so hurried. I scarcely cried till she was gone—she did not, so I kept my tears back. Perhaps her father prejudiced her against us. She was fond of me, but I am sure she always disapproved. Ah, well, she is gone: let us talk of other things, this saddens me."

"I should fancy she must be a rather disagreeable girl—a kind of Minerva and Mentor, and that sort of thing," said Vaughan.

"Ah, you do not know what you are talking about," cried Nathalie, impatiently. "I could tell you so many charming things—but I suppose you do not remain here long?"

"That will depend on you," he replied. "Would you like me to stay?"

"Oh, mamma will be charmed to make your acquaintance."

"Please don't treat me to a propriety answer," he exclaimed. "Shall I stay?"

She gave him a merry, coquettish glance, but her color rose under his prolonged gaze. There was a little vase of flowers on the rustic table by her side. She took out a Marguerite, and began picking off leaf after leaf, looking at him from under her downcast lashes, as she said—

"He shall stay—he shall not—he shall stay—he—oh, Mr. Vaughan, the Marguerite says No!"

There was real disappointment in her voice; one of her chief weaknesses was a strange faith in omens and superstitious fancies and practices of all sorts.

"You did not do it fairly," said Darrell. "Once you picked off two leaves at the same time."

"Are you sure?" she asked, anxiously.

"Quite sure. I shall stay—it is destiny."

He laughed, but he spoke seriously nevertheless. Nathalie's head was in a whirl. As she had often said to Elizabeth, her theories were immense; but practically she was very ignorant of matters concerning which she thought and talked much. This handsome man, with his soft voice and fascinations of speech, coming so unexpectedly upon her, and finding the way to stir at once her fancy, dazed and bewildered her. Now, for the first time, she remembered Monsieur La Tour. It seemed as if a cold wind blew, without warning, straight over her naked soul. She looked pale, and absolutely frightened.

"Oh, I forgot!" she sighed.

"What is that?" he asked.

"Monsieur La Tour will be back. Did not Marie tell you?"

"She told me nothing about any such person —who is he?"

"I—I am to marry Monsieur La Tour," she replied.

Vaughan rose quickly. As he turned away, she caught one passionate exclamation from his lips. Presently he came back, and held out his hand.

"Farewell, Mademoiselle L'Estrange," he said, in an odd, choked voice. "You are right—I can not stay."

Without another word of adieu, he was gone.

"I think," observed Vaughan to his familiar, as he took the road back to Vevay, "that I made as neat an ending to the scene as one could wish. What a fascinating creature she is! Hum! Well, *coûte qui coûte*, I shall not go away yet, in spite of Monsieur La Tour and the philosophic Miss Crauford."

Susanne, roused from her slumbers by the hurried passing of her guest through the salon, came out on the gallery in search of Nathalie. She began a voluble dissertation upon the gentleman's charms. Nathalie recovered herself enough to rise and go away. She could not endure the sight of a human face or the sound of a human voice. She hurried to her bedroom, locked the door, and there she moaned and wept like a crazy thing. She should never see him any more; he had come and gone like a dream. Was it that he loved her? Ah, he had come because of this; he had loved her from seeing her picture. Now he was gone! She had had one glimpse into heaven, and been cast back upon the bleak rocks! Life had just roused itself, a real life, and been snatched away! Nothing lay before her but misery and anguish, and Monsieur La Tour—how she hated him! The old idea of running off and going on the stage beset her; the morbid whim for suicide; a

score of impossible and absurd ideas flashed up. But it was all reality to her. She suffered; she was half mad with pain. This was the man Fate meant her to love, and he was gone forever.

Vevay promised to make a pleasant resting-place for a time. Vaughan had met several young Englishmen with card-playing propensities, and passed a jolly evening. That night he ventured on a dose of hasheesh for the first time for weeks, having discovered, from the effect of his later indulgences, that he must beware how he played with the drug. He had missed the poison terribly; for a while he was much oppressed and upset; no other stimulant took its place. But Vaughan had no intention of becoming a slave to the habit; he meant to keep it, a useful servant when brilliant efforts were needed. So he tried the hasheesh before going to bed, just to be certain that leaving it off for a season was the only thing necessary. His attempt proved perfectly successful. Not only was he treated to a gorgeous vision, but, before his faculties escaped control, he found himself able to finish a bit of writing which he had hitherto failed in completing to his satisfaction—a passage in a political article for a review. Vaughan had no mind to be forgotten by the public, and his speeches and papers similar to the present were not unfrequent.

For reasons which it is not necessary to dwell upon here he had deferred trying for a renomination to Congress. The Administration was one opposed to his politics, yet the causes seized on for opposition by his party in the House and Senate chanced to be matters which he could see would hereafter render those men personally unpopular. If he accepted a nomination and won his seat, it would be impossible to separate himself from their interests. Better to wait. Two years from this autumn there would be a Presidential election. The party to which he belonged was sure to bring in its nominee. Then he would go to Congress. During the two closing years of that Presidency he might take a diplomatic appointment, if questions giving promise of an opportunity to distinguish himself should arise with any foreign government. In the mean time he wrote, as I say, occasional brilliant articles, made effective speeches, and managed to keep himself before the world as a rising man of whom great things were to be expected.

While in London he had been called on to deliver an address at a meeting of some international society, and contrived to perform that most difficult oratorical feat—the satisfying of people both in England and America. The London newspapers openly said it was a pity the Washington Cabinet did not send a man like him, young as he was, to represent his country at the Court of St. James, instead of the dull old "fogies" usually chosen; and of course the New York journals sneered at the British impertinence, but praised Vaughan immensely.

What Darrell proposed to himself by dawdling in Switzerland he did not take the trouble to think. He knew that Cromlin had gone to California, so he was not pressed for time where his interests in the codicil were concerned. In truth, Vaughan was a more visionary person than he himself realized ; capable of very reckless actions, clear-headed, as he could show on occasion. But his bold schemes had hitherto succeeded ; he had unbounded faith in his own powers and his luck—the only god he recognized.

I do not mean that he was an atheist. Darrell Vaughan was simply a heathen, and his deity an odd cross between fatality and chance.

He had an ardent craving for great wealth—for acquiring lands upon lands—for the power that wealth gives. He had not done ill for himself in certain transactions with a set of men at that time all-powerful in the municipal affairs of New York. But Vaughan had been very careful, and kept his record clean : whatever disclosures might in the future menace the clique, he was safe.

He meant now to gain the heritage for which his uncle had given him a chance. Elizabeth Crauford's fortune, added to that and the riches he already possessed, would render him almost a millionaire. The pleasure of thwarting Launce Cromlin counted for something in his plan, too. Darrell nurtured no melodramatic and mediæval enmity toward his relative ; in fact, he rather liked the young fellow personally. But he did hate Launce's honesty and purity of life. Neither quality could be sneered at, for he had to admit that Launce was brave and manly. To surpass his consin—leave Cromlin's career a poor thing in comparison with his own—had always been one of his strongest determinations. He would have hesitated at no wrong to accomplish this, from trying to make Launce show as a villain to shutting him up in a mad-house, if that had been possible. Best of all would be to see Launce struggle unsuccessfully, obliged to turn to him for help. He would fling him bounty with great satisfaction. If he ever came to need that, he might really hope for Vaughan's regard.

A lover of pleasure, passionate, sensual—an ugly word to write, but I can not cure myself of the habit of giving things their true names—Darrell Vaughan had inward enemies to fight against much more potent than he knew. Indeed, he did not make any fight. All he wanted was to preserve a fair exterior in the world's eyes. He trusted to his own self-control for keeping within bounds, as he trusted to his magnificent *physique* standing the wear and tear to which he exposed it.

The next morning Nathalie set out for a walk, up over the hills toward Chaillet, followed by her old woman. Vaughan joined her : he had been keeping watch over the house, and saw her leave it.

Her smile of recognition, the glad light in her eyes, would have caused him to linger had he been on his way to the church to join the woman he meant to marry, trusting always to his luck that the delay should work no harm to his prospects. The possibility of carrying Nathalie L'Estrange off, yet not allowing the gratification of his passion to interfere with the marriage he had sworn to make, occurred to him as he hurried forward to meet the girl.

"I had a hope of seeing you," he said, eagerly. "I meant to have gone away this morning, but I could not. Did you think me very rude yesterday?"

"Yes," she answered ; "very rude! In France people do not end a visit so abruptly."

Her smile would have made much harsher words sound pleasant.

"You knew why I went away?" returned he.

She shrugged her shoulders, but face and eyes belied that affectation of carelessness.

"Listen," he said — they were speaking French. "You admitted yesterday that acquaintance, friendship, love even, were not matters of time. I went away so abruptly because the news of your engagement struck my heart like a blow from a sharp knife. I have no right to say this ; it is rude, unheard of, what you will—but it is the truth. Will you answer me one question?"

She had turned away her head. She signed him to go on.

"Do you love this Monsieur La Tour?" he asked.

"Mamma chose him for my husband," she replied, after an instant's hesitation. "You know how such matters are arranged in my country."

"Oh yes," he cried, bitterly ; "a bargain, an affair of buying and selling. And you are sold to him like a slave in a market—to this old man ! I asked about him last night. You, with your beauty and your genius, are to be bound to him ! It is horrible, horrible !"

"I hate it !" ejaculated Nathalie, setting her little white teeth hard together. "Every day I have wished myself dead ! There, are you answered ? I care nothing for forms ! It matters not to me that we are what the world would call strangers. I am glad to speak out to some human being."

"Nor are we actually strangers," he said. "Our mutual friend's letter to your mother has told you all about me. But that is of no consequence. In any case we should have felt at the first glance we knew one another—it was destiny."

He talked and she listened. It was rubbish, but clothed in such beautiful language that it appealed eloquently to her mind, excited by romances, and ready to grasp at any brilliant sophistry as the real and true.

Soon after she returned to the house. He followed, and made his call upon Madame L'Estrange. She felt able to receive him to-day, and was charmed with his manners and conversation.

Four days passed, and on each of them Vaughan managed to see Nathalie out of her mother's presence. He was wild about her—ready to believe he had never loved any woman till now; but the idea of sacrificing his future for her, of taking to wife a penniless girl, the daughter of Nina de Favolles—Tracy—L'Estrange—whatever she called herself—never once occurred to him.

Any excitement was always pleasant; any adventure out of the common appealed to his fancy. At least, these days were a new sensation; these *tête montée* conversations with Nathalie were like reading a chapter in an original novel. But the mad idea which had at the first crossed his mind started up as a possibility, and was strong within him when he went out to meet her on this fourth day.

Nathalie's old woman knew that she met Vaughan, and walked with him, but she held her peace. Nathalie paid her well for her silence; and as there was no one who tried to buy disclosures, she was not tempted to sell her knowledge.

And this day Vaughan told his love—not that he had hesitated to talk of it before, but now he forced confessions from her lips, and Nathalie felt that she was ready to trust him, stranger as he was. Stranger! she would have laughed at the word. She seemed to have known him for years—all her life. The realization of her wildest dream had come—her visionary hero had taken earthly shape, and stood before her.

They were standing on the hill, back from the road by which the old woman sat as usual, munching chestnuts and calculating what her gains would be at the end of a month.

"Hark!" exclaimed Nathalie. "That was Susanne—surely it was the voice of Susanne."

Vaughan drew her hastily back among the trees, and they stood listening.

"Where is Mademoiselle, I say, you silly old thing?" demanded Susanne's piercing tones.

"I am telling you, or I would if I got a chance," returned the other, raising her cracked voice too. "Mademoiselle has just stepped up the hill for the view. 'Rosine,' she said, 'sit you here; the hill is too steep for your old bones.' Always thoughtful is Mademoiselle."

"You are a chattering magpie," interrupted Susanne. "Which hill, when there is one on every side—cabbage?"

"La, la! Just call; she will hear. Why climb when there is no need?"

Then both voices shouted—

"Mademoiselle! Mademoiselle!"

"What is it, Susanne?" called Nathalie.

"Quick—come home, quick! Monsieur La Tour has arrived, and Madame is in hysterics with joy! Come quick, I say!"

Susanne had commenced the ascent—there was no time to lose. Nathalie cast one despairing glance at Vaughan, and fled.

CHAPTER X.

MILADY'S CELL.

LAUNCE CROMLIN's voyage was a short one. He reached New York in less than eleven days from the date of his leaving Liverpool.

Those bright, golden days were not unpleasant to that dreaming Launce. The ocean was calm as a lake; there were fine sunsets to watch, agreeable people on board, and Launce was soon a favorite, as he rapidly became with most persons.

He was sorely disturbed by the news of his uncle's failing health, and the long delay of his letters. He had expected to arrive at Montreux weeks before, and so had ordered all his correspondence to be forwarded there from London.

The summons home had been a great happiness. He regretted deeply now that he had allowed pride to prevent his seeking his relative long before. Even yet he was ignorant what had caused the old man's anger or brought about this new change of feeling. Mr. Vaughan only wrote—

"I find that I have done you a great wrong—may you and God forgive me! I am ill—breaking fast, though I may still last a long time. But I want to see you. Will you pardon your hot-headed uncle and come? Explanations I can not give in a letter. I will not trust my shameful suspicions to paper. Come to me, my dear boy, that I may hear from your own lips that I am pardoned."

Further lines breathing love and tenderness, but not a syllable to throw any light upon the cause of his estrangement.

Launce Cromlin was six-and-twenty—an enthusiast, an artist who was beginning to win a name in both Europe and America. He had proved that he possessed, not only genius, but the ability to work patiently and hard, to submit to apprenticeship and routine, as even genius must do if really great results are to be gained. Sir Galahad, his artist associates used to call him; yet among the most reckless there was not one but thoroughly respected and honored him. A brave, straightforward, noble fellow—manly in every sense of the word; a man whom other men liked too, though he did keep his youth free from the vices with which, under a score of pretty names, so many of his compeers laid up for themselves a bitter harvest of regret in the future.

Many times during those sunny autumn days, as Launce sat on deck watching the glorious sweep of the mid-ocean waves, and trying with colors and brush to obtain hasty studies which should hereafter be useful for tints and forms, he dreamed of the romantic incident which had marked his day at Montreux. He smiled often at his own folly, and told himself he was as silly as a fellow in a romance, yet the beautiful face of the insensible girl whom he had held in his arms still haunted him. After all it was not surprising, Launce thought. Hers was a countenance to strike any artist. He made a study of the face from memory; it would serve admirably some time. He could imagine a picture that might be very effective. Say a long sweep of sea-beach with the surf tumbling in—great masses of rock like those on the Cornish coast, or at home upon the shore of Maine; a stretch of ocean in the distance, with just those reflections across the waves which he was trying now to catch; upon the sands a woman's figure lying, the face upraised—the face he had painted from recollection. But not a dead face—Launce never could think of depicting it as such. The picture should suggest a tragedy, but not death.

So he dreamed and read novels, and made acquaintance with his fellow-voyagers, happier and more light-hearted than ever at the thought of the clearing up of the cloud between himself and his uncle, and the quiet days took their course. Land at last! The great steamer passed up the Narrows, through the beautiful bay, and the mighty city was reached.

It was still early in the morning when Cromlin found himself once more among the busy streets of his native city. His first business was to rush off to his bankers, in the hope that he might find letters from his uncle. There were none. Then he went to an old friend of his relative, who might have news. The man one wants is never in the way; he whom Launce sought had strayed somewhere into the country. After this there was no step Launce could take to gain any information. He knew that Mr. Vaughan had gone to California years before, and could think of no person with whom the reticent old bachelor would be likely to keep up communication. Who his bankers or lawyers in New York might be, Launce had no idea.

Darrell was undoubtedly in California—his uncle had spoken of expecting him; once there, he would of course remain several months. Still he sought for him a little; very uselessly, for he neither knew Darrell's friends nor place of abode. Launce had been absent for five years, and even before that he and his cousin had not been intimate. There was no quarrel between them, but their ways of life were different. Launce, too, knew Darrell better than most people. Yet after the renunciation of Launce by their uncle, Darrell had behaved well. He had hunted his cousin up in Europe, professed himself in ignorance of the cause of their uncle's anger, volunteered to do what he could to set matters right; and altogether acted in so frank and sympathetic a manner that Launce reproached himself for sundry hard thoughts he had indulged toward his relative.

But no tidings had since reached him from Darrell, though Launce had given him a general address at a London banker's. Darrell also knew who his bankers were in New York, which had made Launce hope he might find news from him there.

There was no use in wasting time. He must send a telegram to San Francisco, announcing his arrival, and must recommence his journey with the least possible delay. Inquiries brought the information that a steamer was to sail for Panama on the following day. Launce drove down to Bowling Green and secured his passage, principally occupied in execrating the impudent hackman, who proved, like his brethren in general, a disgrace to New York, and in lamenting that the wonderful rail which was to connect the Atlantic and the Pacific coasts was still a hope of the future.

He reached the Everett House again. As he was descending from the carriage he saw a hack laden with luggage pass, and at the window he beheld his cousin's face.

"Darrell!" he called.

The carriage whirled on. He could have sworn that Darrell's eyes met his; it must be that he had not recognized him. Launce offered a preposterous reward to his hackman if he overtook the carriage, sprang back to his seat, and off they dashed. All he gained was a rapid drive down Broadway, a half hour spent in a press of vehicles at Fulton Street, a quarrel with the hackman, and a narrow escape of arrest by the police as a criminal or madman, from his excitement at the delay.

While eating his dinner that night, Launce glanced idly over the columns of an evening paper, and read Darrell Vaughan's name among the list of the passengers on a steamer which had sailed that day for Liverpool.

Launce's brain was in a whirl. Had Darrell gone in search of him? The possibility of deceit or treachery did not suggest itself to his mind. Such thoughts do not come readily to a man like Cromlin. Could he at that moment have looked into the state-room of the steamer, where his cousin lay very sea-sick and miserable, he would have seen a triumphant smile on his pallid face; and if Vaughan's thoughts could have been made audible to him, they would have run something like this:

"A narrow thing indeed, by Jove! Ugh! this cursed sickness! He will go straight on to California. A month to go, a month to get back—more at that season—and a hunt for the Craufords, should he push over to Europe. Bah! you are 'played' every way, Master Launce, as usual!—Steward, are you never coming with that brandy? Bring a bottle of champagne too."

Long weeks after that night Mr. Carstoe was sitting one evening in the library of the villa at Moysterville where he and Darrell Vaughan had held so many friendly chats. The house had not been rented, and, according to an agreement with Vaughan, he made it his head-quarters, as the housekeeper refused to stay and take charge of the lonely place with no better guard for her mature charms than Jack, the lame gardener.

He was awaiting the arrival of his old employer's other nephew. Launce, on his arrival at San Francisco, learned that his uncle had been dead for months, and that his former agent, Mr. Carstoe, was then at Moysterville. Particulars Launce could not gain: he would go on. He telegraphed to Mr. Carstoe that he might be expected. He was broken-hearted at these tidings. It seemed so hard that his uncle should have gone before he could once more hear words of kindness from the lips of the man he had loved so well. At least he must have left letters—some explanation of the mystery which had so long separated them. No one so likely to know as this Mr. Carstoe: he would go in search of him. Of the fortune—of his own share therein—he had no time to think; his mind was full of his sad loss, and the bitter disappointment of having arrived too late.

He was worn, tired; another man might have fancied himself menaced by illness; but Launce, never having been ill in his life, set all his odd sensations down to the score of fatigue and trouble, and hastened to reach his journey's end. So this dark autumnal evening Mr. Carstoe sat awaiting the arrival of his visitor, wondering in his slow way why on earth the young man should have come to California. He must have seen his cousin in New York, or, if they missed each other, must have received the letters which would make all matters clear. It was useless for Mr. Carstoe to go to the station in the dark, for he and the young gentleman were utter strangers. Mr. Cromlin knew where to come; all Mr. Carstoe could do was to wait for him in the villa, and be certain that the housekeeper had a good dinner prepared in the guest's honor.

And Launce arrived. Late that night he and Mr. Carstoe still sat in earnest conversation. There were no letters for Launce; Mr. Carstoe had himself gone over the papers of the deceased at Darrell's request.

"The whole thing was terribly sudden, though he had so long been in poor health," Mr. Carstoe said. "I am convinced that matters would have been different had he not put off too long. I said so to Mr. Darrell Vaughan—I repeat it to you."

Launce already knew that his cousin inherited the fortune—let him have it. He did not care for the money, but to have come too late—that was what hurt. The manner of the bequest to himself would prevent his ever touching it; he could receive nothing from Darrell's bounty or condescension.

Mr. Carstoe told things in a slow fashion; but the facts of the will, as most important in his eyes, came out first, and he finally got to the affair of the codicil. Launce was struck dumb. Even in the dull misery of his mood there rose a vision of that beautiful face which had so often of late haunted him. Had it been Fate which showed her to him that day? Time enough for such dreams; there was more prosaic business on hand now.

"A full account of these matters," Mr. Carstoe was saying, "your cousin and I wrote to you at your address in New York, to be forwarded."

"What address?" asked Cromlin.

"Noble & Brothers, Exchange Place."

"I never even heard their names that I remember," said Launce.

"Very odd," replied Mr. Carstoe. "Your cousin thought the letters would be sure to reach you there."

"The letter written me by my uncle—how was that sent?"

"To a Mr. Sandford, in New York. By the way, he is dead too—I saw a notice in an Eastern paper. An answer came from him after your uncle's death: he had forwarded the letter for you to a London banker, but did not mention the name, so your cousin thought we had better send ours to Noble & Brothers."

"A strange insanity on Darrell's part," said Launce, dryly.

"A series of lamentable errors on everybody's," observed Carstoe. "Sir, I am heartily grieved. Mr. Vaughan was a peculiar man—a difficult man; but the most honorable and straightforward one I ever knew. Sir, he was a good friend to me."

There had been neither wine nor punch to quicken Mr. Carstoe's halting speech to-night. He spoke stiffly, with hesitation, but what he said had at least the merit of clearness.

"You are a good man, Mr. Carstoe," returned Launce, seizing his companion's hand, and causing Carstoe to look embarrassed and miserable by this impulsiveness. "See here, sir, I have a sad weight on my mind; I want to know if you can help to clear it up."

Mr. Carstoe waited; he knew what was coming. Launce briefly related the story of his uncle's having suddenly refused to hold any communication with him in that letter in which he had disowned and cast him off.

"Now, did he ever talk to you about it, Mr. Carstoe? Do you know what he fancied I had done? He was a stern man, but never unjust."

Hesitation would only have been as foolish as it would be unkind.

"He did tell me, after finding out his error through Mr. Sandford's investigations," Mr. Carstoe said.

"What did he think?"

"That you had falsified a check he sent you," replied Mr. Carstoe.

Launce uttered a cry. Mr. Carstoe thought he was fainting, but he soon recovered himself.

"Tell me all you can," he said.

The agent gave the details. He could even recall the time at which the check had been sent—Launce's twenty-first birthday. After a while Launce spoke.

"I never saw the check," he said, slowly. "My uncle had arranged for my first year's expenses in Europe while I was with him in Vermont; that was the last money I ever received. I only wrote him once before sailing. I had wanted to keep my broken arm a secret for fear he should defer my journey. I never saw that check, Mr. Carstoe!"

"That agrees with Mr. Sandford's idea that the bank teller must have been in the plot. But who could have got the check, and how?"

"Heaven knows," groaned Launce. "There is no way to find out now—no step to take. Why, it's like an awful dream!"

He stopped and passed his hand across his forehead.

"Remember that at least your uncle lived to believe in your innocence," Mr. Carstoe said, greatly moved.

"Thank God! Did he talk about me—did he seem to care for me?" Launce's voice broke.

"He talked about you constantly during that last fortnight—mostly of the time when you were a boy. Ah! he had loved you dearly all the while. I was with him more than any body. Well, sir, I know he meant to change his will. I supposed that Smith had drawn up a new one at the time the codicil was written. I expected to find that you and your cousin shared equally. I told Mr. Darrell so the night he arrived here. I am bound to say he expressed a hope that I might be right; he was greatly attached to you and your uncle—very happy that your innocence had been established. But when the will was opened I found the change had not been made."

"I don't care for the money," cried Launce. "At least he knew I was not a villain. Good God! how could it have come about? And he's dead, and there is no clew?"

"None," said Mr. Carstoe. "I know what I have told you, and I know nothing more."

He went over the details of the last days: Milady's two visits; Mr. Vaughan's seizure during his conversation with her, Carstoe himself being absent. On the previous night Smith the lawyer had been at the house. Mrs. Simpson and Anthony Turner had witnessed papers; but that was an occurrence too frequent to be important. Mr. Carstoe only mentioned it casually to show that up to the very hour of the paralytic stroke Mr. Vaughan's mind remained clear.

"I got back that evening," he went on, huskily. "He knew me once—tried to tell me something."

"But you could not understand?"

"No. There were only broken words. I caught, 'My boy—my boy—set right—time—I—'"

Mr. Carstoe's voice faltered. Launce remained silent. After a while, the lawyer continued—

"I understood when we opened the will. He had not made the change I supposed completed when the codicil was drawn up. That was what troubled him. But even if I had understood, it would have been too late then—too late, poor man!"

Mr. Carstoe paused, spread out his hands, and turned away.

"God bless you!" cried Launce, wringing his hand. "You have given me great comfort."

Mr. Carstoe put his head straight on his shoulders, and looked into the fire, more wooden than ever of aspect, to atone for his late weakness.

"Your cousin arrived the next day," he continued. "The old gentleman never knew him, nor any body, though he lingered for more than a week. As I mentioned to you, poor Smith was killed only the day of Mr. Vaughan's attack. It was a week to be remembered in Moysterville —two citizens so prominent—"

"Did you ever see that woman again?" demanded Launce, ruthlessly interrupting this bit of eloquence.

"Ah! she could only have come to beg, or worse; probably her visit was a blind."

Then Mr. Carstoe told the story of the stolen jewels, and the lucky chance by which Darrell Vaughan had discovered her guilt. Launce listened attentively to the tale, the interest and excitement of the whole conversation since his arrival causing him to forget the peculiar physical sensations which had troubled him for days.

"And the woman saw my uncle twice?" he said at last.

"Yes; she came two days in succession. After her first visit, Mr. Vaughan told Mrs. Simpson to be sure and admit her when she returned."

"And she is now in the penitentiary?"

"She has not been taken there yet; she is still in the jail here. About the time she was to be sent, a great fire broke out in the women's ward of the penitentiary. The damages were so great that they had none too much room for the prisoners already there."

"I remember now," Launce replied; "they mentioned it in San Francisco. It is supposed that it was set on fire—a plot for the escape of the convicts."

"Yes; and several did get away, but were retaken."

"So the woman is still here in the jail?" Launce said, after a few moments' thought. "Mr. Carstoe, I shall go to see her."

Carstoe looked surprised and puzzled.

"You don't suppose she could throw any light on the matter which troubles you? Mr. Vaughan got his information from Sandford."

"I don't know that I expect any thing. All the same, I shall go to see Milady, if I can get the permission."

The next morning Mr. Carstoe occupied himself in procuring the necessary permit—not difficult to obtain, since it is he who asks it for a nephew of the late Mr. Vaughan.

The two go to the jail together; Mr. Carstoe even accompanies Launce into the women's ward, and with him follows the keeper down the corridor into which Milady's cell opens. Mr. Carstoe has no intention of sharing the interview—he did not mean to come so far; but somehow a painful, irresistible fascination has led him on.

The doors of all the cells have a square window secured by iron gratings. The shutters are open at this hour; at almost every loophole some haggard or evil face peers out at the passers.

"There's Milady taking a peep too," the turnkey says in a low voice, when they have nearly reached the end of the passage. "It's unusual for her to stand there."

Both gentlemen see her distinctly. Mr. Carstoe hesitates, then stops; at the same instant Milady disappears.

"I'll go back and wait in the matron's parlor," Mr. Carstoe says to Launce. "I didn't mean to come—I wouldn't have seen her for the world."

Launce nods, and passes on with the keeper.

"I've brought you a visitor," the man says, looking through the bars. "I hope you will be a little more civil to Mr. Cromlin than you generally are to people."

He unlocks the door, stands back for Launce to enter, and closes it behind him.

Milady is seated in the farthest corner of the cell, her head resting on her hands. She still wears the rusty black-silk dress, and the faded shawl of Indian cashmere is gathered over her shoulders.

Launce stands silent for a few seconds, but as she neither stirs nor looks up, he says gently—

"I want to talk with you a little, if you will let me."

Milady raises her head quickly, and flashes her stormy eyes upon him.

Launce's first thought is that an insane asylum would be the proper place of captivity for her—those eyes can only belong to a mad woman. Then, artist like, he is struck by the picturesque shadow of beauty which hangs about her still—a mere shadow, which some way in connection with that wasted face is more appalling than any ugliness could have been.

"What did he call you?" she asks in her hollow voice.

"My name is Cromlin," Launce replies.

She is half out of her seat. He has the same feeling which strikes any beholder each time she moves—that she is about to spring at him like a panther. But she sinks back on the bench. A strange light, which for an instant altered the expression of her eyes, dies out. Singular changes pass over her face, but Launce can not interpret them. They are like a wild mingling of hope, resolve, doubt, and then a quick, insane cunning and suspicion.

"Carstoe was with him," she mutters.

"What did you say?" Launce asks, still speaking in that kindly voice. He has not time to reflect that such is the case, but his mind is full of pity and sympathy for the creature. "I did not hear."

"I said you must catch a bird before you can put salt on its tail," returns Milady, with one of her dreadful laughs. Her countenance has resumed its usual sullen, defiant look, yet there is a certain eagerness in her eyes, and she watches him narrowly.

"When you first came to Moysterville, you went twice to see old Mr. Vaughan," says Launce. "He was my uncle."

"'Oh, my prophetic soul,' dear Hamlet!" sneers Milady. "Hadn't you better send for the marines if you want to spin a yarn? I say, Buffer, a drink would be a blessing."

Yet Launce noticed the eagerness in her eyes —the suspicion in her face. He knows they have a meaning; that if he could only find out the significance of both she might be induced to talk earnestly.

"I think," Launce says, "that you put a wrong construction on my visit—you do not really believe that I am Mr. Vaughan's nephew."

She starts again at the name, but once more the suspicion masters the eagerness in her eyes. As if it were a reminder to herself to keep impassible, untouched, she mutters anew—

"Carstoe was with him!"

Launce would give much to catch the words. It seems to him that if he could do so he should have the clew he wants whereby to interest the woman and give her faith in him. But he strains his ears vainly; only a hoarse murmur is audible.

"I am sure my uncle was kind to you," Launce goes on, not studying his speech, trusting to his intuitions to say what will be most likely to influence her. "I loved him very dearly; we were separated for years; he thought ill of me—believed that I had committed a great crime."

Does Milady give a gasping breath—almost a groan? He can not be sure. He had turned away his eyes for an instant, and when he looks up at the sound, she is leaning back, her face as blank as the wall behind her.

He goes steadily on in his explanation.

"Before his death he sent for me. He had discovered that I was innocent, but there is nothing among his papers to tell me how. I thought if you knew the least thing, if it were about that you went to him, you would be kind and generous enough to tell me. It could do you no hurt, and would take a great weight off my mind."

Under the cover of her shawl Milady twists her hands hard together. She will not look at him; she bows her head; she fights against her willingness to believe, and fortifies herself anew by that whisper. In his earnestness, too, Launce has overdone his work. She can not fancy any human creature speaking softly to her, unless from a desire to cheat and deceive. He waits, encouraged by her silence to hope that he has found the way to her confidence. But she is quiet so long that he adds—

"If you would tell me! Perhaps never in your whole life will you have an opportunity to do any person so great a favor. I think you would always be glad of having done it."

"He reels it off well," exclaims Milady. "I say, you're a preacher, and you must be worse than the most of 'em, because you're so much more glib."

"I have told you who I am," replies Launce. "The keeper mentioned my name. Why Mr. Carstoe is here, and could tell you."

"No; he's only a fool, after all," mutters Milady. "Why, you can't be a preacher—it's too bad. I was just going to swear at you. It wouldn't be half the fun if you're not a parson."

But Launce will not yet relinquish his purpose. He feels that he has committed an error in mentioning Mr. Carstoe, so he tries to set it right.

"You think he is your enemy. Why Mr. Carstoe pities you from the bottom of his heart. He would be the first to head a petition for pardon if you would even now give information that could put justice on the track of those bad men who led you on. He would do it even if he never recovered the jewels."

"Ah," says Milady, "we've got to that! It's the way he interests Carstoe in keeping up the game. Sail ahead, young man!"

"He—whom do you mean?" asks Launce.

"Your friend the Devil," retorts Milady. "Handsome Devil isn't he—oh, we women!"

Each word has its meaning, Launce feels sure, aimless and coarse as her answers sound, if he could only catch the right clew.

"You were with my uncle when that attack came on," pursues he. That first appeal had seemed to affect her—he will follow it up. "I can not help believing you had some strong motive for those visits; at least tell me if they in any way bear upon this mystery which has darkened my life for years."

"Ten years," mutters Milady; "he said so! And after that, ten years! Didn't you hear the judge repeat it? He'd been taught his lesson too."

A sense of discouragement comes over Launce. The pain and lassitude of the last few days make themselves felt again, and it is an effort to concentrate his thoughts.

"You'll not help me?" he says, wearily.

"How much was your share to be?" asks Milady, with that look of half-insane cunning. "Are you to be paid any way? I thought that Devil was satisfied, now he has me safe. 'Ten years, and then again ten!'" Her voice becomes a groan, but she quickly bursts into a laugh, and adds, in her hardest, most defiant fashion, "I'll go you a pile of Mexican dollars against a cent that I live through and come out. I will live—I *will!*" she fairly shrieks, shaking her clenched fists. "Live and come out—Devil! Devil!"

"Think—just by giving these men up to justice you could be free very soon," urges Launce.

"They could not harm you; you would have friends—be kept safe—"

"'Come into my parlor, said the spider to the fly,'" sang Milady in a hoarse contralto, laughing still, always that crazy cunning in her eyes.

"If I could only tell what it is you suspect—whom you fear," says Launce, his tired faculties growing confused under this feeling that her reticence concealed a mystery.

"Devil! handsome Devil!" croaks Milady.

"Let the rest go," says Launce; "at least you would cheat the Devil a little by this favor I ask. Only tell me if your visit to my uncle threw any light on the crime he suspected me of."

"Do the dead ever get out of their graves?" whispers Milady. "I thought I saw Jem last night." But in an instant she is laughing, and screams out, "Lord, if Jem could come back, what a kettle of fish! But he's safe six foot under ground, and I'm as good as buried—Devil! Devil!"

She is becoming greatly excited. The keeper has warned Launce that she is subject to moods so like insanity that he believes she will end soon a hopeless maniac. Cromlin is himself growing more conscious of fatigue and weakness each moment, now that he has lost the hope which brought him here. But a new thought strikes him—he will try one further plea.

"If you will not help me, or even tell me whether it is in your power," he says, "I will not be so hard and unkind as you are. They tell me you have a child; let me know where it is and I will find it, and send you word of its welfare."

Milady is out of her seat; she has sprung at him lithe and dangerous as a panther. He has only time to avoid her clutching hands by a quick movement. She totters against the wall, weak, half-fainting, her features convulsed, her eyes like nothing human; but he hears broken words as she gnashes her teeth till the blood-specked foam flies from her lips.

"*That* was it—Devil! Devil!—to get the child—a hold if I came out—the child!"

Then with a shriek she falls prostrate upon the floor, writhing in awful spasms.

The turnkey comes, the matron and doctor are sent for. Launce is obliged to go away. He joins Mr. Carstoe, and they wait until news is brought that Milady is better, though still wandering in her mind.

Launce Cromlin has had no intention of making any stay in California. This night he goes to bed early, so oppressed by distracting thoughts that conversation or connected meditation is an impossibility.

He sleeps brokenly, and lives through dismal experiences in his slumber. Sometimes Darrell is trying to drag him over a precipice. Sometimes Elizabeth Cranford is on trial for the theft of the jewels, and he is endeavoring to save her; while his uncle stands by in his shroud, making signs that he wishes to speak words he is powerless to utter, and Elizabeth's face changes to that of Milady, and Darrell is laughing hideously at both.

Then he wakes, sleeps again, and a worse confusion follows. Now he is imprisoned among red-hot iron bars, now freezing to death in a snow-pass of the Sierras—always seeing Darrell and scores of other familiar countenances, and hearing his uncle's voice.

The morning comes, and when Mr. Carstoe ventures to call his dilatory guest to breakfast, he finds him raving in the delirium of the terrible Chagres fever, and the next three months are little better than a blank to Launce Cromlin.

CHAPTER XI.
OUTWITTED.

GOOD, prim, ceremonious Monsieur La Tour! It was fortunate that he entertained the strictest and most ancient ideas in regard to the panoply of reserve and timidity in which demoiselles ought to be wrapped, otherwise the reception he got from Nathalie must have struck an ominous chill to his heart. But his notion of the greeting proper under the circumstances was to bow low over her hand, to imprint a decorous kiss there-on, to offer a long-winded compliment on her appearance, and express his overwhelming delight at seeing her in elegantly correct French, which sounded like a jumble of quotations from Boileau and Telemachus.

Madame L'Estrange leaned back among her pillows and watched the scene, with her haggard features and eager eyes softened into contentment. The scene was so precise, so proper, so dull, that she liked it; her one desire for Nathalie's future was quiet and respectability. Susanne stood behind Madame's sofa, ostensibly arranging her cushions, in reality watching Nathalie, with an odd expression, which might have disturbed the girl had she noticed it. But Nathalie was too busy with the rush of rebellious thoughts which oppressed her to observe Susanne. She did perceive that Monsieur had bought a new wig in honor of his return, and she longed to knock it off and step on it. She had hurried into the house with some mad idea of crying out at once that she would never marry him—never; of defying her mother, and daring the full brunt of her wrath. But once in the room, her courage failed. The light clasp of Monsieur's fingers seemed a hold that she could not break. If, indeed, any wild words she might utter were to free her from him, she knew that confinement or a convent would be her portion. Excitable as she was, her natural artfulness came to her aid and restored her reason. Her one hope lay in cajoling and wheedling both mother and betrothed—gaining time—if she could only do that!

Susanne, watching her always, saw the sudden change in her face. Nathalie grew smiling, talked gayly, said courteous things, indulged even in fun, in raillery which would have called down disapproval from her mother had not Monsieur appeared in a state of high delight with her conversation. Susanne gave a long sniff of suspicion.

"She means mischief," thought that shrewd personage. "Eh, well, it is lucky that I have eyes in my head. Once married, Monsieur must look after her himself, and I do not envy him his task; but until then—no, no, Mademoiselle! You are very crafty, but you are no match for Susanne yet, and I shall see that you do not go straight to the devil, as you are inclined."

Monsieur displayed the presents he had brought. It would have been impossible for Nathalie not to derive satisfaction from the sight of ornaments, even at her last gasp. She tried on the bracelet and necklace, and fluttered the pretty fan, and was happy for five minutes. Then she remembered Vaughan, and longed to dash the baubles on the floor, and give way to her rebellious impulses, but had sense to perceive that by so doing she would ruin her one faint hope of escape. The hope was wild, mad,

and she knew it, but she clung thereto notwithstanding.

Monsieur remained all the afternoon and evening. Nathalie found no opportunity to slip out
of the house, though she was half crazy from her
belief that Vaughan would return, and be lingering somewhere near toward sunset. At that
very hour she was obliged to walk with Monsieur
on the lawn—Madame actually permitted it—
obliged to sit with him under the poplar-tree
and listen to his talk, which grew more lover-
like than ever before.

If she could tell him—he seemed kind-hearted
—but tell him what? That she could not marry him because she loved a stranger, a man
whom she had only seen a few times in all?
Nathalie could not do this; the utter insanity
of such an avowal struck even her. No, she
must wait. If she could only see Vaughan!
He loved her—surely he loved her! Now that
the time was shortening so terribly—Monsieur
returned—Vaughan would break through all ordinary rules, and find means to save her.

While Nathalie tried to listen to Monsieur's
conversation, and to quiet herself with the belief that she should yet escape her bonds, Susanne was warning her mistress.

"He!" cried that astute individual, with ab-
rupt disregard of Madame's shattered nerves.
"We have held together many years, and I am
not going to desert Madame now. I may have
my faults—time enough for perfection when one
gets to heaven—but I shall not do that."

"What are you talking about, Susanne?" demanded the sick woman, irritably.

"Use your eyes, Madame—use your eyes!"
cried Susanne, shaking herself up and down with
great energy.

"What does the creature mean?" asked Madame more peevishly, yet in a good deal of trep-
idation.

"Do you want a wedding—do you want to
be sure she is safe out of harm's way?" continued Susanne. "Do you trust that quiet and
submission, and you knowing women?"

"*Mon Dieu!* what is it? Tell me, Susanne;
you will make me ill—you will upset my night."

"That is just what must not happen; you
must keep all your wits about you, and be able
to act," returned Susanne. "Look here. I en-
gage to watch her for three days and nights; if
she is not married then, I wash my hands of the
consequences."

"*Mon Dieu! mon Dieu!*" moaned Madame.
"What is it—what has happened?"

"Nothing yet; but marry her at once, or she
will refuse. I saw it in her face to-day. The
devil is in it that Madame can not understand!"
cried Susanne, fiercely, as poor Madame shook
and gasped and stared at her in nervous dread.

"This is it, then! That young American has
been hanging about. She has met him twice.

I got it out of that old idiot of a Rosine. I saw
him plainly enough when I went to call her, but
I made no sign."

It required immense self-control on the part
of Madame to restrain the hysterics and spasms,
which would have left her powerless. For a
few seconds she wrung her hands and uttered a
jumble of prayers and imprecations. Susanne
delivered a brief lecture on the propriety of showing common-sense in a case like this.

"If you lose any time you will lose her," said
Susanne. "Swallow your medicine quick, and
be strong."

The cold drops of perspiration stood on Madame's forehead; her teeth chattered as if they
would break the wine-glass Susanne held to her
lips; but something of the old, resolute will was
yet left in the enfeebled frame, and she would
not give way. It required very slight explanation to make her understand the case thoroughly. Feminine weaknesses or insanities could never take Madame much by surprise, after her
varied experience of life.

"There is no harm done," said Susanne. "It
struck me Mademoiselle had grown very fond
of her promenader, and yesterday it all came
over me in a flash—I can not tell how, but it
did! That old Rosine had an important air, and
Mademoiselle was odd. Eh, well, it is no matter—I saw him!"

"I can not think easily, I am so dull now,"
moaned Madame.

"The marriage must take place at once, of
course. Monsieur will want it. Every thing was
ready, even to the license, before he went away.
Does not Madame see?"

"Ah, yes! I shall tell him I am worse; there
must be no delay. Oh, that wretched girl!"
cried Madame, with sudden anger in her voice.

"Bah! one is not a woman for nothing," returned Susanne. "Take good care, Madame;
be very sweet to her—give her no chance to re-
bel; there is no telling what she might do. Come
now; you are better—you can manage?"

"Yes; but, Holy Virgin, I shall die after—I
know I shall; this agitation will be too much for
me."

"And so you ought," was Susanne's mental
comment; but she spoke some comforting words,
and was altogether very helpful and amiable.
Indeed, Susanne quite enjoyed the excitement
and the plotting, after the decorous dullness into
which their lives had so long ago slipped without break or variety. "Let Madame trust me;
all she need do is to give Monsieur a hint that
he may have his wife any day—he will be eager
enough—I shall manage the rest! I am equal
to the occasion—yes, indeed! I know my own
talents, the saints be praised, and I am not wicked enough to undervalue them."

"Susanne, if you never lose sight of her—if
we succeed—I will not wait for what I have put

you down in my will. I shall give you five hundred francs the morning of the marriage," said Madame, catching her attendant's hand between her bony fingers.

"That is only fair! I am proud in the right way, thank God, and am willing always to accept my due," said Susanne. "Let Madame be perfectly tranquil; I have a scheme. Ta, ta! how quick one's invention is at times. Hark! they are coming back. Do not lose a moment in speaking to Monsieur."

Madame raised herself on her elbow as the betrothed pair entered, and gazed anxiously at her daughter. She could read the impatience—all the varied feelings which showed in the girl's face under its assumed calmness. That very effort at composure frightened Madame more than ever; it was unlike Nathalie; she must mean mischief indeed.

"Dear child," said Madame, "go with Susanne for a little; I have to talk with our good friend here."

Nathalie hurried along the gallery to her salon, and made for the outer door. It was scarcely yet twilight; she might still find Vaughan. But on the threshold she met Susanne, and Susanne said in a tone of cheerful interest—

"I just saw that handsome American go past. He was walking; but a carriage stopped, and he drove off in it with the two gentlemen."

Nathalie would have liked to scream—to go into a fury—any thing as a vent to her disappointment. But, after all, Susanne was not to blame. She turned back into her salon, and sat down among the shadows until she was again summoned into the presence of her mother and future husband.

Monsieur spent the evening—the evening which Nathalie thought would never end. There was a change in Monsieur's manner: something even more tender and gallant than usual, but which betrayed a certain air of proprietorship. He was in wonderful spirits, too; he reminded Nathalie again of an elderly sheep trying to frisk himself into the belief that he was a lamb. The carriage came for him at last; he had made his adieu to Madame. As he approached Nathalie, she shrunk back from the smile that rendered his face eager, kind and gentle as the smile was. He did not content himself with kissing her hands—he leaned forward and pressed his lips upon her forehead.

"I have Madame's permission?" he asked, laughing.

"I shall so soon lose all claim to direct," returned Madame, laughing too, "that I may as well resign my authority at once."

Nathalie smothered a little cry of fear and disgust. A few more pleasant words passed between her mother and Monsieur, then he left the room.

"I shall go to bed," said Madame. "My dear, on the day after to-morrow we must part for a time; you will be Madame La Tour."

"So soon? No—I can not—I will not!" gasped Nathalie.

"So soon? Odd words to apply to a marriage that has already been delayed five whole weeks beyond the original time," said Madame in an icy voice. "Can not—will not? Stranger words still from a daughter to her mother, especially when she speaks of marrying a man to whom she has been betrothed for months."

Madame's stony calmness rendered Nathalie more hopeless.

"He came back so suddenly—I can not—oh! he might give me a week," faltered the girl.

"Mademoiselle is dramatic," sneered Madame, preserving her composure by a powerful effort, conscious that it was her greatest stronghold. "I am willing, if it amuses you! One thing is certain: of course, at this late day, you contemplate no real opposition? You accepted Monsieur La Tour; you wished to marry him; you will do so on Thursday."

"I did not know—I was a child—I—"

"Pray do not force me to go further, and say that you are an idiot," interrupted Madame. "Bah! what is this? I am told that American girls do such disgraceful things—break off their engagements at the last moment. You have a mother who does not understand such savage customs. Silence!—go to bed! I know you are not in earnest; you just want a little romance, but it is not proper; besides, I am too feeble and ill to enjoy it with you."

"My mother!—oh, my mother!" cried Nathalie.

She thought she could make an eloquent speech, but no words came. The rigid laws which surround an unmarried woman in France were full in her mind. The utter futility of softening or changing her mother struck her too. The recklessness that stood her in place of force of character was gone for the time; her temper gave no aid. Frightened and miserable, she burst into passionate tears.

"Good!" thought Susanne, watching the interview from behind the dining-room door. "We shall not have much trouble, after all.".

She began to carol a pleasant ditty, as if she had just entered, and wished to announce her approach.

"Is Madame ready for me?" she called, in her most respectful voice.

"Yes; come in, Susanne," replied her mistress.

"Wait," pleaded Nathalie; "let me speak—let me tell you! Susanne, go away for a while."

"What did Mademoiselle say?" asked Susanne, entering. "Yes, she is quite right; Madame ought to be in bed. Ah, Mademoiselle is always thoughtful, and we are to lose her so soon—so soon!"

"You dreadful old woman—you wicked old woman!" sobbed Nathalie.

It was not in the least as she would have expected to behave, but she felt so powerless—such a child.

"Joseph, Marie, and Saint Geneviève!" ejaculated Susanne in a shrill staccato. "Eh, eh, what we all need is sleep! Mademoiselle is nervous—she shall have some of Madame's drops."

"Mademoiselle is inclined to prefer a convent to marriage, but I fancy the night will bring wisdom," observed Madame in her icy voice.

"Ta, ta! girls always feel like that when the wedding-day gets so near. It is nothing—a mere nothing," pronounced Susanne, cheerfully. "She does not really mind, we do not mind; and Monsieur knows that tears are quite en règle, so he will not mind."

"Susanne, I would like to murder you!" exclaimed Nathalie.

"Dear heart, only listen!" returned Susanne, affecting still to consider the whole matter a joke. "But we must not play any longer. Madame needs to go to bed; she will be ill otherwise."

"I am ill!—I suffer!—oh, oh!" It struck Madame that she might as well now yield to her real agitation. If Nathalie received a thorough fright, that would finish the work her mother's firmness had begun.

Usually the girl was ordered away when these attacks came on; but she was detained to-night, made to help, and Susanne pretended to be horribly alarmed, though in reality the seizure was nothing compared to many she had witnessed.

Not a word of upbraiding did Madame utter. When she could speak again, she fixed her great eyes on Nathalie, and said faintly—

"It is possible there may be no wedding after all on Thursday; there may be a funeral though."

Nathalie was sent off to her room, and her terror was so great that she thought less of her own misery than of her mother's words, and no mode of escape would suggest itself to her weary brain.

The next morning Nathalie found Madame sweet and amiable; anxious for her society too, but showing symptoms of spasms if Nathalie so much as moved quickly.

Susanne faithfully fulfilled her promise of watching. Rosine came up-stairs on some pretense, and managed to convey a letter to Nathalie. This Susanne could not prevent, so she appeared blind. A little later, Nathalie went out on the gallery. She dropped a folded paper, apparently by accident. Rosine was picking up twigs and sticks about the lawn, conveniently placed to seize the note. As she entered the passage on the ground-floor where the *fermier* lived, Susanne loomed before her.

"Mademoiselle desired me to take the billet," she said; "it was not for you to pick it up."

Rosine demurred.

"Give me that note, or I will break every bone in thy accursed body and suck thy black blood! —dolt! fish! cabbage!" cried Susanne, so fierce of aspect that Rosine yielded the prize without a struggle. "You to be trusted with such delicate matters—set you up, indeed! You are to go by train to Lausanne, and see if that vile embroidery-woman has finished the work we gave her. Be off at once, laziest and ugliest! Fly to catch the train; here is money. Make any blunder, and I will eat you without salt at precisely seven o'clock to-night, tough and black as you are, vile Swiss!"

And Susanne snapped her teeth together with a noise which froze Rosine's blood.

So the old woman was disposed of for the day. Monsieur appeared: Monsieur, in a state of gallantry and pleasant agitation, full of old-fashioned compliments for Nathalie, which nearly drove her out of her senses. But Madame had prepared him to find her odd, capricious, in tears perhaps.

"It is always the way," she said; "girls invariably get frightened when the time comes. Ten to one, she will beg for a few days or say she hates you. It is nothing, trust me; I know my sex; a mere affair of nerves, no more."

Monsieur, in his goodness, was prepared to be patient and considerate to any extent, but Nathalie did not alarm him by tears or other passionate outbreak. Indeed, she was upheld by a vague hope—of what she did not think at all clearly. Vaughan had written and begged her to meet him. What she expected she could not have told; certainly even in her romance not that he should ask her to fly with him, and that she should consent to go. She had sufficient practical sense in spite of the extravagance of her ideas to remember he was a stranger, well as it seemed to her that she knew him.

Susanne left the house on a little affair of her own, leaving Nathalie safe for the time between her mother and Monsieur. Susanne strayed about until she met Darrell Vaughan. She informed the American that she came from Nathalie; the young lady had not been able to write. She begged him to be very careful—not to come near the house, nor even send her a note, for a day or two. Susanne promised to meet him for a moment on the following day, and was profuse in her wishes to serve them both. She never pocketed money with more satisfaction in her life than she felt in storing away the gold piece Vaughan put in her hand. Having to plot and plan, lie and cheat the two young people, made Susanne feel at least ten years younger. Be it said for her, too, that she was fond of both Madame and Nathalie in her way, and had no mind to see the girl ruin her future by any act of mad folly, and Susanne's ideas of the lengths to which her sex would go under sufficient inducement or provocation were wide indeed.

The next day Nathalie found no opportunity even to speak with Rosine; wherever she moved, Susanne was beside her, amiable, and in her most conversational mood. She tried to vex the woman; Susanne was not to be irritated. She had suddenly developed a patience that was little short of angelic. Nathalie was completely hemmed in — powerless. She broke down at last, enraged her mother, and alarmed Monsieur by an hysterical outburst. Susanne pounced upon her immediately; this was what she had been waiting for. She put her to bed, dosed her with *tisanes* that had several drops of Madame's morphine mingled with their nastiness.

"Ah," thought Susanne, quite touched by her own talent and virtue, "I shall never get a fitting reward in this world for all my sacrifices; but they ought to count in the next."

Susanne thought of several little sins she could commit on the strength of these present efforts for good, which she regarded as a sort of absolution taken out in advance. She saw Vaughan again, and set a time for him to come to the house—Thursday, at two o'clock.

"I can not stop to answer questions. Be in the chalet grounds at that hour," said she, and was gone, chuckling over this last stroke, which would give a dramatic finish to the business.

There was no escape. Nathalie comprehended that Susanne had outwitted her, but was ignorant of the means. One other attempt at a scene was put down by her mother with a high hand.

"I give you a choice," she said; "the wedding or to start for the convent—as a novice too. Do you prefer marriage or taking the veil? One or the other—I will not be disgraced—I am a dying woman."

It was Thursday afternoon. Darrell Vaughan approached the chalet gates; he saw a carriage drive past and take the road which led up to the station. Susanne was standing on the door-step, her handkerchief at her eyes.

"We have lost her," said that worthy woman; "Mademoiselle was married half an hour ago."

She extended her hand. It might have been to point toward the station; it might have been to receive any little reward which the American should feel disposed to bestow upon her.

So Vaughan set out on his journey that night, going as far as Brieg by the rail, that he might have daylight for crossing the Simplon. He was furious. He knew that he had been saved from an insanity which might have endangered his whole future, but he was furious nevertheless. He had never before failed in any scheme upon which his fancy—his heart he would have said—fixed itself. Brief as the dream was, it had taken a powerful hold of his mind; he felt almost ready to throw up his entire plan, let every

' E

thing go, and follow Nathalie. But he could not be crazy enough for this. He must set out on his journey; the rage and mad desire would pass.

CHAPTER XII.

A NEW EXPERIENCE.

PISA is a stupid old place, that is to people who crave society. But Mr. Crauford found a few acquaintances to make up his whist-table, and was content. This satisfied Elizabeth. She dreaded nothing so much as the seasons when her father was seized with a whim of thoughtfulness on her account, and insisted on a sojourn in some resort where balls and gayeties could be found. Not that she was too lofty and visionary to enjoy these pleasures, but a dread always haunted her that such things were a waste of time.

She was given to reading authors who are eager for reforms, and tell us eloquently about the misery there is in the world, and Elizabeth wanted to be "up and doing" instead of casting in her lot among the butterflies, agreeable as their holiday existence might be in certain ways.

She was happy in the dear old town. She enjoyed straying about the Campo Santo or marveling over the beautiful Cathedral, the Baptistery, the Leaning Tower — that most picturesque of all groups of buildings, standing in the grass-grown square where every thing is so still, where the bells sound dreamy and indolent, and the very beggars are too lazy to rise and persecute any unfortunate stranger who may approach. The place carries one back centuries. One would not be surprised to see Galileo saunter past, nor be startled if a troop of Crusaders halted to say a prayer in the church before setting out for the Holy Land.

The Craufords found a charming apartment in a faded old palace which had once been the home of some almost royal family. Elizabeth delighted in the vast salons, that still contained many articles of the ancient furniture, curiously carved chairs, wonderful inlaid cabinets, and the like. There was a balcony, too, from whence she could look out over the distant hills, and watch sunsets and the moonlight, and lose herself in those dreams which were a source of reproach to her, much as she enjoyed them. She feared that they too were a sad waste of time.

She told herself that she had been very idle of late, and prepared to make amends. She brought out her wisest, heaviest books, and pored diligently over musty tomes, afraid that she found them slightly dull, wishing for some real occupation, fearful that her life was a very useless one, and wondering vaguely about the illimitable future, which must ever be so attractive to the young.

Elizabeth Crauford was an enthusiast and a worshiper of idols. Of that latter necessity in her nature, no better proof could have been afforded than the ardor with which she struggled to throw a halo about her father. In his case, if ever she failed, a tender pity might still keep her heart soft; but in other instances of disappointment, a father hard contempt would be the feeling left in Elizabeth's mind toward the object which proved unworthy her worship. Most of her ideas were extreme, as was natural at her age. Duty and self-sacrifice were somewhat confused in her thoughts. It was to be feared that she would often mistake the latter for the former, and bring much pain upon herself. She was singularly clear in her reflections and analyses, in spite of this. She might have become that usually to be dreaded character, "well-regulated," had not her impulsiveness and imaginative tendencies stood in the way. Warm-hearted and affectionate, but a very proud woman too. I was wrong to employ that word. She was thoroughly a girl. It would not have been easy to predicate her future character—so much, with her peculiar organization, would depend on whether she found happiness or the reverse.

She was a beautiful girl too. Not tall, but somehow her figure gave the effect of height; a free, graceful carriage; a face full of promise, possessing a beauty beyond mere girlish loveliness; a mouth which, in repose, looked, as Nathalie had said, a little sad, almost stern sometimes, but which had a world of delicious smiles, when she would permit them their freedom; a complexion exquisitely fair, too pale perhaps ordinarily; a low, broad forehead, and rippling masses of hair that had the tints of bronze in its waves. The eyes were gray or hazel according to the light—eyes which softened easily or grew black with excitement. A peculiarly sweet, rich voice; an earnest, truthful mode of speech, which gave one a feeling of respect and confidence. A carefully educated young person, with a love for languages that extended even to the grand old tongues which have no echoes left save in the depth and strength they have here and there given to the weak, musical dialects which have sprung out of their dead grandeur. Elizabeth was a little ashamed of her ability to read the Latin poets and to understand Plato. Nothing less like the awful creature conjured up by the term "blue" could be imagined. I may as well confess the extremity of her sins at once: she could even make her way among the crabbed Hebrew characters. When about fifteen, she had spent a year in the society of an old relative who was a clergyman, with failing sight, and Elizabeth had plunged into the study that she might be able to aid his purblind eyes. She guarded her secret as carefully as if it were something disgraceful, and her father would undoubtedly have been shocked. He believed in pretty accomplishments for young ladies — decorous piano-forte playing, feeble drawing, a good accent in French and Italian—but Hebrew! No scented dandy of Piccadilly or Murray Hill, with an inability to pronounce the letter r, could have been more horrified than Mr. Crauford had he known the truth. Fortunately he lived and died without ever suspecting it.

To do something with her life—not be something—was Elizabeth's pet dream. If her father had been a learned man, or ambitious, she could have aided him. She was very useful, and attentive a daughter as if she had never dreamed dreams; but while alive to the practical side of existence, Elizabeth thirsted to gratify her visionary and enthusiastic propensities. Some one to look up to and worship; some one who out of his greatness might stoop to make her poor gifts and studies of service in his cause. Failing this, to be a sort of sister of charity; employ her money to found some wonderful institution for good, wherein she should toil humbly, no human being ever knowing that her efforts and wealth had been the foundation of these results.

All her thoughts and plans were vague enough—this was excusable at her age. Indeed, I am free to admit that she was probably much more lovable for this very reason. She had too slight faith in her own abilities to render her either bold or forward in her hopes. I suppose she thought occasionally of loving and being loved—a youthful soul without such fancies would be as unnatural as is a flower without perfume—yet she was oddly shy, perhaps foolishly so, even with her own thoughts, where these matters were concerned.

I think she had more than once dreamed of wedding a missionary. Not that the pictures drawn of those unrecognized saints often interested her, even when done by admiring hands who put their hearts into their work; but the idea of such self-sacrifice appealed to her strongly. She doubted if love or marriage would come to her. Certainly there was little prospect that any man of her own age would be attracted toward her. Elizabeth feared that she was dull and proud; and she had no opinion whatever of her own beauty. She often complained to herself, when she caught sight of her image in a mirror, that she looked like a statue or something cut out of a picture—one of those straight-nosed, broad-browed, serious-eyed women, who might serve as a model for a pre-Raphaelite artist, but possessing nothing that one could call loveliness, or that would please a man, young like herself. It was very grand, no doubt, to think of being loved by some elderly sage, some philosopher, who had long since left his youth on the steep road of fame up which he had so gallantly traveled; still — Elizabeth smiled and blushed, too, in recognition of her own folly—that life would appear brighter, fuller of color, if the love of a hero, possessed of youthful aspirations like her own, might be granted. It never would. Indeed, she could not be said to dwell upon such fancies. Having no direct aim, her visions were all impassible; but, dreamer as she was, the apprenticeship she served in humoring and waiting on her father might have qualified her to share even the destiny of her fancied missionary.

The soft Italian days floated by. Elizabeth, when not absorbed by her parent's caprices, was busy with her books, or her music or drawing; but to what end became a question that haunted her more and more. "They also serve who only stand and wait!" She had often to repeat that glorious sermon in a line to herself during this season, afraid she was growing impatient and discontented. But you are not to get the idea that she was either morbid or restless. She only wanted to be sure that she was doing the best with duties as existence offered. Elizabeth's conscience was a rather uneasy one. Not unseldom you may see that in consciences which are devoid of spot or stain. Perhaps they flutter restlessly just because they have no weight to steady them, for I observe that the heavily laden ones usually seem to bear their burden blithely enough.

One day Elizabeth was sitting in her favorite nook, near a window of the inner salon, a window which opened upon the balcony. She was at work on an illumination—a quaint old-fashioned task which seemed just meant for her. She was dressed in a white robe of some soft, yielding material, that fell about her in broad folds, and swept away over the floor in a train which she had the art of managing as few women can do. There were bits of vivid blue at her throat and waist, a knot of blue flowers in her hair. The wide sleeves were open almost from the shoulder, and displayed the rounded beauty of her arms, as they rested on the crimson covering of the table. A ray of sunlight stole in through the open casement, and cast golden reflections about her head—not like a crown, she seemed too spiritual for that thought —like a halo. Had one been fanciful, one might have gone further, and likened it to a virgin martyr's symbol. Behind her, through the window, showed a background of towers, a castellated sweep of buildings, the river; still beyond, the glory of the mountains and the amber radiance of the sky.

Her father entered suddenly with a guest; so quietly, too, that Elizabeth, absorbed in her task, was unconscious of their approach till they had nearly reached her. Then she sat quite still, for her rather short sight had not made out the second figure, but she supposed it a gossip of Mr. Crauford's who often visited them.

"My daughter, Mr. Vaughan," said her father, just as Elizabeth had discovered that the guest was a stranger. "Elizabeth, Mr. Vaughan is the nephew of a very old friend of mine; you have often heard of his uncle. We must make Mr. Darrell welcome for his own and his uncle's sake."

So Elizabeth rose in her slow, queenly fashion, looking like some vestal that had been called down from a noble dream—like some vision of ancient romance—like any thing rather than an ordinary creature belonging to this prosaic century, and stood face to face with Darrell Vaughan. She regarded this claimant presented for her favor with a serious gaze, finding it difficult to get quickly enough back from her abstraction.

"You are very welcome, Mr. Vaughan," she said, and the words, which otherwise might have sounded a little stiff and studied, took a pleasing depth and earnestness when uttered in that marvelous voice, rendered sweeter by the look of pleasure which softened her lips into an almost childlike smile.

Vaughan was quite able to appreciate the picture which had met his eyes as he walked up the room. Now the living figure stepped from its frame, and he was able to recognize, also to admire, the grace and spiritual beauty that showed in face and form and brightened the grave eyes which met his with an odd mingling of sovereignty and maiden reserve.

Vaughan perceived that he had arrived at a new experience, and the new and strange were always attractive to him.

CHAPTER XIII.
THE STONE-FIGHT.

MANY hundred years ago a tolerably lofty stone wall surrounded Pisa, over against which the Florentines often sat down, armed with battering-rams and all the heavy implements of an ancient siege. Within these walls a broad road circled the city, and in those days the inhabitants at one gate considered those dwelling outside the others almost as great strangers as they did the Florentines. In those times, too, Pisa was celebrated for stone-fights, waged between boys of the different quarters, either brought about by deliberate challenge or the reckless incursion of a troop beyond the limits of their own territory. The battles with the Florentines have long since degenerated into mere wordy contests; but the moss-grown walls remain, the white road encircling the town remains too, and here still may be witnessed every now and then a relic of mediæval barbarism — a repetition of the famous stone contests.

The morning after his arrival in the quaint, dull town, Darrell Vaughan went out for a walk.

He crossed the Arno by the bridge of the old fortress, and, passing through one of the few sunny streets, took the broad highway which follows the walls. He had scarcely met a human being or heard a sound. Suddenly the rush of feet along the paved road roused him, the shrill tones of scores of young voices, the whiz and whir of stones. He turned an angle and found himself in the midst of a retreating army. He could not have believed there were so many children to be seen in the dead old place. Boys of all ages and sizes, from six years up to sixteen, were fleeing, hotly pursued by a larger crowd of similar age and size.

Shrieks and imprecations made a hideous din. It was wonderful also to see the childish faces, usually so careless and good-natured, roused into a fury or set in rigid passion, which gave them the look of the old Tuscan portraits one finds in mouldy picture-galleries. The retreating foe wheeled about — wheeled so quickly that they took their pursuers by surprise. Again a volley of stones darkened the air. Down went more than one combatant on either side. Yells of rage and triumph rose more deafening than ever.

Vaughan found his position by no means agreeable or safe. The missiles were flying about his ears like hail, and the struggling hosts paid as little attention to him as two armies of ants do to a philosophical human being marveling over their battles. So Vaughan ensconced himself in a niche where a very deformed figure of the Virgin resided in a diminutive chamber which sadly needed scouring, and stood still to watch the fight, so exactly similar, save in the modern costumes, to the famous encounters of old, out of which so often grew fierce disputes and quarrels that disturbed the whole city for weeks, and were the means of one half the town frequently being ambuscaded by the other.

A stone did invade the Virgin's sanctuary, and somewhat injured her nose; but Vaughan was not a nervous man, and kept his stand. Suddenly from a side street came a tall, rather bowed male figure, and Vaughan laughed heartily at the surprise and horror in the face as the new-comer discovered himself unexpectedly in the midst of this hail-storm with retreat cut off, for a frenzied onslaught of the besieged brought a party between him and the entrance to the street up which he had passed.

The unfortunate man tried to run first one way, then another, and only turned helplessly round and round like some mammoth French toy wound up by machinery. The combatants did not seem in the least aware of his presence: the stones whizzed over his head; he ducked here, skipped there; the boys ran against him; twice he was actually carried along in a rush of a small party skirmishing on the flanks.

Looking closer, Vaughan perceived that he knew the face; it was the dignified Robert Crauford, made so unwilling and alarmed a participator in this Pisan relic of Middle-Age amusements. Vaughan enjoyed his absurd predicament; but it really was fraught with a great deal of danger, and it occurred to Darrell that here he had an opportunity to ingratiate himself in the elderly gentleman's favor. He had seen enough of Mr. Crauford in a single visit to know that any personal matter must always appear of vast importance to him. This fight, in which he was forced to take at least a passive share, would be the most formidable danger any human creature had ever run since the days of Thermopylæ.

So out dashed Vaughan — scattered the foes right and left — brought them, by good round execrations in fair Italian, enough to their senses to perceive that they had cornered two strangers. The stones ceased to fly — the leaders on either side condescended to explain. Mr. Crauford recognized Vaughan, and clung to him desperately. His forehead was bleeding from a little cut. Altogether he considered the affair of such magnitude that as soon as he could find voice he announced his intention of bringing the matter before consuls, embassadors, the King of Italy himself, on the ground that the majesty and freedom of Columbia's happy land had been menaced in his (Robert Crauford's) august person.

While he talked, on swept the two armies along the highway, and left Vaughan to soothe the frightened man—indignant he called himself, but frightened was the adjective which more correctly expressed his appearance. He had lost his hat—it lay trampled out of all shape at the side of the road; he was covered with white dust raised by the armies; hoarse with shouting; his hands were stained with the blood which trickled from his scratch — a wound he styled it; altogether, he was in very pitiable case.

Vaughan helped him down the street till they found a carriage; once seated therein, and a kerchief bound carefully about his bumpy forehead, Mr. Crauford could rush into ejaculations of gratitude, mingled with expressions which showed that he regarded Vaughan as a very fortunate person to have been able to succor Robert Crauford, Esq., in a moment of peril.

"You did a gallant thing, sir," he said. "My life would not have been worth the purchase an instant later."

By the time they reached his house the affair had assumed gigantic proportions, and as he had managed to smear the blood over his face, hands, and shirt-front, his appearance at first alarmed Elizabeth. Even when she discovered there was no real hurt, she felt inclined also to regard Vaughan as a hero and a friend. Darrell perceived that his morning's stroll had been a lucky business, and admired the Pisan youths for persevering in the barbaric sports of their ancestors.

So in the very beginning Mr. Crauford conceived an enthusiastic admiration for Darrell

Vaughan, and speedily elevated him into a prophet and the hope of the future. It was not often that Mr. Crauford bestowed more than grudging praise, or yielded other than a doubtful belief in men's motives; but in this case all was different. Mr. Crauford seemed to have developed a need of idol worship, and he put Vaughan on the pedestal vacant in his soul.

During the first few days of his sojourn, Darrell devoted himself almost entirely to her father, and he could have chosen no course which would so rapidly have ingratiated him in Elizabeth's favor. He appeared different in every way from young men with whom she had hitherto been thrown in contact. He neither talked frivolity nor was interested in the racing calendar, as, in her somewhat contemptuous opinion, Elizabeth had supposed must be the case with masculines under forty. Fiery denunciations of wrong and injustice — eloquent diatribes against youth wasted in idleness and elegant vice — words vague, but energetic and golden, which betrayed some deep purpose within, some lofty aim for the future, which, if necessary, he looked ready to follow out to martyrdom: such themes were often on his lips, and proved additional aids toward gaining her sympathy. She listened to this talk, never stilted nor sententious, and her cheeks glowed and her heart warmed. These were the desires and motives she had hoped to find in his age and sex, but had only met with disappointment until now.

The speeches he had delivered in Congress, the articles he had contributed to solid reviews, the addresses which created an excitement in the two great capitals—Mr. Crauford showed Elizabeth all these; it was she who read them aloud, sharing fully in her father's admiration.

"I did not think they would fall under your eyes," Vaughan said, when he came to know the facts. "How very considerate you are in every thing that concerns your father; for I suppose you do not care about such matters."

"Why should I not?" she asked.

"Indeed—well, I have no reason—but I fancy young ladies do not usually. I was thinking last night you must have found me awfully dry and dull. Ever since I came here I have been riding my hobbies unconscionably; somehow Mr. Crauford's sympathy led me into it."

"I hope it may still lead you on," she answered; "and I wish you would believe in my sympathy too."

Just her pet dreams and aspirations were those which showed themselves to be his favorite rules and plans of life: a man who meant to devote his existence to political philanthropy—that is, one who entered politics for the express hope of doing the most good for the greatest number of his kind—it sounded wonderfully well. Then he loved books, poetry, art; he worshiped the beautiful and true in their highest forms. Eliza-

beth was ready to believe in her father's prophet, and bow in reverent esteem before his idol. That idol had a marvelous faculty of making Mr. Crauford see with his eyes, and yet flattering the worthy gentleman into the belief that it was by his own eagle sight both were guided.

It was impossible, of course, to avoid giving Mr. Crauford the letter which had been found among Edgar Vaughan's papers, and that letter left Elizabeth's choice unfettered between his two nephews.

"Dear me!" said Mr. Crauford, perplexed. "This is very awkward; I did not understand this."

"Because it was a delicate and painful subject, which I did not like to touch upon in my letter to you," Vaughan replied. "You will perceive that this was written only a few weeks before my uncle's illness."

"Well?"

"He made a will dividing his fortune between us, his two nephews. New circumstances came to light, which showed him that unfortunately his first judgment of Lance Cromlin was correct; he made complete changes on that account. His whole property was left to me; if I chose, I was at liberty to pay my relative ten thousand dollars. You can judge for yourself whether he would have wished the codicil in regard to this other property to hold; only sudden illness prevented its alteration."

"Dear me!" again ejaculated Mr. Crauford.

"There is, too, another way of looking at it," pursued Darrell. "My uncle was a gentle-hearted man; he may have thought Lance should still have this chance for retrieving his past; whether you and your daughter would be willing to give it to him is a question for you to decide."

"Impossible! I blame your uncle; he might have—why, there is no telling what trouble he might have caused! A man who had committed a forgery—a—"

"That is a secret between us," Darrell said, softly.

"And where is he now? Does he know of this matter of the will?"

"I suppose he does by this time. Carstoe and I wrote; it was our duty."

Mr. Crauford bounced about in a state of wretched excitement. "Suppose he were to hunt us up?" he asked.

"Then you would be at liberty to close your doors against him if you saw fit."

"I should think so. Why—"

"A very winning fellow is Lance; I never could resist him! Where women are concerned, I believe if they had seen him commit a murder he could manage to make it appear a heroic act."

"Good Lord!" quavered Mr. Crauford. "*Good* Lord!"

"Miss Crauford is a girl of remarkable sense

and judgment," Darrell continued; "but once interest that keen sympathy of hers, and it would blind her judgment. Launce would be able to show that his uncle had come to believe in his innocence. It would not then be difficult to convince her that he had died in the belief; that the fact of the will, which in our eyes proves the contrary, went for nothing; that he would have altered it—given Launce a share of his property had there been time."

"Good *Lord!*" exclaimed Mr. Crauford, querulously.

"I learned to love your daughter before I ever saw her! I love her well enough I think—I know—to be unselfish. If I believed it were for her happiness, I could—yes, I would—bring Launce to her myself, and go my way—"

"Nobody wants you to go away," interrupted Mr. Crauford. "Now don't complicate things by talking like that! Oh, my head! What a neuralgia I shall have!"

"Of course the bare possibility of your daughter's becoming interested in such a man is painful," Vaughan said; "but the plan you suggest settles all difficulty—your decisions are so wonderfully clear and rapid!"

Mr. Crauford looked elated and embarrassed, as a man might who had never arrived at a decision in his life; but he believed that he had here, only he was not quite certain what the resolve might have been, luminous as it appeared to his companion, so he said—"Well?"

"Launce, I have reason to believe, is in California; once the ten thousand dollars in his hands, he will think of nothing else till he has gambled it away—so that rids you of him."

"Elizabeth would not know him; she would despise the rascal."

"If there were not several things in his favor. Let him convince her that he had suffered unjust suspicion—"

"Then what are we to do?"

"Persist in our original resolve. Say nothing whatever to Miss Crauford about my cousin. As you said, that will be the wisest course."

It was a comfort to hear a positive plan of action clearly and definitely announced; a keen pleasure, in spite of the worthy gentleman's agitation, to pounce on it as his own.

"I think we have arranged it for the best, indeed," said he.

"The letter for your daughter which my uncle left is not written in a way to rouse any question; it simply speaks of the happiness it would have been to call her his niece—pleasant, general phrases, you know. The letter was sealed like yours, but Mr. Carstoe wrote at his dictation—Mr. Carstoe told me."

Mr. Carstoe had never read a syllable of either letter—was ignorant of their contents.

"It is all very odd, very troublesome," sighed Mr. Crauford.

"Yes; as you suggested, the best thing now is to put the codicil out of our heads," returned Vaughan. "You are good enough to like me, to be willing to accept me as your son-in-law if I can succeed in winning your daughter's regard."

"That with all my heart," said Mr. Crauford, more energetically than he often spoke. It was a memorable speech from this one fact—that he never contradicted it, he who lived in an atmosphere of self-contradiction and retraction, and mental uncertainties of all sorts.

Mr. Crauford's imagination displayed just now a brilliancy which it had never done in his countless unfinished poetic efforts. He pictured to himself a being who was a cross between Mephistopheles and the Duke de Richelieu—a man brought into the world for the express ruin and destruction of female peace in one way or another—a creature with delightful, devilish fascinations, and great talents perverted—a mass of incongruities, which could never have held together—and he called this figment of his fancy Launce Cromlin.

The desire that his daughter should marry Vaughan would have caused him to rush into open, unadvised partisanship, had not the astute young gentleman held him back. An odd personal motive also aided Mr. Crauford to keep silence concerning the will and provisional bequest. He had, as I have said, always been jealous of Edgar Vaughan—jealous, that is, of the memory he believed left in his wife's mind of her earliest suitor. If Elizabeth wedded Darrell, he wished to feel that his former rival's plans and wishes had nothing to do with her decision. It would be a constant source of irritation to think that after death the man gained an influence over the daughter as he had retained while living a place in the mother's recollection.

Then, too, Mr. Crauford greatly enjoyed the possession of a secret; the sense of importance, and the absurd feeling that he was in a certain way thwarting his dead rival by excluding his expressed desires from participation in the affair, kept Mr. Crauford's little soul puffed out like the plumage of a pouter pigeon, and rendered him very happy.

The days and weeks went on.

At length a letter from Mr. Carstoe reached Darrell—it had been sent to London, and forwarded from thence by his bankers. Darrell knew that Launce Cromlin was very, very ill, and his recovery far remote, though the physicians believed that his strong constitution would ultimately conquer. So Vaughan could even rid himself of the idea that haste was necessary in the carrying out of his projects, and his contentment nearly equaled Mr. Crauford's own.

To peripatetic Americans and English in general, Pisa is a place to visit in the interval between two trains; but to people who have sat down there in the quiet, Pisa and its environs make a delightful memory. There is a pleasant drive to the sea and the bay in which poor Shelley was drowned, with a pine-wood casting long shadows over the waters, and a glorious view of Spezzia in the distance. There is a famous old Pilgrim church near where the ancient harbor of Pisa is supposed to have been—an old church, with broken marble columns and faded frescos, erected upon the spot where Popish legends declare St. Peter first set foot on the Italian shore.

Like a thorough, understanding church-woman, Elizabeth was prepared to refute this tale, and prove by the most credible of the primitive historians that the great disciple never left the East, but met with martyrdom upon the banks of the Euphrates, thereby destroying the very claim on which the Romish power asserts its right to sovereignty over all branches of the Catholic faith. There is a fine Carthusian monastery some six miles back among the blue Pisan hills; from thence an excursion up a steep mountain, on whose summit are noticeable ruins—a mountain called *La Verucca*, a name suggestive of something so odious and unsightly that one never cares to translate it into English.

So the days passed pleasantly indeed, and brought about a closer companionship between Elizabeth and this man who had so unexpectedly crossed the monotonous course of her life, brightening its sameness by the charm of his presence.

Vaughan was almost constantly with them, and never had she found society so suited to her taste. His marvelous faculty of adapting himself to the habits and fancies of others served admirably here. He quickly comprehended enough of Elizabeth's enthusiastic nature to enable him to take the lead in the expression of ideas and dreams which filled her mind—doing it so well that often it seemed to her she owed their clearness and even their dawn to his suggestions. Altogether, two months passed in daily intercourse between Elizabeth Crauford and this young man. From the first she had been led to suppose his visit to Europe ordered after great and prolonged mental exertion, otherwise she would have objected to ease and repose. There was so much work to be done in the world—its needs were so vast—that she must see a necessity for any body's resting in order to excuse the delay.

The time came at length when she could not fail to perceive that Vaughan had some special motive in lingering with them—when it became equally plain that her father saw and approved this motive.

So a new and unknown restlessness entered Elizabeth's life, but it was a very pleasant one.

If any spirit guide could have made plain to her the fact that in this man she saw only the shadow of her lofty ideal without consistence, she would have been astounded to discover how this thought had lain at her heart and she been still ignorant of it.

She grew to believe thoroughly in Darrell Vaughan—to accept him as the embodiment of her hero who was to struggle for right, and win tangible results in the form of general good. A hero who toiled neither for fame nor ambition; who chose deliberately the hardest path—put by the dreams which would have induced him to become either poet or artist—accepted the world's dusty high-road—the hardships and wearinesses of a politician's course—simply because the age needed a man capable of doing this for philanthropy's sake.

That she could be thought worthy to have part or lot in this grand destiny—grand, whether success or disappointment crowned its efforts, since the aim was there, and some portion of good must be wrought—filled her with pride and gratitude.

She believed in him—she would have shrunk from no sacrifice which might aid in his work. There was no task so humble, no drudgery so severe, that she would not have gloried in it for the work's sake.

Sometimes, even when not soaring off on the wings of hobbies and noble endeavor, there was a rare charm in his presence. At other moments the man who sat by her seemed suddenly to change. A veil lifted, as it were, or a haze came between her consciousness and him. It was all vague; something she did not understand enough to dwell upon with any clearness. There were lights in those eyes sometimes—smiles on that handsome mouth—variations in his manner—twice, almost a confusion and incoherency in his talk (passing quickly, to leave a strange luminousness behind)—glances, tones, things so different from his usual seeming, that she shrank almost affrighted.

These intuitions seldom really affect us; we look back and recognize them later, but the soul is as powerless to make its own prescience palpably felt by our mortal consciousness as it is to put before us clear gleams of that soul's experience in lives antecedent to this—experiences which can no more have had a beginning than they can find an end, if eternity be that soul's portion.

The day came when Vaughan put his hopes into words, and then, indeed, the romance and poetry assumed their proper place, and Elizabeth the enthusiast dreamed that she was straying away into Eden, and felt no fear—only a beautiful joy at knowing her hand clasped in this man's, ready to believe her heart within reach of his forever. Did he love her? He would have said so, and credited his own words. Vaughan could no more help longing for the possession of a beautiful woman than he could for wine, hasheesh—any excitement; and Elizabeth was a new experience. To put humanity into the statue—

fire—passion—the idea was pleasant. That she would only turn into an ordinary woman if he succeeded, did not trouble him; he did not even stop to think that then she would become a weariness, and fare as others had done.

Great wealth—great reputation—boundless power—Vaughan meant to have all these. Honor and virtue were lovely abstractions to him, like the mythological fables which clad them in glorious shapes and called them gods. Sin, as sin, was just as much an abstraction, however agreeable indulgence might be. He was as incapable of feeling shame in the gratification of his appetites as he was of remorse at flinging out of his path, by any means, an object which interfered with his course. Put spiders in a bottle: the smallest will be devoured by the next in size, and so on until there is only one bloated monster to be seen. Vaughan would not have called the conqueror a monster—he would have admired him as a visible expression of strength. He carried the same creed through all spheres of life and action. He would have told you, too —if he had chosen to let you get at his secret thoughts—that any fresh sensation which the soul craved, whether upward or downward, pure or vile, was an experience offered that soul, and a part of its development. To reject the temptation because it interfered with what men term right or decency would be an act of consummate folly and a relic of priestcraft.

When Vaughan had told the story of his love —had dwelt on the bright future which her companionship was to render still better worth the living—Elizabeth asked for a week's reflection. It was all beautiful. The thought of having won such affection filled her with a sweet trouble. It was herself only that she doubted—was she worthy? Her own unfitness for marriage had been a rather firmly settled creed in her mind, but the old theories faded and lost their force now.

"I will wait any time that you set," Vaughan answered to her request. "A week—it seems a long while! Perhaps I have been too bold— it did not come from arrogance or vanity though, I am sure. Let me try to tell you how it was. My own heart was so moved, I think it seemed to me impossible that yours could remain untouched. I might have known you were too noble—too—"

Elizabeth stopped him by a little sign. A vivid color tinted her cheeks, and her eyes looked at once earnest and disturbed. It was an effort to speak, but she struggled bravely.

"It is not that—please do not misunderstand me—it was of myself—the doubt of my own fitness—"

"Elizabeth, Elizabeth!" he cried, uttering her name for the first time as her broken sentence died unfinished; "you do care—you do!" He was bending over her; she felt his kisses on her hands; yet this first show of passion startled and troubled her, though she could not put the feeling into words. "I beg your pardon," he said, drawing back. "Ah, can you not understand—I love you—I love you! I am only human—you have been a sort of beautiful abstraction all your life—my whole heart and soul have gone out to you, and I could not call them back."

But it was not any exhibition of passion or eagerness which touched her. He saw this. Such outbursts only troubled, almost terrified her. Tenderness—calm affection—those vast plans for the future, that hope of sharing in his work—these were spells which had drawn her toward him: to their potency he must still trust.

He told her of having seen her miniature and those letters—of the dream which sprang up in his heart before their first meeting.

"I have another secret, too," he added; "you must hear that now."

Then followed the story of his uncle's project —of the condition which in his will he had attached to the fulfillment of that desire.

He placed the dead man's letter in her hands, and left her to read it.

CHAPTER XIV.

BACK TO LIFE.

THE glorious sunlight of a spring morning shines into the room; the window is open; the breeze enters too, whispering softly, bringing the voices of the birds and the scent of the early flowers on its wings—a room in the Californian villa where old Mr. Vaughan died, the large, cheerful library which he had fitted up with the care one naturally bestows upon an apartment that is to be the favorite shrine in the sanctuary of home.

Launce Cromlin sits here this morning, leaning back in his easy-chair, a little weary from the effort of having been helped out of his chamber for the first time since that terrible illness struck him down. Launce has been away off close to the gates of Death since then, so close that often in moments of semi-consciousness he seemed to hear familiar voices call to him from the other side, and wondered dreamily that those friends did not open the great portals and let him through. Before his reviving faculties reached even such vague, disconnected attempts at thought, there were long weeks of wild delirium, followed by still longer weeks whose record must always remain a blank—when the soul made no sign to denote its presence in the earthly tabernacle—when for days and nights, and nights and days, it needed the skill of physicians or sage nurses to be certain that a faint ray of the mysterious power we call vitality still lingered in the dull, senseless frame.

He has been well cared for—that seemed to Mr. Carstoe a plain duty; but the quiet, reticent man has gone beyond the exactions of this chill word. Were Launce his son—that dreamson who sometimes finds a place in the solitary old bachelor's musings, practical as he is—more earnestness and devotion could not have been displayed. So to-day they have moved the convalescent into the library. Strength and its accompanying restlessness have begun to return, and life is to go on once more, and slip gradually back into its ordinary channels. Launce is always hungry or sleepy, or reversing the order of those requirements, and Mr. Carstoe and the stiff housekeeper are delighted with his prodigies in both lines. Launce begins to wonder in his quaint way whether his proper soul did not make its exit during that long blank, and the soul of a cormorant or some antediluvian creature with huge appetite take advantage of the rightful owner's absence to assume possession of his corporeal frame.

"Mercy sakes! he aint flighty again, is he?" asks the housekeeper, in an audible whisper, when she hears Launce expressing his absurd fancy to Mr. Carstoe.

"No, no, Mrs. Simpson; I am all right," Launce replies, laughing.

"Then the best thing you can do is to stay so," observes Simpson, erect and rigid. She has come in a sort to regard Launce as her property after all the care she has bestowed, and is inclined to show her interest by scolding him now and then—a liberty which he finds rather pleasant than otherwise. "So please don't let us hear any talk about your being any of those creeturs that aint to be found any more than Jonah's whale. We had enough of that when you was stretched on your back and knowed no better," adds Simpson.

"I suppose I talked an awful lot of rubbish?" Launce says.

"I suppose you did," retorted Simpson, arranging the sofa cushions, just to have the satisfaction of doing something for this patient who will soon pass from under her charge. She does her work so deftly, and looks so preternaturally grim when most solicitous, that she affords Launce a great deal of amusement.

It is Sunday, so Mr. Carstoe has leisure to spend the whole day with the young man, and Launce makes him talk till Simpson several times bustles in and scolds them both. Simpson has an idea that men are only gigantic children, and need to be grumbled at on every possible occasion.

The doctor pays his visit, and pronounces the convalescent doing as nicely as possible; and Simpson, ready to cry with delight, fairly scolds the doctor too, and remarks generally that she doesn't like "to hear folks shout till they're out of the woods"—that's her way, and she's never yet seen any reason to change it.

But it does not appear that in this case the physician has shouted too soon. Launce, as the days go by, gets gradually stronger, and the youthful face, that looked so like a mask during those awful weeks, has begun, worn and emaciated as it is, to catch the tints and expression of returning health. The mental lassitude, the difficulty to grasp and hold thought steadily, passes too, and once more life looks warm and hopeful, and Launce longs to be busy with its interests and labors. Mr. Carstoe comes in one morning while Launce is trying his strength in walking about, and wondering how long it will be before he can again use pencil and brush. Mr. Carstoe has letters in his hand—the letters he and Darrell Vaughan wrote to apprise Launce of his uncle's death. The agent has had them returned.

"I wanted you to see," he says, finding Launce able to talk and occupy himself a little, "that there was no delay on your cousin's part or mine."

Launce looks at the address upon the envelopes, and looks at the wrinkled, kindly face before him. If there were some reason for managing to delay these letters, Mr. Carstoe knows nothing about it—of that Launce is certain. He reads the pages, and smiles rather scornfully at the possibility of his accepting a legacy left him on such terms. He is too just to feel angry with his cousin on that score—at least Darrell had nothing to do with the bequest or its restrictions. His letter, too, is kind, affectionate even—just a little patronizing perhaps, but at this Launce can afford to be amused.

"Have you heard lately from Vaughan?" he asks.

"Not very lately; one letter in answer to mine about your illness. He was extremely glad you were here with me."

"It has been a lucky thing for me that I did reach you before that fever came on," Launce replies, stretching out his hand.

Mr. Carstoe grows shy and awkward at once. He does not like to be thanked, and seems fairly ashamed of himself.

"Well, well, you are going on famously now," he says.

"Yes; I shall soon be able to get away."

"Dear me; yes, of course," observed Mr. Carstoe in a regretful tone, rubbing his nose the while. "Naturally; but you must not hurry too much. Let things work awhile; we don't want any risk of getting that fever back."

"Upon my word, although I have been such a bother, I believe you and that good Mrs. Simpson will be rather sorry to have me go," says Launce, laughing, though he chokes; for he is still weak enough to be easily touched and made childish.

"Sir," says Mr. Carstoe, scowling as portentously as if he were about to utter some awful threat, "the Lord forbid that I should speak for any female, especially one as capable of speaking for herself as Mrs. Simpson. But *I* shall be sorry, and so will she—I can take it on myself to say so much for her."

"It was falling among good Samaritans indeed," Launce answers. "I shall be sorry to leave you both, Mr. Carstoe. I have wasted a great deal of time though. I want to be up and doing. You see I have not stumbled over several hundred thousand dollars, and must make my way in the world."

"Just so, just so," observes Mr. Carstoe, musingly. "It would have been different if there had been time, I am sure of that."

"Perhaps so; but indeed I am not caring about the money. Of course every body would like to be rich; but I have my profession, and I may say, without vanity, that I have not done ill."

"I am glad of that; very glad."

Mr. Carstoe is remembering the impression Darrell had produced on his mind in regard to this young man, and decides that Vaughan was mistaken utterly in his estimate of Cromlin, although usually so clear and correct in his judgments.

"I don't know much about your business—I suppose that is not the proper word; but I have enjoyed looking over those sketch-books of yours, and—and—so has Mrs. Simpson." Mr. Carstoe finishes his sentence with this jerking mention of Simpson simply because he is shy about expressing his feelings. "Now I should think—I don't mean to offer suggestions—but being here among new scenery as it were—mightn't you, for example, do something among our mountains, and so on, a little?"

"I should be glad of the chance; but you see I am anxious to go back to Europe—I left very suddenly." Launce feels himself coloring, and hastens to add—"Some time I shall hope to come again to California and see it thoroughly."

Mr. Carstoe is thinking of the codicil, and, slow man though he is, has a perception that Miss Crauford is in the young man's mind; it is Miss Crauford, not the money—somehow Mr. Carstoe is certain of that.

"Just so, just so," he observes, running his hands through his short hair till it stands up like a gray iron netting all over his head.

"Now if you are at leisure I want to have a little talk," Launce says. "Would it bore you to go over the conversation we had the night of my arrival? I get it confused when I try to think. I believe I must have been ill even then, though I recollect our visit to the prison."

It is all made clear to Launce again—all except that impenetrable mystery which shrouds the evil deed his uncle so long believed him to have committed: there is no light to be thrown on that.

"Thank God, at least he lived to know I was innocent!" Launce says. "But Mr. Sandford's letter does not in the least clear up the matter."

"All the papers your uncle left are in that cabinet," Mr. Carstoe observes, pointing to a massive, ancient piece of furniture at the end of the room. "You may like to look over them some time; I will get the keys and leave them with you. I know your cousin would like to have you—he and I searched them together. When you see Mr. Darrell you will find him prepared to be friendly and considerate."

Launce glances at the patronizing letter, and smiles again. Catching that smile, Mr. Carstoe wonders if Cromlin feels a certain bitterness toward Vaughan on account of his good-fortune. It would be natural, he thinks, if it were so, but not in keeping with the idea he has gained of the young man's character. He thinks, too, what a pity it would be if enmity should grow up between the two, and would gladly do or say something to remove any angry feelings from Launce's mind.

"Very kindly in all ways your cousin spoke of you," he continues after a pause. "It seems hard, it really does, that your uncle did not live to make those changes in his will which I feel confident he intended."

"That he wanted to do it is enough for me," interrupts Launce, his face clearing. "I am not grudging Darrell his luck, Mr. Carstoe; don't think that."

"I am sure you are not!"

"You remain agent of all the property, I believe you told me," Launce says.

"Yes; your cousin's conduct has been most generous to me. I thought when I met with the last loss—the jewels, you remember—that there was nothing before me but worse drudgery than that of the past. His liberal offers not only make me comfortable, but will enable me to lay by a fair competency for my old age—something more, if property in this region continues to increase in value as it has done for the last ten years."

"I am glad of it; very glad. I am sure you deserve success."

"You are very good to say so, Mr. Cromlin. At least I have worked and tried honestly; I can affirm so much in my own behalf. I could not, however, have hoped for such advantages as Mr. Vaughan has given me."

"A good salary—"

"More than that—percentages upon lands that I sell or rent, and other means of saving. Had I been a relative instead of his uncle's man of business he could not have dealt more generously."

It is new in Launce's experience of his cousin to find him thinking of any body besides himself. But he does not say this: his conscience suggests that perhaps he wrongs Darrell—has, without knowing it, cherished harsh thoughts and suspicions in regard to him. Launce has no mind to be on bad terms even in thought with his relative. Probably the course of their lives will not often run parallel, but Darrell is almost the only relation he has in the world, and there shall be no ill-feeling on his side.

Mr. Carstoe disturbs his meditations by uttering aloud and abruptly those to which his own thoughts have wandered.

"There is another matter, Mr. Cromlin, that we may as well arrange now."

"What is that?"

"About the ten thousand dollars."

"Well, what about it?" Launce speaks quickly, and sits up with sudden erectness, and a brighter light in his eyes.

"It can be paid you at any time. Your cousin mentions in his letter to you that you have only to apply to me—he had made all the necessary arrangements for me to—"

"Excuse me," interrupts Launce, "we need not go into that matter, Mr. Carstoe. I have no intention of touching the money."

"Now really, on reflection, is it wise? Pardon my seeming to—"

"I understand; you are very kind, and I thank you. But there is nothing to be said, Mr. Carstoe. I do not want Vaughan's money, and I shall not take it."

"But it would be a gift from your late uncle."

"No; it would be Darrell's bounty that gave it. I could not take it, and there is an end. If my uncle had lived to change matters, that would have been different. I can not accept any thing left me in that way. The business does not even admit of discussion."

"Well, you must be the judge, I suppose," sighs Carstoe.

"Yes; it is an affair of feeling, perhaps. Do believe that I meant what I said when I told you I did not grudge Darrell his fortune. If it were mine, I would give the whole just to clear up that dark business. I mean to find out by what means my uncle was so grossly deceived in regard to me."

"But that is of no consequence now. Your uncle was convinced. His letter to you—what he said to me—proves it."

"Yes; and it is a great comfort. Let the money go; I shall be able to earn all I need. But it is horrible to think that some wicked plot separated me so long from him; that is what hurts! I loved him better than I ever loved any body; and to remember all these years, when he was in failing health, that I could not be with him—that—"

Launce breaks off, and turns his head. Mr. Carstoe is afraid that agitation may do him harm, and wants to get his thoughts away from such painful meditations. He thinks what a fine thing it would be for Launce if he could only win Miss

Crauford and the two hundred and fifty thousand dollars, for Mr. Carstoe has struggled hard enough to know what money is worth.

"I—you—well, as you do me the honor to talk about your affairs, would it be a liberty if—"

"No liberty, whatever it may be; go on, Carstoe," says Launce, thinking how little one would expect to find so much delicacy and kind feeling as he has learned exists under that awkward, grim exterior.

"Only that I am sure your uncle's wishes would have weight—now it seems from the codicil that he desired you to try your chance—in short, did you ever happen to meet the young lady, Mr. Cromlin?"

Launce's thoughts have gone back to that brief meeting. He seems to see the beautiful face lying pale and helpless on his shoulder. His cheeks wear a tinge of color, and his eyes soften as he answers—"I saw Miss Crauford once; I am not acquainted with her."

Mr. Carstoe looks the other way, and rubs his hands softly together. He does not know much about romances, but it seems to him that he has stumbled on a sort of idyl or poem, and he delights in it, little accustomed as he is to exercise his imagination. Launce perceives this; smiles, but not scornfully, at so odd a corner in this cold, legal mind, and, partly to please Mr. Carstoe, partly to gratify himself, he relates the incidents of that one meeting with Miss Crauford. He does not mention those after-dreams which have haunted him so persistently. Launce is not given to confidences. Mr. Carstoe listens attentively, and enjoys the story, and, in his silent fashion, reads Launce's face, and, middle-aged and toil-worn as he is, can construe its language as plainly as if the young man had put his pretty fancies into words.

"I gathered from what your cousin said, though I could not tell how," observes Mr. Carstoe, "that he had no mind to occupy himself with the possible results of the codicil; that, in fact, he had interests of a—a tender nature elsewhere."

Mr. Carstoe is almost as shy about pronouncing such words as an old maid would have been, in spite of his beard and his years.

"I know nothing about Darrell's affairs," Launce replies; and Mr. Carstoe feels that the subject is done with. But he would like exceedingly to know how Miss Crauford looks, for the life of him he could not tell why. Mr. Carstoe has not read a novel in thirty years—probably not more than three before that, say "The Children of the Abbey" and "Charlotte Temple" among them—but he certainly has a latent taste for romance all the same.

"A bachelor's life is a lonely one," he says, making an attack on that unfortunate nose of his. "I think Mr. Vaughan found it so. I gathered, too, from what he told me just before his last illness, that at one time he had been attached to this young lady's mother."

Launce is interested, but Mr. Carstoe has not much to tell, though Launce's youthful fancy has no difficulty in clothing the bare skeleton in glowing colors.

"There is a miniature in the cabinet, too," says Mr. Carstoe. "I have an idea it was the portrait of Mrs. Crauford."

Launce is eager to see it; so Mr. Carstoe gets the keys and opens the cabinet. Launce sits still in his chair; somehow he can not find courage yet to look in the receptacle filled with mementos of his dead uncle. Mr. Carstoe returns with a small velvet case in his hand, and gives it to Launce.

A painting on ivory of a beautiful girl-face—the very face he had once, for a few moments, studied so eagerly; only then the eyes were closed, and now they regard him with a sweet gravity. A name is written in pencil on the satin lining—Laura Marlow. Launce can not remember how he knows, but he does, that this was the maiden name of Mr. Crauford's wife. He gazes at the portrait for some minutes in silence, and Mr. Carstoe gazes silently at him. As Launce looks up, he meets the other's glance, and both are slightly confused. Mr. Carstoe fears that he has been indiscreet, and Launce wonders if the vague, sweet fancies in his heart are visible upon his countenance.

"It would make a fine study for a picture," Launce says, carelessly laying the miniature on the table. "I should really like to keep it, but I suppose it is my cousin's property now."

"You could give it to him when you meet; there could be no impropriety certainly in your taking it," replies the other.

Launce suggests no further scruples; he puts the case quickly into his pocket, with a keen pleasure in the possession of that treasure, which he half feels to be folly, yet would not check if he were able.

Now Mr. Carstoe is obliged to go into the town, and leave Launce to his own devices for the day. The hours do not drag: Launce can read a little, sleep a little; partake of the savory messes Simpson the rigid serves up to tempt his palate, and dream a great deal, though in a vague fashion, of the possible future which may meet him beyond the seas. He shall soon be able now to undertake the voyage—very soon. It is odd, but among those delicious dreams, wherein Elizabeth Crauford's face makes the brightest radiance, slight thoughts of Darrell or his possible plans intrude.

The day has gone on to afternoon. Launce, in walking about the room, stops for an instant near the cabinet. He perceives that Mr. Carstoe has left the key in the lock—probably that, if so inclined, Launce may have an opportunity to look over his uncle's papers.

The young man sits down before the cabinet, opens the portion arranged as a desk, pulls out drawer after drawer, and examines the papers tied up in orderly packages. There is nothing of much importance, nothing of mystery or romance; yet he touches every thing tenderly, and is moved and softened as memory after memory comes back of that dead man whom he so fondly loved. In one compartment he finds letters written by himself—letters labeled in his uncle's hand, "From my boy." These have been preserved, even through those dark years of suspicion and anger. Launce is young enough to feel his eyelids grow moist, and man enough to be proud of the weakness. He looks over the letters—several written when he was a mere boy, others not long before the break between him and his relative. There are not many of them; just a few retained, as if, even in the height of his anger, the old man had not been able to deprive himself of reminiscences of what he once believed the youth actually to be.

Nothing to bear upon the strongest thought in his mind, however. Mr. Carstoe was right. Neither in pocket-books, notes, nor papers is there the slightest allusion to that dark mystery. Probably in this life no light will ever be thrown upon it. What good could disclosure serve now? If he might know the exact means by which he had suffered that injury, the very hand which wrought it, what purpose could it further? There is no desire or idea of retribution or vengeance in Launce's mind; for the world he would not burden his soul with such a weight.

He lingers for a long time over the relics in the cabinet; commonplace ones enough, but sacred to him from the affection he bore the dead man. He begins at length slowly to lay the papers back in their place, and to close the drawers and compartments.

One of the inner drawers does not shut entirely. Launce struggles with it somewhat—not that it is of any consequence, as it does not interfere with the closing of the portion arranged as a writing-desk, inside which it is situated. At another time he would not have noticed—he might have examined the cabinet often without doing so—but in his softened mood he regarded with almost morbid tenderness every thing his uncle's hand had touched so near the last conscious hours of his life.

The drawer will not shut, so he tries to pull it out, that he may discover the reason. But the drawer is no more inclined to come out than to go in—an obstinate, pig-headed drawer as ever an old carved cabinet owned in its interior. Launce tugs with such strength as he possesses, and the drawer squeaks in querulous resentment, but is at length obliged to yield. It flies out with such force that Launce in his still weak state is fairly thrown backward in his chair.

He sees now what held the drawer—the cover

of a book, the leaves hanging down behind out of sight. Launce pulls the volume forth and looks at it. A thin blank-book, with pages of writing here and there—a journal, broken and disconnected, kept by his uncle during the last months of his life—one little entry on the very day of his fatal seizure.

Launce does not clearly understand, he retreats in horror from the suspicions which strike his mind. He does not want them cleared up! If Milady were here before him, ready to answer any questions he could ask, Launce feels that he should fly from her presence. Oh, let the secret rest!

CHAPTER XV.

PLATO'S DISCIPLE.

Mr. Crauford fell ill. For years he had considered himself an invalid, constantly prophesying untold suffering and speedy death as his portion; but hitherto the former had refused to have much to do with him, and the latter showed no inclination to shorten his mortal span. Now among the soft Italian spring days Mr. Crauford caught a low fever. At first the malady promised to be of little consequence, not grave enough to alarm even his daughter, accustomed to see him take to his bed on the slightest provocation. But the days went on—grew into a fortnight. Elizabeth became very anxious, and the doctors were forced to acknowledge that the disease proved more deeply seated and obstinate than they had anticipated.

One never can predicate, from previous knowledge of any human being, how he will support an illness serious enough to suggest to his mind the possibility of a not distant departure from this mundane sphere. Mr. Crauford had always been the most nervous and captious patient that ever tried a physician's good temper, but from the beginning of this attack he exhibited a fortitude which caused the doctors, previously unacquainted with him, to regard his character as one of unusual force and self-control. The truth was, Mr. Crauford had seized the occasion to become a hero in his own eyes. I suppose at the bottom he did not really believe himself about to die, but he thought he believed it, and his inordinate vanity and craving for admiration, added to a feeling that this critical state rendered him an object of interest and importance, caused him to enact a kind of ancient stoicism quite wonderful to witness.

Vaughan had been absent on one of the little excursions wherewith he diversified the quiet of his present life; but he returned as soon as he heard of Mr. Crauford's illness. He trusted that chance, or the lucky star which had thus far ruled his destiny, would bring to a fortunate conclusion this period of suspense fraught with such dangerous possibilities. He proved the kindest of friends to Elizabeth in her trouble, and the most patient of nurses to the sick man. Mr. Crauford was more submissive to him than he had ever been to any living creature, and Elizabeth quickly acquired the habit of leaning upon his advice and consolations, reproaching herself for not having hitherto esteemed the gentleness of his nature as it deserved.

Mr. Crauford's illness, and above all the state of high mental grandeur into which he saw fit to soar, afforded Vaughan the opportunity that neither his craft nor good-fortune had been able to bring near.

He strengthened the physicians in their view of the sick man's temperament; and when they admitted that the disease proved more serious than they had expected, though still perfectly hopeful as to its ultimate results, Vaughan at once opened his batteries. They were grave interests affecting the whole fortune of this gentleman's daughter, which ought to be definitely arranged. Mr. Crauford was, as they saw, a person of unusual coolness and fortitude, but if later he became enfeebled in mind and nerves, his anxiety would go far toward preventing his recovery. The physicians acknowledged this, and advised Vaughan to encourage Mr. Crauford in setting straight any matter important enough to cause him uneasiness. There certainly was a great lack of vitality. While anticipating his recovery from this attack, they could not deny that a future illness might be less successfully combated, and at his age it was best that all business connected with his daughter's well-being should be arranged. Of course he must not be agitated; but from what they could judge of the patient's character, Mr. Vaughan's certainty that such a course would be the surest means of preserving the tranquillity of spirit so necessary seemed to them correct.

After the physicians had gone, Darrell sat meditating until disturbed by the entrance of Gervais: the sick man desired his presence.

Mr. Crauford was very Roman indeed this morning. He had a copy of Plato lying on the bed-cover; he could see his face in the mirror, and he fancied that he must look very much as Cato or Cicero did when stricken by disease, and was determined to render these closing scenes of his earthly pilgrimage as impressive as possible. An under-current of thought which went on in his mind concerning the feasibility of a voyage to Greece the following autumn, might have suggested to an unprejudiced person a doubt as to the depth of his belief in that speedy departure of which, for days past, he had talked in grand phrases; but Mr. Crauford's admiration of his own mental strength was disturbed by no such humiliating consciousness.

He would have liked to rise, wrap his dressing-gown about him in toga-like folds, and so appear more Ciceronian, and he regretted the years had not left him bald, that after his decease a correct cast might be taken of his wonderful head. But he was too weak to sit up, and he could not bring himself to sacrifice the still luxuriant locks of which he was exceedingly vain. So he stretched one hand out upon the copy of Plato, and extended the other toward Vaughan as he entered, and did his best to offer the appearance of an ancient Consul reposing in the curule chair.

"What I want," said Mr. Crauford, as the visitor seated himself by the bed, "is frankness. That the medical men have come to a decision in regard to my state I know—it is only fitting that I should be made acquainted with it."

"I think so myself," Vaughan replied. "With ordinary invalids the less they know about themselves the better; but with your marvelous firmness and clear-sightedness, it would be simply an insult to your great mental powers to treat you in this way."

These words were as honey and manna to the listener's soul. Nobody had ever flattered him so outrageously, and in consequence he believed that next to himself Vaughan was the most remarkable personage of the century—falling a long way behind his own rank of course, but still coming next.

"I am a dying man, my young friend," said he; "you and I know it—to minds like ours the thought is free from those terrors which cause weaker souls to shrink."

"At least I fear that you are very, very ill," Vaughan replied, gently.

Mr. Crauford had elevated Plato in his hand while uttering that fine sentiment, but at Darrell's response he let the heathen philosopher fall with a crash.

"Eh—what! Have the doctors—they don't think—" he began more eagerly than was in keeping with his assumption of the Ciceronian style.

"They are hopeful—confident of the favorable result finally," Vaughan hastened to add.

Mr. Crauford recovered his dignified composure, and signed Vaughan to pick up the heathen.

"Plato grows too heavy for my frail hands," he said, with a self-compassionate smile. "My young friend, the doctors deceive themselves, or they deem it wise to deceive me—not easy, not easy to do."

Vaughan paid a neat tribute of admiration to his perspicacity, and noble powers in general, then continued—

"While differing from your opinion of your state, I hold with our great man yonder"—pointing to Plato, as if he made a third in the interview—"that it is always a proof of wisdom to have one's worldly affairs as carefully arranged as if one expected to set out immediately upon that journey into the unknown."

"The very thing of which I wished to speak," Mr. Crauford said. He had not thought of speaking of any thing of that nature, but he now believed it was with some such purpose he had sent for the young man. He tried to think of any affair of importance which ought to be arranged, but his money matters were all in perfect order; so the only thing which suggested itself was in regard to those masses of fragments he fondly believed poems. He seized with avidity upon this new idea.

"I leave my work unfinished," he pursued; "but there is much which in careful hands might be given to the world. That must be your duty, Vaughan."

Darrell laughed internally at the idea of his ever meddling with those chaotic heaps of weak rhymes and stolen fancies, as he replied—

"If it were to prove necessary, of course the task would be my delight; but, my dear sir, you will live to do it yourself."

Mr. Crauford shook his head at the possibility, looking rather puzzled to discover what important business could still remain, as it was evidently not of the manuscripts he had been thinking. Something urgent had been in his mind since he had sent for Vaughan to speak of it; but what? Darrell saw his perplexity, and was prepared to clear away the mists.

"That part in any case we may consider settled," he said; "but I know what from the first has disturbed you—the thought of your daughter."

"Yes, yes," Mr. Crauford answered, immensely relieved to find out what care had oppressed him. Of course it was about Elizabeth he had intended to speak; but what had he meant to say? "A father's heart, Vaughan; a father's heart!"

"I can judge a little from my own—a lover's feelings," Vaughan said, laying his hand on the sick man's, while his face softened with that smile which made it seem so earnest and noble. "At least she would have always one faithful affection in which to trust. I know you were thinking that too."

Of course. Still Mr. Crauford was no nearer the light.

"I think I have read clearly what has been in your mind," continued Vaughan; "my love for Elizabeth, my veneration for you, make me clear-sighted. But why should you leave yourself room for anxiety? I myself believe that, ill as you are, you will recover—"

"No!" interrupted Mr. Crauford; "no!" And he held up Plato again, as if the Grecian's spirit had revealed the future to his eyes.

"Then, believing that, why, as I said, leave room for care?" said Darrell. "I know you have been asking yourself that question also. Will you let me try to answer?"

"Try; I will listen," replied Mr. Crauford, glad so easily to find out what interrogatory he had been putting to his soul.

"You both believe in my earnest affection," Vaughan went on. "Elizabeth's answer to my plea was virtually a consent—she only asked for time. In urging her to marry me at once—as I think has suggested itself to you in viewing this matter from every side, after your habit—you leave your mind completely at rest—"

Mr. Crauford broke in with some hasty exclamation. He seized on this new excitement as joyfully as he had accepted his *rôle* of Stoic. There was no doubt whatever in his mind that he had been pondering the very thing Vaughan put into words. Mr. Crauford's inner vision contemplated a hurried picture of a marriage by a death-bed, himself, Ciceronian to the last, bestowing his farewell blessing on his child and her new-made husband—something white and grand floating off over their heads directly after — his departing soul probably. He was charmed with the tableau; it was very real, and yet perfectly destitute of painful reality. It is not easy to explain the jumble his faculties made of the business. He contemplated doing a fine death-scene, but for all that, he did not see himself actually dead and cold. He could consider a voyage to Athens in the same breath; but he was dying, he knew he believed that. Let him bless his daughter and her husband before he soared off to join Plato and other kindred natures in a higher sphere.

The two conversed for a long time. When Vaughan ceased talking there was no mistiness nor uncertainty in Mr. Crauford's mind. He was perfectly satisfied that since the beginning of his illness he had been brooding these weighty matters; that he had sent for Darrell to unfold his wishes; that every suggestion had come from himself; that the young man's share consisted simply in agreeing to his decision.

He wanted Elizabeth summoned; he was wild to have his project carried into effect. Vaughan himself hurried in search of her.

"I have been waiting for you ever since the doctors went away," she began. "Gervais said you were with my father. I know it annoys him sometimes if one interrupts a conversation, so I stayed here. Tell me what the physicians say this morning."

She was very anxious, very beautiful in her anxiety; it was a great comfort to his æsthetic sense that she did not make her nose red, nor sniff, nor display trouble in a disagreeable manner.

He did not spare her. He seemed to be breaking the verdict gently; but he let her believe that the doctors were very doubtful how the illness might end. He liked to console her in her grief; she was picturesque and stately still, troubled and shocked as she was, so he enjoyed the interview. He proved so tender, so kind,

how could she help trusting him—help believing that he was noble, and earnest, and true as some chivalrous Paladin of old?

But her father wanted her; she must wipe away her tears, and be composed and brave. Vaughan warned her that, above all things, perfect tranquillity must be preserved in his presence—no wish or idea thwarted. She should hear the truth! It would be useless to question the doctors—even if the sick man grew worse, they would consider it a duty to deceive her; but from her friend she might rest assured she would meet entire frankness, however painful the effort.

She was so utterly alone in the world, this visionary, enthusiastic creature; under all her dignity and pride she had such a tender, loving heart—she so craved affection, some superior strength upon which she could repose in complete confidence. She had never in her life been thrown into such intimate companionship with any man—never seen one who comprehended her dreams and aspirations—one whose own plan of life was so marked and, broad, so replete with noble aims and determinations.

He was gentle and tender too; the softest woman could not have been more kind and sympathetic than he proved in her affliction. No wonder she clung to him—believed in him wholly—felt humiliated in her own esteem that at first she had not rated his goodness so highly as it deserved.

She went away to her father, and that modern version of the antique was at once so pathetic and sublime over the speedy cessation of his mortal sufferings, that, unnerved by sleepless nights and watchings, more than ever alarmed by Vaughan's apparent fears, Elizabeth lost the last trace of courage, or even ability to reason, and almost believed that her father was positively dying before her eyes.

He managed to make his whole meaning clear—the plan which he was convinced he had unfolded to Vaughan. Elizabeth was too weak and shaken for any exhibition of the control and decision natural to her; she could only cry out, as the weakest girl might have done—

"I can not!—I can not! It is too sudden! —I can not!"

Then Mr. Crauford rushed into a violent excitement, and Elizabeth remembered Vaughan's warning—the consequence might prove fatal. She could only try to soothe him by loving words; but he was as obstinate as ever in his weak, inconsequent way, and got speedily back to the idea which had thoroughly taken possession of his mind.

Elizabeth could not deny that this man was more to her than any other had ever been; indeed, these last days had almost convinced her that she loved him; but the haste was abhorrent to her—the idea of a marriage under such circumstances in every way distasteful.

"I could not die in peace remembering that I left my child helpless, alone in the world," Mr. Crauford said over and over, as if he were about to leave a small orphan of ten years penniless on the earth.

Indeed, Elizabeth felt desolate enough, but she could combat this.

"If it were to happen—but it will not—oh, it will not—I should not be alone; there is my Aunt Janet—I could go to her."

"Think of the journey; and Janet is an old woman—an impossible old woman," moaned Mr. Crauford. "You could not live with her—nobody could! I tell you, Elizabeth, I could not rest in my grave to leave you so; and you care for Vaughan—you would have married him in a few months; why not a little sooner, if it will please your father? I shall not have many more favors to ask at your hands."

"Ah, papa, dear papa, don't speak like that!" She knelt by the bed and tried to comfort him, but Mr. Crauford would not be comforted; he would moan and shake, and forget his Roman firmness, and terrify her half out of her senses by his looks and conduct.

That night Mr. Crauford was worse. Vaughan had stayed at the house, and as Elizabeth was completely exhausted, he persuaded her to go to rest. In the middle of the night the sick man was seized with a kind of nervous spasm, and wanted his daughter. Darrell had no objection to her being alarmed by his appearance, though perfectly certain the crisis was not a dangerous one.

Poor Elizabeth could only feel that she was to blame. Had she gratified her father instead of ~~crossing~~ him, the attack would not have taken place. She felt terribly guilty and wicked, but she retained composure enough to go on doing whatever she could, so white and ghastly that a heart of stone might have pitied her despair; but Vaughan never offered a word of hope: he was tender, kind, but he allowed her to see that he was sorely alarmed.

Toward morning the crise yielded to the physician's remedies. Mr. Crauford slept, and was perhaps no worse on the following day, though certainly somewhat weakened. At all events, his desire to urge forward the marriage was as strong as ever; Vaughan took care there should be no falling off in that respect; and having all his life been the most changeable and capricious of men on every subject, great or small, submitted to his decision, it was wonderful to see how Darrell's influence held him firm here.

Later in the day Vaughan comes into the great room where Elizabeth sits alone in the shadow—comes so softly that she does not hear his step—is only roused from her confused reverie by his voice calling softly—

"Elizabeth, Elizabeth!"

There is a tone of inquiry in the passionate utterance which she comprehends; it asks the question she had been vainly trying to answer during her troubled meditation. She looks up with a start, trembling at the light in his eyes, the eagerness in his voice.

"Do not be afraid," he says sadly. "Think of me only as your best, your truest friend."

"I will—I do," she answers.

"Will you listen to me? Will you let me tell you what seems to me right, Elizabeth?"

She knows that his wise counsels and tender words are to be added to her father's persistence. She knows too—unable to decide whether the tumult in her soul is fear or some softer emotion—that circumstances, or fate, are too potent for her will. Indeed, her power of judging seems gone now that a dread of clouding her father's last earthly days is added to the balance against her unreasoning hesitation. He must judge for her—this hero, this brave, earnest man, who has shown himself as gentle and loving as he is strong.

So it comes about that one evening, weeks after we last saw Launce Cromlin, Mr. Carstoe returns home, and brings the latest New York papers to amuse his guest; for, in spite of his desire to be gone, Launce is still a prisoner. Some slight imprudence or exposure—perhaps some mental agitation, which the doctor has not taken into account—caused a relapse, from which he is only now recovered.

But this time he is radically better—quite strong, in fact; and the day of his departure is set, sorely to the chagrin of Mr. Carstoe and Simpson. Indeed, the fiery-haired is utterly disconsolate at losing her occupation of the last months, and visits her grief so heavily on the heads of all about that Launce laughingly tells Mr. Carstoe he will be obliged to advertise for a troublesome invalid, whom Mrs. Simpson can spoil and tyrannize over to her heart's content.

While the agent has gone away to consult that despotic female sovereign in regard to some household arrangement, Launce opens the newspapers, and idly turns the pages.

He comes upon a gossiping letter from an Italian correspondent; and as any thing concerning Italy always possesses a charm, he reads on and on, and at last reads an account of a marriage which took place in Pisa the very day this epistle was penned. The bride mentioned is Elizabeth Crauford, and she has wedded Launce's cousin, Darrell Vaughan.

One thing and another detain Mr. Carstoe, so that it is deep in the twilight when he re-enters the library. Launce sits there in the gloom, his head resting on his hand, his eyes gazing abstractedly toward the western sky, along which a single line of yellow light still lingers.

Twice Mr. Carstoe speaks before the young man hears; then he rouses himself, and is composed and cheerful. Before they part for the night he gives his companion a pleasurable surprise.

"You will think me a very capricious fellow," he says, "but I have changed my mind. I shall not go East this year. I have decided to follow your advice. I may never get to California again, so I shall visit the wonderful mountain scenery before I return, and perhaps paint a picture or two. I have been idle too long."

Darrell Vaughan has won in every way. He has won—whether honestly or not matters little to Launce. What does matter, is the loss of the beautiful dream which has been with him during many weary months. He marvels somewhat at his own weakness, at the hold which so baseless a vision has taken upon his soul, but neither astonishment nor indignation at his own boyishness changes the fact.

The truth remains—Launce has lost a hope so precious and fair, that life looks dull indeed deprived of its radiance.

CHAPTER XVI.

AFTER TWO YEARS.

PAGES of pretty poetry have been written upon the misery women suffer from seeing their idols turn into common clay. The poetry is nice to read, but no fate can be more galling, more replete with daily and hourly suffering, than that of the woman who has such an experience forced upon her, if said idol chance to be her husband. The worst feature in the case is that there remains no tinge of romance, no æsthetic glow which would at least fling a certain dignity about the trouble. Most women could pardon a great crime free from selfish meanness, or, have the consolation of regarding the perpetrator as a kind of fallen angel, still glorious in a Lucifer-like way at least; but what flings the oracle off his pedestal is to find him full of small vices, heartless, regardless of others—all his brilliant theories mere words, his whole life a sham.

Elizabeth Cranford had been two years a wife—years over whose details I must pass almost in silence, since, slight as many of them would seem, I should need my whole volume to chronicle their course.

The autumn after their return to America Vaughan received a nomination for Congress. The contest was very sharp, and he encountered defeat—his first failure. Just after that he was preparing to address some great meeting. The speech would require much care, must be in every way a brilliant effort. Elizabeth had gone one night to a party; Darrell was too busy to spare the time, but had insisted on her accepting the invitation.

It was very late when she returned; Vaughan had not yet come up-stairs. She dismissed her maid, and sat for a while waiting his appearance. Three o'clock struck at length; it seemed wrong for him thus to spend the whole night in labor, as he had not been well for several days. She was afraid of annoying him by intruding into his study, still she could not make up her mind to go to bed without warning him of the hour. She stole down-stairs in her dressing-gown, and knocked at his door. There was no answer. Thrice she knocked; then, growing almost alarmed, turned the knob. The door was locked.

He might have fallen asleep. She tried to think that; all the same, she could not subdue the anxiety which troubled her. She remembered a staircase leading from his dressing-room to the study—a staircase reserved entirely for his own use—possibly she might gain admittance in that way. She hurried back up-stairs, through a sleeping-chamber, into this apartment, and on down the stairs.

The fear of vexing him—she had already learned that it was always well to avoid the possibility—caused her to pause even when she reached the lower door. She knocked several times; there was no answer—no sound. She opened the door, and entered. The fire had died out in the grate; the room felt cold and chill. She saw Darrell lying back in his easy-chair, the table strewn with pages of manuscript.

She called his name. No response followed.

"Poor fellow," was her thought, "he is completely worn out! I must awake him; I am sure he will not be vexed."

She went up to him, and laid her hand on his shoulder. He did not stir. She shook his arm, calling again. He might have been dead for any show of life he evinced. Now she looked closely at him: the eyes were partially open, blank, unseeing; the muscles of the face drawn and rigid. She lifted his hand—it was cold; as she released it in terror the arm fell back supine and nerveless. She was thoroughly frightened; she turned to ring the bell; she must awaken somebody—must have assistance. As she moved, the loose sleeve of her robe swept the papers upon the floor; some heavier object fell too with a dull, metallic ring. She stooped and picked up a little silver box, opened it, and saw a mass of greenish substance, which she recognized.

Her husband's secret was clear now. She had known for months that he had a secret. She understood the odd manner which had several times puzzled her—the incoherent conversation, the strangeness of voice and look. Vaughan sought his inspiration in hasheesh.

Elizabeth gathered the papers together, glancing over them as she did so. A few pages of a speech—a brilliant opening—after that, paragraphs more hastily written, but full of force; then sentences unfinished; then mere broken words. There lay the pen on his knee: it had fallen from his hand as he sank back com-

F

pletely overcome by the effects of the poisonous drug.

Elizabeth was familiar with the workings of the potion : she comprehended that he had taken an overdose, and that, after quickening his faculties for a brief space, this death-like lethargy had come upon him. She could not tell if he were conscious of her presence, but she fancied not. It was useless to attempt to rouse him ; indeed, it might be unsafe.

She stood there, white as a ghost, and looked down at him. Across the pain and trouble which disturbed her features swept an expression that was almost loathing and contempt. In these brief instants she decided upon her line of conduct. Expostulation would be useless—worse ; it would form an element of actual discord and disunion.

The day which had witnessed Vaughan's political defeat showed his wife a new phase of that complex character she was studying too rapidly for her own peace. He had, for the first time, given free rein to his temper ; twice before she had been shocked by a perception of the fierce capabilities hidden under that polished exterior ; but this time there was no attempt at self-restraint, and the brunt of his fury fell upon her. Some word intended to be kind and consolatory—some suggestion which piqued his self-love or obstinacy—ont burst the storm, and a mad one it was.

Without a word Elizabeth had turned and left the room, but the one look of haughty scorn which flashed on him was a reproof Darrell Vaughan would never forget nor forgive. When he came to his senses he was able to put by for a space the recollection of that glance ; but it would return. As yet the spell of her beauty still possessed its influence. He cared for her in his material, passionate fashion, so he made his peace. Elizabeth would have shrunk from excuses put into language, would have disliked that he should thus humiliate himself, so she accepted his tacit repentance at once.

She thought of all this now as she stood looking at his pale, distorted face, from which the fire and energy had gone out. The mask had lifted ; the real man was there—coarse, brutal, sensual—all his glorious theories, the pretenses which had hitherto ennobled his countenance in her eyes as they had done his life in her esteem, gone utterly.

She crept away to her chamber, and left him there alone. She would keep his secret ; no perception that she had penetrated it should come up to anger or disturb him.

Day broke ; the chill, gray dawn stole in through the curtains and startled her like some importunate watcher of her misery. It had been a terrible vigil: a communing with her own soul, a study of the future, full of import to a character like Elizabeth's.

At last she heard her husband's step on the stairs. She closed the door into his dressing-room, put out the lights, and got into bed. He had the habit when he worked or came home late of sleeping in a chamber the other side of the hall. She heard him enter that now.

They met at luncheon. He was listless, weak, and miserable. Labor was an impossibility, yet the speech must be finished ; on the evening of the following day it was to be delivered. He had sent for her to his study to ask some question in regard to a matter he had intrusted to her care. His petulance and nervousness he was quite unable to conceal, and he told her frankly that he found himself completely upset and his work not half done.

"Perhaps I can help you," she said. "I see you have copious notes there ; at least I might arrange them for you to elaborate."

He hated the idea of receiving such assistance, but the position was a critical one. Elizabeth sat down at the table, and toiled over the fragments of the address. She not only put them in order, but she elaborated them herself, spending the whole day and almost the whole night over the address. He took it then, and roused himself to read and alter. In truth, he delivered the speech as she wrote it, but he did not admit this, and he almost hated her that he was compelled not only thus to recognize her powers, but to use them in his own behalf.

When they had been married a year, Mr. Crauford returned from Europe, and very soon after his arrival died quite suddenly. To the last the old faith in his son-in-law remained undisturbed. His fortune he left entirely at Vaughan's disposal. Darrell was now a very wealthy man. Only an inconsiderable portion of Elizabeth's own property had been secured to her ; the wedding was too hurried and Mr. Crauford too indolent to think of such matters. A part of her mother's fortune descended to her in a way which kept it independent of the man she married. She found herself fettered and hampered. Her schemes for doing good met with no sympathy from Vaughan save when they could serve to cast a lustre about him and redound to his credit. During the early days, while he still maintained a show of sympathy, excuses and reasons were offered. At length she heard plainly that she was going out of her province ; meddling with affairs which did not belong to her ; trying for notoriety as a philanthropist in a manner he deemed unbecoming. This taunt was a hard blow, but she bore it. I do not mean that she was a model of patience —she often rebelled, flamed into anger—but she shrank from contention ; harsh words hurt her like blows, and the idea of quarreling with her husband filled her with horror—any submission was better than that.

Up in one of the northern counties was a small estate, which had been a part of Mrs. Crauford's marriage-portion, but not among the property she owned independent of her husband. It was a place both father and daughter held in love and reverence. It had been Mrs. Crauford's favorite residence. She had beautified the house, embellished the grounds, spent years in the task. She was an admirable artist; the walls of several of the rooms were wainscoted with wood, and the panels painted by her own hands in landscape and figures. On a hill at the back of the grounds Mrs. Crauford was buried: they made the husband's grave beside her.

Twelve months after Mr. Crauford's death a new railway was projected which would pass near this country-seat. The company offered Vaughan an exorbitant price for the place. A cutting through the hill where the graves were would lessen almost by millions the expense of building the road, and the other lands were admirably situated for the site of certain factories they proposed to erect.

Darrell had gradually acquired the habit of accepting his wife's services in his literary labors and the immense correspondence which his political life forced upon him. Elizabeth was glad to be of use; she never shirked her tasks nor complained of fatigue, and he did not spare her. To himself he would not have admitted that she did any work beyond the skill of an ordinary amanuensis, but in all ways she was like a quicker, more comprehensive portion of his own intellect—able sometimes to seize and make palpable thoughts which only vexed him by their vagueness. He refused to acknowledge this truth to his own consciousness, but he felt it, and the knowledge kept up a constant *sourde* irritation in his mind.

So it happened that the first news of the company's proposition reached Elizabeth herself. She was opening and reading aloud letters; she came upon this; glanced at the commencement, and flung the sheet down with an expression of horror.

"What is the matter?" Vaughan asked.

"It is too dreadful—I can not read it!" she exclaimed, putting the letter into his hands.

While he read she turned away to a window, trying to subdue the thrill of indignation and grief which shook her. It was an actual insult and desecration offered to her dead, this vile proposal.

Vaughan read the letter through, folded it up, and laid it on his table. Surprised by his silence, she looked back, her features still quivering, her eyes bright with tears.

"Let me answer it at once," she said.

"Don't think any more about it," Vaughan replied; "I will attend to it."

"But did you ever hear of a proposal so absolutely base and revolting?" she demanded.

"My dear Queenie," he said, calling her by that pet name, after a habit he had when wishing to be particularly kind or tender, "business men have not leisure for sentiment."

"At least they might be human," returned she. "To propose carrying their road through a burial-place—it has been consecrated—"

"Very likely they knew nothing about the graves being there," he observed, as she stopped, half suffocated by emotion. "Don't think about it—there is no use."

"You will answer at once, Darrell?"

"Of course! Come, you are upset by this; dress yourself and go out. I can't have you worried by those beasts' stupidity."

He came up to her, passed his arm about her waist, kissed her forehead with a gentleness which was growing rare of late. She felt grateful for his sympathy, and, with her usual consideration, forebore to trouble him by any further display of emotion.

She went out to drive, paid several visits, and all the morning was thinking that during the past weeks a change for the better had come over their lives. Only once since her father's death had she discovered any trace of Vaughan's having yielded to the fatal fascinations of the poison. No hint of her knowledge had passed her lips: she could not be certain whether he suspected that she had gained the clew to his secret.

To-day she felt more hopeful than she had done for months. It was much to her that Darrell accepted her assistance; she was utterly incapable of such self-gratulation and complacency as he imputed to her in his thoughts. She did not in the least realize what his growing literary success, his efforts as an orator, owed to her patient toil and her clear, luminous intellect. She labored without selfish feeling, and would have been more astonished than the world had she perceived the full extent of her part. If she thought at all, it was only that Vaughan, like many men, was too impatient and excitable to work out and elaborate his own brilliant fancies or clear reasonings; she was blessed with a kind of faculty (she did not dream of calling it talent) to understand these, and an ability under his directions to put them in the shape requisite for others' comprehension.

She had been trying of late to lay by her forebodings in regard to their future; her perception of her husband's faults; her consciousness that, glitter as it might, his course was animated by motives very different from those noble aims of which he had talked so glowingly during the days of their acquaintance in Italy.

She reproached herself with having been guilty of too harsh judgments, when she perceived that this hero whom she had mounted upon so lofty a pedestal was only human after all. That he had grave faults, inexplicable contradictions of character, even startling weaknesses, was no reason why she should dare to rise up in condemnation, without waiting to discover whether he meant to struggle against these temptations. She told herself that she had thus armed her soul in the first shock of disappointment, and now she was obliged to admit that he did strive against his inner foes; his conduct of late enabled her to believe this. She exulted at this proof of his strength, and blamed herself more severely than another could have done.

Gradually he would outgrow his faults; ambition would limit itself to rightful bounds; this love of wealth be kept from warping and blighting his character; his temper fought down and conquered.

He could not be a sham—a pretense. He must believe in his own aims, and he would press on toward their realization.

More than ever she was thinking these things to-day. Life looked brighter to her than it had done for a long time. Not content with doing her husband full justice in her esteem, she would have him reinstated in her heart—that proud heart which required the object of its affection to be lofty and pure, or risk awakening an estrangement, a terrible shrinking at once physical and mental, which would turn her very soul to stone, or wear out body and spirit rapidly in the contest.

Days passed. Vaughan was in the most sunny of his moods—careful, tender—fairly like the worshiper who had wooed her under Italian skies, and been at once lover and friend. Success had come to every undertaking during the past weeks. His name was to be brought up again as a Congressional candidate, and this time triumph was certain, for he had resumed his relations with the municipal party, at once the most powerful and corrupt that the annals of our history could furnish. He concealed the fact of this coalition from his wife as carefully as he did from the world at large, and managed so well that not a suspicion was roused in the minds of honorable men who were among his supporters. The municipal leaders were as anxious as he that no inkling of the truth should escape. Sundry schemes, which they hoped by his assistance to carry through Congress, would be much surer of success if entire secrecy were preserved as to their electioneering efforts in his behalf.

A fortnight elapsed. Vaughan left home suddenly; he told Elizabeth that business called him to Albany—he might be absent three or four days.

The second morning after his departure Elizabeth was seized with a desire to visit Northcots, the place where her parents were buried. She had only been there a few times since her return from Europe. Vaughan owned a country-seat in another county, and one excuse or another on his part had kept her away from Northcots, the real reason being that he had conceived a strong dislike to the pretty spot.

She would take Margot and go up there for the day and night. An old servant of her mother's had always lived at the house and kept it in order. It would be a sad pleasure to have a day of quiet memories in the haunt where so much of her childhood was spent. She had been dreaming, too, all night of her mother—odd, perplexing dreams; pleasant at first, changing suddenly to dark, painful visions. She awoke depressed and absurdly anxious; it would do her good to visit the place.

It was still very early when she summoned Margot and announced her determination. They were in ample time for the morning boat, and it was a pleasant sail of a few hours up the beautiful river, with the landscape on either hand brightening into the glory of spring.

They left the boat and drove off among the hills for another hour, to the quiet hamlet near which Northcots lay.

The carriage reached the entrance to the grounds. The gates stood open; they passed through. Elizabeth was leaning back in her seat, forgetful of her dismal fancies of the night, when Margot, with her head out of the window, muttered a surprised exclamation.

"What is the matter?" her mistress inquired.

The Frenchwoman turned upon her a face utterly blank with astonishment. There was no time for further words; the carriage had halted on the lawn.

"Why do you stop here?" Elizabeth asked, as the coachman appeared at the door. "And you are driving over the grass. What do you mean?"

"I couldn't get along the road, ma'am," he answered; "and 'taint much matter about the grass now."

He stepped back, and she descended from the vehicle, looked up, and stood transfixed with horror. The sward was littered with furniture, men were bringing out of the house great panels of wood, and putting them in boxes which were placed on the veranda. The grass had been ruthlessly trampled, the early flowers trodden down.

Elizabeth grew so white that Margot, who had reached her side, called out in terror. Her voice roused Mrs. Vaughan; she moved forward across the lawn, and entered the house.

"What are you doing—what does this mean?" she asked one of the men busy over the boxes.

As she spoke she saw that they were packing the painted panels. The man she addressed was a mechanic from the village, who knew her by sight.

"It's just the masther's orders, av ye plaze, ma'am," he answered.

Elizabeth felt dizzy and faint. There was a sense of unreality about the whole thing too; it was like the continuation of her evil dreams.

She could scarcely persuade herself but that in another moment she should awake and find herself leagues away from the spot.

"Where is Mrs. Anderson?" she inquired.

"Faith, ma'am, it's me belafe she's keenin' in the kitchen," returned the Irishman, staring at her in open-mouthed surprise.

Elizabeth hurried past him, down the corridors, catching glimpses of dismantled rooms as she hastened on—still feeling that it must all be a hideous dream; another moment and she should awake.

On through a back passage without meeting any one—into the kitchen, usually a model of neatness; but the same disorder reigned here as in the other parts of the house.

"Mrs. Anderson!" called Elizabeth.

"Who is it?—what do you want?" returned a voice from a porch off the kitchen.

Elizabeth passed out; at the farther end of the veranda stood Mrs. Anderson, with her sleeves rolled up, her cap awry. She was packing all sorts of kitchen utensils, and crying heartily as she worked. At sight of her young mistress she uttered one scream, half pain, half wrath, dropped a pile of plates with an awful crash, and sat flat down on the floor, covering her face with her apron, and sobbing as if her heart would break.

"Are you all crazy!" exclaimed Mrs. Vaughan. "Get up this minute, Prudence, and tell me what it means."

Mrs. Anderson only held her apron more closely over her head, rocked herself to and fro, and moaned—

"I'd never ha' believed it of you, Miss Elizabeth—oh, Miss Elizabeth! The place she loved so—and never even to give me any warning—oh, it has broke my heart—broke my heart!"

"Prudence!" called Elizabeth again, going toward the old woman, her voice grown suddenly tremulous and weak—"Get up, for Heaven's sake get up, and tell me what has happened."

The housekeeper quickly drew the apron from her face, stared for one instant in wonder at the pale countenance which met her gaze, and gasped—

"I don't believe she did it—I don't believe she knowed a word!"

"Knew what?" repeated Elizabeth. "Get up —tell me—tell me."

"Don't you know it's sold?" demanded the old woman, rising.

"Sold—what is sold?"

"The hull place—the very graves out on the hill-side!" cried Prudence. "Oh, Miss Elizabeth, say you didn't do it—say you didn't!"

A mist gathered before Elizabeth's eyes; the woman seemed suddenly retreating to a great distance; the veranda heaved under her feet, and a roaring like a sea deafened her—then every thing was a blank.

CHAPTER XVII.

NORTHCOTS.

WHEN Elizabeth came to her senses she was seated in a chair, her bonnet off; Mrs. Anderson and Margot were bathing her forehead, holding hartshorn to her nose, and talking incoherently in their respective languages.

"Miss Elizabeth, Miss Elizabeth!" moaned Prudence. "Laud's sake, she's jist like dead!"

Margot's voice rose shriller still. The noise was insupportable to Mrs. Vaughan.

"Don't!" she said feebly, holding up her hand. "Give me some water."

Prudence put a glass to her lips; Elizabeth managed to drink.

"Madame is better!" cried Margot.

"Yes, yes," Elizabeth answered slowly. "Go away for a few minutes, Margot—I want to speak with Mrs. Anderson."

"Oh, deary me! oh, deary me!" groaned Prudence. "She didn't know—she didn't know; I said at first she didn't."

"Did you say the place was sold?" Elizabeth asked. "I could not have heard that—you did not say so, Prudence!"

"Oh, Laud's sake! oh, mercy on us!" sobbed the old woman, breaking into a fresh torrent of tears.

Again Elizabeth checked her.

"Please don't," she said; "I think I am not well—every noise sounds so loud. Try and tell me what it all means."

"Mr. Vaughan haint told you!" Prudence fairly shrieked, regardless of the caution she had just received. "I never heerd the like—your own property too—your own dear mother's afore you—and she pulled out of her grave actilly—oh Lord! oh Lord!"

Elizabeth caught at the arms of her chair— every thing began anew to totter and reel.

"If you don't tell me, I shall die," she whispered. "Prudence, Prudence!"

"It's sold, I tell you; and they wanted me to believe it was your work," cried Prudence. "Sold, every acre and foot—house and all—even to the graves. Oh, that was what cut me worst! I said to Mr. Vaughan I'd lived—"

"Has Mr. Vaughan been here?" broke in Elizabeth.

"Why, he's here somewheres now, else down to the village. Didn't you even know that?"

"Go and find him, Prudence," said Elizabeth.

A hot indignation sprang up under her pain —the outrage was so flagrant, so atrocious. She could hardly realize it yet; even now that she knew he was here, she could scarcely force herself to believe he had not only sold her old home, but allowed the graves of her parents to be desecrated. Then her indignation inspired her with a sudden resolve; she called Prudence back.

"Tell those men to stop their work," she exclaimed. "I will not have another thing touched—not a thing."

The old woman shook her head sadly.

"Taint no use now," she replied; "it's too late, Miss Elizabeth; the place is gone, unless—why, law, you must ha' signed the deed if it's reg'larly sold."

Elizabeth remembered that two days before her husband's departure she had been ill with a torturing nervous headache—a headache caused by several hours of unremitting toil for him when already sorely fatigued. Darrell had come into the room where she lay half asleep, apologizing for disturbing her, but it was necessary she should sign her name to two deeds; he was about to sell some wild lands he owned, and, of course, required her signature. She was too ill to ask questions or to think, and after that she forgot the matter. She recollected now how gentle he had been—bathing her forehead, holding the papers so that she could write without lifting her head! All the while he had been basely deceiving her! Oh! it was impossible; he could not be so vile! She would doubt even the evidence of her own senses rather than credit this!

"Say nothing to the men," she said, as these thoughts whirled through her brain. "Go and find Mr. Vaughan."

She remained there for what seemed a very long time. Once Margot came and addressed some question to her, but she motioned the girl away; speech was too painful to be attempted during this suspense. Twice she rose with the idea of going herself to seek Darrell—sat down again, deterred by the recollection that their meeting ought to be without witnesses.

Mrs. Anderson came back at last; she had walked rapidly, and was in a pitiable condition between weeping and fatigue.

"He haint around, my deary dear," she said; "he's driv off with some o' them men; but I left word with every body to send him on to the house as soon as he got back."

She must wait; until she had seen Vaughan she could not even command the workmen to stop: they might answer that they were obeying her husband's orders! The sound of hammers, the tread of feet, the murmur of voices, came up every now and then, and shook anew the composure she was struggling so hard to attain. She rose at length, determined to get beyond the reach of these noises, which struck like blows upon her heart.

"I will be back presently," she said to Prudence, who was not yet sufficiently restored for conversation.

"But you haint had nothing to eat," she expostulated, roused into thoughtfulness at once.

"It's all upset, but I could manage sumpthing."

"I'm not hungry—I can't eat, thank you,"

Elizabeth replied. "Give Margot some luncheon if you can."

She passed down the steps, and hurried through the shrubberies which extended toward the hill. At first Prudence did not comprehend whither she was bound; but when she saw her take the path that led to the gates dividing the grounds from the ascent, she exclaimed—

"Good Lord! she mustn't go there! Why that would be worse'n all the rest to her!"

She dashed off in pursuit, calling on Mrs. Vaughan to stop. Elizabeth was so engrossed by the terrible thoughts which agitated her mind and the awful pain at her heart that she did not hear. Suddenly the old woman stood still, muttering—

"Mebby she hears and means to keep on. Wal, going won't make it really no worse, arter all. What it all means is more'n I can make out, only that husband of hern has been at some villainy, smooth as he looks. I know more about him'n she does. La! if I'd a chose to speak—but there, she was married to him, and what was the good?"

She walked back to the house, where she was joined by Margot. While Prudence did her best to prepare something for the Frenchwoman to eat, the pair held an animated conversation, though neither could understand a fourth part of the other's talk—a fact which seemed to render both more emphatic and voluble.

Elizabeth pushed the gates ajar, and entered the grove which extended along the side of the hill. It was a pretty place. The afternoon sun streamed in through the branches of the maple-trees; a tiny rivulet ran singing along; the voices of the early birds sounded joyous and clear. As she mounted, glimpses of the valley below opened to her gaze, with the distant mountain peaks standing up purple and soft beyond.

This wood had been a favorite haunt of her mother's; there was not a path, not a nook, but was replete to Elizabeth's mind with some association of her childhood—that childhood which her mother's love had rendered so happy. At the top of the hill a smooth, level sweep of greensward spread out, carpeted with violets and daisies, groups of stately elms and solemn pine-trees guarding the spot. In the centre, under the shade of a magnificent willow, rose the tomb in which less than a year since she had seen her father laid to rest by the side of the mother whose memory was the most sacred treasure of her heart. She reached the summit, and looked toward the grave. She had scarcely noticed Prudence's words—certainly had not taken in their import. The marble monument had disappeared; the gigantic willow lay prostrate on the ground; all about were signs of awful havoc and desolation.

Elizabeth felt her senses giving way again; she sat blindly down on a bench, and hid her face in her hands, trying to lift her mind enough out of its confusion and the physical weakness which unnerved her.

There was no possibility of further self-deception where her husband was concerned; he had sold the property—actually torn her parents' remains out of their consecrated resting-place in his greed. She could only meet him once more; could only remain long enough to hear him admit his guilt; beyond that her endurance would not go. She was too shocked for tears—too much horrified even for anger. She could only sit there and shiver, while the spring wind drifted through the branches of the fallen willow, and roused a low complaint which sounded in her ears like the moan of grieving spirits.

At length the dull echo of footsteps on the turf roused her; she looked up, and saw her husband upon the other extremity of the hill in company with two men. She rose, and with all the force she could muster, called aloud—

"Mr. Vaughan!"

He heard; stopped for an instant irresolute, then turned, dismissed the men, and walked toward her. She sat down again, and waited; wrath and sorrow seemed alike to leave her heart. She felt cold and stiff as if an icy wind had blown over her. A strange longing to fly crossed her mind as he approached—a shudder disturbed her whole frame; she was like a person watching some noxious thing which she had no power to escape.

He came on, wearing his usual calm, pleasant expression; there was neither confusion nor remorse in his countenance. When quite near, he exclaimed—

"Why, Queenie, I could scarcely believe my eyes! Where on earth did you spring from so suddenly?"

He had passed by the house; Mrs. Anderson had told him of his wife's arrival, so he was prepared for the interview.

"What put it into your head to come up today, of all others?" he continued, as he reached the bench. He held out his hand—stooped to kiss her. She shrank from his caress, and kept her arms folded across her bosom; but he was resolutely blind.

"Will you explain to me the meaning of all this—this—" She had got so far quietly, but now her voice broke. She waited in silence, never moving her eyes from his face—eyes which, unconsciously to herself, regarded him with a horror and repulsion he was quick enough to perceive. Still he appeared to notice nothing uncommon in tone or manner—not a shade of surprise crossed his features.

"I am sorry you happened to come to-day," he said, gently. "I meant to have had everything arranged before I told you, so that there might be nothing painful to you in the matter."

"It is true, then?" she asked, slowly. Her

voice sounded unnaturally composed now. "You have sold my mother's home—you have not even left my parents quiet in their graves!"

"Let me explain to you—"

"I could not believe it—I doubted the evidence of my own senses," she continued, in the same low tone, which still rang out with a strange power. "I thought I was mad—I wish I had been! I wish Heaven had been merciful enough to let me die yesterday."

"My dearest Queenie!"

She shivered anew at this utterance of the familiar pet name he had caught from her father, but neither face nor voice lost their stern rigidity. She went on unheeding—

"At least I might have died honoring you—believing in your truth, your manhood! Darrell Vaughan, you have not only desecrated my parents' graves—not only trampled my heart down under your iron will, but you have destroyed my faith—left me alone in the night, almost without hope in my God!"

"Don't say any more," returned he, still speaking kindly, though a frown darkened his forehead. "You will be sorry afterward—you always are, you know, when your temper leads you to judge me hastily and say harsh things."

"I think I shall never be able to feel sorry again," she answered, and a quiver shook the sternness of her voice; "I think I shall never have the ability to feel grieved or repentant any more."

He was astonished at the horror, at the unutterable despair, which had seized her. He had expected tears, anger, sorrow of a certain sort, but nothing like this. Positively he could comprehend no reason for such excessive feeling. He had meant to keep his secret as long as possible, never doubting that after the first outburst he should be able to soothe and bring her to acknowledge the reasonableness and common-sense of his procedure.

"Now, Queenie, let us talk it quietly out," he said, sitting down beside her, and speaking with resolute patience.

"Did you not promise me that nothing should be done? Did you not profess as much horror as I when that infamous offer came?" she asked.

"I had not considered the case—I did not understand it fully, any more than you do now," he replied.

"Did you or did you not promise?" demanded she.

"Yes, yes; but—"

"And you broke your word."

"Elizabeth!"

"You went away on a journey; in regard to that you spoke falsely. Can you deny it?"

"I have no intention of denying any thing," he answered, in the same self-restrained, compassionate way. "I did it all from affection and a wish to spare you pain."

"To spare me!" she repeated, pointing toward the open grave, while her eyes seemed to pierce his very soul with their steely light.

"I must insist now on your hearing me," he said more firmly, but still with the forbearance one would exercise toward a rebellious child that needed to be brought back to reason. "I meant to write, rejecting the proposal."

She motioned him to go on, touching the palm of her left hand with the fingers of her right, and continuing to do it at each new statement, as if jotting them down to compare the aggregate—never once releasing him from the thraldom of her eyes.

"The president of the railway came himself to see me. Now you know, Elizabeth, that one can not hinder a road being carried along a certain route if it is considered absolutely indispensable. There must either have been a long *détour* or this cutting. I could not help yielding."

"The *détour* would have been one-half mile," she said, when he paused; "it was discussed in your presence and mine a year ago. The cost of that *détour* we could have paid if necessary."

This seemed to Darrell a proposal so insane that he involuntarily shrugged his shoulders.

"Since this must be done," he continued, "it seemed better to sell the house and land. You would no longer have cared to come here, and the company were willing to pay largely for it."

"The company of which you have become one of the chief directors," she replied. "I suppose you count on at least another fortune from your share in the factories that are to be erected over my mother's home—fresh millions from the proceeds of the road which runs across my father's grave?"

"Of course you can't reason—no woman can," exclaimed Vaughan impatiently, yet with a certain aggrieved inflection in his voice. "I have done every thing that a human creature could to soften matters—stayed up here myself, superintended every thing, even to the taking down of those old painted panels—and the thanks I get are reproaches and insolent looks, as if I had been guilty of some fiendish outrage."

"Oh," she cried, with a sudden bitter passion, "there are enormities even fiends would shrink from; there are acts so dastardly that only a man could perpetrate them."

"I see you are determined to quarrel, Elizabeth; if you insist upon it, we must. I have borne your taunts patiently, but I warn you there are limits to my self-control."

"I think I was wrong to say that, though I can not be sorry," she answered, more quietly.

"That's right! Now do be a dear, reasonable girl!"

She struggled for a moment with her pride and anger, then a sudden eagerness came into her face. She stretched out her hands with a pleading gesture.

"It is not too late!" she exclaimed. "Go to these men—buy back this place—give all my fortune—it would be enough, Darrell. Darrell, I have no one but you in the world; leave me my love, my faith! Do this—oh my husband—for our future peace—for our souls' safety—do it!"

"I would do any thing for you, Elizabeth," he replied; "but this is impossible! I am powerless! I was forced to sell—"

She interrupted him by a groan.

"Spare me any more falsehoods; at least you can do that."

"You call tenderness and thoughtfulness falsehoods!" retorted he.

"If my prayers have no effect, if my suffering do not move you, then think how this action will appear to the world! What excuse can you offer?—how right yourself in men's esteem?—and you prize that."

"Good heavens!" cried he, "men are not babies! Why every body thinks it so wise and sensible on our part. The clergyman here, your friend, said it was just what ought to be done. He admired your common-sense. I gave you the whole credit! I said, what was the truth, that if we were both to die we could not be sure this place would be preserved—it was not a regular burial-ground—it was much better to have the bodies removed to the new cemetery near, a very pretty place. I have purchased a lot—"

She threw up her hands again, this time with a gesture that pleaded for silence.

"I must explain," he said. "You must be brought to see the thing in its proper light. You accuse me of thinking about money, you talk so much about doing good—you are full of grand schemes—can you make no sacrifice to accomplish them? The new resources which the road and the factories will afford us make such designs more practicable—"

She interrupted him again. She knew too well the hollowness of such promises. No philanthropic scheme would ever appeal to this man, except it flattered his vanity or added to his aggrandizement.

"I think we must end here," she said. "Oh, go away; leave me my life to myself!"

He stared at her in bewilderment.

"You had better talk intelligibly," he sneered.

"I want to live alone—can you understand that? I want to escape an atmosphere of deception and treachery."

"Oh yes; now I understand! To gratify your vindictive disposition you want to pose as a martyr before the world—you want to ruin my whole career! This is your idea of wifely duty that you used to talk so much about before our marriage!—this is the conduct your loudly vaunted religion teaches you! If your churchgoing, your prayers, your Lenten observances, and all the rest of it, have taught you no more than this, you had better turn schismatic or heretic, and see if some sensible modern faith can not appeal to your reason a little, since the old creeds and apostolic benedictions have failed to touch your heart!"

"I want my life free!" she repeated. "At least leave me the ability to pray, to trust in my God. I think even that would have to go."

"Now see here," he exclaimed; "we will end the matter once for all! I have done nothing which could afford you a pretext for leaving me in the eyes of the law. According to your doctrine and your Bible, there is only one sin on my part that could liberate you; you can not accuse me of that! I have been a faithful husband, loving and kind! I am ready to be so still; to forget your unjustifiable language. At all events, we shall not separate! If you prefer war to peace, take it."

"Any thing for quiet," she moaned; "any thing."

"However you may judge my conduct, you are bound to believe I meant to act for the best, since I assert it solemnly. So to leave me would be only to gratify your temper; you would ruin me socially, politically, just to do this! Think a little; could any sin be greater than that? Try to cover up your purpose under what fine names you might, the truth would remain; you would live to feel and to upbraid yourself more bitterly than you have me."

He had triumphed by making others believe that this sale of the property, this removal of the graves, was with her consent and participation. He triumphed anew by appealing to her sense of duty, her dread of doing any thing wrong, her fear that her motives might be actuated by passion or evil temper. She was conquered in every way. Had she gone, that mocking appeal of his to her Bible would have brought her back. She had no right to leave him; she must stay, must endure.

She sat silent for a time. He studied her face furtively, reading her thoughts as completely as if she had put them into words. He could have smiled at the ease of his victory. But from the first he had known he should succeed; final defeat never menaced his will.

At last she turned her eyes toward him again. The fire had died out of them; the hardness out of her face; she looked utterly helpless and crushed. It was no mere submission to his edict which broke her resolution; no hesitation in regard to expediency or the world's opinion. His words had reminded her that she had no right to shrink from the duties she had accepted, the vows she had made. Life might become henceforth a martyrdom, but she must bear it. Straightway that active, living faith which animated her soul whispered the dear words wherewith the Holy Spirit encouraged His disciple—her weakness would be made perfect in His strength. It was

hard to believe; difficult in this, the most fearful trial she had known, to keep any hold of the old faith. But she clung to it, torn, broken as she was; clung to it as she might have done to an actual representation of the holy cross; and once more in the life of a human being was renewed God's precious promise that no creature shall be tempted beyond his powers of endurance, since with the temptation comes always the means of escape—faith in the Father.

"I want to go home," she said, faintly; "let me go home."

"Yes, dear, yes!" Never had his voice been sweeter, his face more kind. "You will just have time to reach the station comfortably. I would go to town with you but I want to be certain every thing in the house is properly attended to. I shall be down the day after tomorrow."

At least a season to herself was granted—a space to garner up her strength in solitude; it was much in this hour of need.

She rose to go.

"Good-bye," she said.

He had conquered. He liked peace. He was still enough under the spell of her beauty to be greatly influenced thereby, and she looked very beautiful in her suffering and prostration. It would have been a new pang, an added horror, could she have understood that his strongest reason for self-restraint and gentleness rose out of the passion of his sensuous nature.

"I'll go down to the house with you," he answered; "but let us say the real good-bye here. You are a brave girl. You will try to believe I meant to act for the best? Kiss me, Elizabeth; let us be at peace."

The handsome face bent toward her; the eyes, soft with a sudden eagerness, gazed into her own. She shrank away, moaning—"I can't, I can't! Let me go!—oh, let me go!"

Another man, with a temper so hasty as Vaughan's, might have been roused to anger, but he only felt a kind of pleasure in her hesitation. It would be like winning a fresh heart, gaining a new experience, to woo her back to an acceptance of his caresses. But now he only said—"Come, then, let us go! We'll not talk of these things any more. We will both forgive and forget! In our whole lives, probably, no such strong cause of difference will ever arise. I meant for the best; one day you will see it too."

She did not answer.

"You are not angry still?" he asked, presently.

"No," she replied, in a tired voice; "I am not angry. Leave the matter; you said we were to leave it."

They walked on toward the house. After a few moments he spoke of the pretty landscape, the cloud effects, the prognostications of the farmers in regard to the coming season. Another man would have done this to avoid the embarrassment of silence, after a scene like that they had gone through, or to keep his mind or hers from dwelling on it; but it was not Vaughan's reason. He noticed, and was thinking of the matters he talked about; he had conquered, and was prepared to be cheerful and at ease; curious also to see how much self-control she could exert.

Margot and Prudence were standing on the kitchen-porch when they reached the dwelling. Elizabeth spoke kindly to both women, and before going away arranged that Mrs. Anderson should still remain in her service. She was so composed that most people would have believed her convinced of the wisdom and necessity of her husband's conduct. But Prudence was too shrewd to be deceived, though of course she held her peace then and afterward.

To pass through the denuded dwelling again was more than Elizabeth's fortitude could support. She requested Margot to have the coachman drive round to the back entrance.

Vaughan helped her into the carriage, and took his place beside her. Prudence alone caught the one last despairing glance her mistress cast toward the hill as they drove away.

Vaughan talked pleasantly, and Elizabeth made a pretense of listening. Margot was there; no human being must obtain a glimpse of the awful gulf across whose depths she regarded her husband. The effort and the struggle had begun.

CHAPTER XVIII.

BREAKING HER BONDS.

THE slow, dull sweep of a sluggish river, the stretch of a meagre village along its banks, here and there a factory sending up clouds of black smoke which render the narrow streets still more dingy and close. An open square in the middle, with an old gray church. From this square, a stone bridge arching the stream; beyond, a steep hill, along whose side rise sombre, frowning houses, guarded by high walls. On the summit another square, surrounded by still more stately and sombre mansions, likewise jealously guarded by lofty walls and huge oaken doors.

This square is so dull and silent that the one in the village below seems a carnival scene in comparison. There is a church here too, so ancient that the columns along the front need the support of iron stays. The tower is moss-grown and covered with ivy; a clock within strikes the hours in a solemn voice, and the bells ring out with a muffled sound, as if they had grown weak and hoarse from age. There is a fountain in the centre of the square, backed by a huge black cross, on which hangs a bronze

figure of the Crucified; but the fountain does not bubble and laugh after the habit of its kind; it only rises and falls into the cracked marble basin with a dolorous murmur, so like a human complaint that a fanciful person might almost deem it the moan of the tortured shape above. A line of solemn cypresses extends along the church, and adds to the gloom. No matter how brightly the sun shines, it is a sombre, chilly place, that makes one shiver. So horribly silent too! Occasionally a flock of pigeons darts down from the belfry and circles about; but they are not talkative pigeons—dark of plumage too, whispering a little to one another, stepping gingerly over the broken pavement; altogether so still and shadow-like that one imagines them the ghosts of the cloistered nuns who have died out of the grim convent at the back of the church. There are never any children playing about, to rouse pleasant echoes by their blithe young voices. One might sit there half a day without seeing a creature pass, unless when toward sunset the gates of the great houses open, and give passage to elderly figures, who saunter about almost as noiselessly as the pigeons, or an old-fashioned carriage drawn by sedate horses rolls out of some courtyard, and passes slowly away toward the poplar-bordered road beyond the hill.

Leave the square, go along the street which leads to the poplar-bordered road with its monotonous landscape. More tall houses, more jealous walls, occasional glimpses of dull courtyards and prim gardens through the iron gates, which are kept as carefully locked as if the place were in a state of siege. The last of these mansions, on the left hand, is the largest and gloomiest of all, with hideous turrets rising above the roofs, and knots of chimneys, so twisted and contorted they are really painful to look at. Within the great gates a dismally clean court, a garden at the right and back of the dwelling, but a garden as dreary as a churchyard, with tall yew-trees and discolored marble vases, that remind one of funeral urns.

The house has vast corridors, suites of rooms where scarcely an article looks younger than the days of Cardinal Mazarin—rooms which might be imposing enough filled with bright furniture and gayly dressed crowds, but which suggest no more idea of comfort or home than the dreary old convent that turns its back virtuously on the dead square we have just left.

It is autumn now—deep in November. Just three years since Monsieur La Tour brought his young wife to this dwelling, which to him is so precious and beautiful.

Only a twelvemonth after their arrival here Madame L'Estrange died in this house, and so an additional sense of desolation and gloom darkens it to Nathalie's eyes. That was a strange death-bed. Nathalie is a creature whose emotions are usually as evanescent as they are easy to excite, but to this day she shudders when she recalls that season. The weight of a secret which Madame L'Estrange had carried about her so long—only once breaking the silence in a few vindictive whispers to Mr. Crauford the day they met in the Swiss chalet—became too oppressive when death stared her in the face. Holding fast to Nathalie with her wasted hands, transfixing her with the unnatural fire of her sunken eyes, she gasped some the secret, and wrung from Nathalie a promise which both knew there was scarcely a probability Fate would ever put within the girl's power to fulfill.

Can Nathalie ever forget that scene? Other memories shall come and go, the most important events of life will leave only a transitory impression on her mind, but she will never forget that hour.

She is thinking of it now, when we find her sitting out in the dreary garden, a book lying unheeded on her lap, her gaze wandering away toward the pile of gorgeous-tinted sunset clouds in the west. She never pays much attention to the beautiful in nature unless there is some one with her to point it out. She is so occupied with dreams and fancies, which always have herself for an aim and centre, that she has slight leisure for any thing else when a musing fit seizes her. She has grown a more hopeless visionary than ever. When she is not reading novels, or putting her wild fancies and borrowed theories upon paper, she is imagining some wonderful thing which is to happen—some stirring sensation, which shall shake her life out of its present monotony—make her a heroine of romance, whose fate will afford the scribblers of another generation ample material for poems and tragedies, over which future dreamers will marvel and weep.

Directly after Madame L'Estrange's death, her husband took her down to Italy. They visited all the famous cities—sailed over to Sicily, and Nathalie wrote an account of her wanderings. Feminine authorship was a thing opposed to all Monsieur La Tour's creeds and prejudices, but he could not oppose his young wife's will. The book was published; a noted *littérateur*, who had been fascinated by Nathalie in Rome, used his best efforts to give the work a temporary success. Nathalie tasted the first draught of a most intoxicating cup and craved more.

After the return from Italy, she was forced to accept existence in the old house for a considerable season. Monsieur La Tour was seriously out of health, and the physicians insisted upon his remaining here to try the beneficial effects of his native air. But the spring before this period of which I mean to write Nathalie did succeed in getting up to Paris, and obtained glimpses of excitement and gayety which rendered the thought of life in this dull place more insupportable. She had written a little romance,

full of French sentiment, impossible situations, theories at once so appalling and absurd that a reasonable person could not have told whether to be shocked or amused. But the story possessed a certain grace and ease of style, adroitly enough modeled upon that of one of the most famous French authors of our day; and this book too had its brief triumph.

There remained one serious drawback to Nathalie's satisfaction, however—she dared not put her name to the work. She was afraid both of Monsieur La Tour's anger and the verdict of people whose countenance she desired. The book was one which, if known to be hers, would have left no society open to her outside the Bohemian literary ranks of Paris; and insane as she was to fling off her shackles and be free, she dreaded the possible results. Marital law and the authority of relatives are very powerful in France. If she went too far, she might find herself deprived of her freedom, and kept so securely confined that she would have no opportunity even to make her woes public.

So this summer she came back to the old house. What a life!—how she hates, loathes, chafes under it!—breaks often into active rebellion, and renders poor Monsieur La Tour the most miserable elderly man in all France. He loved her so fondly—he loves her still; but now he knows that she has not in her heart so much as a gleam of tolerance for him. She does not attempt to disguise the truth; she taunts him with it whenever he opposes her whims or one of her black moods seizes her.

She execrates the staid, respectable people about—grand titled people, who, having slight vestige of their ancestors' fortunes left, are doubly grand and stately to atone for the loss. There are dull dinners occasionally—evening receptions, where the women bring their embroidery into the cold, gloomy salons—where weak lemonade and sweetened water are drunk—where girls and youthful married ladies are expected to listen submissively to their elders—where Nathalie is regarded with a certain wonder and doubt because she has written a book, though every body is kind to her on her husband's account, and few even among the women can resist her loveliness and her charms when she chooses now and then to rouse out of her apathy and dazzle them by her wit and her marvelous powers as a *raconteuse*—a style of amusement irresistible to French natures.

How long shall she be able to endure it? That is the question Nathalie asks herself over and over. Vain, frivolous in many ways, Nathalie is an odd compound. She married believing that at least in flirtation she should find a constant source of amusement, and yet even when the opportunity offers it does not amuse her. In Rome she managed to make Monsieur La Tour several times uncomfortable, but, as she told herself, *le jeu ne valait pas la chandelle.* In Paris the same effort with the same result. Into the dull old place come now and then handsome or agreeable youths to visit their relatives. Nathalie subdues these at once—horrifies the whole circle—distresses her husband ; but she does not amuse herself. When the youths, obedient to the creed of Frenchmen, feel it their duty to make love to her, she is bored, and discovers that they are vapid and shallow.

What the girl wants is universal adulation : to have a world at her feet, or some such impossible nonsense. The applause bestowed upon a successful actress would be delightful, but one man's worship, a *tête-à-tête* of tender words, even if the situation be dramatic, has none of the relish she expected it to possess.

So she tells herself it is because she has really loved, and she moans and wrings her hands and makes a god of Darrell Vaughan's memory, and chooses him for the hero of her novel, and enjoys all the misery she can manage to procure.

Here she sits in the quaint garden to-night, as pretty a picture as the fancy of a poet ; older, more matured than when we last saw her ; not beautiful according to strict rules—far from it, indeed—but with an inexplicable charm and witchery about her. She is just one of those exceptional natures, those impressionable beings, who seem at one hour animated by a good angel, the next possessed by a demon. Often it almost appears as if such creatures were brought into the world to work evil, while always straining after some unattainable ideal—some vast theory which shows foul and false under the glowing hues in which its devotees enfold it, with faith too, many of them, in the purity and right of its doctrines.

There she sits, perfectly unconscious that a crisis in her destiny is even now at the threshold—that the long-wished-for cause which shall nerve her into positive revolt has at last arrived.

She is roused by a hasty step on the gravel walk—by Susanne's voice close at her side. Susanne is little changed, only that she is very gorgeous in attire, and usually very grand in manner—putting on as many airs with the servants of Monsieur La Tour's household and those of the neighborhood as if she had always been confidential maid to the Empress of Russia. A more unfortunate person for Nathalie to have about could not be found. Susanne delights in plots and intrigues ; is ready to lie to any extent ; enjoys the thousand small ways in which Nathalie deceives her husband, and considers their detention in this dull place a heartless tyranny on Monsieur's part which deserves condign punishment.

"Madame ! Madame !" exclaims Susanne, clattering up on her high heels, with her head-dress fluttering.

"How you startled me !" Nathalie says, peevishly. "This horrid hole is so still that the least noise makes me nervous."

"*Chut !*" whispers Susanne, as warningly as if there were somebody near to listen, quite regardless of the fact that she shouted at the top of her voice as she ran up. "Come this way ; something has happened."

"What a mercy !" returned Nathalie, rising slowly. "Now I am sure it is just a bit of your nonsense ; tell what it is, and be done."

But Susanne will only utter hissing exclamations, and refuse to speak till she has drawn her mistress some distance from the house, behind a thicket of laurustinus. Then she begins—

"I saw her come in ; she asked for Monsieur, so I knew she meant mischief, the old cat ? I just whipped into the little passage back of Monsieur's study—"

"Who came ?—what do you mean ?" interrupts Nathalie, giving her shoulder an impatient shake. "It must be Madame de Mercœur, I suppose."

"She divines at once !" cried Susanne, triumphantly. "Ah, Madame has reason to suspect her of being an enemy—the monkey-faced old wretch !"

"She has come to tell my husband about Monsieur Frédéric, I conclude," pursues Nathalie. "Well, let her ; I do not care."

Madame de Mercœur is a countess — one of the magnates of the place, as poor as Job and proud as Lucifer. She has always been kind to Nathalie, on account of a life-long friendship with Monsieur La Tour ; but she has never liked her, and has been loud in her diatribes upon the folly of that worthy gentleman in his marriage. But of late she has cause to feel active animosity toward the creature. Less than a month since her youngest son, a naval officer, came home, and fell hopelessly blinded by the first of Nathalie's smiles. In the end Madame surprised the youth in the garden on his knees before the enchantress. That was bad enough ; but the crowning sin proved Nathalie's conduct at the discovery. So far from showing confusion, she appeared triumphant — laughed at the boy and bearded the mother. The climax had come, and Nathalie was not sorry that Madame pounced upon the scene. It had been all very well to let Monsieur Frédéric write her letters, to reply in pages of equally exaggerated trash ; but to-day he had screwed his courage up to the point of revealing his passion in open language, and, as usual when an adorer reached this stage, Nathalie's interest in the sport flagged, and the youth became a bore.

Nathalie has not scrupled to repeat the whole story to Susanne, mimicking the Countess and her hopeful to the life. Indeed, she would have revealed it just as unhesitatingly to her husband, only that since the scene she has chanced to be in an amiable mood where he is concerned, and does not wish him to have the pain of giving up his old friend's society. Madame fled from the neighborhood with her boy the day after her discovery, but Nathalie had this morning heard of her return, and is not in the least astonished at this visit.

"I am sorry now I did not tell Monsieur myself," she says; "but after all it is of no consequence; let Madame make her moan."

"Ah, but it is worse than that," cries Susanne. "She has found out that you wrote the book—they are quarreling."

Nathalie turns pale, but answers recklessly—

"It had to come sooner or later! Well, there is nothing he can do; he dare not shut me up."

"Men dare do any thing," answers Susanne.

"Not with a woman like me!" cried Nathalie, proudly. "Let me alone, Susanne; I want to think—I must reflect."

Nathalie's reflections do not go beyond vague resolves of angry defiance, but she enjoys the excitement, alarmed as she is, and even contemplates with satisfaction the idea of martyrdom—not carried to an unpleasant extent.

Madame de Mercœur has not rested till she found some weapon wherewith to smite her insolent foe. Through a gossiping correspondent she has learned that Nathalie is the author of the much-talked-of novel—a work which the coterie of the select in Du Bourg regard with horror. Monsieur La Tour has himself publicly expressed opinions of unusual violence concerning the book, declaring it unfit for any woman to read.

Poor Monsieur! With unscrupulous ferocity Madame intrudes upon his quiet and pours out her tale. The little idyl in which Nathalie has indulged with the susceptible Frédéric admits of no doubt. There are the letters; one of them is held before Monsieur's eyes; but when he discovers what it is he turns away. The story in regard to the authorship of the romance he refuses to credit, though in his heart he knows that it is true.

"To-night I shall have a copy of the journal which gives her name," cries Madame. "We shall see what you can say then."

"It will be no proof," replies Monsieur; but his troubled heart sinks under a fresh pang. It seems to him that he must die of shame and grief; but he bears up, asserting again that the story will be found to have no foundation. Madame de Mercœur pities and blames him all in a breath, and is so bitter against Nathalie that at last he fires up, and more than hints, though with great courtesy, that of course Nathalie's youth, beauty, and great talents render her a mark for the envious to shoot arrows at—those unhappy ones who have lost their beauty, and possess no especial mental gifts to supply its place. This is hard on Madame, who has been a belle in her

day. She fires up in her turn, and tells him roundly that the whole set—all this great world in little—has decided to countenance Nathalie no longer. Her conduct has brought misery into more than one hitherto peaceful household; strange stories in regard to her birth have been for some time afloat; this history of her authorship has added the crowning sin to her wrongdoing! Nathalie is to be tabooed—made a social pariah; the magnates of Du Bourg will send her to the wall, and gather their garments closely about them as they pass, lest her touch should contaminate their purity.

Then Monsieur rises, and, pale as death, asks his visitor if she have any other communication with which to honor him. She accepts the hint, and goes out with scanty leave-taking. Though even in the height of his wrath and pain, Monsieur can not forget his old-fashioned ceremonious politeness. His icy courtesy brings Madame a little to her senses—she is not to be outdone in that line, and their bows and obeisance are a sight to behold.

The door closes; Monsieur falls back into his *fauteuil*, and sits there, looking five years older than he did an hour ago—sits pressing his hands to his forehead, trying to collect his thoughts, to decide upon some course which shall be at once right and as merciful as he can make it toward Nathalie.

The room is filled with the gray shadows of twilight before he rouses himself from his meditation—is roused from it rather by the measures of a clear, youthful voice which float up from the garden. Nathalie is returning to the house, singing in very recklessness and defiance. Just then a servant taps at the door—enters with a parcel, and Madame de Mercœur's compliments; she sends the journal of which she was speaking to Monsieur. Madame has had the decency to seal the newspaper, that it may be safe from the prying eyes of the domestics.

"Will Monsieur have lights?" Monsieur only shakes his head; the roll which the servant has placed in his hand drops from the nerveless fingers. The man thinks Monsieur lays the package on the table; but it is not so. He has reached the door, then his master speaks for the first time.

"*Mes compliments respectueux à Madame;* if she is not occupied, I should be glad if she would come and read to me for a while."

The servant goes out; Monsieur bows his head on his hands, and sits still. Presently there is a light step in the stone gallery—the tones of the merry song which reached him from the garden a little time before again fill the sombre room with their melody. The wrinkled hands which support the head, grown so gray during the past year, shake nervously, but he does not stir.

Once more the door opens; Nathalie pauses on the threshold to exclaim—

"What a dungeon of a room — like all the rooms in this old den! If I am compelled to live here much longer, I shall pitch a tent in the garden; that is bad enough, but it is a degree better than this awful barrack."

"You do not like this house?" Monsieur says, seizing upon the chance her words have made to get at once to his purpose. "You would not mind going away?"

"Mind! Why Patagonia, wherever it is, would be Paradise compared to this place." Nathalie is rather nervous — somewhat frightened; but she keeps up a show of courage — overdoes it, in fact, so that it looks like bravado. "Martin said you wanted me to read to you — I must have a lamp."

"One moment, please! Come in, Nathalie." She enters, and closes the door.

"Well, then!" she says in her defiant voice.

"About going away first," he continues, looking at her with a gaze so wistful and sad that it ought to soften her heart; but she is not in a mood to be touched. "I think it may happen," he goes on slowly, after another pause; "indeed, I can see no other course to pursue, at least for a time."

"So much the better!" she cries. "We shall go to Paris."

"No, Nathalie; to Languedoc — to my sister's."

"What!" she almost shrieks, preparing to rush into a fury without loss of time. She has subdued him before this by a display of temper; he so dreads to see her behave unworthily that he often yields a point to escape the humiliation — perhaps he will now. "To your sister's — the awfulest old dragon in all France! I'll not go — I remember my one visit there! I tell you I will not go — I'd rather stay here even than endure that purgatory."

"Unfortunately, you have rendered it impossible," he says, still speaking in the same slow, sad fashion — he is too depressed and broken for anger. "We must go away for a while. I will even relieve you of my presence, but I must place you under proper guardianship. There is no one so fit as my sister — no one who, misjudge her as you may, will prove so kind, so lenient a friend, if you permit her."

"And now, having announced your lordly will, perhaps you will condescend to explain what all this means," cries Nathalie. "You can neither drive nor frighten me, I warn you; I am not a woman of that sort."

"Child, child!" he says, reprovingly, yet with a quiver of pity in his voice, as if trying to soften his own judgment in regard to her by this name.

"Let us get at the bottom of the matter at once," pursues Nathalie, hotly. "That old demon, Madame de Merceur, has been with you. What falsehood did she bring this time? Brave man — gentlemanly conduct to listen to complaints of your own wife!"

She will neither coax nor plead; she will bear down upon him with the full weight of her will; he shall yield — beg for forgiveness; Madame, and all the rest of her enemies, shall see that their malice has only served to leave him a more submissive slave than ever.

He does not recriminate; one might almost think he had not heard her cruel words, only that the gray head bows lower, and the sad eyes, which watch her always, grow misty and dim. His hand stretches out and takes up the newspaper — he breaks the seal. He has no need to search for the paragraph he wants — Madame has folded the journal so that it meets the eye as it is opened, and she has drawn a wide line about it with very black ink into the bargain.

"Will you read this?" he says, his utterance growing still more difficult.

Nathalie takes the paper — goes closer to the window, and glances at the marked paragraph. She is so delighted with seeing her name, so charmed by the fulsome compliments paid her beauty and genius, that she absolutely forgets the danger which menaces her, and cries out ecstatically—

"Oh, how it praises me!—signed 'R. V.' Why that is Monsieur Valmont, the most celebrated critic in France."

"Nathalie!" The name is groaned out with such mingled pain and horror that she comes back to her senses. She remembers the exigencies of the moment — is more angry than ever at the idea of restraint or opposition just when such incense and triumph are offered her.

"So this was the old cat's errand!" she cries. "Eh bien!—afterward? You have not read it; stay, you shall hear how the world estimates the woman you and your miserable idiots of neighbors deem a child — a frivolous butterfly, that needs counsel and guidance. Listen then!"

"No, no; I don't want to hear," he exclaims, brokenly.

"'The much-talked-of romance, "Le premier Pas," whose audacious theories astonished limited intellects as much as its pathos and dramatic plot touched heart and imagination—'"

"Nathalie! Nathalie!"

But she reads on unheeding—

"'This eloquent appeal against the unjust tyranny of our social laws — this bitter, ironical exposition of the iron rule of marriage—'"

"I tell you I will not listen!" he interrupts.

"Bah!" she cries, contemptuously. "Of course you can not understand or appreciate! Skip that part then. 'This work, assigned to so many different writers, is, we are credibly informed, the production of a lady already favorably known as the author of "A Winter in Italy" — a lady whose beauty, grace, and varied charms for a little time last spring fascinated the literary circles of Paris—'"

"Nathalie! I beg! I entreat!"

"'A certain Madame Nathalie La Tour,'" continues the young voice, shrill with triumph. "'One sees that she has written from her inmost heart. The details of an actual experience are here unfolded. She transcribes a drama which she has lived. She—'"

By a sudden movement Monsieur's trembling hands almost succeed in wresting the paper from her. She retreats, calling out—

"You shall hear! you shall! Listen to this bit: 'She has placed herself among the foremost disciples of the school to which so many of our great writers belong. She boldly avows her hatred of the tyranny of marriage; her belief that love is too holy and powerful to be shackled by men's petty laws—'"

She is interrupted again; it is only a groan this time. Still she reads on from another sentence that has caught her eye.

"'The incidents of the heroine's marriage, the selling of her to a rich, elderly man, the defeat of her lover's efforts to save her, are all said to be actual experiences—'"

"It is not true—at least that is not true."

"It is!" she cried, flinging the journal down; "it is true! There, then, do your worst! I have suffered enough—been submissive too long; I will give my wrongs full voice at last."

She stops, alarmed at the possible consequences of her own recklessness, but the bowed form before her does not stir. She picks up the newspaper and hides it in her pocket; this tribute to her vanity is too precious to be rudely treated. Then she hears a rustling of other papers. She sees that Monsieur is extending toward her a package which she recognizes at once—her letters to Monsieur Frédéric. One of them has been separated from the rest—it is open.

"I have not read these," Monsieur says; "that single page I read; it was placed in my hand before I knew what it was."

Nathalie's quick eyes fasten on it; a passage in which she bemoans the weariness of her life—the utter lack of sympathy with her husband; a rhodomontade as overstrained and untrue as possible, though she tried to believe herself in earnest as she wrote.

"Go on—go on!" she says. "What do you mean to do now?"

"Take your letters, Nathalie," he answers; and still no thrill of anger sharpens his mournful voice. "Child, child, I have tried to see what was best to do. I want to act aright. It is so hard to know! I can not leave you to yourself—to the consequences of your mad folly."

"Are you silly enough to suppose I cared for that young idiot?" she asks. "The coward, to give up those letters! You ought to kill him! I played a little drama just to tease his mother."

"I know—I know. Of what men call sin in a wife, I hold you innocent, Nathalie. I am not thinking of that. If I were your father I could not be more anxious to help you. I can see but one way."

"To send me to Languedoc? I'll not go."

"Here we can not stay, Nathalie. I could not live among my old friends and see my wife avoided; the talk of every servant's tongue; the scorn of those I honor and love—"

"Your friends are idiots, fossiles," she breaks in. "Take me among real live men and women of our century—people who can comprehend me. Let me have my life!"

"Never! I put aside the danger you would run—the sin on my part of throwing you in the way of temptation—"

"Bah!"

"But I can not as a Christian; as I fear to offend my God, aid you in promulgating the dreadful theories you have imbibed from bad books—theories whose evil you do not half understand."

"You forget to whom you speak!" she interrupts again. "You have the honor to be allied to a woman who has already given proofs of her talent! Do not presume to set your puny judgment, your old-time scruples and superstitions, against the verdict of the world."

"Ah, child, can you not see! You have only gained a little notoriety among a set of people glad to hail a young, respectable girl as one of themselves: this is not fame—this is not literary reputation."

"My book has been translated into Italian and English;" she exclaims. "I saw only the other day that it had run through three editions in America! I have another finished—ah, what a work! It shall be published too—your tyranny can not prevent that."

"If it inculcate similar doctrines, I must prevent it," he replies. "Write books fit for a woman to pen, for women to read, and I will not interfere."

"I defy you!" she cries.

"Then you must listen to my will, and you must obey," he answers. "Nathalie, in France a wife can not easily dispute her husband's law. Painful as it is, I must insist on obedience."

She laughs aloud as she stands before him, her eyes dilated, her face convulsed with passion.

"Let me hear your will—your regal decree!"

"If you could only trust in my tenderness—if you could believe what my age and experience make clear to me," he pleads.

"Genius has no need of either," returns Nathalie, grandly; "its intuitions are unfailing."

"You have a whole life before you," he continues. "The time must come when you will see in their full horror the ideas and theories which look so beautiful to you now—"

"Which are to become the hope of the future," she breaks in again, with a majesty that would have amused a less interested listener. "I expect persecution — all reformers and apostles must; I do not shrink."

"The time to die will come at last," he goes on, unheeding her interruptions, his voice growing lower and more tremulous. "Child, there are sins enough which affect one's own soul to repent at that hour; do not add to the weight the awful memory that by your written words you have done incalculable harm to the souls of others."

"I can not argue with you," retorts she contemptuously. "It is useless to attempt to make you understand! Yours is a narrow, priest-ridden nature—I am a philosopher: the very word is beyond your comprehension."

Absurd as the speech is, he can not smile; he can only grieve over her blindness and perversity, wondering by what means he may save her from herself—from the effect of evil teachings and evil books.

"Let us end the discussion here," he says wearily; "for the present, at least."

"I told you arguments were useless," she replies, almost ready to believe that she has conquered, and will be allowed to pursue her own course unmolested. But the flattering delusion is quickly dispelled, for Monsieur adds—

"As soon as you can prepare, we will set out on our journey."

"What?" she cries.

"I told you we could not remain here—it is impossible; we must go without delay."

"To Languedoc?"

He bows his head.

Nathalie stands for an instant dumb with rage and terror, then bursts into a torrent of angry speeches which he does not notice. She sweeps out of the chamber, and leaves him alone in his grief and desolation—the terrible solitude of an old man, whose one hope of earthly happiness has been dashed into ruins.

"It has come at last," Nathalie says this night to Sosanne. "At least I can depend on you. I have already arranged a plan—he shall not wreck my life in its very opening."

"How will you manage, Madame?" asks Susanne, greatly impressed by her looks and words. "What will you do?"

"Do?" she repeats. "Go to America—he can not touch me there: to America!"

But even as she utters the name her mother's dying words come back, and Nathalie shivers and turns pale, mad and reckless as she is.

CHAPTER XIX.

LAUNCE'S PICTURES.

It often happens, especially in the history of married lives, that even when some important crisis is reached no events of consequence follow,

although at first it has seemed impossible that existence should ever settle back into the groove from which it has been so rudely shaken.

After that interview with her husband, in sight of the empty grave which his greed for wealth had violated, Elizabeth Vaughan went home. For several days she was left to herself; then Darrell returned, but was called away immediately to Washington, so that almost up to the time for their departure into the country she was granted a season of solitude.

She needed this season to reflect—to face her life with its present pain, its future dreary possibilities. The hero about whom she had tried to cast a glow of enthusiasm so bright and warm that she could believe even her heart joined in the worship was flung down from his pedestal forever. One course remained—the fulfillment of her wifely duty; and to satisfy her conscience this could take no narrow scope. She must put from her mind bitterness and wrath; she must struggle against contempt and distrust. It was very hard, but she did try—faithfully, constantly.

When Darrell reached home he found her tranquil, cheerful, and no allusion was made to their last meeting.

The summer went, the autumn came, the winter, with its round of society duties, which, under other circumstances, might have possessed a certain pleasure for Elizabeth, if only she were not forced to think she was wasting the time.

Most people regarded her as a beautiful statue, with nearly as few human sympathies as her stone prototype. The few who learned to know her marveled what struggle was going on in the pure soul; but she made no confidences.

Scenes between Vaughan and herself were rare; now and then his fiery temper broke out, but ordinarily peace reigned in the house. He was less and less at home. Business, pleasure, led him about, and his numerous schemes occupied him greatly. He was a very successful man—honored, courted. This period was the heyday of his triumph. Few reports to his discredit got abroad; he was still careful in his conduct. Elizabeth's empire was rapidly wearing away. There were times still when her beauty filled him with fierce passion, and he could scarcely tell whether he loved or hated her—when he would have burned her soul up under his kisses if he could.

Elizabeth Vaughan lived to endure the most horrible form of degradation which can befall a pure woman, and pure as she was, she could not shut the humiliating truth from her soul. She belonged to a man who prized her beauty because it appealed to his sensual nature—valued her mental gifts only as they could be employed in his service. A slave in an Eastern seraglio could not have been placed on a coarser level, and here this woman had to live.

Thwarted in every laudable ambition; fettered even in the expenditure of money which was her own; obliged always to preserve for the world's sake, for duty's sake, the semblance of respect, an appearance of trust in what she knew to be the hollowest sham ever hidden under a golden exterior, lest it should be her hand that rent the veil and showed him to his fellows as he really was, thereby rendering him so utterly desperate that no chance of redemption would remain.

And she still tried to hope for this; tried to believe that he would grow out of his faults; and always just when some noble word, some worthy act, seemed to promise a fulfillment, a cruel fate would force the truth upon her, and she was doomed to see plainly the selfish motive, the studied craft hidden beneath.

Her life was not an idle one. She gave not only all the money she could for the charitable purposes which had been the dream of her girlhood, but actual superintendence, real, honest work, to atone for the limited means in her control.

The season advanced. Of course there was the usual round of balls and dinners; constant festivities at their own house or abroad. Elizabeth did her part—perfect in dress, calm and dignified in demeanor; and so the days passed.

It was toward spring once more when business brought Mr. Carstoe on from California—the first time he had visited the East in many years. Vaughan had need of his services in some company or project. He could trust Carstoe's honesty and ability; and where the former quality at least was concerned, Vaughan's faith in most of his kind was exceedingly limited.

Carstoe was often at the house, a devout admirer of Elizabeth's; and she learned to enjoy greatly his quaint conversation, and to appreciate the stern integrity and perfect uprightness of his character. Not an extraordinary person in other respects, Carstoe impressed one as far beyond the common run of humanity as regarded these virtues. It was a keen pleasure to Elizabeth to study his nature for this reason; a comfort, in the midst of the dissimulation and scheming which surrounded her, to watch this grave, plain, elderly man, so firm to his convictions, so honest to his word. Absolutely his society gave her a feeling of rest. Most things on which she had placed her faith looked so shifting and unstable that his immovable rectitude was like a prop to her tired soul.

Mr. Carstoe was the most unassuming of men —proud, too, in his quiet fashion, and utterly incapable of pushing or forgetting his position; but he was rather petted by both husband and wife, and their kindness and consideration came like a gleam of sunshine into the loneliness of his life.

Mr. Carstoe's respect and admiration for Vaughan were as unbounded as ever. If he could have brought himself to accuse Mrs. Vaughan's character of a fault, it would have been on account of her manner to her husband. She was unfailing in all essentials of deference and respect, but less

impulsive and demonstrative than Carstoe (always a little visionary when love and marriage were concerned) could have wished. But he felt certain it was only her manner; of course she loved him, and they were a very happy couple: Carstoe would have gone to the stake in support of that belief.

Side by side on the elevation which Vaughan and his wife occupied in his esteem, Mr. Carstoe placed Launce Cromlin. Naturally he could not be long in the society of Launce's relatives without mentioning the young man's name. It was the first time Elizabeth had ever heard it spoken except joined to slighting allusions or open condemnation. Her father had told her something of Darrell's cousin. As Mr. Crauford had made a *bête noire* of Launce, he was loud in his censure: according to him, Launce was a cross between Caligula and a modern rake. When she asked Vaughan, his hesitation and hints were as expressive as her father's sweeping though vague censures. Of the reasons for his uncle's distrust she knew nothing, and indeed she forgot all about Launce Cromlin until Mr. Carstoe brought his name abruptly into the conversation.

"Didn't know he was in America," Vaughan said.

"He is not, but he has sent several pictures over, and they are attracting great attention," Mr. Carstoe replied. "The very best judges pronounce that he has won for himself a foremost place among our artists."

"Really I have not even heard the paintings mentioned," Darrell observed, disdainfully.

"They are only recently arrived—yesterday's papers began to speak of them; but they had been exhibited in London, and they established his reputation there."

"Dear me; well, I am very glad that Launce has won a little notice, however ephemeral," returned Vaughan, carelessly.

Nothing is perfect—there are specks on the sun. The one blemish to Darrell's perfection in Mr. Carstoe's eyes was this underrating of his cousin. But he was too wise to make matters worse by arguments or expostulations.

"I suppose you have not seen Mr. Cromlin's pictures yet?" he said, turning to Mrs. Vaughan.

Elizabeth roused herself—she was falling into the bad habit of growing abstracted and preoccupied. During the last half-hour, while the two men talked, her thoughts had been traveling worlds away, or brooding drearily over the life which looked so different from her girlish dreams —the life so void of fruition that it was hard to be patient—hard to remember that "they also serve who only stand and wait."

Several times while conversing, Mr. Carstoe had glanced at her in a meditative, questioning way. He had been some weeks now in the habit of seeing her daily, and of late, absurd as it seemed, he had occasionally caught himself wondering if it were possible that her happiness and content could be less complete than he had supposed them.

It was growing a very sad countenance, that beautiful face of Elizabeth's—graver than suited her youthful loveliness; acquiring, too, a self-restrained expression, which ordinary observers called pride and haughtiness, but it possessed a different significance to the few capable of closer, clearer judgment.

More than once Darrell had glanced toward her likewise, but with a feeling of irritation which he found it difficult to restrain. He was talking particularly well, and it irked his vanity to perceive that he had only one listener. Had there been twenty people in the room, and a single person among them appeared indifferent to his eloquence, he would have been annoyed. But this increasing habit of absorption or reverie on Elizabeth's part irritated him hugely. It was as if her soul soared off beyond his control; and though what he called love was rapidly wearing out of his heart or fancy, he chose to dominate her still.

So now, when she started a little as Mr. Carstoe roused her suddenly by speaking her name, Darrell said with a laugh—

"She has not heard a syllable! My wife looks a sibyl, and is as abstracted as a Sappho."

It sounded only like pleasant raillery to other ears, but the remark was meant to sting, and Elizabeth understood its full significance. The more he taxed her talents in his service, the more he sneered covertly at her powers, making it evident that he considered her devoured by vanity and self-esteem for which her mental gifts or achievements offered no foundation.

"I beg your pardon, Mr. Carstoe?" returned she, interrogatively.

"I was speaking of Mr. Cromlin's pictures," Carstoe answered.

"Launce, you know — my cousin," Vaughan explained, with a polite sneer in his voice: it was always there when he spoke of his relative.

"Yes," Elizabeth said. "I have seen a few of his pictures since we came back to America; they seemed to me to show great talent."

"Now that settles the matter!" laughed Vaughan.

Mr. Carstoe laughed too, thinking the words a merry jest, under which, while pretending to speak lightly of his wife's judgment, his great love and admiration for her were plainly visible. He worshiped the beautiful woman — Mr. Carstoe knew this. Elizabeth paid no attention whatever; did not seem to hear; though she never grew hardened against such petty insults from her husband, however much she might despise them—a proof that she still had some feeling left where he was concerned.

She went on quietly speaking of the paintings to Mr. Carstoe.

"Those were youthful works," the lawyer said.

"These new pictures are far beyond any thing he has done before."

"You must go and see them, Queenie," added Vaughan, in his kindest voice. "Indeed, we ought to buy one or two, if there are any for sale."

"Several I know are already sold in England," Mr. Carstoe observed, "and others since the exhibition opened here."

"Then we must make haste," said Vaughan. If Launce was achieving reputation—though the bare thought made Darrell grind his teeth—it suited him to appear the munificent patron as well as friend of his cousin. "Don't forget, please, Queenie dear! I shall try and look in myself, but I am awful busy just now."

"You wish me to select and purchase one?" she asked.

"By all means."

"There's one I fancy greatly," Mr. Carstoe said. "It is an Italian scene — a balcony and garden back, and a beautiful woman and child in the foreground."

"Italian?" repeated Vaughan. "Ah, that will be the picture to choose, Queenie— we like any thing that reminds us of our magic land."

She caught the sneer again. Italian! The word carried her back to those days under the soft Tuscan sky when her dreams looked so near fulfillment—when the idol which her enthusiastic nature craved for worship seemed to have descended at her side, as unexpectedly and in a shape almost as glorious as the gods were believed sometimes to appear in the old days of mythological credences.

Here he sat now opposite her; handsome perhaps as ever, though the face looked worn—from toil and mental effort the world would have said; from dissipation and evil courses she knew, and could not soften the terms, try as she might.

Here he sat mocking her in his cruelty by reference to that season whose every memory he had trampled upon and sullied; captious and irritable from a sleepless night, in a mood to enjoy hurting her in all possible ways.

"Besides buying one of these," pursued Vaughan, "we'll have one painted specially for us when Launce gets back. Say your portrait, Queenie—in that old palace salon, with the Pisan mountains showing through the window—yon in mediæval costume, and I'll be coming toward you as a Crusader just returned—some business of that sort. Nice idea, eh ?"

"If you fancy it," she replied, without showing any trace of annoyance. "You must choose some other lady for the mediæval princess though —I don't mean ever to sit for my portrait again."

Just then she was called out of the room by the arrival of visitors, and made her escape gladly.

Vaughan and his guest went back to the discussion of the business matter which had brought the latter to the house. But Darrell did not forget that it would be well to prevent any danger of rash disclosures on Mr. Carstoe's part. So before he renewed the business talk he must needs praise his lovely wife, and at the same time mention sundry oddities in her character.

He made Mr. Carstoe understand that Launce Cromlin's name was tacitly tabooed in the house, and that from certain feminine repulsions in which Mrs. Vaughan indulged. She was a very proud woman—a very peculiar woman; and the stipulation in that will of his uncle's had been a wound to her pride.

In his wooing and success Darrell had received no assistance from the dead man's request and the letter left for Elizabeth Crauford — just the reverse, in fact; and it was only love that had enabled him to triumph over the distaste or obstinacy which the details of that codicil had roused in her mind.

"As for Launce," pursued Vaughan, "he would never have stood a chance. Mr. Crauford had a hopeless prejudice against him—would not have allowed him in his house. He had known of the forgery affair; I tried to set it right — to show him how convinced my uncle was of his innocence: no use though."

"But surely Mrs. Vaughan would not be so —so unyielding?" Mr. Carstoe said.

"Ah, she never knew what made the trouble between Launce and my uncle. She only thought he had been wild and reckless, as he was; but of course I never told her of that—indeed, we just don't talk about him. I like Launce—I always shall; but I have no hope of ever changing her prejudices—all the Craufords are the same; otherwise my wife is perfect. I suppose there must be some flaw in every thing human."

"I am sure when Mrs. Vaughan meets Cromlin she can not help liking him," Mr. Carstoe said.

Darrell shrugged his shoulders hopelessly.

"I'd be glad to believe it," he answered, "but I can't. At all events, it is better not to talk about him—above all of that wretched codicil; it is the one thing she can not speak or think of with any calmness."

"Of course I never should mention it," replied Carstoe; "it would be an impertinence on my part."

"Oh no; we both look on you as a friend; but it would tease and annoy her."

"And that I certainly would not do for the world," returned the lawyer, his face beaming with satisfaction to hear himself called the friend of these two objects of his highest esteem.

So then Darrell could return composedly to the business affairs.

A few days after this conversation, Elizabeth went to see the pictures—went again and again, for they delighted her. She did become the possessor of one, though it was paid for out of her own means, and she refrained from speaking of Launce to her husband; she had long since perceived that Darrell was always irritated at the mention of the man.

Mr. Carstoe found her in the gallery one morning when he had taken advantage of a few hours' idleness to have another peep at the productions of his favorite. Remembering Vaughan's caution, he was careful to keep the conversation upon the grounds it would have assumed had the artist been an unknown or indifferent person to both. So he was somewhat surprised when Elizabeth said suddenly—

"I forget if you told me that you knew Mr. Cromlin?"

"Yes; I know him well."

"Indeed? I had an impression that he usually lived abroad. You have not been in Europe?"

"Never. I met Mr. Cromlin in California, the autumn after his uncle's death," Carstoe replied.

Every thing connected with old Mr. Vaughan was interesting to Elizabeth; she wondered now that she had asked so little about him of this man, who had been his trusted friend.

"After? Then he was not with Mr. Vaughan either at the time of his death? My husband likewise arrived too late—at least his uncle never knew him: it was very sad!"

"Very sad!" echoed her companion.

"But I remember now," continued Elizabeth; "Mr. Cromlin and his uncle were not friends. It is a pity Mr. Vaughan could not have lived to see how he has grown out of his youthful errors — for he must have done this: those paintings tell not only of genius but patient study—study that has been the habit of years."

"Cromlin is one of the most industrious men I ever knew," returned Mr. Carstoe, warmly. Since she chose to talk of Launce, Carstoe's fidelity to his friendship obliged him to give the young man the full credit that was his due. "Most artists, they say, are spasmodic and irregular about work. Cromlin is as methodical and patient as if he were as dull a plodder as—as I am, say, instead of a genius."

"Did he go to California to study new scenery?" she asked.

"No; he did remain with that view, but it was not the reason which brought him there."

"What, then?"

"You have forgotten, I suppose," he answered, feeling a little uncomfortable. "He hoped to find his uncle still alive; the letter Mr. Vaughan wrote begging to see him did not reach its destination for many weeks. Launce sailed for America, hurried on to California, but his uncle had long been dead and buried."

"He sent for Mr. Cromlin? Then he had ceased to be angry with him?"

Mr. Carstoe bowed. Elizabeth wished to know more of this young man. His pictures inspired her with such admiration that she wanted to believe, if possible, that he had overcome those vices which, always in a vague fashion, she had heard laid to his charge.

"I do not know the cause of the difficulty between the uncle and nephew," she said. "My father seemed to think the subject a painful one to my husband, so I have never asked. Have you any objection to telling me?"

So after all the husband and wife misunderstood each other's avoidance of Cromlin's name. It was all owing to Mr. Cranford's prejudices and errors. No task could be more grateful to the old lawyer than that of righting Cromlin in the esteem of any person who misjudged him. It was doubly a pleasure to attempt the work with this woman, whose good opinion he deemed an honor almost matchless.

It was better that she should know the whole. That very suspicion in regard to the forgery under which he had at one time lain had better be told. Darrell had kept the truth from her because he did not comprehend her feelings, but Carstoe was sure that she desired to think well of her husband's cousin. This story and the final discovery of his innocence by the uncle now dead would help more than any thing to enlist her womanly sympathies in Cromlin's favor.

He told the history in his slow, clear manner —Edgar Vaughan's grief at having believed the boy he loved capable of crime—then Launce's arrival, his sorrow for his relative, his delight in feeling the old man had discovered his innocence —the impenetrable mystery which enveloped the affair—Launce's illness—all the details of his Californian life.

Elizabeth listened, while a strange wonder awakened in her mind.

Mr. Carstoe made, too, certain allusions to the codicil in Mr. Vaughan's will; they came back to her afterward.

Now she was thinking most of another aspect of the affair. Why had Darrell never told her these things, instead of vaguely expressing opinions of his cousin which were calculated to impress any listener with a sense of the man's unworthiness?

Darrell hated Launce Cromlin; she could not help wondering why. And, too, the dead man had meant to make a new will—a more even division of his fortune. Vaughan knew this; but here she dreaded to doubt him; she would ask no questions; it might be an offer had been made to Cromlin and refused.

Still the fact remained that during all these years he had allowed her to think ill of his relative; had taken no pains to set her right—far from it indeed. Elizabeth hated injustice; this was a new shock and pain. Well as she knew Darrell, now it was misery to have this fresh proof of his utter hollowness, the entire sham of his pretense of generosity and justice.

"I fear you are not well; you look pale," Mr. Carstoe said. "I have tired you with my long story."

"Not in the least," she replied, calling back her thoughts with an effort. "I knew very little of Mr. Cromlin; I have always misjudged him. At least I am a just woman; I am glad to change my opinion."

"Then I may tell you honestly that I am delighted this conversation has come about," Mr. Carstoe said, making a ball of his unfortunate gloves, which he rolled between his long hands, while the ugly old face lighted pleasantly. "I do so thoroughly honor your husband that I can not bear to have any estrangement between them! I should not of course have ventured to speak unless you had brought the subject up. I —I—am sure Mr. Vaughan would like to see his cousin, to invite him to the house. Ah, I am very glad there can be no objection, that you feel differently, that—"

He had been stammering dreadfully all through the sentence; now he broke down in hopeless embarrassment, afraid that he had presumed too far in his earnestness.

Vaughan had given him to understand that he feared she, Elizabeth, would desire to keep him aloof from his cousin; this was evident; but what could it mean—what could have been the motive? Oh, it was useless to search for the reason; perhaps only a wish to make her appear in a harsh, unpleasant light. It seemed petty to suspect him of such intentions, but he had so often done similar things to prejudice people whom she esteemed that she could not help supposing he had been actuated by a like feeling in this matter.

Her face changed, and her eyes grew at once stern and troubled. She was glad to leave the subject, once more assuring Mr. Carstoe that she had no dislike toward his friend such as he had imputed to her; that even her vague prejudice had vanished under this explanation.

Then she bade the old man farewell and went away, trying to put from her mind this fresh evidence of her husband's untiring efforts to present her in a wrong light to those about them.

CHAPTER XX.

A COUSINLY OFFER.

ONLY a few weeks later, Launce Cromlin returned to America. He had begun to reap the reward of his years of patient labor, though the ideal for which he toiled was so far from reached that the praise bestowed upon his work affected him little. It was pleasant, because his broad, generous nature yearned to give and receive sympathy, to be in the fullest accord with his kind. It was like scenting the fragrance of sweet flowers, this appreciation which floated his way—nothing more. Only the second night after his arrival, some lion-loving dame, who had known him in Europe, begged his presence at one of those *réunions* in whose pleasantness she found the triumphs which gratified such necessity of success as her nature required—not a lofty form of the longing perhaps, but since she was capable of nothing beyond, one could only demand that she should do her part well, and that she did. It was late when Launce appeared. Of course, he had first to run a gauntlet rather annoying to any man not spoiled by vanity, but he let his hostess have her way, and, fortunately, the persecution was soon ended by the arrival of forest kings of larger growth—a foreign diplomatist, a noted warrior, and the like—and Launce was left free to follow his own devices.

Presently he heard music; a violin and harp were discoursing eloquently in a salon beyond, and he passed on through the brilliant rooms till he reached that where the heavenly voices made a welcome silence. How many among those present kept quiet from a sense of decency, how few from a comprehension of the language uttered, Launce was not misanthropist enough to ask himself; had he been, the golden harmony appealed too subtly to his own faculties for him to have found leisure for the question.

The imprisoned souls in the instruments ceased their melodious cry, and the murmurs of the listeners rose, rather making one feel as if a crowd of gnats were buzzing their commendation of nightingales, believing, too, that the nightingales had sung for their benefit. Launce found that while listening to the music he had been watching a lady seated at some distance; and, though he had not known it while absorbed by the duet, he perceived now that all the time he had watched because she struck his fancy as looking like the personification of the harmony which had thrilled his being.

A woman, young and beautiful—a woman whose very attire showed that artistic keeping and perfection were a necessity to her in the merest trifles. A dress of one of those marvelous new tints for which the eye is as grateful as the ear for a new strain of music. Bands of dark Roman gold, in which were set antique cameos, encircled the white neck and arms, and heightened the glory of her hair—hair that was bronze in the shadows, and took tints like those of a yellow topaz in the light.

Another moment and he was far enough down from the height whither he had followed the spirit voices to see more than the perfection of the dress—the grace of the attitude, the beauty of the face, into whose fairness the music had brought her very soul; he saw that the features were familiar. A second's perplexed wonder, and he knew that he was standing in the presence of the woman whose image had for a brief season cast so lovely a light of dreams across his later youth.

At the same instant a hand touched his shoulder—a pleasant voice said in his ear—

"Launce, old boy! How glad I am to welcome you home at last!"

As he turned and faced the speaker, Cromlin remembered still another fact in connection with this lady—she was his cousin's wife. While Vaughan hurried on with gay, friendly greetings, a quick repulsion shook Launce—a half-determination to check this affectionate enthusiasm by chilling words. Once more his gaze wandered toward Elizabeth. She was speaking now with some one, but her eyes were fixed on Darrell and himself. It seemed to Launce—it was an insane fancy, and he knew it—but it seemed to him that he saw a strange pleading in the glorious face, as if she comprehended the sudden impulse and entreated forbearance. The whole was only a whirling fancy of a second, then Launce allowed his hand to be shaken, and the salutations proper between such near relatives were given and returned.

"I only saw your arrival in this morning's paper," Vaughan continued. "I went at once to your hotel, but you were out; then I met Mrs. Sumner, and she said you were to be here to-night. How nice it is to see you back, and what an amount of work you have been doing lately!"

Just the slightest possible inflection on the final word, as if to express the contrast such industry offered to Launce's past; but Launce was rather amused than irritated thereby.

"One does not like to prove exactly a drone in this busy old hive of a world," he answered, smiling.

"No, no," returned Darrell, "I always knew you would feel that sooner or later. I had faith in you."

The words must have been audible to several persons standing near—people who were their mutual acquaintances. Launce understood perfectly the light in which Vaughan meant to make him appear, but he could afford to smile. Besides, no ill-timed evidence of annoyance under this affectionate patronage could have helped his case. Indisputable facts and the future must prove the falsity of the impression which Darrell desired to produce, and Launce had schooled himself in that most dignified of virtues—patience.

Vaughan's hand still lingered on his arm; he was led forward; they were standing before Elizabeth, and her husband said—

"Greet your new relative—wild man, not of the woods, but of the studio! Queenie, here is this wretched boy, Launce Cromlin, at last! Scold him well for not coming to our house when he landed."

The words were so gayly spoken, that one

needed the most delicate intuitions to seize the covert insolence and condescension lurking beneath the cousinly familiarity. Both Launce and Elizabeth comprehended—it was like a jar in pleasant music—though neither face betrayed any consciousness.

Mrs. Vaughan looked at the new-comer with a gravity which the faint smile about the serious mouth sweetened, but did not brighten.

Still Launce thought the little she said the most delightful welcome he had ever received.

It was the voice which made the spell—so unlike ordinary voices, that sound as if the world's dust had spoiled their ring. This voice of Elizabeth's seemed never to have been used to utter petty deceits or miserable trivialities. It was as different from tones familiar with such verbiage as a cathedral organ kept sacred to the expression of music's holiest utterance is different from a shrill piano in a hotel, degraded by the touch of every common passer-by.

The words were simple enough—Elizabeth was never pretentious or affected. She had even outgrown the fault almost universal among full-idead natures—that of talking over the heads of chance auditors. Best of all, she could listen. Had nine persons out of ten been capable of analyzing their impressions (that rarest gift), they would have discovered that the chief charm of her society lay in this—she could listen.

Vaughan stood by the two for a while, talking pleasantly; then he strolled away into the outer rooms. The harp and violin began another angelic dialogue. When the silvery speech ended, the newly introduced relatives—it seemed odd to both to remember that they were such—conversed for a while longer. But other people came up presently to claim Mrs. Vaughan's attention, and Launce recollected that any further lingering in her neighborhood would be contrary to the small laws of etiquette.

An hour after he met the husband and wife as they were leaving the drawing-rooms.

"We must ask Launce to come and see us," Vaughan said, as he caught sight of his cousin. "Nothing so absurd as coolness between relatives. Besides, I wish to show him that I approve of the change there is in his life; it probably won't last long, but it is right to encourage him."

Elizabeth made no answer; she was not irritated on Mr. Cromlin's account—only ashamed for the man who spoke, who had forced upon her a knowledge of the hollowness of such virtuous pretense on his part. But Vaughan was thinking of his intended patronage—of getting all the glory possible for himself out of his relationship with Launce, under cover of that same condescension, and did not notice her silence.

"Let me see," he continued. "Suppose you invite him for the day after to-morrow—we have some people coming to dinner, you know."

Of course Elizabeth gave the invitation, and Launce accepted it without really thinking of what such acceptance implied. But he did think of it on his way home, and had no mind to be drawn into an apparent intimacy with his cousin, or to become his debtor even for ordinary social kindnesses.

Before he went to bed he wrote a note to Darrell, and told him, not this, but his cold regrets that circumstances (which he did not attempt to explain) compelled him to retract his promise left that intention perfectly evident.

He sent the billet to Vaughan the next morning, and just after he had done so, Mr. Carstoe came to pay him a visit, and to reiterate his satisfaction at Launce's success, in a blundering fashion as comical as it was sincere. Then the good man rushed into praise of Vaughan, having it always in his mind that slight prejudices existed between the two cousins, and anxious to make each respect and admire the other as thoroughly as both in his convictions deserved.

Launce would not pain him by any expression of doubt in regard to Darrell's worth or good feelings toward himself, and Carstoe received his silence as a sign of assent to his own exalted opinions.

In the midst of their conversation some one knocked at the door.

"Come in," said Cromlin, supposing it to be a servant; and Vaughan entered.

"I was in too great a hurry to recollect ceremony," he said in his pleasantest voice. "Good-morning, Launce. Ah, Carstoe, how do you do? I am glad to find you here."

"Good-morning, good-morning!" cried Mr. Carstoe, fluttering and rubbing his hands with delight at this visit, which seemed a proof of his assertions in regard to Darrell's friendship for his cousin.

Launce spoke some pleasant words of greeting, as he might have done to any ordinary acquaintance, but Vaughan hardly waited for him to finish.

"Now, see here, Launce Cromlin," returned he, "that's all humbug, and you know it. You're not a bit glad to see me, and I don't want politeness—I want the truth! I came here on purpose to have an explanation—and I'm glad to find Carstoe—he'll do me justice, if you won't."

"Sit down, Darrell," said Launce, cordially enough, but not paying the slightest attention to his cousin's half-injured, half-affectionate outburst.

"Well," laughed Vaughan, "if I were a dignified fellow, I'd not do it—I'd not come near you; but I can't behave in that way. Now, Launce"—his voice grew serious, even pleading—"tell me outright, are you angry with me?"

"Not in the least," replied Launce.

"Come," said Vaughan, "that's something,

for you always were a frank fellow, at least, and meant what you said."

"That applies to both—to both," murmured Mr. Carstoe, rubbing his hands harder than ever in delight at this prospect of a thorough understanding between his friends.

"Thanks, Carstoe," returned Vaughan.

"I beg your pardon, I didn't mean to interrupt you," said the agent, confused at finding he had uttered his thought aloud.

"I depend on you to help me set myself right with this wrong-headed man," continued Vaughan.

Cromlin perfectly comprehended Darrell's drift, and the light in which his cousin meant to make him appear — impulsive, boyish, hotbrained, perhaps envious and jealous; but he felt no inclination to anger—rather amused, in fact, at Darrell's craft.

"Mr. Carstoe has been sounding your praises for the last half-hour," said he, smiling; "but let me tell you, once for all, Vaughan, you don't need any setting right with me."

"How he says the words!" cried Darrell, petulantly. "Now don't put a fellow a thousand miles off with your stateliness! See here, Launce, I am going into the middle of matters at once. I wish that confounded will had been at the bottom of the sea—"

"There need be no question about the will," interrupted Cromlin.

"Yes, there need and there shall," returned Vaughan. "Launce, you ought to have had more than ten thousand dollars. I wouldn't have said so once, because I should have thought you would only waste it. But if my uncle could have known how you would work, how steady you would become, he'd have left you more."

"Ah," said Launce, composedly, "so you thought me a spendthrift—dissipated. On what did you base your belief?"

"I don't think I could tell," replied Vaughan, with delightful frankness. "I had an idea you were very wild—as a young fellow; just what my uncle thought."

"I never had any reason to think my uncle believed ill of me until the time when he cast me off without explanation," Launce said, still retaining his calmness.

"And I never knew why either till just before his death," Darrell said. "I told you that in Europe. He told me only that he had been disappointed; that he had found you to be utterly worthless and vile."

"But, thank God! all that was cleared up in his mind," Mr. Carstoe broke in.

"Yes, thank God!" echoed Vaughan.

Launce did not speak.

"Fortunately," continued Vaughan, "nobody knew of that sad business except Mr. Sandford: he died just after our uncle learned the truth."

"It strikes me the truth is not known," observed Cromlin. "My uncle was satisfied, yet it was only circumstantial evidence on which he based his conviction of my innocence."

"It's enough to drive one wild!" cried Vaughan. "But it is only the mystery that is a worry now. It's of no use to think; the matter can do you no hurt—will never be heard of; you ought to put it out of your mind, Launce."

"I think I have done so," he replied. "Pray don't fancy that I am making a melodrama of myself—weaving a plot—meaning to devote my life to finding out who was my enemy, and what induced him to work such villainy."

"No, no; I am sure not,". said Vaughan. "Better to let it go! Carstoe and I worried and thought, but it was of no use. Perhaps it was not even an enemy—just some fellow who found himself in a corner, and helped himself out of a scrape by using your name."

"I don't care to talk about it," returned Launce. "It is done and gone. Time may clear the mystery—Time does odd things, you know."

"Ah!" said Darrell, but did not follow up the vague ejaculation, which might mean any thing or nothing.

"Let it go," said Mr. Carstoe. "At least that can not stand between you two."

"Nothing must stand between us," said Vaughan. "I suppose Launce thinks I did wrong in never writing to him after we met in Europe. But my uncle was so violent, so set against him —excuse me, Launce, I must say it—that he prejudiced me too. I admit that."

"It was natural," sighed Carstoe; "you know it was, Cromlin."

"Once for all, Vaughan," said Launce, "there is no need of explanations; I have no hard feelings toward you."

Vaughan rose impulsively from his chair, and put both hands on his cousin's shoulders.

"Prove it," he exclaimed, "by taking not only what the will gives you, but a proper share of the fortune my uncle left. I hinted at this in my letter to you; I was afraid of vexing you by speaking outright, but I must now. Carstoe, tell him it would be right—tell him to put by his pride and let me have the pleasure of doing this. Ah, Launce, be a sensible old boy, and do what I want."

Of course Cromlin felt terribly irritated; he was tempted to push his cousin away and answer roughly. He believed the whole a bit of hypocritical acting; but, after all, he had little beyond vague suspicions of Vaughan. The blotted lines he had found in their uncle's note-book were not a proof. Nothing could be gained by giving expression to his doubts. He felt that Darrell was not true — how far he had been guilty of actual treachery he could not fathom. It was better to be silent; he did not want his life marred by contention or hatred. His doubts did not make him angry; he tried to accuse himself of injustice in considering his cousin a hypocrite, but though unable to do this, it was contempt he felt, not indignation.

Mr. Carstoe was immensely touched by Vaughan's generosity. He knew that it would not be accepted; but it was noble and just, and Cromlin would give him due credit.

"Now speak, Launce—say you will," added Vaughan.

Cromlin looked up in his face; he was sure he caught a sudden gleam of anxiety in Darrell's eyes. He could have smiled to think of the confusion he should cause if he were to accept the lofty-sounding proposal.

"Don't let petty scruples stand between us," said Vaughan. "What do you care if the world does say I gave the money? Are we not cousins? —and who need know?"

It was a little argument that might appeal to Cromlin's pride in case the warmly urged plea should have made him falter in his determination.

"We will have done with this matter too," Launce said. "This question of money must not come up between us again. I have all I want without asking yours."

Mr. Carstoe heard only the quiet resolution in the voice. Vaughan perceived the undertone of mockery, which made him doubt whether his cousin were fully impressed by his generosity.

"At least you will take the ten thousand dollars," he said.

"I shall not take a penny!" exclaimed Launce, sternly. Then he caught firm hold of his waning patience, and continued—"Now we are done with all that; let us talk of pleasanter matters."

"There is just one other thing—it is difficult to speak about," Vaughan began, with a neatly assumed hesitation.

"The codicil?" said Launce. "Not difficult at all; but there is no necessity."

"After all, that was a matter Fate settled independent of every thing and every body," returned Darrell, with a triumphant laugh. Then he added, more gravely, "I need hardly tell you that my wife knows nothing of that sad story—about the check: you understand. I fancy her father—a dreadfully prejudiced old party—gave her an idea you were a very naughty fellow; but with your new line of conduct you'll soon live down every body's prejudices."

His new line of conduct! Whether he commended or was affectionate, Vaughan managed to be annoying. Launce only bowed and held fast to his temper. Mr. Carstoe was too busy now to notice what either said or did. He felt dreadfully guilty toward Vaughan, though he could not repent having told the wife the whole story, since it had been the means effectually of clearing Cromlin in her eyes.

"Come," said Vaughan, "I have not wasted my time, after all, this morning. That note does not count, Launce; we shall see you at dinner to-morrow?"

There was no possibility of refusal now, unless he really meant to quarrel. Launce wished he had left the matter where it was in the beginning —at least he might have been spared Darrell's grand proposals and affectionate demonstrations. But he was not by any means done with the latter. Vaughan remained, talking of his friendship, his willingness to forget, his desire to have faith in the future, till Launce scarcely knew whether to laugh or turn him out of the room, and at last felt rather confused. He almost wondered if he were unconsciously a Prodigal, whom it was magnanimous on Darrell's part to receive with open arms and loudly expressed forgiveness—the sort of forgiveness which holds a full recognition of the culprit's faults, and redounds abundantly to the credit of the forgiver.

Finally Vaughan got round to the subject of his cousin's pictures, and talked agreeably and well. Several portfolios of sketches lay on a table. They began turning them over, and discussing their relative merits as subjects for finished pictures.

Suddenly Launce felt the table shake under a quick movement Vaughan made. He held a sketch in his hands and was staring intently at it. Launce glanced over his shoulder, and saw that it was a scene in water colors that he attempted in California after his illness—Milady in her cell. It was one of the most forcible of Launce's studies—the expression and life-likeness of the woman's face were wonderful.

"Not bad, is it?" said Launce.

Darrell turned toward him with a murderous scowl: his countenance livid — his eyes black with anger—yes, with an absolute dread added, Launce felt.

"Where did you get this?" he asked, hoarsely.

Mr. Carstoe had been seated by the hearth examining a book of engravings. He came up now and looked at the sketch.

"Milady!" he said in a low tone. "Wonderful!"

Darrell controlled himself by a violent effort. Launce perceived it, and laid the sketch down.

"You saw the creature, then?" he asked.

"Yes," replied Launce. "I had an idea— an insane one—that she might be able to throw some light on that secret."

"Ah!" returned Darrell.

"I told Mr. Cromlin she could not," observed Mr. Carstoe, too busy with the drawings to look at the cousins, who were gazing straight into each other's eyes, Launce confused and puzzled rather than suspicious. "She only treated him to a crazy scene."

"Ah!" Darrell said again. "What did you think of her, Launce?"

"She seemed to me half mad: I could make nothing of her talk."

"Her visits to Mr. Edgar Vaughan were undoubtedly an attempt to make a way for a burglary," Mr. Carstoe said.

"No doubt of it," Darrell replied.

He began to speak of other matters, and presently took his leave, gay and sparkling to the last.

After Vaughan had gone Mr. Carstoe fell into one of his states of embarrassment. Launce knew that he had something to reveal. It was his way in such cases to flutter and bounce, and behave generally like a fly hitting his head against a window-pane.

It was only to confess to Launce that he had told Mrs. Vaughan the story of the forged check —that is, as much as was known; old Mr. Vaughan's first anger and his final recognition of his nephew's innocence. .

"I could see she was prejudiced," he said; "it was her father's doing. I couldn't help setting it straight. I suppose, considering the codicil and all, you know, it was a delicate subject to Vaughan—don't you see?"

"Oh yes, I see," returned Launce wearily, then tried to rouse himself. "It was very good of you, Carstoe. I am much obliged all the same; I am not likely to see much of my cousin or his wife."

"But you feel that he means to be kind; that he is friendly, as I told you he was?" demanded Mr. Carstoe, anxiously.

"Oh, of course — of course. Vaughan has about the most charming manners of any man I ever met."

So Mr. Carstoe was enabled to think that the slight clouds which might have separated the two had been swept aside, and he rejoiced in the knowledge, privately designing to relate the whole interview to Mrs. Vaughan, because he considered it greatly to the credit of both cousins.

CHAPTER XXI.

READING THE LETTER.

So Launce went to the dinner and called twice at the house afterward. He met Vaughan and his wife almost every night at the parties and receptions from which he could find no reasonable excuse for staying away, though Launce was scarcely more of a society man than artists in general.

Elizabeth's life, or rather she herself, reminded him always of a beautiful strain of music which some one insisted on playing in the wrong key, and that not from ignorance, but cruelty.

They talked a great deal together, always upon general subjects, of course; but Launce's perceptions went deeper into the reality of her existence than those of the world about. He saw beyond the veil of resolute composure which

her associates called coldness and haughtiness. To him, in spite of its beauty, her face was the saddest he had ever seen. The eager longing, the great want, the bitter disappointment, the struggle for patience—they were all visible to his sight. The subtle sympathies between their natures, which Elizabeth herself did not as yet realize or reflect upon, enabled him to look straight into her soul through the disguises which pride and wisdom alike taught her to bring to her aid.

So a fortnight went by. There came one evening a note to Launce—an invitation to another of Vaughan's dinners. It was a little thing, but somehow the thrill of pleasure with which he held the billet and gazed at the lines Elizabeth's hand had penned roused Cromlin for the first time to a perception of his own state of mind.

He did not go out that night, though he was due at a house where he would have met Elizabeth. He stayed resolutely at home, because he was forced now to recognize the reason of the new delight he had of late found in such scenes. The result of his meditations was a resolve to cut short his stay in town—to depart at once.

Elizabeth's face haunted him, the memory of the old dream had returned, and its golden light rendered her still more beautiful to his sight. So Launce knew that the prudent and only right course would be to go away; and he was not a man to hesitate for an instant after he perceived the truth.

At present he could conscientiously assert that it was the recollection of his bewildering vision which caused him unrest; but if he lingered he might later be obliged to admit a more humiliating fact, and feel, too, that the fresh trouble had been brought about by his weakness in having remained in spite of his own convictions that he ought to go.

The time would come—must come—when he could meet this woman and recollect only that she was his cousin's wife, in no way connecting her with the rudely dispelled dream which during a few months had lifted his life into fairyland—a dream which, perhaps, must always haunt him with a vague feeling of disappointment, as though he had lost some precious treasure, without which existence would lack a certain fullness and perfection.

But now he must go—go without delay. He called the next morning at Vaughan's house to make his farewells. A resolution once formed, he did not dally: he was going away on the same evening. He tried first to write a note; a good many notes were attempted, in fact, but none suited him: either they sounded stiff or contained polite falsehoods; and he so wanted to see her once more—just once. He was prepared to be inexorable with his weakness, but it was scarcely in human nature to have resisted the pleasure of that last visit. Darrell had gone out, but the servant thought Mrs. Vaughan was at home. While Launce waited in a reception-room, the notes of a piano rang softly down from the apartment overhead, marvelously sweet, as the voice of that much-abused instrument really is when some rare player succeeds in rousing the soul hidden under the cold white keys. The music ceased. Presently the man came back: Mrs. Vaughan would receive the visitor. When Launce entered the chamber—half library, half morning-room—where Elizabeth read and worked, she was standing near the piano. He could have sworn, when the tones struck his ear, that her hand awakened them. She moved forward to receive him with a light in her eyes which he comprehended had no connection whatever with his arrival. The interrupted melody was still whispering to her.

"Unless you will be good enough to go on," he said, after the first salutations, "I shall wish I had stayed down-stairs—I could hear you there."

"I had found a book of masses and fugues that I picked up in Germany," she answered. "I will play you something else if you like. I keep these for my own private delectation, because I can seldom persuade any body to be fond of them."

"I know the collection," he said, turning over the pages. "It is a rare old book; how fortunate you are to possess it."

So she played and he listened; then they wandered into talk suggested by the music. The picture of Launce which Elizabeth had purchased hung near the piano-forte. It gave him a keen feeling of pleasure to see that something of his had found a place in her favorite retreat; but when she spoke of the painting, he did not attempt any small compliment to that effect, such as one would have paid an ordinary woman.

He knew intuitively that the room was a haunt she loved, and its arrangement her own design. The walls were hung with gray of a somewhat severe tint, which suited Launce's artistic eyes, because it brought out the pictures so admirably. Of these there were not many, but every painting was a gem—a couple of veritable Titians among them, and a copy of a Raphael by Giulio Romano, preserving the spirit of the master as only he could do. The purchase of these three works had been Elizabeth's sole girlish extravagance. A gallery in Venice was being denuded of its treasures during one of her visits there, and she had not been able to resist these, though the cabinet Madonna alone was almost priceless, for many art-judges declared it an original Raphael, and had fought numerous battles in regard to the matter.

But in spite of the gray hangings, and the size and lightness of the apartment, it looked neither sombre nor cold. The carpet was like a bed of leaves that the frosts have turned to a golden brown; rays of vivid color were scattered here and there; on the walls, against shields of bright-tinted velvet, were placed rare cinque-cento plates and Etruscan cups. There was antique carved furniture, which had been brought from some ancient palace across seas, covered with pale silk that had flowers and quaint devices woven over it in blue and silver. Rare vases stood upon the tables; a glorious marble nymph lived in a recess at one end of the chamber; stands of odorous blossoms brightened every corner: the whole place looked not only luxurious and picturesque, but home-like and womanly.

A room that was a poem, Launce thought; as plain to read as any written expression of its owner's pure tastes and lovely fancies could have been. And the woman herself, sitting there in the midst, with her pearl-colored robe falling about her in statuesque folds, filmy lace and ribbons of bright color lighting it up—every attitude she assumed as graceful as a picture—the sad, proud face glorified by the lambent eyes and the dark splendor of her hair—hair such as the old masters delighted to paint, which altered in its hues with every movement of her head, just as her eyes changed color with each passing emotion.

Those eyes! he could not tell if they were brown or blue. Black he would have said when the long lashes partially veiled them for an instant—then positively golden in their radiance as they shone out full again, luminous with some sudden thought. He did not know that few people ever saw her look as she did while their pleasant conversation took its course. It was so seldom nowadays that she met any one who cared for the subjects upon which she liked to talk; so seldom she could sufficiently forget the disappointment and emptiness of her life to grow visionary and enthusiastic, as had been so easy in the old time; but Launce's earnestness and enthusiasm affected her unconsciously.

From music and Launce's "St. Agnes's Eve" to reminiscences of foreign lands, to the books which treat of art and kindred subjects, and Cromlin ventured to fall foul of sundry great critics, whose dogmatic assertions most people consider themselves bound to accept for gospel.

"You are very bold," Elizabeth said with a smile. "It quite takes my breath away; though several times, in Paris and London, I have met those men, and felt a rebellious desire to contradict the magnificent theories they poured out with a sort of pitying condescension for the weak intellects of their listeners."

"It seems to me absurd," Launce said, after they had pursued the topic a little further, "to talk about gradations in art—I mean for one set of art servitors to rank itself above another;

for instance, that the historical painter should put himself on a grade above the delineator of landscapes, or the sculptor above them both."

"Now I think I do not catch your meaning," Elizabeth answered. "What is your creed?"

"I should style Art a grand soul calling to men out of the infinite; all forms of art, as we term them, only the voices of that soul wherewith she strives to lift men toward the light—up to the beautiful and true."

"Yes, I understand," Elizabeth said. "Music, sculpture, painting, poetry—Art's voices calling to men."

"In certain ways all blend. We say of a statue, it is a poem; of a poem, it is a picture; of a picture, it is a dramatic scene; of a great actor's effort, that it is the picture and poem put into action."

"Yet the latter critics rank the lowest, because it is so ephemeral in its influence."

"They might as well say a flood of sunshine is lost, or that the world has forgotten Apelles, because the actual works themselves have perished."

"And you admit of no independent forms of art?"

"The thing seems to me an impossibility. Art must remain one and indivisible. The expressions or voices of the great soul unite in harmony — no voice perfect in itself — needing the whole to make the diapason complete. Leave out a single tone—music, poetry, acting, what you will—it is like an organ with one key silenced."

"Yet some particular form — expression, if you please—appeals much more strongly to each man's mind than the others, as a rule."

"Naturally enough. No human being can take in the glorious whole in its completeness; that would be to comprehend the spirit which controls the voices; it would be comprehending Infinity."

"And so many mistake the voices altogether!"

"Of course. There are numberless false voices shrieking through the world. Men rush after and believe in them, as men believe in false Christs, too deaf and blind to distinguish between the false and true. There are so many pretenders—in literature, sculpture — men who think of money only, or who arrogate strength to themselves, forgetful that they are but the mediums through which Art makes herself audible."

"I think the promulgation of your theory might bring about a little desirable humility among the servants of the great God," Elizabeth said.

Launce laughed.

"I just remember," replied he, "I have been talking as dogmatically as the critics I presumed to assail."

"There is a vast difference between assertion and the expression of earnest conviction," returned Elizabeth.

"At least it is very civil of you to offer me that loophole of escape," Launce said, laughing still.

Presently a clock in the adjoining room warned Launce that he was making a visit of unconscionable length, for he remembered already to have heard it strike the hour—a few minutes before, it seemed to him, time being so entirely a relative term.

"We shall have the pleasure of seeing you to-morrow night?" Elizabeth said, as he began to express his contrition for the long stay.

Her words brought back the reason for his call.

"I had forgotten that I came to bid you good-bye," he answered, and the words sounded very sad in his own ears. "I leave town this evening. I must beg you to accept my excuses, and make my farewell to Vaughan."

"You do not return this spring?"

"No; certainly not this spring."

"I am sorry," replied Elizabeth, frankly.

Launce only bowed. His lost dream-world looked perilously fair, the reality cold and gray. He seemed to catch a glimpse of the two, both visible, though separated by more than the breadth of a universe, and this woman standing between, in her glorious loveliness.

Then he recollected that just at present his business was to speak certain fitting words, and take his departure. It was like going away from the last gleam of radiance wherewith that dream-realm had flooded his soul.

So there came a brief silence. Elizabeth remembered once, in an out-of-the-way part of Spain, entering a beautiful garden, and spending the whole morning there, while she awaited the conveyance which was to carry them forward on their journey—a spot she was not likely ever to visit again. Perhaps for that very reason the lovely haunt had always kept a prominent place in her recollection.

Whenever she thought of it she could fairly hear the murmur of the fountain as it plashed into its marble basin, the cooing of the doves as they fluttered about it, the humming of the bees among the orange-flowers, the patches of shadow under a group of cypress-trees—could catch the glory of the distant Sierra, and the marvelous white clouds that drifted across the opal sky.

She thought of the spot now, and mentally compared this hour spent with Cromlin to that day. She was not absolutely regretting the fact that they were not likely to meet soon again or often, yet for this reason the morning was a thing to treasure as she did the memory of the Spanish garden amid whose beauty she should never wander any more. Then both became suddenly aware of the silence, and began speaking of ordinary things. As Launce took his hat from the table, some careless movement scattered a pile of photographs which Elizabeth had put there to arrange in an album.

Launce picked up the pictures with a laugh-ing remark upon his own awkwardness; then he perceived a portrait of his uncle among them.

"Is it like?" Elizabeth asked, bending her head to see which had attracted his attention, as she noticed his face grow suddenly grave.

"It was taken not long before his death; Mr. Carstoe showed me one," Launce said. "I had not seen my uncle for five years. He must have changed a great deal. The face had aged, and it used not to look so careworn—so hopeless and despondent."

He sighed, remembering how great a share the black clouds which had risen between him and his relative had in causing this alteration. Elizabeth comprehended what was in his mind, and said gently—

"But he knew at the last—he had this great happiness. You must always remember that."

"Yes," he replied.

But he was thinking of the sympathy there was between him and this woman. Few and brief as their meetings had been, it was already a marked and pleasant thing, this ability that each possessed to divine the feelings and fancies of the other. Then he remembered that he had no right to dwell upon this thought. It must be put away along with all the host of bright chances which his last dream had held — the treasures never touched, the happiness never to be grasped, the whole round of golden possibilities that lay buried in the irrevocable past, with those saddest of human words engraved upon their tomb, "It might have been!"

"Every thing connected with his memory is very dear to me," Elizabeth continued, softly. "I like to talk with Mr. Carstoe about him, to make myself feel that I really knew him."

"You would have loved him dearly, I am certain," Launce replied.

"I have a letter that he wrote me," pursued Elizabeth. "I suppose you did not know that. Such a beautiful letter! I could not speak of it to any other friend, because it holds a secret which was his; but I should like you to see it."

Again Launce only bowed his head. He was too much surprised—more than that—too much annoyed, to answer. That she could speak to him of the strange arrangement the dead man had devised whereby his two nephews were to have equal opportunities of winning her regard —to him, the loser—showed a lack of tact and delicacy of which an ordinary woman might have been guilty from frivolity, vanity, or coquetry; but coming from her, the speech gave him a positive shock.

Elizabeth had opened her writing-desk and taken out the letter.

"I always keep it here," she said, "it is so loving and sweet. It seems to bring me so near him."

Still Launce did not speak. She looked up. He had grown pale; his mouth was set hard and stern under his drooping mustache. There was not only grief, but an expression of disappoint-ment, of absolute reproof, in his eyes, which start-led her.

"I beg your pardon," she said; "I am afraid I have pained you. I thought you might like to see the last letter he ever wrote. It was thoughtless of me to forget that just for this rea-son it would be—"

She hesitated, and Launce said coldly—

"Not for that reason."

The color rose in her cheeks; she was hurt rather than angry. Darrell or Mr. Carstoe had told him of the romance of Mr. Vaughan's life which this letter revealed, and he thought it in-delicate for her to speak of the matter. Such judgment—above all, the betrayal of it—was not only unjust, it was an impertinence. She felt a sudden pang of disappointment in her turn —the man's nature was not what she had sup-posed.

"I see you think I have done wrong," she said, and her voice sounded at once tremulous and proud. "We do not think alike. To me the little romance is very beautiful and sacred. I did not even suppose you knew—my husband or Mr. Carstoe has told you—"

She stopped again. She was terribly annoyed; almost angry enough now to have left him, had he not been a visitor in her own house.

"I believe we misunderstand each other, Mrs. Vaughan," Launce said, coloring too.

"Yes—we do—since you can find any impro-priety in my speaking of the cause which makes your uncle's memory so dear to me," she an-swered. "Under other circumstances he would have been simply my husband's relative—a man entirely unknown to me. But the fact that he loved my mother makes me feel—"

"I did not know," he interrupted quickly. "You are misjudging me, Mrs. Vaughan—in-deed you are."

"Excuse me," she exclaimed, impulsively. "I told you I had a hasty temper—I have been positively rude."

"No, no!" he said.

In truth he did not know what to say; he was utterly bewildered. One thing was certain: she had been thoughtless—she had not shown indel-icacy or a want of tact. She was thinking only of the romance which connected her dead mother and his uncle in her mind—so full of it that she did not remember the terms of the codicil or the share given to him (Launce) therein.

"Yes, I was rude," she continued, with the rare smile that made her face almost childlike in its sweetness. "I forgot that you do not know me well—that your uncle's loss is always a grief and pain to you—that to hear an almost entire stranger laying a claim to his affection would naturally give you a sort of odd, jealous feeling."

"But indeed it is all a mistake," he said, earnestly. "I know nothing about the romance; tell me, please."

"You shall read the letter if you like," Elizabeth replied. She glanced down the pages as she spoke. A new pain, in which her companion had no share, struck her heart. She was wondering if the dead man could know how yielding to his plan had utterly wrecked her happiness—if he could see the weariness, the disappointment of her life. How could he be at rest up in the heavenly light knowing? Yet if those gone forward into the eternal sunshine do not perceive what befalls their loved ones on earth, how can they be near, as we believe they are?

Then the trouble died; Faith brought an answer. They might see; they might sympathize, and yet be at peace; for they behold what we are ignorant of—God's plan. They understand how our present tribulation is for the soul's development, and worketh out an eternal weight of glory.

The light came back to her eyes—a look of inexpressible patience and trust fairly transfigured her mournful loveliness.

Of what was she thinking?—where had her soul gone? Launce gazed and wondered, but he could not ask.

How petty and miserable it had been in him for one instant to hold her capable of an unworthy thought or act. He had no part in her past; she had never seen him before her marriage. It was natural she should forget that the codicil (whose terms were detailed, of course, in the letter) could ever in any way have affected him. To attempt explanation was an impossibility; no conversation upon that subject could ever take place between them: she was Darrell's wife—Darrell's wife!

His head whirled; the hand he was extending for the letter trembled so that he let it drop upon the table. Elizabeth, still full of her fancy, did not observe him. He wanted to break the silence —to talk—to get away from the wild thoughts that stung. He meant to ask for the letter; in his pain and bewilderment he asked instead—

"May I see the codicil?"

As soon as the word was uttered he realized what he had said, but she betrayed no confusion. She only looked surprised as she answered—

"I never saw the codicil; the will, you know, was drawn up in California."

"I think my head is quite astray this morning," returned he, trying to smile.

Then he became so utterly confused that he added—"I meant the letter. You must wonder whether I am more boor or idiot to have mentioned the other."

She was still more surprised at what she took for embarrassment, and said laughingly—

"Oh, I am not an engaged young lady to be nervous about the matter."

But it was difficult to speak lightly of that request of the dead man which had brought her such misery. Had she been a happy wife the romance might have formed a pleasant enough story to discuss with her intimates—but now! Before the speech fairly ended, Launce saw her brows contract—her face suddenly lose its color. All he could think was that she, for the first time, remembered the dead man had meant him also to be considered in that bequest.

"I had forgotten—"

Then she stopped short after this beginning. She had intended to say she had forgotten to add that the letter gave no mention of the codicil. Of course Launce interpreted the unfinished sentence to mean that she had forgotten he had any part therein.

She did not end the phrase. She wished to leave the subject, for fear it might call forth some complimentary words—some expression of pleasure that his uncle's wishes had been realized. She did not want to hear such speeches and be obliged to utter falsehoods in answer—say things which would imply content and happiness. Her heart was too sore for such deceit: so she paused.

But it was unfortunate that she stopped, because Launce felt bound to answer what to him her words implied. His confusion was gone — he felt cold and tired—but he was calm enough.

"Under other circumstances it would have been a matter I could not mention," he said. "I never thought—nor did you, I know—to speak of it—but—"

She did not really hear his words—only fancied that after all he was going to utter the compliments —the congratulations; and she said hastily—

"No, no!" Then got her senses back enough to remember that a refusal would be a sort of tacit confession that her marriage had proved a mistake and disappointment. "I shall let you read the letter now."

He took it from her hand and read the pages, while Elizabeth sat thinking of all that lay between her and those bright Italian days when she had first perused those lines.

"I loved your mother," Edgar Vaughan wrote. "Your father won the prize I coveted. As I look back over my long, dull life, I find always that love and disappointment standing out the most important events in my whole past. It has been my dream that your mother's child might become connected with me by ties which should bring you close to my side. If life is spared I shall tell you these things with my own lips. If my pilgrimage is near its end, I desire that at least you should read this confession of my hopes and wishes. I am ill and suffering now—perhaps even this letter will not sound clear and coherent. Two weeks ago a great joy came to me—only yesterday a new blow struck my heart. I am too old and broken to bear either happiness or pain.

"In the trouble and confusion of my thoughts it is a rest to pen this letter. I write with your mother's picture lying beside me—with those beautiful eyes smiling at me like a promise of peace that awaits beyond this weary world. They tell me you resemble her. I know much of you, my child, though you may scarcely have heard my name.

"This is what the foolish old man has dreamed, dear Elizabeth. I hope to see you my nephew's wife—I hope when spring comes to be able to seek you with him. But if that last great pleasure is denied me, one day he will give this letter to you himself, after he has told you his own story. For he will love you. That certainly is as strong in my mind as if a voice from heaven had whispered it. Your mother, when she comes to me in my dreams, has never failed to utter that promise. How good and noble he is you will perceive for yourself. The tale of his youthful struggles—his patience—his fortitude—you will learn from him.

"It is a conviction in my mind that he will win your affection. I try to believe that I shall live to see you happy together; but if that may not be, I want this brief record to prove how dear you are to me—what the tie is that knits my soul to yours. Perhaps I shall never tell even him the secret of my past, but when I am gone, and this letter is in your hands, you will tell him, and you will both remember that I see and enjoy your happiness."

While Launce read, Elizabeth sat occupied with bitter reflections. His blundering mention of the codicil had roused a score of painful memories. Of course, when Darrell and Mr. Crauford spoke of it to her, they explained its conditions as referring only to Darrell himself. Elizabeth had expressed a wish that after their marriage the two hundred and fifty thousand dollars might be wholly devoted to charitable purposes. Vaughan had promised this—had arranged with her the precise uses for which the money should be employed. When they returned to America, and she found that he did not resume the subject, she spoke of it. At first he put her off—the property was somewhat encumbered; after a while that portion should be used as she desired. But when he began to throw aside his disguises, he openly laughed at her folly in expecting him to carry out a pledge which he called the romantic nonsense of a thoughtless moment.

Launce read the letter to the end, growing colder and colder—with anger now—a stern, hard indignation against Darrell Vaughan.

His suspicions, that even in this matter Darrell had behaved treacherously, became a certainty now. The entry he had found in his uncle's old note-book took a fresh significance. That entry had been penned on the very day of his paralytic seizure—the letter to Elizabeth bore the same date. He spoke of a great happiness which had come to him two weeks previous—that was the news of Launce's innocence. Only the day before that writing he had received a new blow—the entry in the journal proved that the pain was in no way connected with Cromlin.

A sudden light struck Launce's mind. The nephew Mr. Vaughan had spoken of in that letter was Cromlin himself! In the will which had never been discovered—the will which Mr. Carstoe believed had not, after all, been made—Mr. Vaughan proposed no division of his fortune between his nephews. Mr. Carstoe thought such had been his intention—Launce knew that it was not so. Something had decided him to leave Launce sole heir: it was of Launce he wrote to Elizabeth.

Cromlin knew this as well as if the dead man's ghost had come back and uttered the fact. How had Darrell managed?—how deep was his guilt? Useless to question; in this world there would never be an answer.

Launce cared nothing for the fortune—Darrell should have been welcome to it. But this woman—this glorious, peerless woman, this reality of his dream—swept out of reach of his life by Darrell's falsehood, Darrell's skillfully woven web of deceit and sin!

Launce could have cried the whole truth in her ears as she sat there before him in her pale, sorrowful beauty. The devils that tempt us all at times fought fiercely in his soul, bidding him do this. He recognized Elizabeth's unhappiness—he knew, without a word of explanation, just what her life was. She had been hurried into this marriage by her father's illness; by her tender feeling toward the dead lover of her mother in that mother's girlhood; deceived by Darrell's specious eloquence, his charming manners, his noble promises; and she had lived to know him as he was, as Launce knew him—vile, base, degraded.

Yes, to tell her the whole truth, that was his impulse. He shut his soul against the insidious whispers—he held fast to his reason, and conquered. He believed in honor—he believed in God. He could neither insult this woman by the revelation of his love, which any explanation of the truth must be, nor could he even ask her to sully her soul by pity for his pain—his terrible loss.

He must get away; he could not trust himself longer in her presence. He must not see her again until time had given him strength to support the burden which this day's knowledge rendered so much more difficult to bear.

He arose—he felt that he almost staggered—he knew there was a terrible revealing in his face.

"I shall say good-bye now," he said.

Elizabeth held out her hand; he hesitated—he dared not touch it. His hesitation made her look up: she saw his face, pale, shaken with trouble and anguish.

She could not understand, but she could not question him. Something—that letter—memories of his uncle—what, she knew not, had shaken him to the very soul. His gaze was on her, mournful, despairing—as she had seen, in the dismal vigils grown familiar, her lost hopes stare at her with their dying eyes.

She longed to speak some words of comfort, but in her uncertainty as to what had caused his pain, she feared hurting him still more.

"Good-bye," she echoed, softly.

He touched her hand with his cold fingers, and went quickly out of the room.

CHAPTER XXII.

BACK TO THE CODICIL.

ELIZABETH sat there a full hour after Cromlin left her; then Mr. Carstoe was shown into the room.

He had taken advantage of a leisure morning to go searching among all the hot-houses for a Californian plant of which he had spoken to Mrs. Vaughan. He found it at last hidden in the depths of a botanical garden among the fastnesses of Brooklyn, and brought it away in triumph.

He was amply rewarded for his trouble by Elizabeth's thanks and admiration of the glossy-leafed thing, but his mind was a good deal distracted by a chance meeting with Launce, who had been on the way to visit him and say farewell.

"Mr. Cromlin is going out of town," he said, dolefully.

"Yes," Elizabeth replied; "he was here to bid us good-bye. His departure is sudden, I think."

"Very," said Carstoe. "He is going to visit some friends in St. Louis, and means to wander on into the far West for the summer. If I go back to California in the autumn, I shall not see him again."

"He is a great favorite of yours."

"Yes; I rank him and your husband side by side. I feel honored by their goodness in liking me," he said, in his stiff, jerky way. "And you like him now, Mrs. Vaughan; I did not overrate his pleasant ways?"

"I like him very much," Elizabeth answered. Mr. Carstoe rubbed his gloves into a ball at once—a sure sign of satisfaction with him. Indeed, he felt his tongue pressed against the roof of his mouth, and only just saved himself from clucking with delight, like a hen or an indecorous school-boy, growing quite red with dismay at the idea of having gone so near such an atrocity in Mrs. Vaughan's presence.

"It has been so pleasant to see him here at the house on friendly terms," the lawyer continued. "I'm sorry he is going. It must have been a sudden idea. He said nothing about it when I saw him yesterday, and I thought he looked pale and worried."

It had not been her fancy then, and the change had come upon him during their conversation. She feared that she had distressed him by the sight of his uncle's letter.

"I have had no opportunity to tell you something which happened a few days ago," continued Carstoe, presently. "I knew your husband would not, because it was so much to his own credit—indeed, they both behaved admirably, as one might be sure they would in any matter."

"Mr. Vaughan has told me nothing," Elizabeth said.

"He went to Cromlin, and offered to share their uncle's fortune—was earnest and splendid about it—wasn't it fine?" cried Carstoe, enthusiastically.

"And Mr. Cromlin?"

"Oh, he would take nothing; but he admired his cousin's behavior, and appreciated it. They will be fast friends always now, those two," Mr. Carstoe said. "So many men would have behaved differently. But Cromlin is so frank, so large-minded. The two cousins are a great deal alike, in fact," he added, with a delightful faith in his own powers of comparison and ability to read character.

"I believe the will left Mr. Cromlin ten thousand dollars," Elizabeth observed, speaking more to keep the old man from fearing that she lacked interest in the topic than for any other reason.

"Oh, yes; he'll not take even that though; but I did not mean about the money. In the other matter plenty of men would harbor resentment, or try to feel themselves ill used."

"What other matter?"

In his earnestness Mr. Carstoe had touched on a point which he felt himself unjustifiable in alluding to. He grew confused again, and colored till his bald head shone.

"I beg your pardon—I do beg your pardon for mentioning it; and Mr. Vaughan had cautioned me—he said the codicil was—did—had always—"

Here he broke down completely, and sat such a picture of embarrassment, done, too, in as violent a purple as ever the most insane pre-Raphaelite employed, that Elizabeth would have pitied his trouble had she not been too much startled by his words to notice it.

The codicil again! The recollection of his allusion in the picture-gallery, disregarded at the time, flashed upon her; Cromlin's agitation—annoyance even—of the morning, came back too. The codicil! How far was she in the dark? What possible part or interest could Launce Cromlin have had therein? Something there was which she did not in the least understand. Mr. Carstoe had said that in Cromlin's position many men would have harbored resentment against her husband.

Dared she question further? If the answer were to bring some new proof of Vaughan's duplicity — though she could not imagine how this would be possible—she should feel guilty at having done any thing to render the fact patent to her mind.

Her face changed so painfully that Mr. Carstoe was almost out of his senses from a fear that he had hurt or annoyed her.

"I wish I'd been born dumb!" he exclaimed, penitently. "Mr. Vaughan would never forgive me—quite right, too, after his caution! He told me the subject was unpleasant to you, and here I go blundering at it full tilt, like a bull at a red cloth!"

"I am not annoyed," Elizabeth replied. "I can not explain; but indeed, Mr. Carstoe, I am not vexed with you."

There was a secret—a secret which Vaughan had cautioned this man to keep from her. She did not wish to hear another word; it could serve no good purpose.

"You would be vexed if you were not an angel!" cried poor Carstoe, and then shuddered with horror at his own boldness, becoming so utterly bewildered that he stumbled on from bad to worse. "I only wanted to show you how just and honorable Cromlin is. Many men would have hated Vaughan—thought he took an unjust advantage—tried to think so, at least —for of course there would have been no ground to think—"

Another breakdown. Elizabeth was only wondering how she could avoid further revelations without strengthening his dread of having offended her. But to Mr. Carstoe her silence was the surest confirmation of his fears, and he stammered—

"Now just when you had learned to like Launce (of course I've no business to call him so), I go bringing these stupid things up! Such a noble fellow! Why, when the news of the marriage came, he had only the kindest wishes for you both. Of course, he would have gone to Europe long before that, if his illness had not prevented. He never told me so, but I gathered it from what he let fall."

Then he stopped again, and panted and puffed, and Elizabeth's eyes, fastened upon him full of trouble, only dazed him entirely, and on he dashed, perfectly incapable of checking his own speech.

"There seemed a fate in it, did there not? As if no wish of his uncle's in regard to him were to be carried out. The new will not drawn up—then Vaughan won the prize for which the codicil meant both nephews to have a chance; but of course Launce could have none, since Vaughan was lucky enough to gain your regard."

He could only choke and gasp now—he was past further words. In his whole life Mr. Carstoe had never spoken so fast nor blundered so horribly.

Elizabeth's limbs trembled under her; a tumultuous throbbing at her heart sent a dizzying pain to her head. She had seized the full import of Mr. Carstoe's broken words.

Even when he wooed her for his wife, Darrell Vaughan had acted a false, treacherous part. The codicil had been entirely misrepresented to her. Scores of incomprehensible remarks of her father's came back; she understood them now: they confirmed her dread. Then she felt shocked at her own suspicions. She told herself that she had harbored doubts against her husband until her judgment was positively perverted. She condemned too harshly; she was too ready to think evil of him. She must hear more; a clear explanation might show her that she was at least unjust in the present instance. Whatever had been done, it could not be so vile and treacherous as the idea upon which she had fastened.

"Mr. Carstoe," she said, suddenly.

He half jumped from his chair, still staring at her open-mouthed, as he had been doing for several seconds.

"Oh, I do beg your pardon—I do!" moaned the wretched man.

"But there is no need," she replied, able still to keep her voice steady. "Pray don't worry yourself any more. See, I want you to explain that codicil fully to me. It is not only that I wish to show you I am not annoyed, but I would like you to go over all the details."

Her composure brought him out of his maze, and after a little he grew less vivid in tone (to use an artist's phrase), and was able to speak without tumbling his words over one another.

"I dare say you remember the codicil," Elizabeth said.

"Yes, indeed—word for word; it was so odd, you know, that it made a strong impression on my mind. But of course you saw the copy I drew up for Mr. Vaughan?"

"Still, you shall go over it, if you please," was all she said.

With his legal memory for dry facts, stimulated by the romantic interest which the case had always possessed for him, Mr. Carstoe was not likely to be at fault in recalling the codicil. He gave the exact terms as if he had been reading them aloud.

Elizabeth listened to the end, then knew that in her effort to soften her judgment of her husband she had put the possibility of doubt beyond her power. She was not past the capability of suffering where he was concerned: she suffered now, as only a pure, upright nature could have done.

She could not wish that she had remained in ignorance of the truth as to this or other matters.

Better to see her idols crushed into the dust than bow before false deities. To her mind, devotion to a false god must be enervating and pernicious, insensibly leading the soul from the right path. How much her stern judgment might have been softened had her heart cried out in defense of the poor clay image from which the shining gauds that wrapped its deformity had one by one been torn, I can not tell. But when she married, Elizabeth's feeling for her husband had been hero-worship. The first perception of the difference between the real man and her ideal came too soon for her whole heart to have joined imagination and enthusiasm in that cult.

She suffered keenly enough, but she was not broken-hearted. Her pride was lacerated, her faith stricken, her sense of womanly purity outraged; but the ache was over the disappointment, the loneliness, the desolation, for she craved love and sympathy; it was not the death-like agony of a heart which bursts under its burden. Suddenly a new thought started up in her mind: the recollection of the words she had this morning spoken to Launce Cromlin. He must believe that she had known the contents of the codicil. What could he have thought of her mentioning it? She understood now his annoyance and surprise: he had believed her vain, coquettish, unwomanly. She felt her face burn with shame and mortification; but a deeper pang followed, for presently she recollected the after-conversation—the change in his manner. He had comprehended that she only knew what the letter expressed, that the real significance of the codicil had never been explained. This was almost worse to bear than to have had him deem her silly or unfeminine; for now Darrell Vaughan's baseness was not a secret confined to herself—Cromlin had divined it.

But she heard Mr. Carstoe speaking, and hurried back from her painful reverie.

"Thanks for your patience," she said. "You are right, Mr. Carstoe; your friend is a very generous man."

"Then I haven't vexed you and made mischief after all?" he cried, ecstatically. "I am so glad you like him—appreciate him as he deserves. I was sure you would."

This cool, practical man of business—the most commonplace and trusty of mortals in that respect—was, I have told you, an old romance-weaver in his way. He would have kept a professional secret even in regard to an enemy with unfaltering caution; but he could not resist the impulse to share with Elizabeth a little secret of another kind. He wanted by every means to soften her heart toward Launce; besides, he was so carried on by the romance of the thing that he could not repress a betrayal which could harm no one, of which Cromlin would never be made aware.

He winked and blinked so portentously that Elizabeth perceived he had something else on his mind; but it was something agreeable, she could see by his face.

"You look as if you had something pleasant you would like to tell me," she said.

"Yes—I would; only it is a bit of a secret."

"But you know we women are said to like secrets," she answered, cheerfully.

"In a way it is," he continued; "nobody told me—it was only by putting two and two together that I made it out."

"Yes," she answered, not interested, but wishing to be good-natured and set him thoroughly at ease after his recent embarrassment.

"You see—only think—Cromlin had seen you before your marriage, Mrs. Vaughan!" said Carstoe, eagerly.

"Seen me?" she repeated, in surprise.

"Yes; in Switzerland—at Montreux—the very day he got the letter recalling him to America," returned Carstoe, delighted with his idyl. "You had fainted; he carried you up a hill. You must remember—there was a young lady with you."

He waited for her to answer.

"I remember," she said, rather coldly. "I did not know it was he."

"No, of course not; that made it so romantic," and Mr. Carstoe fairly beamed. "He had to hurry off to catch the train. Well, poor fellow, after all his haste he was weeks and weeks too late. Just fancy; in New York he saw Vaughan pass in a carriage, but could not make him hear—and Vaughan was driving down to the steamer."

She wished he would stop; she could not have told why the whole story pained her, but it did.

"I told you how ill he was," pursued Carstoe, in his voice of pleased mystery. "During his fever he used to talk in a wandering way about that meeting. He remembered the codicil too; and I know he had dreamed as young men will—it was natural."

He waited for an assent, but none was audible.

"When he was better, I showed him a picture of your mother I had found among his uncle's papers—wonderful resemblance to you—and—and—he kept it. Then, just as he was getting able to travel—meaning to go over to Europe, you can guess what for—came the news."

Carstoe paused to shake his head and sigh. "Poor fellow; I carried him the paper myself—I had no idea what was in it. So then he changed his mind very suddenly, and stayed a long while in California. How hard he did work! And that's all," concluded Carstoe, drawing a long breath. "Quite a little romance, was it not?"

Elizabeth had no opportunity to reply. The door opened, and Vaughan entered.

"Ah, Carstoe," he said, "just the man I wanted to meet! Queenie, dear, I have scarcely seen you to-day! You look rather pale; you stop in the house too much."

He walked up to her chair, stooped, laid one hand caressingly on her shoulder, and kissed her forehead. She neither shrunk nor spoke, but a chill that was like the coldness of death smote her very soul: the touch of his lips seemed an absolute pollution just then.

Mr. Carstoe sat silently watching the two, and again a vague suspicion crossed his mind to see Elizabeth so quiet and unmoved under her handsome husband's evidences of affection. But Vaughan did not appear to notice any thing peculiar in her manner.

"Poor Ribston died suddenly this morning of apoplexy," he said. "I shall have to go into harness sooner than I expected."

Ribston was the member of Congress whom Vaughan would have succeeded the next winter in the natural course of events; but now he would be obliged to go on to Washington for the remainder of the spring session, which might "drag its slow length along" for several months to come.

CHAPTER XXIII.

A LAST APPEAL.

In this age of railways and telegraphs, elopements of any sort are rather prosaic matters, and so Nathalie La Tour discovered when she began to carry into execution her plan for escaping what she considered her husband's insupportable tyranny. But at least there was the secrecy and excitement to give a glow of romance, and Susanne proved an invaluable coadjutor, enjoying the idea of the flight as much as if she had been a youthful heroine going off to join her Romeo.

The first thing was to gain time, so Nathalie took to her bed, because as Susanne in her wisdom observed—

"Arguments with men are just breath wasted; they can carry one off whether one scolds or cries; but they can't take one, pillow, nightgown, and all, and that is where we have them, the saints be praised."

Nathalie offered no further opposition to her husband's will. She was sullen and taciturn, acting so well her *rôle* of injured wife that a more acute person than Monsieur La Tour would have been deceived. The journey to Languedoc was deferred for a week. Suffering as he was in body and mind, the old man pitied Nathalie sincerely, and strove by gentleness and consideration to soften somewhat the verdict he had pronounced. He shut himself up in the house; he could not bear to meet his neighbors' eyes—to feel that they were commiserating him; worse

still, were condemning Nathalie. He was stung to the soul by this disgrace which had struck the life he had kept always upright and pure; but, terrible as this was, he thought more of Nathalie and her future than of any thing else. The man's ideas ran in a narrow channel, restricted by the prejudices of long years; but he thought vigorously enough, and his perception of justice and right was more independent of his prejudices than is that of many men who pride themselves on their broad views and theories in regard to social freedom.

He trusted that time and proper influences might work a great change in Nathalie—teach her the falsity and wickedness of the doctrines she had espoused. His ideas of the ways by which this teaching was to be effected were utterly erroneous, but he walked by such light as he had. His sister was a woman upright and gentle, whose whole life was a psalm of goodness. He really believed that her example must have its effect on Nathalie, quite forgetting that to his wife's mind psalms had no meaning. Then he had great faith in the advice of a certain Curé who resided near his sister; the books which had helped to disorganize Nathalie's judgment were to be kept out of reach, a course of reasonable literature substituted in their stead.

For himself, nothing could be done. Nathalie did not love him. He could no longer court deception here. For months trust in her affection had been slowly dying out of his heart as the sun fades from a landscape, leaving it each hour colder and more dreary; now the last ray was gone.

While he meditated over the means by which Nathalie might best be aided, and prayed for strength to bear the burden that seemed heavier than his age-weakened shoulders could support, the wife was arranging her flight. She had a considerable sum of money by her; the little income she inherited from her mother was received from funds in England—her husband could not touch that; and her books had brought in enough; so that her fancy built glowing hopes for the future.

She wrote to a friend in Paris—a literary woman, whose acquaintance she had made during the memorable spring spent in the enchanted city—one of the band of modern philosophers whose practice went beyond Nathalie's most daring theories. Even in her first excitement it was hard for Nathalie to give up Paris, and there would have been her rightful sphere; life any where out of its charmed influences must be dull in comparison. But there could be no safety for her in France; expatriation was the price she must pay for liberty.

Her letter received a speedy answer; Susanne managed its reception with the art of a *soubrette* in an old comedy. The philosoheress was ready to assist her young friend by every means in her power. She had at once seen a publisher in regard to Nathalie's new book. Best of all, she and a party of friends were just setting off to spend the autumn and winter in Italy. Nathalie must join them; break the yoke under which her soul had so long groaned; seek freedom and companionship of natures able to comprehend her exalted needs—natures eager for the regeneration of mankind and the glorious light of liberty, undimmed by the blight of old prejudices and worn-out religious creeds.

These glowingly expressed theories were all real and beautiful to Nathalie—a gospel to which she clung as tenaciously as a blind man to some vain support which he has convinced himself is his one refuge. She would defer her journey to America for a time. In Italy she should have leisure to translate her novel into English, and make arrangements for its publication in London and New York. Her name would go far and wide; she should have the world at her feet.

But Susanne had no intention of leaving her own or her mistress's wardrobe behind, and she contrived, by the assistance of a friend in the village, to get the principal part out of the house, and sent on the road to Italy.

Monsieur La Tour was so completely exhausted that for a few days he could only lie on his bed in a darkened room, wondering what error in his life had rendered necessary the terrible punishment which now befell him. In the case of another, he could have believed it only a trial sent for the further purification of the soul, but he was too humble to accept so hopeful a view in his own case.

One morning he awoke to know that a fresh blow had fallen—Nathalie was gone.

At Genoa she found her friends awaiting her, and together they journeyed down to Naples. Nathalie's book was published under her own name; the translation she made would appear in England and America in the spring. She fancied herself on the road to fame and fortune, and for a short time believed that happiness was at last reached.

But that winter was not all sunshine. The female philosopher and her band were disappointed in Nathalie; she was good at theory, but beyond this she did not go. The women grew venomous because she took no lover, the men spiteful. Still there was the *éclat* of enrolling this young, lovely, and, in certain ways, gifted creature among their band, and the consolation of having other people believe that her daily life was in keeping with the laxity of morals in her books.

On the whole, Nathalie was glad when spring took the entire set back to France. She had fears of being made a prisoner if she set foot on Gallic soil, so the only course was to reach Ostend by Switzerland and Germany. The journey was a hard one, and Susanne very troublesome whenever she became fatigued. Nathalie began to think that even the exalted career of a new-light teacher was not free from small cares and vexations, and it had been just the trifles in her former life which had seemed so unendurable.

London appeared a howling wilderness to her eyes, and she hated it with a feverish energy, which only French blood can feel in its full extent toward the damp shores of Albion. A few hangers-on of newspapers came about her, a few theatrical people; but there was nothing brilliant —no ovation: not even women to envy her the admiration of the stiff Englishmen she detested. Nathalie felt existence to be as bitter as ever she had done in the dreary house in the French provincial town.

She began to yearn for America. Since Paris was a heaven closed to her, New York looked the next brightest spot, and she waited impatiently for certain money matters to be arranged so that she might sail.

It was late in June before any fresh excitement came to her, and as Nathalie only counted life by sensations, the time seemed very long. But one morning a packet of newspapers was brought in. They were several numbers of a semi-monthly journal that had been started in New York, called the *Bohemian*, avowedly the representative of a little set in that city who believed in their own importance, and had not the slightest doubt they were destined to revolutionize the world. Nathalie found long reviews of her books—numerous personal notices—descriptions of her beauty—bits of romantic incident supposed to have been actual experiences in her girlhood—a poem or so which chanted her praises —and eager assertions that America was the field for her genius.

She laid down the papers actually convinced that it was the voice of the whole vast continent which she had heard. At last fame had come! Yes, there was her field of operations—her Elysium! She was a recognized priestess at length, and innumerable worshipers were eagerly calling her to appear and occupy the shrine they had erected in her honor. There were letters too— letters from men and women who belonged to the newly established coterie of Bohemians. There were epistles from youths in poetry and madder prose, declaring the ardent love with which she had inspired them. Their souls called her soul across the vasty deep, and so on; the plain English for which would have been that, as the worshipers possessed no money for the voyage, she must float withal their reach if she desired to test their devotion.

In addition to these eloquent communications, she received a letter from the leading proprietor of the *Bohemian*. He proposed that she should come to America, buy a share in the newspaper, and assist in conducting it. Between her books and her editorial influence she would be able to accomplish the grandest work that the age could offer any woman.

The newspaper itself reiterated this last assertion, declaring that she was the true apostle for whom the world had been waiting—her genius the immaterial divinity for which true souls had sighed so long!

In truth, he was a sufficiently shrewd man this chief owner of the lever that was to move the universe. The journal could not live longer without assistance, and Nathalie's moneyed success had been as much overrated as such successes usually are. This philosopher, with a practical vein under his theories, and a keen eye to interest beneath his floating locks and dreamy brow, saw clearly all the advantages of electing this handsome woman (who could come with a well-filled purse in her pretty fingers) the anointed Queen of the Bohemians. That was the title the newspaper offered her: it sounded very sweet in Nathalie's ears as she repeated it over and over.

She must answer the letters at once! Her brain was so dizzy and her hand so tremulous that she could scarcely write. This was the happiest hour of her life—she had found her throne and crown!

The first thing was to secure the newspaper. The long-headed philosopher had spoken of the necessity for a speedy acceptance if she decided to join in the great work. There was an American woman, with talent, money, and influence, eager to be chosen as sovereign, and she had a clique to support her claims. But to him, the long-haired philosopher, and to all the furthest-sighted of the band, there could be no doubt—they wanted Nathalie. Still (here he showed talent which his printed writings seldom exhibited) a certain portion of the contract money must be forthcoming without delay, in order to crush the hopes of the New York literary lady and her faction. He explained clearly how the affair could be arranged through a publishing house in London.

But eager as she was, Nathalie's usual lack of continuity of thought caused a new idea to strike her in the midst of her reply. She must write to the poetess who had honored her with an epistle. What she considered an apt quotation from Mrs. Browning suggested itself, so she preluded her rhodomontade with—

"How dreary 'tis for women to sit still
   On winter nights by solitary fires,
And hear the nations praising them afar."

Then she paused to read the newspaper tributes again, wishing for an auditor to share her triumph. Susanne would be better than nobody! At least Susanne would express unqualified delight, even if she did show it by standing on one foot and uttering incoherent phrases.

But when she rang she found that Susanne had gone out; the lodging-house servant said a gentleman had just called. Nathalie supposed it must be some literary acquaintance—perhaps a person connected with the press, who could get mention into London journals of this success which her genius had achieved. Indeed, it might be a friend who had already heard of her triumph, and had come to offer congratulations. She bade the woman show the guest up at once. The door opened again; Nathalie looked down the dimness of the dull, gray room and saw her husband standing there, like a ghost among the shadows.

She uttered a cry of fear. Her first impulse was to flee. He had found her; she might be dragged back to the purgatory of her old existence just in this crowning moment of success.

"Nathalie," he called, in a slow, tremulous voice; "do not be frightened, Nathalie."

"I'll not go back!" she cried. "I'll kill myself first! Never, never; don't come near me; don't try to touch me!"

He had advanced half-way up the room, but he stopped at the sound of the wild words and the sight of her frightened face.

"I have no power over you," he said; "think a moment, and you will remember that."

She sat down in a chair, trembling still from the effects of her terror, but able to recollect that out of France he had no authority whatever. Then a sudden anger took the place of her fright; but as she turned toward him with insolent words on her lips, they died unuttered.

Somehow, to look into his face was like looking into the possibility of a life which made her hopes and dreams show shrunken and deformed. The idea was too vague for her to seize it—indeed, her vanity and her warped mind would have rendered this impossible; but the thrill shook her—only long enough to check that cruel speech—then was gone.

He stood there with his head a little bowed, his eyes fixed upon her. Oh, the piteous hopelessness of that glance! Every thing in his attitude and appearance aided the inner voice which had tried to make itself audible to her blinded soul—the vision which had sought to lighten the darkness where she groped; but she was deaf and blind alike to all.

"I don't know what you want; I can't see why you should come!" she exclaimed, fretfully.

Had she ever contemplated this meeting, she would have fancied herself equal to the emergency; proud, haughty, like a priestess confronting a heretic who had come to attack her altar. But she was taken by surprise, and could only wail out a peevish remonstrance.

"I think you should know, Nathalie," he answered gently. "Whenever I could learn where you were I have written."

"I never read one of your letters," she broke in; and again was conscious that she had not assumed the tone fitting her dignity as the acknowledged apostle of a new faith, and paused.

"I wish you had done so," he continued. "I am not eloquent, but you might have seen my heart, perhaps, and felt that at least I wanted to help you."

"Help me—you!" she cried, scornfully.

She saw him tremble a little.

"May I sit down?" he asked. "I am getting old, you know, and the long journey has tired me."

She ran and placed a chair for him; she could feel sorry to see how pale and worn he looked, though her pity roused no pang of remorse. Her intense egotism precluded the possibility of her seeing that she had erred. All faults were on his side. She was a victim, not so much from his deliberate causing as from the tyranny of ancient creeds and laws—but she was a victim.

"I wish you had not come; it would have been so much better not!" she heard herself saying in the same fretful tone, wondering at the same time why she felt childish and weak, and could get at none of the grand phrases with which she would have expected to overwhelm him.

As he seated himself, he took her hand—gently, but so firmly that she could not release it, and, looking in her face again with his sorrowful eyes, said—"Nathalie, do you ever pray?"

Straightway there rose before her the memory of her mother's last hours, that awful death-bed, the dying woman's agony of supplication and fear, her calls upon Virgin and saints—and Nathalie shuddered.

He let her hand go; she got to a seat near, and sank into it. She turned her gaze from his face—it was an effort to do so—and fixed it on the letters and newspapers. Her courage came back; her spirit rose indignantly at this temporary assertion of power by the old superstitions and mummeries in which she had no faith.

"To live for the beautiful and true is prayer," she cried; "to keep the soul free from superstitions; to reach forward to the ideal, to the living centre of magnetic influence. But you can not understand; why do I speak?"

"Let us, then, talk of things in which we can understand one another," he answered.

Nathalie shrugged her shoulders. She wanted to make a comparison about some dull, slow, creeping thing presuming to imagine it could comprehend a bird soaring and singing above its head, but she was still sufficiently softened by the wave of emotion which had touched her to refrain.

"I made the journey on purpose to see you, Nathalie," he continued. "I should have gone to you in Italy when I heard you were there, but I was very—I was not just fit to travel."

She knew that he had been prevented by severe illness; but somehow to feel this irritated her, as did his checking himself in the mention of it through consideration for her.

"I wish you had left every thing as it was," she said. "I can not think why you came! I shall never go back; you ought to have known that. Go back? As well ask a skylark not to fly when it has learned to use its wings. There, it is all said now; do not let us talk of it! I have no wish to say harsh things, but I will not be reproached or lectured; I am free."

She felt herself very magnanimous to speak with such mildness.

"Will you let me tell you why I came—exactly what thoughts were in my mind?" he asked, gently.

"Oh, tell me, then," she replied, with a sort of fretful resignation.

"All those weeks when I was prevented seeking you I had time to think," he continued in the same subdued, patient tone. "You are very young, Nathalie. Many things will look so different to you when you reach my age."

Nathalie shivered, only at the idea of growing old. The thought of age was hateful to her. It was dreadful to look at him and remember that some time she must be thus — bowed, wrinkled, gray-haired. She called it cruelty on his part to force such reflections upon her mind. "The idea of coming all the way from France to talk of that!" she said, angrily.

"Only because it has to do with what I want to say. Don't be impatient, Nathalie! I am slow; I do not explain myself well. Let me try to tell what I mean in a few words."

He was about to make the offer against which his priest had warned him as dangerous for his own soul—what the Curé called condoning sin and crime; the offer which his sister had implored him to relinquish, because if he succeeded in the errand he would only bring new and harder suffering upon the last years of his earthly life. But plain and commonplace as he was, narrowed as his mind had become from living in the little round which education and example had taught him to consider the only safe one, Monsieur La Tour could rise above these restraints, because his love for Nathalie was strong enough to thrust self aside. He paused, not because the opportunity to plead his wishes brought up any selfish consideration, only to try for words which should be most likely to influence her.

"Well?" cried Nathalie, sharply. She had glanced back at the newspapers and letters. She longed to return to her pleasant task. It was too bad to have her time wasted; to be dragged down to earth by such antiquated talk when she was eager to soar off into the realms of transcendentalism and latter-day philosophy.

"If you would be content to stay with me—to let me be like a father to you. Listen, Nathalie"—for she had made an impatient movement to rise—"I do not mean you to go back to the old home—we would live where you chose. I would only ask you to wait awhile—to study—to think before you publish any more books—to examine well the doctrines which seem so beautiful and broad to you—before you help further to promulgate them—"

"Stop now?" she broke in. "Why, do you know what position I have already won for myself—my books translated—my name famous? Read these!"

She ran to the table, seized the newspapers, and brought them to him.

"I don't need to look at them," he said. "Oh, child, child, can you not understand! This is not fame."

She smiled at him with a grand compassion; she could not even be angry. He was utterly blind, earthly, soulless. Outside the crime of having married her, he was a good enough plain creature. She had shaken off her bonds—she was free! She could afford to look leniently down on him from the height to which she had risen.

"You ask impossibilities," she said. "I could not wait if I would! Destiny has pushed me on—my work lies before me—I must do it."

"God have mercy on your soul!" he murmured.

"Bigot!" retorted she, and went back to place her precious papers upon the table. She stood resting one hand upon it, and glanced toward him. Nathalie could undergo numerous emotions and changes in an instant. She felt sorry for him, because he must be deprived of her society —that seemed, indeed, a terrible punishment for his error in having made her his wife. She must have married somebody and been wretched—it was her destiny—else how could she have successfully preached against the miseries of wedlock? She recollected a verse of English poetry about suffering and song and crushed grapes and wine, but it was not worth while to quote it to Monsieur, whose comprehension of the language was limited to the utterance of a few phrases whereby man, the animal, makes known the needs of his stomach.

And Monsieur looked at her and realized how helpless he was to fulfill the mission which had brought him, and with his usual humility blamed himself. If he could only speak as he ought— if he could only find eloquent words which should be like a sudden light whereby she might see the dangerous precipice on whose edge she stood! His own pain he could bear—he was old and ugly and dull—it did not matter! But this creature, so full of youth and loveliness, it was awful to think of the future she must bring upon herself, the harm she might do others.

Most men in his position, cheated of their love —horrified by the distasteful notoriety brought on their name—would have had their opinions too warped by passion not to give the harshest

color to Nathalie's conduct, believing that in theory and practice she was alike depraved. But this man, narrow as many of his ideas were, did not do this; he was capable of the heroism of putting himself out of the question; and when a human being can accomplish this, his judgment of a fellow-creature is a very different matter.

"If I could say what I ought!" he exclaimed, suddenly.

She shrugged her shoulders with impatience. Why would he not go, and let her alone? Her mind was full of herself again; these letters to answer, this brilliant offer to accept, the first taste of fame to indulge, and here he was dragging her down to commonplace discussions, just as if she were still a slave, sitting in the old prison of a house in France, and liberty only a dream.

"We can neither speak a language the other is able to comprehend," she said, magnificently. "I have no desire to say unkind things, but I wish you would go away, Monsieur."

He rose.

"Yes," he said, "I weary you—I have always wearied you. Wherever I have been wrong, Nathalie, I beg your pardon."

"Never mind," she answered; "I do not blame you now. In the daily irritation and misery of my life, when the chain that bound me galled my soul always, I was excitable and impatient; but that is all over."

"Oh, Nathalie!" he cried; "think — only think! Remember what the world will say and believe of you; what it says of your associates, of those women who—"

"Haven't I told you that it does not matter?" she broke in. "We expect persecution and misapprehension from the common herd—all reformers must. Why that very faith to which you cling—worn out as it is—did not its first proselytes struggle even to martyrdom in its support? Do you think I am less brave?"

This unconscious blasphemy was terrible to the poor old man. He held up his hand, saying sadly—

"Not that, Nathalie! Say any thing else you will, but let my religion alone."

He saw now that the case was hopeless; he could not move her in any way. His sister had been right; this visit had no effect but to bring him a new pang—a keener suffering; he had better go. It was a horrible alternative, but he had no choice. His own misery, the utter wreck she had made of his closing years, he could have borne, but his agony went beyond personal feelings. He had struggled for Nathalie's soul against the tempter and been worsted. To him it was not only that in her madness she risked honor and reputation here, but he believed in eternal happiness or eternal punishment! He dared not think; he could only shut his eyes and pray to God to send a ray of light before it was too late.

"If you should ever want me, Nathalie," he said at last, "you will know where to find me. You will come?"

"Oh yes," she replied, indifferently. "I do not dislike you. Now that we are free from one another I can judge you more leniently."

"In God's sight we can never be free from one another," he said, solemnly.

"Rank nonsense!" exclaimed Nathalie. "If you would only read my last book. There is no answer to my arguments if you go by the light of reason; but you would not! You only see by what you call faith, and there is nothing that so enfeebles the judgment! To doubt is the right, the loftiest attribute of the mind!"

He would go. To linger only increased his distress for her—always for her.

"One thing more," he said. "I have arranged with a banker here to pay you an annual sum in addition to your income; I have made it as large as my duty to others would permit."

"Oh, very well. One must think of money as one must of other coarse needs of the body," she replied, grandly.

She stood waiting for him to go; she did not want to be softened by further appeals.

"And is this farewell?" he asked, after a brief silence.

"Our paths separate unavoidably," she said. "I have a great work before me; I can not be trammeled in any way."

"Oh, Nathalie, Nathalie!" he cried, in a voice sharp with agony. "Come to me, child; come! For your soul's sake—by your mother's memory —by that death-bed, I implore you to come!"

She shivered and grew frightened anew, but this weakness only angered her.

"Let me alone!" she exclaimed. "I am not a child to be scared by such folly; let me alone! I will not go back; I will not! Say another word and I shall hate you as bad as ever! I'll do any thing, no matter what, just to make it impossible for you to come any more with such silly offers."

"You are right," he answered; "it is useless to trouble you. I am going now, Nathalie; I am going."

Again he gave her a long, yearning look; he loved her so! He had gone through his youth, past middle age, and love had never come to him till he met this wayward girl; and now she had broken his heart and was endangering her own soul.

His gaze troubled her; she wanted him gone. It was not that she was too hard-hearted to pity his suffering, but she could not understand it. He was old—love could have no meaning to him; and to expect to fetter her genius and youth down to his petty life was an insanity fairly ludicrous.

"Farewell, Nathalie," he said; "farewell."

He held her hands for an instant; she heard his lips murmur a broken prayer; then he went slowly out of the room, looking wistfully back to the last, as if there still lingered a hope that she might relent, might bid him return; then the door closed.

Nathalie cried a little from nervous excitement, but the sight of the papers and letters soon restored her composure, and she forgot him in her engrossing occupation.

After a while Susanne entered in a state of intense excitement; she had seen Monsieur in the street, had hurried round a corner to escape, and flew home to warn her mistress.

"But he has been here," said Nathalie. "Bah! Don't weary me with such trifles, Susanne! Listen to this; let me translate these reviews and letters. Oh, Susanne, I am famous at last!"

CHAPTER XXIV.

COME TO LIGHT.

AUTUMN was come again.

In the spring Elizabeth had gone to Washington with her husband, when he took his seat in Congress. Some measure, momentous for the time, whatever might be its effect on the future about which Conscript Fathers talked so eloquently, was occupying the attention of both Houses. Vaughan's first speech was in regard to this bill, and proved a great success.

Try to shut her eyes as she might, Elizabeth could not help knowing that Vaughan fought against his convictions in the interest of his party; but she presumed to pass no judgment. She saw other men, called good and great, doing this daily. If such action was a necessity of politics, she could only feel that another illusion had vanished—another barrier been set up between her and any possibility of sympathy with her husband's career.

Vaughan worked hard, and Elizabeth was aware that his recourse to stimulants had begun anew. At this time she felt obliged to speak, but the result was only what she had feared. Darrell, enraged at her discovery, punished her in a thousand painful ways for her "prying insolence"—the name he gave her attempt at expostulation.

The summer was spent at their country-seat, with the house always full of guests. In September Elizabeth went to visit her old aunt, Janet Crauford, and Darrell received an invitation to attend the Chief Magistrate and Cabinet upon one of those "presidential tours" which have grown into a custom of late years, and prove more expensive than a "royal progress" under their republican name.

Toward the middle of October the husband and wife again met at their house in town.

It was hard for Elizabeth to be patient in these days. Life had closed about her so circumscribed, so narrow, that she felt like one shut in a cell into which there could only enter just air enough to prevent suffocation. Disappointed in her dreams—thwarted in her aims—not even allowed to make a rightful use of the fortune which she regarded as a stewardship—bound to the man through whom these and other troubles came, and forced into the knowledge that greed and avarice contended in his soul with darker vices, which were dragging him so rapidly down that soon the hollow fabric of his reputation must crumble, and he lose the one restraint which could keep him from deeper degradation—the approving verdict of the world.

She endeavored to learn the lesson of not looking forward—sought to live each day by itself; trying to see how she might best use this discipline for the development of her own soul. But this was a pain too; it seemed so petty thus to concentrate life upon herself; it was sad to think she had not been considered worthy to be of use in her day and generation.

She was young still, and grand dreams are so natural at her age!

She visited her hospital—attended to the wants of her poor—went into society, since her position rendered this a duty—and so time wore on. What would come after? Over and over she asked herself this question—asked it as hopelessly as the young do when existence closes about them, dull, purposeless, and gray, and no efforts, no struggles, can show a path toward the light. But she tried to bear—tried to be patient.

At least her home was just now untroubled by angry words or contentions. Vaughan had returned in one of his most genial moods. He was immersed in business, but the men she saw about him at this time gave her a hope that for a while, at least, his habits of dissipation were kept in abeyance by the engrossing interests of politics and the numberless other schemes in which he was engaged.

Launce Cromlin also came back. He meant to sail for Europe toward winter, and various matters demanded his presence in New York before setting out on his journey, from which he might not return for years. Vaughan went to see him, insisted on being friendly, inviting him to the house with such urgency, and causing Elizabeth to add her persuasions, that Launce could not refuse without downright rudeness. The quiet and hard work of the past months had helped him to overcome the feverish restlessness which beset him in the spring. He could meet Elizabeth, confident that no wrong thought, no weak grieving over thwarted possibilities, troubled his mind. Then, too, he was going away; half their lives might pass before they should meet again.

Mr. Carstoe was still in town, but he had near-ly completed the business which Vaughan had intrusted to his charge, and would soon return to his post in California. His society always cheered Elizabeth, and was a great pleasure to the solitary woman. She had grown attached to the quiet, elderly man. He was so honest, so straightforward, so earnest and good in his simplicity, that his visits came like a breath of fresh mountain air into the close, vitiated atmosphere of her life.

Then Vaughan was called away by business. Some difficulty had arisen in regard to the title to a tract of land which he owned in Virginia, and it was necessary to attend personally to the matter.

He had been gone ten days, when one morning a letter from him was brought to Elizabeth as she sat alone in her favorite room. He seldom wrote nowadays during his absences unless there were a necessity therefor. She opened the envelope and found a hastily written note, beginning with a decorous "Dear Queenie," and going at once into the business details she had expected to find—following by good wishes for her health, a hope that she was amusing herself, and winding all up with the information that he was "her affectionate husband."

There was food for mournful meditation in the epistle, just from what it lacked. Whatever may be the circumstances which have caused the estrangement, the desert is, indeed, reached when husband and wife are only kept together by a community of worldly interest, a regard for the decencies of life, or a sense of duty: perhaps they suffer most who are detained by the latter bond.

But Elizabeth had often enough thought of these things: she was glad that just now she lacked leisure. She hastened to put the letter out of sight and attend to the request it contained. Darrell needed certain deeds and papers; he hoped that by aid of these the people might be induced to compromise and prevent the necessity of a lawsuit. He told her where she would find a number of keys, which boxes she was to open, the engrossing whereby she would recognize the documents. To read the directions one would have supposed Vaughan the most methodical of men; but Elizabeth had too often had experience of strange lapses of memory on his part to be much surprised when, after patient search, the papers were not discovered in either of the trunks he mentioned.

These boxes, along with a variety of others, were in a light closet off Vaughan's dressing-room. It was possible she might find the papers in some other trunk. Several of them were not locked—their contents unimportant; nothing, at least, like the documents he had described. Then she perceived an old packing-case; this was locked; none of the keys she had brought were of use. She went to her chamber, took a bunch of her own keys, and at last succeeded in opening the trunk.

It had belonged to old Mr. Vaughan; his name was on the lid; there were various packages of papers in his writing. Every thing connected with the dead man's memory was precious to Elizabeth. She turned over the contents with a carefulness which, had her husband seen, would have called forth a contemptuous smile for what he would have termed a bit of sentimental folly: perhaps it was such; but it is not a bad thing for any human being to possess the capability for that sort of romantic sentiment.

There were numerous deeds among the great mass of documents, pamphlets, and similiar matters which filled the trunk, but those Darrell wanted were not there. She had taken every thing out; there was a heavy writing-desk and other articles not easy to lift, but she called no assistance, knowing how great was her husband's dislike to have any one meddle with his papers. Nothing but an urgent need could have induced him to commission her to search among them. But the deeds were not there. She put the contents back, and was closing the trunk when she perceived a little box that had fallen out; it was tied about with a cord; she had no hesitation in opening it because it had belonged to old Mr. Vaughan. It might be some relic that would be pleasant to keep. She had discovered a variety of trifles—a seal, a carved paper-cutter, and the like, which she meant to retain. So she opened the box, raised the cotton which lay next the lid, and the gleam of jewels caught her eye. There were a number of unset diamonds, a stud, a ring, and a large emerald. Elizabeth knew enough about gems to be certain that these were valuable; the ring struck her fancy from its quaint setting. She put it on her finger, and took the box to her own room.

Her maid chanced to enter at that moment, and raised her hands and voice in horror at her mistress's appearance.

"Only look in the glass," moaned Margot; "only look."

Elizabeth did look, and could not help laughing: her dressing-gown was decorated with festoons of dust, and her face adorned in the same fashion. She hastened to dress, that she might write to Darrell and tell him how unsuccessful her search had been; but before she began her letter there came a telegram. She was not surprised on opening it to find a message that Darrell had discovered the papers among those he had taken with him.

These lapses of memory, which would have been the merest trifles in the case of another, had a painful significance to Elizabeth when Vaughan was concerned; for she knew their cause, and she knew too that they, like other symptoms which proved the baleful effects of the poison to which he yielded more and more, were

increasing rapidly. It was so dreadful to do nothing; to sit still, and see the man rush on to destruction—and yet she was powerless; pleading or expostulation from her only made him worse.

They came to tell her that visitors were below. She went down to receive them; spent a half-hour in that frivolous talk which is so inexpressibly wearisome when one has heart and brain full of anxieties and cares.

Just as these guests were taking their leave, Launce Cromlin was announced. He did not often visit her, but it was always a pleasure to see him come; it was a little lifting of the dull mist which closed over her life to talk with Launce, to see some one who lived in the higher world of work and art in which her dreaming girlhood had been spent.

She was playing to him, and he standing by the piano; chancing to look down at her hands, he noticed the ring, which she had forgotten. Later he spoke of it, and she drew it from her finger, and handed it to him.

"It is very quaint, is it not?" she said.

"Yes," he answered. "It is an old Spanish setting; you may occasionally find such in California; they came, I suppose, from Mexico—nobody knows how old they may be. I suppose you picked this up in Europe?"

"No; it belonged—at least I think it must have belonged—to your uncle."

Then she told him about her discovery of the box of jewels—went to her room, and brought them for him to look at. They both arrived at the same conclusion in regard to the stones—that old Mr. Vaughan had purchased them in California; they had been put aside, and had escaped Darrell's notice, if, indeed, he had ever examined the trunk.

"Probably Mr. Carstoe sent that trunk because he saw it contained papers and deeds," Launce said, "and neither he nor Vaughan ever examined its contents carefully."

While they were still looking at the gems, a servant came in with a message from Mr. Carstoe—he wished to know if Mrs. Vaughan could receive him. Kindly as Elizabeth treated him, he was always careful in his humility not to trespass upon her goodness. This cordial friendship she showed him was the most beautiful thing that had come into his commonplace existence for years and years. He felt as if a lovely flower-garden had suddenly opened beside the narrow, wearisome path he had so long trodden with patient feet, and he could not enough marvel at God's graciousness in allowing the dullness of his way to be thus brightened.

As Elizabeth moved forward to receive him, holding out her hand with her customary friendliness, he caught sight of the gleaming circlet upon her finger. Its resemblance to that ring which was connected with one of the most painful episodes of his life was a mere chance, of course, but it set him thinking of that time. Between the reflections thus called up, and the usual confusion which beset him on entering any feminine presence, he became so nervous that Elizabeth began to talk on the first subject that suggested itself, and Launce good-naturedly tried to aid her in restoring the shy man to composure.

Elizabeth was absently turning the ring about on her finger, and the action reminded Launce that he still held the open box of jewels in his hand.

"See, Carstoe," he said, "what Mrs. Vaughan found this morning among some old papers of my uncle's."

He moved to Carstoe's side, holding out the box; a ray of sunlight struck the gems, and their radiance flashed full in the startled eyes of the old man.

"And this ring," Elizabeth added, drawing the jewel from her finger, and adding it to the contents of the box.

At the same instant a servant entered: Mr. Vaughan's lawyer had called, and desired to see her at once. She made a hasty excuse, and left the room without noticing the look of horror that had paled Carstoe's face, or the amazement with which Cromlin stood regarding him.

"What on earth is the matter?" asked Launce, as the door closed. "Are you ill? You're as white as a ghost."

Carstoe extended his trembling hand, and took the box. He held it for a while, staring down at the gems, which flashed out rainbow hues in the sunlight, speechless and immovable. Launce spoke again, but he did not answer—evidently did not hear. Presently he let his hand sink upon one knee, as if the tiny box had been some heavy weight which he could with difficulty support. Launce stood still and watched him, utterly confounded. It was not a sudden illness that had seized the man; in some way the jewels were connected with this inexplicable agitation.

Carstoe lifted the ring and examined it closely. His face was that of one who had stumbled unwittingly upon some dreadful discovery, and was trying to doubt the evidence of his own senses. He laid the ring upon the broad chair-arm at length, and began taking up the jewels, diamond after diamond. He spread them all out upon the palm of his hand—stones noticeable from their size and purity.

There were also several immense yellow diamonds of unusual lustre, and a great emerald with a tiny nick upon one of the edges. They shone and flashed, and Launce gazed wonderingly from the gems to the white face, and back to the glittering baubles that sent forth new gleams with every movement of the shaking hand.

"Carstoe!" he exclaimed again, fairly terrified by the horror which gathered more heavily on the wrinkled countenance.

"Take them away," Carstoe groaned; "get them out of my sight! I thought I was crazy at first—I wish I had been; oh, I wish I had been."

Launce brushed the jewels from Carstoe's hand into the box, and shut the cover over them.

"Do tell me what is the matter," he pleaded.

"I want to go—let me get away," returned Carstoe, in the same slow, unnatural voice. "I can't see her again yet; say I was ill—any thing. And oh, Launce Cromlin, bid her put them away—hide them—never let them see the light; don't forget that—don't forget!"

He had almost reached the door before Launce could do any thing but stare at him in dumb wonder. Then he hurried forward, saying—

"Let me walk to the hotel with you, Carstoe —you are not well; you oughtn't to go alone."

"Stay where you are," returned Carstoe, in a sharp, imperative tone, that one would not have believed his voice could utter. "You must tell her something—she mustn't suspect—you're quick-witted enough—oh use your wits to some purpose. There's need, for I can't think—I must get away before she comes."

"What do you want me to tell her?" asked Launce, holding fast to his sleeve.

"Haven't I said? To shut them up—hide them; never to let any human creature see them," whispered Carstoe, shaking from head to foot till he fairly tottered to and fro. "Be careful how you do it; don't let her think there's any reason. Say he might not like it; say I could not wait. Take care what you do, Launce Cromlin; there mustn't any trouble come near her—she has enough to bear, God help her. Somehow I understand a great deal that I was blind not to have seen before."

He pulled his arm from Launce's hold, and went out of the room, motioning the young man impatiently back when he would have followed.

Launce sat down, still holding the box of jewels, and waited for Elizabeth to return, feeling as dazed and astray as people usually do when some bit of mysterious tragedy forces itself suddenly out across the decorous monotony of existence.

CHAPTER XXV.

HOLDING COUNSEL.

Two days elapsed before Cromlin saw Mr. Carstoe. He called several times at the hotel, but the clerks told him the gentleman was unwell, and had given directions that no visitors should be admitted to his room. At last Launce grew too anxious to support the uncertainty longer, and absolutely forced his way to the chamber. Mr. Carstoe was up and dressed, and sitting by a window, but he looked as changed as if a long illness had wasted him.

"I couldn't endure it," Launce said, as he entered. "You must excuse my forcing your door, Mr. Carstoe, but I was too anxious about you to stop for etiquette."

"I am glad you have come," Carstoe replied, holding out his hand. "I was going to send for you. I have thought and thought—I can't see my way clear. Launce Cromlin, you're an honest man; you must help me to do what is right."

He did not speak with any excitement; his voice was weak and languid—in keeping with his appearance. Launce sat down by him, retaining the worn hand, and pressing it with gentle firmness. It gave the tired man a sensation of strength, that vigorous young grasp upon his weary muscles. He looked up and smiled.

"You don't need any one to help you do right," Launce answered, speaking cheerfully. "But if easing your mind a little will do you any good, then talk to me. Something that troubles you is making you ill; this is no bodily ailment."

"No, I'm well enough," Carstoe answered. "It's an awful thing, Launce Cromlin, to have your faith in somebody you've trusted knocked away at one blow. And I was so proud of his friendship—not so fond as I got to be of you during that long illness; but I honored and respected him so; and now—"

He passed his disengaged hand across his eyes, and sat silent for a while.

"Of whom are you speaking?" Launce asked; but he knew who was meant. He tried to get away from the conviction, feeling as if it rose out of his own suspicions, out of a desire to believe the worst of Darrell Vaughan; all the same he knew that it was Darrell of whom Mr. Carstoe spoke.

"It seems like an ugly dream yet," Carstoe continued, "for all I have thought of nothing else two whole nights and days. What did you say to her? Did she ask why I did not wait?"

"Eh—Mrs. Vaughan? Oh, yes. I told her you had not time."

"I had a note from her this morning," Carstoe said.

He took from his breast-pocket the dainty billet, and gave it to Launce. It was a pleasure to hold the violet-scented sheet, to read the kindly words of inquiry. Suddenly Launce became sensible of this feeling, and laid the paper down on the table. It was a little thing, but just so resolutely did he put every forbidden thought and feeling in regard to this woman out of his mind.

"Such a dear, sweet letter; so like her," Mr. Carstoe said. "She's an angel, that girl, Launce Cromlin; I feel a better man for knowing her. And God knows what is in store for her!"

"I think she would tell you not to be afraid just because God does know," Launce replied, softly.

The old man's words filled him with a keen anxiety, the more painful from their very vagueness; yet somehow the comforting words came to his lips—uttered themselves, as it were—as if Elizabeth had prompted them.

"Yes," sighed Carstoe; "I'm an old heathen; I keep forgetting that!" Then he asked, eagerly—"Did you tell her—the—the jewels, you know—did you warn her to put them away?"

"Oh, yes; I said she had better."

"But not in a way to trouble her—to make her think there was any thing amiss?"

"No; I am sure not. I said perhaps Darrell had picked them up as a present for her, and had forgotten to have them set. He would feel disappointed if he found she had anticipated him; she had spoken of doing that."

"Yes; and she put them away—all of them?"

Launce nodded. He was thinking how sad she looked, sad and startled, when he spoke of Darrell's having forgotten, and wondering what the look meant. He did not know what a signification his words had to her ears. Those lapses of memory to which Vaughan was becoming more and more subject filled her mind with alarm at the possibilities they suggested.

"If they only had not been found!" he heard Mr. Carstoe say. "I don't see any good it can do. What was the use of my knowing? I'm growing an old man; it's very hard to have such a blow."

Launce could not bring himself to ask a single question further; he had no desire to pry into any of Darrell's secrets—no wish to have further confirmation that his opinion of the man was a just one. He was going away soon; he and Darrell might not meet half-a-dozen times during the remainder of their lives. Whatever this discovery was that had so terribly shocked Carstoe, he would prefer not to hear it. But after an instant his companion continued—

"But you must help me to do what is right, Cromlin; you must help me to do what is right."

"I will do any thing I can—I have told you that," Launce answered, almost impatiently. In spite of himself he was to be forced to sit in judgment on Darrell, and he felt as if he were doing the man a wrong, since he came with strong prejudices in favor of his guilt, no matter what the case might be. "I don't know that you ought to ask my advice either," he continued hastily. "See here, Mr. Carstoe—it is something connected with Vaughan, with my cousin, that troubles you. Now I'm inclined always to think ill of him—to put harsh constructions on his actions; so, after all, I am not a fit person to counsel with."

"Yes, it is about Vaughan," Mr. Carstoe replied slowly. "Your likes or dislikes can't make any difference; it is too plain a case. If I need not believe—if there were any way of—I'm behaving absurdly—excuse me—really my head is so disturbed I think I don't quite know what I say."

"You are worn out from lack of sleep, and staying shut up in the house," Launce said, kindly.

"Why, I believe even yet you don't get near the truth—you don't suspect what it is he has done," exclaimed Carstoe.

"I have not the slightest idea. I know so little about Vaughan's affairs—"

He paused; Carstoe had leaned forward, pressing his hand on Launce's knee—it was pitiable to see the fresh horror and pain which came into his face.

"You remember about my loss in California," he said, in a voice that was little more than a whisper. "The jewels that were stolen from me—the—"

"Good God!" cried Launce.

"Those diamonds that Mrs. Vaughan showed us were the stones I lost!"

Launce sank back in his chair, his face grown as pale as Carstoe's own, and for a few seconds the two men stared dumbly in each other's eyes.

"Why, I can't understand!" muttered Launce at last. "A portion of the diamonds were found in the woman's possession—"

Carstoe interrupted him by taking a little paper from his pocket; he unfolded it, and held up a crescent-shaped diamond stud.

"Do you recognize this?" he asked.

"Yes; it was with the diamonds. How did you get it?"

"It is the mate to the one you saw—the one that was hidden among Darrell Vaughan's things: this is the stud we found on the woman when she was searched," returned Carstoe, in the same repressed, awe-stricken voice.

"You are sure—you can't be mistaken?"

"You know I can not—you know I would give my right hand to find out that I was. If it had been only the unset stones—but the studs —the ring—couldn't you swear to that ring any where, though you have only seen it once?"

"Yes—it is so peculiar."

"And the yellow diamonds—the emerald with the nick in the edge: see, this is the description of them I gave at the time."

He took up an old newspaper from a bundle of letters that lay on the table, and gave it to Launce. It contained an account of the trial. Launce read it through. Then a new horror started up amid the confusion and trouble of his brain.

"Have you thought," he said, "that woman is innocent? She has been four years in prison, and she is innocent."

"Great heavens!" groaned Carstoe, "I have thought until I seem to have almost lost my senses! Cromlin, you remember my telling you of your uncle's sudden attack—of this woman's coming to visit him just before?"

"She had gone to him about Darrell," Launce said.

"Yes! Vaughan must have known it. Either she held some secret of his, and he was afraid of her, or he did it out of revenge; but Darrell Vaughan stole those jewels that day he went to my room. He put the stud in the woman's dress while she was under the influence of some drug—his evidence sent her to prison! There, I have thought it over and over, but I can not get away from the facts; nor can you."

"But to keep the diamonds—"

"He dared not sell them. He put them in the safest possible place; there was scarcely a chance of their ever being found; and after all he has betrayed himself."

"But what is to be done?"

"Haven't I asked myself the question till I'm dizzy and sick? Yes; what is to be done?"

He bent his head upon the table, and groaned aloud.

For many moments Launce sat immersed in thought. His powers of reflection were not disturbed, as poor Carstoe's had been during these weary days and nights, by any shock to his heart —the pain of discovering that one he had trusted and honored was a villain. He had long known that Darrell was this; whatever suspicions he might have entertained of his cousin's utter worthlessness had become convictions during his stay in California.

It was not alone a desire for revenge which had prompted that infernal plot against the woman; she had known some secret, and he had conceived the idea of this charge, not only to get her out of his way for the time, but to render any revelation she might ever attempt without weight.

And during these dreadful years she had languished in prison, and the man had gone serenely on his path, courted, triumphant, untroubled by a single memory of his hapless victim. Strict justice demanded that this man should be given up to the punishment due to his crime; but Launce never for an instant contemplated the possibility of acting thus. Right or not, it was simply a thing impossible to do. It might be tampering with justice, it might be wrong, but Darrell must be shielded from the consequences of his crime. And the woman—the unfortunate creature who at some time had been in some fashion linked with the man's tortuous, evil life— she must be set free: that must be accomplished at any cost, and with the least possible delay. When he thought of her, Launce's indignation rose hotly; and as his fancy painted the picture of that wretched creature wearing out the last remnant of her youth in a prison cell; losing the last shred of faith in man or God in her rebellion against this unmerited punishment; losing, by another's sin, the faintest hope of ever being able to regret or repent her misused life—he felt almost that it was an unpardonable guilt on his part to think of screening the man.

But he could not betray him—he could not! It did not even need that Elizabeth's image should rise in his mind to keep this resolve settled and firm. He did think of her—ah, with such pity! such yearning commiseration! Why, the miserable woman pining in prison on the far Pacific shore was almost to be envied compared to her! Launce realized fully what her life must be: that young face with all the joyfulness of youth gone out of it—those beautiful eyes, heavy with thwarted dreams, with blighted hopes, told their own story. She bore her burden, and would continue to bear; but Launce knew that her husband's character was no secret to her—knew that she lived degraded in her own eyes from this companionship, which must go on till death set her free.

At last Mr. Carstoe's voice roused him. Launce looked up. The old man had raised his head, and was gazing drearily at him.

"Can you see the right way, Cromlin?" he asked. "Is it clear to you what we ought to do?"

"Right or wrong, I shall never betray Darrell," returned Launce, firmly. "That much is clear to me. Never!"

"I am glad; you must decide," Carstoe said, with a sigh of relief. "It would kill her—no, the worst of it would be she would have to live —his wife, you know."

"I have no need to consider his wife," Launce replied, almost harshly. "But that unfortunate woman; she must be set free, Carstoe."

"Oh, that's worse than any thing!" cried the old man. "Her face haunts me like a ghost; just as she looked that day in court, with her awful eyes on Darrell, never moving—never—oh, to think that I have helped condemn a human being unjustly—"

"You can not blame yourself," Launce interrupted. "You could not have acted otherwise; it is useless to dwell upon that. But she must have her freedom now."

"How are we to do that without betraying him?"

"I don't know yet; but we must find a way. Who is the Governor of California now?"

"Charles Howell."

"An old friend of mine; a sort of connection, too," Launce said. "Carstoe, I must go to California at once. I believe I can convince Howell of her innocence without implicating Darrell; nor can she hurt him by any thing she may say or do after her liberation, even if she wished."

"I shall go too," Carstoe said. "I can't meet him again—I can't! I must resign my agency—I— He was kind so far as I was concerned; he more than made up to me my loss. It's a hard blow, Launce Cromlin—a hard blow!"

"I know what you feel. Indeed, indeed I am sorry for you."

"I couldn't look in his face again," pursued Carstoe. "I scarcely know what to write; but he must know that I mean to resign the agency. He can send directions to me in California when he decides whom to appoint."

"When does a steamer sail?"

"On Saturday."

"You must take two places in your own name," Launce said. "I shall let people think I have gone to Europe. We will go on Saturday's steamer, Mr. Carstoe."

"You're a great help and comfort to me," Carstoe said, wringing his hand. "I don't know how I should have managed—I could see no way out! But you're young and quick; and you'll be able to get the poor woman free, you are sure?"

"That must be done, at any cost; but I do not think there will be much difficulty. This is Wednesday. You had better send at once and secure a state-room, Mr. Carstoe; the hotel people will attend to it. Then you must lie down and rest; you are not fit to be up. Don't think any more than you can help. So far as that wretched woman is concerned, we can set the matter partially right. I can't argue, but I must save Darrell."

"Yes, yes."

"Help and befriend her we can. We leave her still a criminal in the world's eyes, it is true; but her past life was such that she was helplessly ruined before. Even if she were cleared of this charge, human verdict would be as severe on her as ever."

"But we may find her a home, make her comfortable, try to keep her from going back to the horrors of the old life."

"That we can and will do! Now let us leave the matter, Carstoe; I am tired and sick with thinking."

"Shall we have to tell him that we know?"

"I see no purpose it can serve. If he finds out that the woman is free, and attempts to trouble her, we must—not otherwise. I can't tell, if the facts were known, whether Darrell could be proved guilty. We *know* he is; but the box belonged to my uncle: they are not Darrell's papers. Oh, well, let it alone; we have decided what to do."

"I am almost afraid to see Mrs. Vaughan again."

"She knows you have been ill. You must tell her some business of your own calls you away. You have nothing more to do here, and can not wait for Vaughan to return."

"I seem to understand so many things now," Carstoe said, after a brief silence. "I used to wonder sometimes at her manner toward him.

It was somehow as if there were a great door shut between them; I can't explain. I half blamed her; I thought she did not fully appreciate him; it seemed her one fault. Now I see! Cromlin, she is a miserable woman—I never admitted it to myself, but she is—she knows that man as well as you or I."

"We can't help her," returned Launce, shortly. "She chose her own life, and must endure it—God help her!"

"Did she choose?" questioned Carstoe, with an odd, perplexed expression crossing the pallor of his face. "I have been thinking of that too. Oh, there's nothing my miserable old head hasn't turned and bothered over."

"Don't bother any more now," Launce said.

"Why no, it's further past remedy than all the rest," returned Carstoe, just thinking aloud in his bewilderment. "But she never knew—I am convinced of that. I could not understand her manner and her questions. Cromlin, she married him without knowing!"

"Knowing what?" asked Launce, quickly, trying to believe that the man's faculties really were a little disordered by the shock he had received, yet feeling all the while that some new disclosure of Darrell's treachery was hidden under his words.

"About the codicil," Carstoe began, then got his senses back enough to realize that it was worse than useless—an absolute cruelty—to speak of the matter. "I don't know what I mean," he added; "I'm a blundering old idiot."

Cromlin had risen to go. He resumed his seat. His face grew firm and hard, and his voice sounded stern and cold, as he said—

"What questions did Mrs. Vaughan ask you? I insist upon knowing."

"It was just a conversation I had with her—I don't remember how it came up—I thought she was prejudiced against you—I wanted her to like you—"

"Well, well?"

"But I've nothing to tell you—it's only a fancy. I did not think of it at the time," stammered Carstoe.

"Think of what? What did she not know?" demanded Launce. Then a sudden light struck him. He half started to his feet; a hot rage thrilled his pulses and blazed in his eyes. But he sat down again; when he spoke his voice was calm. "I want to hear that conversation; you have a wonderful memory for such things; I want to hear every word that passed between you," he said.

It was too late now to retreat. Carstoe told the whole in his hesitating fashion, and when he had finished Launce Cromlin knew as well as if Elizabeth had actually revealed it that Darrell had kept back the fact of his uncle having meant that the two cousins should have an equal chance to win her regard.

He knew this, and the discovery of the jewels rendered it easy for him to avenge the wrong he had suffered at Darrell's hands. But he did not want revenge—not even for an instant did the possibility of such action dwell in his mind. The thought came—he would have been more than human otherwise—but it did not take a second's hold upon him.

Presently he rose and held out his hand.

"I must go now," he said. "I will see you in the morning. Try and rest; have them secure the tickets; but don't attend to any thing else or think any more to-day."

He walked slowly homeward through the bright autumn sunshine, forgetting the long voyage, the duty that lay before him, in the host of thoughts called up by Mr. Carstoe's revelation.

If that illness had not prevented his reaching Europe, how different life might have been! But it was useless to reflect upon mere possibilities—a power stronger than his will had arranged the whole. He must accept existence as it came; the events which, one by one, overtake us we are powerless to govern; but a man's action under the joy or discipline which comes within his own control. Launce was thinking this too, and he did not mean his life to be either wasted or weak. At least Elizabeth had learned to judge him differently from what she had once done—she did not believe him either an idle or a bad man. There was a certain pleasure in feeling this. His way must lead far from hers; now and then their paths might cross for a brief space, but that was all; and it might have been so different—it might!

Darrell Vaughan had kept secret the real conditions of their uncle's will; he had prejudiced father and daughter against his absent relative; Mr. Crauford's illness had hurried on the marriage. All these facts became clear to him as he went over the matter, putting the conversation he had held with Elizabeth the day he read his uncle's letter side by side with Mr. Carstoe's testimony.

Ah, life was not easy—Destiny was a stern task-mistress! Then Launce remembered in whose hands the universe was held, in whose eyes the humblest creature was regarded with pity and love, and got away from the fatalistic theories which haunt us all at times. He believed in God's mercy; he had faith in the Father's loving care; he would not doubt because his way led over sharp rocks and through thorny places.

But it was not easy—oh, it was not easy! He had lost the hope that makes youth beautiful; he had been shown a bewildering vision, whose fulfillment would have rounded his youth into perfection—then it had been snatched away. He had lost it, too, by a human being's treachery. Elizabeth was essentially a just woman; had she known the conditions of that codicil—the full, entire conditions—she would have carried out her part to the very letter—would have decreed that both men mentioned therein must have a chance given, if both desired it.

And if he could have met her—if he could have convinced her of his honesty and truth—oh, it might all have been so different! He found himself thinking this, and turned his mind resolutely upon other subjects. The vision he had cherished was dead—lost; this woman, who wore its likeness, was separated from him more effectually than if worlds swept between. She was another man's wife, and even speculation upon chances which had been allowed no trial was a sin.

CHAPTER XXVI.

WHAT SHE FOUND.

It was a dark, dismal day, threatening a storm, but the rain kept aloof, and the air was heavy and oppressive. Elizabeth grew tired of the confinement of the house, and went out for a brisk walk.

She passed down the Avenue to the Parade Ground, intending to visit a sick woman in Amity Street who had formerly been in her employment. She had nearly traversed the block between Fourth Street and Amity when she saw a group of mischievous boys worrying a cat. At the same instant a little girl dashed out of one of the houses, and flew at the urchins in defense of the frightened animal. To do the *gamins* justice, they were not hurting the kitten—a melancholy-looking grimalkin, with more tail than he knew how to manage. They saw the lady standing on the sidewalk, and retreated around the corner with a war-whoop which might have led one to suppose them descended from Mohawk chiefs instead of heavy Dutchmen or merry Emerald Islanders. The little Amazon seated herself on a door-step, and began to cry—not loudly; in a womanly fashion, wiping her eyes on her apron, while the cat lay in her lap, and stared up at her with an expression of indifference which spoke ill for his character in the matter of gratitude and other proper sentiments.

It was not possible for Elizabeth to see any creature in grief or pain and pass by "on the other side." She crossed the street, and, as she neared the child, saw that one of her hands was bleeding, and she still grasped in it the neck of a bottle, which she had evidently broken in her onslaught upon the boys, for her dress was stained with some dark-colored liquid.

She was gazing disconsolately at the spots, and did not even look up as Elizabeth approached; but the cat saw the intruder, and immediately elevated its back and swelled its tail, as if expecting to be attacked by a new enemy.

The child was an odd-looking thing—too dark and pale to be pretty; but her short curly hair dropped over her forehead in a succession of sunny rings, and her features were delicate and intelligent. Her hat had fallen off, and lay on the stones near Elizabeth, and her dress, though of very common material, had evidently been clean and tidy until that misfortune with the bottle befell her.

Elizabeth picked up the hat, and said kindly, "I am afraid you have hurt yourself. You were a brave little girl to defend kitty; let me see your hand."

The child raised her eyes—great dark eyes, so beautiful that they glorified her whole face, and made Elizabeth wonder that she could have thought the creature plain. She stopped crying, gave the speaker a long, solemn look of inquiry, then glanced at the wounded fingers.

"I didn't know I'd hurt myself," she answered; "but I've broken the bottle, and now Aunt Jean won't have any liniment, for Mrs. Baines hadn't another scrap—not a scrap."

The idea was so dreadful that it put her even beyond the relief of tears. She shook her head dismally, and let the fragment of the shattered phial fall.

"Perhaps we can manage about the liniment," Elizabeth said; "but the first thing is to attend to your hand."

"Why, it does hurt," said the child, in a tone of surprise; "hurts like murder; but I didn't know it! And, oh dear, my dress!—and it was a clean one—and I told Aunt Jean I'd be careful; and now only look—and it was all Moses's following me down-stairs. Oh, Mose!"

Moses was the cat, and he at once proceeded to give another evidence of the ungrateful nature which had before exhibited itself in that contemptuous disregard of his saviour's distress. He deliberately spit at her with all his puny might—whisked his tail across her face—bounded out of her arms, and flew into the house with a sharp meaul of indignation and injured innocence.

"He lives there," said the child; "he'll go up-stairs, and Sally'll let him in."

"Sally is one of your playmates, I suppose?" Elizabeth said, wanting to keep the child's attention occupied, for she had taken the injured hand in hers, and on wiping away the blood perceived that there were two or three bits of glass to be got out of the fingers.

"Yes, ma'am," the child answered. "Only we don't play, 'cause Sally's lame, and walks with a crutch."

"Poor Sally! that is very hard, isn't it?"

"Oh, she was born so—she don't mind," was the philosophical answer. "Oh my!—see here! —you hurt!"

"It is all over now. I will do your hand up in my handkerchief. Is there a chemist's near here—a drug-shop, you know?"

. "Oh, yes, just round the corner."

"Then we'll go there and get some plaster for the cut. Does it hurt now?"

"Not much," replied the small maid. "Why, you're awfully good, ain't you?"

Elizabeth put the hat on the child's head, and they walked toward the shop. There was nobody in but a long-legged, watery-eyed boy, and he took a great while to find the plaster—one of those abortive-looking creatures of whom you would prophesy that he would all his life be behindhand with whatever he might undertake.

"Oh, dear me, ain't I a sight?" Elizabeth heard the child sigh. "It's awful to be so messed, and Mrs. Baines hasn't got a scrap more liniment—not a scrap."

"Perhaps we can buy some here," suggested Elizabeth. "What is it for?"

"Rheumatism in the left arm," replied the child promptly. "But you couldn't buy it any where—it's stuff Mrs. Baines makes herself, and it's all roots and herbs, 'cause she used to live in the country, and knows how; but Aunt Jean don't, and nobody else, I s'pose, though Aunt Jean once lived in the country too, but that was ever so long ago, in Scotland."

During the progress of these confidences, Elizabeth cleansed the blue dress as well as she could by rubbing it with some paper, while the watery-eyed boy peered at them over his shoulder, and quite forgot the plaster he had been sent to find. Elizabeth went to the case herself, discovered what was wanted, and soon had the child's wounded fingers neatly bound up.

"That's better now, isn't it?" she asked, with her slow, beautiful smile, that never failed to carry comfort to the sick or suffering.

"Oh, it's well enough, thank you," was the answer; "anyhow it's my left hand, so I can stuff all the same, and Aunt Jean's got a lot ready for me."

"What?" Elizabeth inquired, somewhat mystified.

"Dolls; she makes the kid parts, and I stuff 'em, and then she sews the legs and heads on."

"So you have dolls enough to play with?" Elizabeth said.

The bright eyes gave her a rather contemptuous glance.

"It's all foolishness," she said; "I've seen too many of them made; but Sally Baines's got a woolen rabbit with a squeak in it—that ain't so bad. She likes dolls though. Aunt Jean made her one once out of a broken-headed one that wouldn't sell, and so she wears a cap; but Sally don't mind."

By this time Elizabeth had paid for the plaster, and was ready to go.

"There is a shop up toward Broadway where they have something that is good for rheumatism," she said; "if you like to go there with me, I will buy a bottle for Aunt Jean."

The little face grew troubled.

"I don't know," she said; "Aunt Jean sent the money to pay Mrs. Baines, and I haven't got any more."

"But I mean to get it myself, you see."

"I'm afraid Aunt Jean would send it back," returned the mite, still shaking her head. "She never takes any thing she don't pay for, and I don't know as she's got any more money to-day; and you don't play with dolls, 'tain't likely."

"But I know some children that I buy dolls for sometimes," Elizabeth said. "If you like, I will go with you and tell Aunt Jean how it all happened. Do you live far from here?"

The little creature interested her, and she wanted to see the place where she lived, and the woman who had charge of her.

"No, not far; it's in Minetta Lane," the child said, still hesitating.

"Shall I go with you?"

"I—I don't know. See here—you ain't a deestrict, are you?"

"I don't believe I am," Elizabeth said, laughing. "What is it?"

"That's what Aunt Jean calls 'em—she's Scotch, you know; and there's another word—"

"Oh, yes—a district visitor?"

"That's it; and how she does hate 'em! They don't come much now, 'cause she told two or three that she had her Bible, and the tracts were no good—not even to stuff dolls, though she did cut some up to fill a pillow, and I sleep on it."

"I am not a district visitor. Aunt Jean can be sure of that," replied Elizabeth.

"I didn't think you looked like one," said miss, with a smile of approval; "and I like your bonnet; they do wear such dreadful ones. And I expect Aunt Jean would be glad of the liniment, for she said her rheumatism was bad enough; but she'll want to pay."

From the chemist's they passed down Bleecker Street to the narrow, crooked by-way, which was in old days the channel of a brook that still gives its name to the lane. The dwellings were clean and decent, and the house at which they stopped one of the most comfortable.

"I live here," said the child. "I don't think the stairs are very steep."

They went up two flights, and Elizabeth's conductress knocked at a door, which was opened by an elderly woman, holding in her hand a half-finished doll. She dropped a civil courtesy, but seemed ill pleased at the sight of a stranger. Evidently her first thought was that another restless seeker after good works had come, prepared to show, by manner and words, that she supposed herself visiting a heathen.

"It's the lady that tied up my hand," the child burst out volubly; "and how it did bleed! But oh, I've broken the bottle, Aunt Jean, and I'm ever so sorry! But she bought some liniment, though I said you always paid, and it was Moses's running out after me that did it, and my dress is spoiled."

She began to sob. The woman tapped her head with the doll's one leg, but not unkindly, and said—

"Don't cry, Megsie—spilt milk, ye ken!" She dropped Elizabeth another courtesy, a little less stiff, and added, "I'm obliged to you, ma'am, for your trouble. It's na' much o' a place to rest in, but if you feel to tak' a chair after climbin' the stair—"

The invitation was given in a doubtful tone, and scarcely came to a legitimate conclusion, still Elizabeth accepted it. Aunt Jean led the way through a dark passage into a moderate-sized chamber, which served as parlor and bedroom, but was scrupulously clean. A table stood near the window, covered with dolls in different stages of development—a rose-bush in a pot on the window-sill. The woman herself looked delicate and ailing; but, though the eyes were keen and the lips compressed, it was not a hard face. Elizabeth felt sure that Meg had a far from unhappy home. Poverty was visible everywhere; but poverty in its better aspect, which struggles and works, and will so struggle to the end. Elizabeth knew the signs. This was a person who would starve rather than descend to beggary—just one of those cases it is a pleasure to assist, and yet difficult. An offer of money to that resolute old body would have been an insult—no penny had ever found its way into her dwelling which had not been honestly earned.

Elizabeth seated herself in the wooden rocking-chair the woman drew forward, and related in a few words her meeting with the child; praising her courage, which had brought about the accident, and the fortitude with which she had borne her hurt, while Meg stood behind her chair and dolefully regarded her dress—at leisure now to indulge a purely feminine distress over the ruin which had befallen it.

"She told me you suffered from rheumatism," Elizabeth added, "and I ventured to bring you this liniment. I thought possibly you had never heard of it, and I know that it is an excellent remedy."

Aunt Jean's gray eyes softened, and she smiled. "I thank you hearty," she said, taking the little bottle Elizabeth held toward her. "I hope I didn't seem rude when I first saw ye: I'd ask ye to excuse it if I did. I'm always thinkin' ony stranger is ane o' the deestrict visitors, and I canna bide 'em, and that's the truth. And I dinna like tracts, and I dinna like my floor muddied, and I dinna like to be speered at for a heathen or a beggar!"

"And I shouldn't like it either," replied Elizabeth; "nor should I have taken the liberty to come, only I did not wish to leave the little girl after I saw that she was hurt."

I

She smiled, and the woman smiled in return: her obstinate old heart was fairly won.

"Dinna talk o' liberty to such as me," she answered, "nae mair than the sunshine wad; it does me mair good to see your face and be spoken to that gait than a quart o' liniment! Megsie, go into the closet and tak' off your dress. I'll warrant we'll get those stains out; so dinna fash yersel', my woman."

"She is your niece?" Elizabeth said, as the door closed behind the child.

"She's nae kith or kin," replied Aunt Jean, shaking her head; "but I feel as if she were. She's been with me ever since she was a baby, and she's like to stay now."

"She has no father or mother, then?"

"She may have baith, or neither; I don't know for sure, and she knows nathing, and it's better she never should. Ye understand?"

The child's little history was easy to comprehend from these few words. Evidently a common enough one; but out of the common was the fact that the poor, nameless waif should have found protection and kindness like these.

"What do you call her?" Elizabeth asked, not liking to question a syllable beyond the account the woman might choose to give.

"Her true name wad be Marguerite."

"That is French."

"Like eneugh; it was her mother's before her, when she had a name, pair soul," murmured the woman.

"How old is she?" inquired Elizabeth.

"Oh, she'll be a bit past eight now, though she does na' look it."

Just then Meg came out of the closet in her ordinary dress, and seated herself on a stool by the window.

"Now I'm ready to stuff, Aunt Jean," she said. "I've wasted a lot of time, haven't I?"

"We'll let the stuffin' bide the day," replied her protectress. "It's like your wee fingers 'll be stiff. Ye may gae up to the auld fiddler body, if you're likin'."

Meg disliked to lose sight of the beautiful lady, but the temptation to listen to the violinist's music was irresistible, and she rose at once, though she looked rather wistfully at the visitor.

"Aunt Jean will call you before I go," Elizabeth said, understanding her thought out of that great sympathy she always had with children. "I am going to sit here awhile, if she will let me."

"Megsie," cried the old woman, "the rose-bush 'ull blossom after this; mind that!"

And Elizabeth thought in her life she had never received a prettier compliment.

Meg went out of the room, and left Aunt Jean and her guest together.

"And you have taken care of the child—worked for her and supported her as if she were your own?" Elizabeth said. "I think you must be a very good woman."

"Eh, the bit she eats is na' much; and she's help to me now," was the cheerful answer.

"You will not be offended at what I want to say?" Elizabeth continued.

"Dear heart!" exclaimed the other; "that voice could na' say any thing it would na' be a pleasure to hear."

"I'm glad of that, Mrs.—"

"Murray—Jean Murray," supplied the woman. "It has been my name aboon forty years; but it's nigh half that time since I lost the gudeman; he died in Scotland. Then I cam' across the water, and I've na' fared ill, first and last."

"Will you tell me something about Meg?" asked Elizabeth, gently.

"I'm drawn to," returned the woman; "that was why I sent her out. Odd times I think I'm growing auld, and nae that strong I was; and on'y this morn I was wondering o'er it, and when you cam' in, somehow it was just as if something said to me, The Lord has found the way. He does, leddy, in spite o' all our frettin', always He does, if on'y a body could remember it."

The simple words of faith struck like a promise to Elizabeth's heart, which had been so bitter during these past days. She was glad, too, of any thing that took her out of herself—gave a hope of being of use to any human being, in however small a way.

"I never have talked to aye a creature about her," Mrs. Murray was saying; "it was naebody's business—the child had me. But since I took the long illness, and these weaknesses coming o'er me—but who was I to tell?—na' the Visitors; my certy, no!"

"I should like to help where the child is concerned, if you will let me," Elizabeth said. "I am not a philanthropist—"

"The vara word. I could na' speak it," interrupted Aunt Jean, in a parenthesis, with a shiver of disgust.

"But I have money, and I have no children," Elizabeth continued; and the quick-witted hearer noticed how her voice saddened, but she gave no sign. "Sometimes I find children I can help, can educate and bring up to learn trades and be useful. I might assist you about Meg; she ought to go to school—to—"

She stopped, for Mrs. Murray made a quick movement, and she was fearful of having annoyed her. Elizabeth had not a particle of the stuff in her composition which helps to make a philanthropist by profession. She was as shy of intruding where humble people were concerned, as careful of hurting their independence or pride, as if they had been formed of the delicate porcelain which enters into the composition of the great. She was a foolish creature in many ways, this Elizabeth.

"It's like having a dream come true!" Mrs.

Murray said, in a low, awe-stricken tone; and a dew gathered over the sternness of her eyes, which had ached under too many troubles for tears easily to dim them. "On'y the ither night, when the pain kept me awake, I lay thinkin' o' it. If on'y there were somebody able to do it, and with a kind heart—if I should be taken! And now you come—oh, leddy, ye maun hae been sent—I'd been a wicked woman na' to let ye do what He puts in your mind; and He's showed the way, too."

"I must think what it would be best to do," Elizabeth said.

"It's not now that help is needed—dinna go believing that," returned Aunt Jean, eagerly. "I'm able to work, and she pays for her keep. She has been to school, too—there are plenty, gude and free, and I manage to dress her decent for that. It's if ony thing happened to me."

"I shall not forget," Elizabeth said. "But there is no reason why all the care of her should come on you. It is only right that you should be paid something for her board when she goes to school, and not have the expense of clothing her."

"I could na' tak' it, ma'am! Forgie me—I canna pit it in the right language—but it wad be like sellin' my hairt, somehow," Mrs. Murray replied. "The claes and welcome, because of her not then having call to feel ashamed amang the ither bairns."

Elizabeth did not urge the matter. After a moment, Aunt Jean added, with a shrewd smile—

"Ma'am, I beg your pardon! But hae ye thocht how ye're takin' me on trust?"

"I am not afraid to do that, Mrs. Murray."

"And ye're ane to gae straight to the hairt an' motives—ye'd be guided!"

Elizabeth laid her hand on the old woman's for an instant.

"Now tell me about Meg's mother," she said.

"Eh, it's awa' back, to begin wi' the commencement," said Mrs. Murray, picking up her glasses from the table, and rubbing them diligently on her apron. "Yes—a'maist ten year. I got a hurt in the street—a'maist rin doun wi' an omnibus in Broadway. The last thing I mind was a leddy in the crowd that got aboot me—the grandest-dressed body—wi' e'en like twa stars. Someway I felt she could understand, and I ca'ed, 'Na' to the hospital—dinna tak' me to the hospital!' Then I tried to gie me address, but I could na' speak anither word. And it was her ainsel' answered me, 'Ye'll not go, gude woman, I'll promise thot.' Then it was a' mirk, and I swounded awa'."

She sat silent for some seconds, still polishing her spectacles. Elizabeth could see that she had to struggle hard to retain her composure.

"I get sae Scotch when I'm a bit movet," she said, apologetically. "Maist times I mind mesel', for I wad na' hae the bairn tak' my way. It seems right ye suld knaw, though it can do nae gude, but ye'll understand what I'm always fearin' for the child—I could na' tell why."

Elizabeth bent her head.

"And when you came to your senses?" she asked.

"Ah!" resumed Mrs. Murray, drawing a long breath like a sob, "when I cam' to I was in a braw chamber, and a doctor there, and the leddy. I was in her house, she said, and I'd be cared for."

She stopped again.

"Were you ill long?" Elizabeth asked, to help her, for it was evident she found the story difficult to tell.

"Nae, nae, I was na' ill—bruised like. In the evening I could rise up. Dear ma'am, I canna bide to think what I did! I thocht I was vara gude and virtuous, a' the same I was a wicked Pharisee."

"I am sure you did not mean to do wrong," Elizabeth said.

"I did wrang, though," answered the old woman, "as ony body does when they thank God they're not so bad as ither folk. She trippit into my room wi' anither gown on—she was aff to the opera, she said. She tauld me she'd need o' an honest body to be her housekeeper and mind the maids. She'd a fancy to me, she said; wad I stop? I was oot o' wark joost then. I'd been to see a place that vara day, and was too late. But that's nae matter."

"So you agreed to remain," Elizabeth rejoined, eager, she could not have told why, to get to the end of the story.

"Aye, that was it! I'll never forget how beautiful she looked, a' in white, wi' jewels in her hair; but her eyes were brighter still—the child's 'mind me o' them, odd times. Eh sirs, she was na' muckle mair her ainsel'; she'd na' hae been ower nineteen, puir soul!"

"Poor soul!" repeated Elizabeth, pityingly.

"Yes. I've telled eneugh; ye can speer the rest. When she'd gane, I sleepit a bit. Wakin' again, her servant came till me, and we'd a lang crack aboot it a'. Then the jade let it oot that the bonnie lass lived wi' a mon wha was na' her husband, and she skirled awa' and telled me how she garred her mistress pay a double wage because o' her ain character.

"Then Mileddy, as she ca'ed her, cam' hame wi' a troop o' freends, and the bizzie said there'd be supper and dancin' and mad doins till daybreak. So off she rin, for the leddy had come up the stair and was ringin' her bell. I could na' to say walk, but I could mak' shift to win alang, and I'd hae creepit on hands and knees to be free the hoose. I did na' reflect that whatever she might be she'd been gude to me, and that it was na' for the like o' me to judge her. Silly doited auld carle, I thocht it a fine Chreestian thing to bear my testimony, as I ca'ed it, against sin!"

She mechanically took some bits of kid from the table, and tried to work, but laid them quickly down, put her glasses off and on several times, while her features quivered as if she were crying, though she shed no tears.

"You believed you were doing right," Elizabeth said, longing to comfort her.

"Eh, dear leddy, I did na' stop to think, I was that full o' mysel', ye ken. Aweel, I got out o' my chair and searched my claes, and though sair stiff and lame, I could hirple alang. As I stepped doon the passage, oot shot the maid in a great takin' to know my wull, and then cam' the leddy too.

"'What do you want?' she says, kindly like.

"'Let me gang oot o' this,' says I. 'For the gude ye've done me ye hae my thanks, but I'd no hae tuk it an' I'd known. I'm an honest woman, and I tell ye the "wages o' sin is deeth!"'

"She sank bock to the wa', like as I'd struck her, and went white i' the face. In a bit minute she began laughing, but not hearty—just reckless like. 'Let ner go,' she says, 'that's the thanks one gets for helping these Chreestians.' I got doun the stair and ont intil the night. As I was ga'en by the perlor-door I heard skirlin' an' singin', an' I felt like Lot a fleein' from Sodom; an' aiblins I was wickeder than she I condemned."

Mrs. Murray sat silent for a time. Her eyes were closed; her lips moved slowly. Elizabeth knew that she was praying. She looked up at last, and went on slowly—

"I hae made it a lang story, but there's little mair. I was awa' to New Orleans; I'd gaen there wi' a sick leddy. She died sune. What wi' wark frae shops an' twa bit bairnies to mind, I was fairin' weel. I'd took some wark hame, and was hastenin' bock, for I'd asked a neebor to sit wi' the weans, fearin' they'd wake while I was gane. The night was mirk, and the wind howled, and the big river a roarin' like the sea. The rain cam' pourin', an' I rin wi' a' my might till I saw a woman crouched in a corner, sair droukit, puir thing! an' holdin' a bundle in her arms. It was a bairn. It began cryin' as I rin past. I stoppit—the mother not hearin'—in a dream like. I caught a glint at her face—ou, it was Mileddy!"

"Did she recognize you?"

"Just at my voice she loupit up wi' a skreigh I can hear yet, an' the first words she said were the hairď anes I spoke when I rin awa' oot o' her hoose. 'The wages o' sin is deeth,' says she; 'the wages o' sin is deeth; ye tauld me sae!' Weel, weel, I took her to my own bit place; it was ane body's wark to get her there, for she'd meant to droon hersel'. Happen it was nae a kindness to keep her here, wicked as it sounds, but I did it."

"She would not stay with you?"

"She bided the night and the next day; she was reicht dour and silent; waur than that—

half-mad like. The mon had flung her aff and gaed his gate; she telled me sae much. She'd come to New Orleans wi' him; her wean was born there. Oh, ma'am, he left her, an' he took anither lass wi' him when he went, an' she was knowin' to it."

"It is too dreadful!" shivered Elizabeth. "Tell me what you did—what became of her."

"Waur than the deeth she was seekin'—waur than the black, black water she meant to bide her trouble under," groaned the old woman. "I took her to my airms, and begged her to let me help her an' the bairnie, in token she forgave my haird words. The bit babbie was in a bad way. She'd no milk for it, and it was nigh stairved. The night, when I thocht the puir body was sleepin' at last, I dozed aff, wi' the bairn beside me. She cam' and stood by my bedside, beggin' an' prayin' me to keep an' care for the wean. I thocht her daft, an' had a muckle wark to comfort her wi' promisin' all she asked. Then she quieted, an' lay doun again, askin' me to pit the babbie by her. I was sair worn mysel', and slept sound till the morn's mornin', an' the bairnie woke me wi' its skirlin'. Dear leddy, it was broad day, and she'd gaed her lane to due penance for her sin."

"But you heard from her afterward?"

"It was lang first—na' ti' I was hame here. When we were talkin', she asked an address that wad always reach me, an' I gied her one, though I was mindin' the babbie, and did na' think o' her meanin' at the time. But I got a bit scrape o' the pen an' a hantle o' money—no news o' hersel', but just the money; it cam' a matter o' three times — plenty too; checks frae a San Francisco bank. I was to write to a man there how the child fared; an' I did."

"But that is a good while ago?"

"Aye! The last news that cam' to me was through an English sailor I knew—just chance. He was here, an' when he saw Megsie he was that scairt he tauld me the story. As ye may think, I did na' let out that the bairn was nane o' me or mine. It was a story about a drunken frolic he had in San Francisco. A parcel o' men robbed him at a drinkin' an' gamblin' place kept by a woman they ca'ed Mileddy. I'd hae known her wi'out the name, just by his account o' her looks. Eh, dear ma'am, she'd gaed from bad to waur. He telled how she was mair like a fiend than a woman, on'y sae beautiful through it a', and gangin' always doun, doun!"

Elizabeth covered her eyes with her hand. Aunt Jean's simple words made the picture so terribly clear that it was unbearable.

"That was the last I ever heerd," pursued Mrs. Murray; "four year an' mair. It's like she's dead lang syne; it's the best to hope. Ony way, she'd be in God's hands, an' after a' that's come an' gaen, He might judge her as mon could na' do."

"And through His goodness you were allowed to save the child," Elizabeth said.

"Eh, dear ma'am, in ane way or anither He warks to bring gude out o' a' the wrang and sin, in His ain way an' His ain time. Whiles it's haird to believe, but He does it."

The touching words from the old Scripture narrative rose involuntary to Elizabeth's lips. She did not speak aloud, but in her heart she cried, "Lord, help thou mine unbelief!"

"It's muckle the bairn need never ken," Mrs. Murray was saying. "The money's a' pit by. I could na' use it—I could na'!"

"You are a good, good woman!" Elizabeth said; and Mrs. Murray only looked at her in mild wonder.

What made up a complete life? Elizabeth was thinking. Perhaps in the sphere beyond this the patient sacrifice of this lowly woman, the tender caring for this helpless waif and stray, should count for more than all the grand achievements, the far-reaching plans for human advancement, which had been the dream of her own visionary youth, even had she been able to carry them out in their fullness.

"I've always kept some bit trifles that I found," Mrs. Murray said presently. "They must have droppit out o' a bundle she had, wi'out her knowin' it."

She went to a trunk that stood in a dark corner, and unlocked it with a key she took from her pocket. She came back to the table, and set a small box down upon it.

"I've aye kept them in this," she said; "they're naught, but I could na' bear not to treat them carefully. Whiles I've fancied always they were just the first he'd given her that she kept after sellin' the rest, for he'd treated her so ill—a woman is aye a woman, ye ken."

She lifted a coral necklace of no great value—a simple ring—some withered flowers—a book. One could fancy, as the good woman said, that these trifles had each possessed a history. Perhaps the coral was the first gift of the man to his victim—the flowers might have been gathered some day the two had spent in the country.

"An' this," Mrs. Murray said, holding up a silver cross, with a horrified look—"a crucifeex! The puir lass pit it roond the bairn's neck hersel'—she's aye worn it till the ither day the ring broke. I had it mendit, and she's na' asked it yet—I've na' the hairt to keep it frae her. Meg kens naething aboot its bein' a heathenish embleem, and I hae warned her ne'er to show it. And the book—it's French, I'm thinkin'. I hae na' looked at the things in years, till I pit the crucifeex here—they're awfu' to me—awfu'!"

She held the book toward Elizabeth. It had been richly bound, but was worn and tarnished. There were stains on the cover—perhaps the trace of tears—who should say?

Elizabeth mechanically opened the volume—

it was a collection of Alfred de Musset's passionate lyrics. On the fly-leaf was carelessly written the one word—"Milady." Here and there on the pages other pencil-marks were visible—passages underscored—in certain places a date scribbled. To an imaginative person the book contained a complete history.

"I'd na' seen the writin'," Mrs. Murray said, looking over Elizabeth's shoulder. "I just saw it was a foreign tongue—French belike; and that aye seems wickedness. It wad be in verse, I'm thinkin'."

"Yes," Elizabeth answered, and still absently turned the leaves whose few pencil records seemed to make plain to her the black tragedy which, like so many another, had passed under the world's eyes without the world's heeding.

Mrs. Murray began collecting the finished dolls, and putting them in a basket ready to be carried to the shop. She had gone to the other end of the room. Elizabeth still lingered over the pages, which possessed a painful fascination she could not dispel.

Toward the middle of the volume she came upon a page that had a couple of lines written on the inner edge; they were partially effaced by flourishes and careless marks, as if some person had done it absently while reading. She moved close to the window to see more clearly. It was an extract from the poem that had been written in a man's hand—then came again the name "Milady"—then another name—not distinct at first, but as Elizabeth stared at it, the words seemed to grow till they rose like gigantic characters before her horrified eyes.

The name was Darrell Vaughan, and the writing her husband's! It was a habit of his as he read to scribble absently on the margin of a page.

She felt dizzy and faint at this fresh proof of the vileness of the man to whom her life was bound, but the shock did not come with the violence it might have done to most wives. She had grown accustomed to proofs of his baseness—month by month, week by week, some new evidence was forced upon her. She tore the page from the book, and hid it in her dress—at least it must not be left for any other eye to discover. She caught sight of her face in the little mirror; she was startled at its stern coldness. In the midst of her weakness and trouble she was conscious of wondering could it be the same face that used to meet hers in the glass?—the face that was once eager with bright dreams, out of which, young and fair as it still was, every trace of hope had worn away?

She drew her veil down, and turned toward Mrs. Murray.

"I must go now," she said. "I have stayed a long time. I will come again soon; I shall not forget."

She was out in the air, hurrying through the streets toward her home. One reflection came suddenly up, and brought a sort of comfort with it. At least she might make it her care that the future of this nameless child should be peaceful—kept far away from harm or evil.

Her husband's daughter, and she was childless! He had often reproached her with it, and sometimes she had grieved because the sweet blessing of maternity was denied her. She thanked God heartily now for the want which had helped to make her life solitary and gray.

CHAPTER XXVII.

FOR HIS OWN SAKE.

ELIZABETH went back to her desolate home, and sat down in the silence. The secret which she had discovered—which had been thrust upon her rather—could not outwardly affect her life. This was the clearest thought in her mind after those long hours of meditation—perhaps the hardest of all to bear. She was married to this man, and neither human judgment nor human law would be on her side if she were to throw her burden down for a cause like the present. She was old enough, had knowledge enough of the world, to understand this. That page out of the dark book of her husband's past was filled up and put aside before her life touched his; she had nothing to do with it. That would have been the world's verdict. Even women—good, pure women—would unhesitatingly say that a young man's weaknesses and follies should not be submitted to a rigid, pitiless examination. No young man's record would stand it. Men were exposed to temptations which women could not appreciate; besides, they often made better husbands if during their bachelor liberty they had gone through experiences "likely to teach them the folly of such things." Over and over Elizabeth had heard these arguments from feminine lips, and had learned to listen in silence. Her soul filled with bitterness, as many another woman's has done, when such theory and practice were forced upon her knowledge, and now it had become a personal matter; yet she was bound hand and foot. Still, she was thinking more of that unhappy creature, a glimpse into whose history Mrs. Murray's words had offered, than of herself. Some wild idea rose in her mind as to the possibility of finding her out if she were alive—trying to help her. There came, too, a wilder idea of appealing to Darrell: begging him for his soul's sake to discover the woman, and save her from the final consequences of misery and sin. It was all she could do; and was not this course a plain duty? Oh, that word! Why, holy and beautiful as it had once seemed to her, it had grown the greatest stumbling-block in her path! She was always bruising herself against it at every turn, and to her piteous cries, her eager questions, it returned no more answer than if it had been a dumb heathen idol, standing up with a smile of imbecile ferocity amid the ruined temple of her life.

What was her duty? what, indeed, was existence for? what part or place had she in the grand universal plan? Her place! A wife, and yet widowed — that most terrible widowhood of the soul! A woman in the fullness of her youth, in the strength of her powers, and no work granted—not even the sweet task of making home pleasant to a loving husband.

Thought was too dreadful, too dangerous; she must get away from it. She could only hold blindly to her faith, and pray that it might not forsake her.

The whole afternoon had gone unnoticed; the shadows of evening were filling the room, and still she sat there, holding the leaf she had torn from that book, trying always to see some gleam of light, some means, at least, of aiding her sister woman, of urging upon Vaughan the need of going back over that disregarded, perhaps forgotten episode, and trying if atonement were possible.

Disregarded! — forgotten! this seemed the strangest, the most unnatural part of the whole matter. Could he have forgotten? Could he be so utterly callous and hardened that not even a memory remained—not a pang of remorse?

Suddenly she heard her husband's voice in the hall addressing one of the servants. He had come back without warning, as his habit was. "Mrs. Vaughan is in the library? Tell them to hurry dinner, please. I am hungry and tired."

Then he entered; she saw him pause on the threshold, and look about. His eyes, unaccustomed to the dimness, did not at first distinguish her, but she saw him clearly. She did not rise —she could not; the paper that fluttered in her trembling hand seemed the sign of a new and sterner barrier between their already widely severed souls.

"Are you here, Elizabeth?" he called, pleasantly enough. "What a fancy you have for enjoying blind-man's holiday!"

He was beside her now, holding out his hand. "How do you do—been well?"

He did not offer to kiss her. She noticed this, confused and troubled as she felt; noticed it, and was glad.

"I did not expect you to-night," she managed to say, and rose slowly, letting her fingers lie passive in his clasp.

"How cold your hand is—the room's like a furnace, though—you stay shut up too much," were his next words. Then he gave a fretful little laugh. "Have you got to the end of your welcome already?" he asked.

"I hope you have been well. Were you successful in your business?"

For the life of her she can think of no other words! That paper is still in her hand; she can neither turn her eyes from it nor hide the page, though she would like to do one or the other.

"Yes, to both questions," she hears him say. Then he adds, "I should think we might as well have the good of what little light there is."

He goes to the window near her chair, and pulls back the curtain which Elizabeth had dropped over the casement when she entered the room hours before.

"Upon my word, this is a cheerful sort of welcome for a man to receive!" he exclaimed, turning toward her again. She is still standing, her eyes fixed on the torn page. Dim as the light is, she can see his name written there; the characters fairly burn before her eyes.

She is at a loss what to do. To leave the matter without making some appeal to him she feels impossible. But whether it is better to wait or in what words to frame her explanation she can not think.

"I will hurry the dinner," is all she does say; there is a kind of relief in falling back for an instant to the safety of some commonplace household matter.

"Thanks. I told Martin. I dare say they will manage. I should be sorry to trouble you," he replied with an elaborate civility, which betrays his rising anger.

If she could talk—get that paper out of sight —keep down to the level of ordinary subjects, if only for a time. To let the matter in her mind come up in a way to cause contention or harsh words would be to add to its loathsomeness. There must be no quarrel; he is dead to her; absolutely dead! What she must say, let her try to speak as dispassionately as if she had been set free from this earthly bondage, and had come back to plead with him.

Just then he notices the paper in her hand. He is always ready with suspicions; he never fails to believe the worst of any man or woman. Some quick thought that he has taken her by surprise is what goes through his mind. She is agitated—confused. Perhaps he has come near some secret. Is it a letter?—does some feeling lie at the bottom of her odd manner?

"What are you holding? what have you got there?" he exclaims, and tries to draw the paper from her.

"Don't take it—don't touch it," she replies, putting her hand behind her.

"I insist on knowing what this means! Give me that letter."

"It is not a letter," she says; "it is only a page out of a book."

"A page out of a book! Then what are you hiding it for?" retorts he, and pulls her arm roughly.

A swift, sudden indignation rises in Elizabeth's soul—a prouder creature never breathed. The scowling, angry face confronting her does not bring any sensation of terror as it might to a weaker woman.

"Let me go, if you please—this instant!"

The voice is very low, but there is something in its tone which brings him back to his senses—something in the haughty coldness of her face which reminds him, as it has done before, that with her no show of threat or tyranny will serve. His hand drops; he retreats a step, and Elizabeth sinks wearily back into her chair.

She realizes that this is no fitting moment to bring up the subject which has been in her mind during these hours since her return home. Months and months ago she decided that another quarrel between them must be fatal. Strife shall not come now; certainly not in regard to this matter about which she feels so strongly the importance of acting aright. It may be that his soul and hers must endure for a period, which to mortal comprehension would seem endless, the consequences of their action at this crisis.

Something of these thoughts, this resolve, he sees in her face—what they mean he can not of course tell. So often he has been irritated, half-maddened by the unknown language written on her countenance—many a time of late he has almost hated her therefor.

"You and I are reaching a point where some sort of explanation will be necessary," he says, angrily. "I don't mean to be met at every turn by obstinacy and secretiveness—mysteries made out of every trifle just to irritate me. If you have any secrets, I advise you to be careful."

"Oh, stop—don't say any more," she answers, wearily. "We have nothing to quarrel about—do not invent reasons—let us have such peace as we can find."

"I want that paper," he persists. "I am determined to know what it is! I wish to understand why my coming home unexpectedly puts you in this state! I have not the slightest intention of playing the part of *un mari sage*, and timing my arrival to suit any little plans you may happen to have on foot."

"If you will not be quiet, I shall go," she says, rising. "Perhaps you will have come back to your senses by the time dinner is ready."

With an unexpected movement he snatches the paper from her hand, so carried away by anger that for an instant he half believes that he holds some secret. Well as he knows her, forced as he is to feel her honor and truth, detesting her sometimes therefor, with one side of his distorted mind, he half believes his devilish suspicions for an instant.

"Now then for your little private letter!" he cries.

"Not yet—don't look at it yet," she pleads. "I meant to tell you, but not with such feelings between us! Oh, of all things in the world over which we might have trouble, do not let us choose this! Let me tell you in my own time—my own

way. Let us try for once to act together and to act for the best."

"It is my opinion that I shall have to end by paying for your keep in a mad-house," is the answer she receives.

She has laid her hand on his arm; he shakes it off.

"I beg you to wait!"

"And I beg you not to touch me," he retorts; "my susceptibilities are as keen as yours. Hands off, if you please! I shall not wait!—I shall read it!"

"Then read—read it and be done," she answers, and once more seats herself.

A fresh sensation of hopelessness strikes her. Even if she tries to do right, something prevents her doing it in a manner which could bring about the good she desires. She can not tell if it be fate or her own error, but so it always happens. He must have his way; she can struggle no longer.

Vaughan is laughing bitterly, scornfully, as he lifts the paper. It is only a printed page, after all.

"What do you mean by such a performance?" he asks. "A nice bit of work over an accursed little—"

He stops. He has caught sight of the writing, and he recognizes it; he deciphers the lines, more, it seems to him, by a sudden action of memory than any thing else.

"*Milady—Marguerite.*

"*Darrell Vaughan—Darrell Vaughan.*"

Something shivers at his heart as if a hand of ice had suddenly been laid there. Were he able to analyze his thoughts, he could not tell whether it is pain—what men call remorse—or only rage. But he feels as if a ghost had started up before his eyes—yes, a ghost, though his materialistic creed would not grant any significance to the word invented to frighten children.

It all comes back—incident after incident of that episode in his life so long perished—of the very day he wrote those lines—the beautiful face which looked up into his as he laughingly penciled them—the face radiant with youth and loveliness! More than this, he sees the crowd in the court-room—that face looks out at him again, awful in the wreck of its beauty, in its apathy of despair. These pictures flash before his eyes as a gleam of lightning reveals phase after phase of a landscape that has been hidden beneath the blackness of a tempest till it looks unfamiliar.

He turns angrily upon Elizabeth.

"Have you been spying—hunting among my things—"

Then he stops, conscious that he has betrayed himself.

"I will tell you how I found it," he hears Elizabeth say.

"Nonsense! What is it any way? I am sure

you must be out of your senses—making a scene over a scrap of an old book."

This with some feeble pretense to cheat not only her but himself—to get away from those flashes of memory that burn and sear somehow as they have hardly done during all these years of secrecy and guilt.

"We must talk about it," Elizabeth says, firmly. "I can not live, Darrell Vaughan—I can not bear my part of the burden unless you will take some means—try in some way to atone."

"Now see here—"

"Stop, stop! listen to me!"

"I shall do nothing of the sort! You have found, Heaven knows how or when, a scrap of an old book, and you choose to build up a romance, and go into one of your fevers, and act when I come home more like a lunatic than any thing else."

She sits upright in her chair now. Every trace of emotion has left her face; her eyes are full upon him with that cold, searching expression he has learned so well—a look that always irritates him more than the most bitter words could do.

"Why you showed me this I can not imagine," he hurries on, forced by his natural dissimulation to keep up this farce of falsehood, however vain and shallow he may feel it to be.

"Don't say any more—don't!" Elizabeth says, and her voice falters. It makes her faint, sick, the miserable attempt to deceive at a moment like this, when all she longs for is to help him into some course of right action. "Let me tell you—I am not angry, I don't mean to make a scene; but you must hear."

"I'll hear nothing more of your absurd fancies; some ridiculous whim; a trick you have gotten up to annoy me," he persists still, and can not stop, though he feels the absolute absurdity of the position he has taken.

"I must tell you, Darrell, for I have found—Milady's child."

She hesitates a little over the words. Even now, after all that has come and gone, after all she has lived through, the misery and degradation he has forced upon her, she shrinks from the task of showing him that she sees his soul as it really is. But she has spoken the words. A brief silence follows.

"Well, what do you mean to do now?" he asks, sullenly.

"It was about that I wanted to speak," she replies. "If that had been all, I would never have told you—I would have cared for the little thing, and been glad to; but there's something more to be done."

He leaves her side, and walks up and down the room among the shadows. Elizabeth rises from her seat and approaches him. He turns toward her, frowning blackly.

"I'll just tell you one thing," he says; "you're the curse of my life, and I hate you!"

The cruel words do not anger her; they do not even cause her pain. What she thinks of at this moment is to succeed in her purpose—to find some appeal which shall move his heart or his conscience.

"There is no need to talk of yourself or me just now," she answers, moving beside him as he resumes his march. "I am not minding for myself—I can't even care about what you say—"

"Because you are stone—ice!" he breaks in, passionately. "All you want is to set yourself up on a pedestal of dignity and virtue, and show how much better you are than other people! Better! Wait till you are tempted; wait till you have blood in your veins before—"

He ends the speech only by a gesture—a movement as if his impulse were to strike, but lets his hand drop to his side.

She must go on—she must tell the rest. Personally she is powerless to act, but she can not endure the consciousness that she has made no effort to aid that hapless woman, to aid Darrell himself in the strife of his evil instincts against his own soul.

"Don't talk of me," she says; "don't think of me if you can help it. I am nothing in the matter."

"Then why do you meddle with it?" he interrupts. "I suppose you mean to do heroics! I should think you were old enough to have learned common-sense. Do you suppose men are angels? Do you think there is any body that has not gone through some infernal folly of the sort?"

"I don't judge you; try to understand me. It is not that. I only want—oh, Darrell! it is never too late to set wrong right; never too late to atone!"

He looks at her now with only an expression of amazement in his countenance.

"Now what have you got into your head?" he asks.

"If she could be found—she went to California—it is long ago—but she might be found—she might be helped. She was ill—suffering; she—"

"Who the deuce told you all this fine romance?" he breaks in. "Now let's finish and have no more words. I've no intention of pretending not to understand. There was such a woman, and I was a young fool! If there was any body deserved pity, it was I. But it is useless to try to make you comprehend that."

"She was so young, so—"

"Will you be quiet? I tell you that you don't know what you are talking about! The woman was one of the worst creatures that ever lived. As for all that stuff—the child, and all that—it might be mine or any body's! Now don't shiver and shake—you've brought it on yourself—try and look at the business in a reasonable light."

"Oh, don't I tell you it makes no difference where I am concerned?" she groans. "Only let let us try to do something. Don't remember I am your wife; just think that we are two friends —that I want to help—that I shall be glad and thankful to help."

"Why, what is there to be done?"

"The child. If there is nothing else to be done, we might—"

She can not finish; he is laughing! Oh, if he had heaped abuse upon her, struck her to the earth, she thinks it would have been little to bear in comparison to this proof of his utter hardness.

"Perhaps you'd like to adopt the brat—do the good Samaritan, so as to have a proof of my wickedness always at hand," he sneers.

"I would take it if you would let me," is her answer; "I would love it. Who knows? Perhaps she might bring a blessing into our home."

"Of all exasperating women you are the worst!" he exclaims. "Now let this be the last time you ever mention the subject. I should think you would be ashamed to mix yourself up with such wickedness—so fine and virtuous as you are."

"And you will do nothing?"

"No! A pretty idea if a man is to hunt up every vile woman that happened to fasten herself on him when he was young and silly! If that were the law, I'm thinking you'd find some of your religious friends with a sort of harem that would astonish you."

She has gained nothing—done no good! That is all she thinks or cares for. She does not even heed the coarse words which at another moment would have hurt her worse than blows.

"I can not bear it!" she cries; "I can not bear it! She was young—she was a woman—she must have been innocent once—"

"Now I doubt that," Vaughan breaks in again with cool irony. "She was born utterly depraved and abandoned. I see what you fancy—that I ruined her life—drove her to sin, as you call it. Nothing of the sort. Why you ought to be ashamed to make me tell you such things. Of course you would blame me—you would be certain I had been wrong! I suffered enough from that she-devil. I hope she's dead!"

"Darrell!"

"I hope she's dead! She nearly ruined me; she— Why she was a liar and a thief! Look here, you needn't talk about hunting her up. I remember now, she was concerned in a murder or something of the sort. I heard of her in California; they lynched her, I think. A wretch —a devil; and you come laying her sins at my door! I'll not endure it. I'm tired of you always trying to believe some ill of me. Let me alone, or I'll make you repent it."

How much is acting, how much genuine rage, Elizabeth can not tell. It does not matter. As usual, she has done harm in her effort to act aright. She is ready to believe ill of him—she feels that; is it strange? She has every reason; but what good can follow harsh words or recrimination? If she had only been silent—yet that seemed impossible. She has accomplished nothing, but she has done every thing in her power. She knows that each word he speaks is false; she can not credit him, though there would be a certain relief in doing so. Whatever she had since grown under the brutalizing effects of an evil life, the woman had loved him. She had been young and fair, and—oh, why think, why torture herself! She is helpless—helpless! Living or dead, the outcast is beyond her reach. It had seemed so easy, as she thought, of ways and means to help, and a wall, a great black wall, has suddenly been built between her and the possibility.

Something for the child she may do—in secret. Darrell Vaughan's child—his eyes, his expression. There is proof there which even he could not resist were she set before him.

When she looks up from that whirl of dizzying reflection she is alone. Vaughan has left the room without her observing it after that last furious tirade. The torn page lies at her feet, where he flung it; she picks it up—smoothes it out— hides it away. She can not destroy the record; utterly worthless as it is, she can no more do it than she could spurn the wretched creature herself if she were to appear suddenly and beg for help. Dead—dead as the penalty of her crimes! Vaughan had said this; it is not true! There seems no reason for doubting him, but, all the same, Elizabeth feels that it is not true.

It is quite dark; dinner must be nearly ready. It is time to dress; every wearisome, petty detail of common life must go on. Shock after shock may come—she may be thrust further and further into the gloom and cold, farther and farther from any hope whereon to steady her mind —but life must go on. The miserable pretense must be kept up: dinners eaten, friends greeted, the whole round of daily existence endured, while her soul stares out into the blackness with aching eyes, and can scarcely find a ray of light to remind her that above all and beyond all, the misery, the sin, there still stretches heaven with its future.

Her dressing-room is lighted, but the maid is not there.

Vaughan enters quickly; he has heard her step. He comes holding a letter in his hand.

"Why didn't you tell me Carstoe was gone?" he asks. "What the devil does it mean—is this your work too?"

"I had no time to remember," she answers. "He told me business called him back to California. If I had thought about it, I should have supposed you knew."

"The old fool has resigned the agency!" exclaims Vaughan. "Now just tell me what that means."

"I have no idea; he did not speak of it to me." She is telling the truth—he sees that.

"Ungrateful old hound!" he mutters.

"I don't think Mr. Carstoe is that," Elizabeth replies, absently. "It seems odd—what does he say?"

"Say—say? Read his letter and see! You may dine without me—I am going out. You have managed a pretty welcome for a man after a month's absence! You're a lovely pattern of a wife—a model of the domestic virtues!"

Then he flings out of the room. Elizabeth reads Mr. Carstoe's letter. It affords no explanation; he only says that circumstances compel him to resign his trust. While in California he will arrange the business matters so that they can be placed in some other hands. If Mr. Vaughan will write at once and appoint a new agent, he, Carstoe, will be glad, as he desires as soon as possible to be freed from his present duties.

What it means Elizabeth does not know, but she feels that the brief, constrained letter has a meaning, and a painful one. In some way his illusions in regard to Darrell Vaughan have been dispelled—he knows him for what he is: so much significance the letter has to her.

They come presently and tell her dinner is ready. She makes some excuse for her husband, but not a soul among the domestic band is deceived. They know very well that Mr. Vaughan is subject "to his little tempers," smooth as he appears to the outside world. They comprehend perfectly that he has left the house under the influence of one of these attacks. They talked it over among themselves of course, and are divided in opinion as to whether the blame rests with the master or mistress of the mansion, and, after a general instinct of human nature, end in blaming both about equally, and finding a certain pleasure in so doing.

CHAPTER XXVIII.

THE QUEEN OF THE BOHEMIANS.

THE autumn had come before Nathalie La Tour's affairs rendered the voyage to America practicable. She was wild with impatience to go. More numbers of the *Bohemian* had reached her, bringing fresh incense of praise, and eagerly demanding her presence in the New World, where, according to the *Bohemian*, a whole nation waited to greet her with the admiration due her genius and her success.

Nathalie had looked forward to attracting great attention on the steamer: of course all her fellow-voyagers would be excited about the presence of so celebrated a woman. Unfortunately, Nathalie's stomach was not of the strongest, and from Liverpool to New York she could only lie flat in her berth, and wish disconsolately that she had never been born. But she could not even be miserable in peace, for Susanne, equally wretched, and no better able to bear it

than if she had been a genius also, lay moaning night and day on the upper shelf, finding slight comfort in peevish complaints against the cruelty of her mistress in having dragged an unfortunate old woman forth to meet an awful death upon the sea, in spite of prayers and resistance. Susanne always insisted upon her unwillingness to go, though she had scolded straight through the summer over the delay in their departure.

But the misery ended at length; land was in sight; the steamer sailed majestically up the beautiful bay, and Nathalie got on deck to catch a first view of the great city where the fulfillment of the future awaited her.

She was, perhaps, a little surprised that the cannon from the different forts did not boom out a welcome as she passed; but when the vessel reached the dock, what she called her triumph commenced.

The editor of the *Bohemian*, accompanied by representatives of the illustrious band which gave the paper its name, came on board to receive her. Nathalie could have wished that most of the party had been differently attired, but consoled her easily disturbed taste by remembering how many examples there were of genius appearing indifferent to such matters.

Lodgings had been procured for her at a French hotel in the upper part of the town, and the very evening of her arrival there was a gathering of the Bohemian clique in those apartments. The editor had told her how anxious these earnest-souled men and women were to welcome her appearance among them, and though she would have been glad to rest and recover her looks a little, the fear of disappointing them, and her own eagerness to taste her triumph to the full, prevented her asking for any delay. Indeed, as she understood the matter, these unknown worshipers had prepared an entertainment in her honor—to be given at the hotel in order to spare her fatigue, but an entertainment of which she was to be the chief guest.

The supper was a good one; nothing had been spared, even to champagne; and the Bohemians—more shame to an unappreciative world, who paid slight attention to the needs of such elevated natures—did not drink champagne every day. A few men appeared in correct evening dress, more or less dilapidated; several with their coats tightly buttoned, in order to conceal the lack of waistcoat. Others made as much as possible of that garment, conscious that it was the best point in their attire. There were long-haired poets, who had pined voiceless until they found utterance through the columns of the *Bohemian*. Men whose pictures year after year were sent ignominiously back from the exhibitions, owing to the malice and envy of the "hanging committee;" but the *Bohemian* was at hand now to give their wrongs a tongue, not to mention interminable criticisms upon those remarkable works. There were women celebrated, through the *Bohemian*—women who wrote, women who painted, women who acted and sang as neither Rachel nor Patti had ever done, though fate and a gross world refused a recognition of their gifts. But men and women, they bowed before Nathalie, and the supper proved a brilliant success.

Many poems were recited in her honor ; she was called on for a speech ; she made one that was loudly applauded. She was crowned with a garland of flowers, and hailed Queen—"Queen of the Bohemians!" Her heart swelled, and Susanne, peeping at the scene through a half-open door, fairly wept with joy, convinced, like her young mistress, that this adulation was the admiring utterance of a whole people—an entire continent.

But the culminating moment was when the prophet of the band rose to pour forth the inspired measures her coming had roused in his mighty soul. This tribute had been left till the last—it followed directly after the coronation, and Bohemia felt that nothing more was possible in the way of honoring its new sovereign. Nathalie was convinced of the beauty of the poem ; every body rushed into ecstasies ; one enthusiastic female kissed the hem of the prophet's robe— a rather greasy black frock-coat, much worn about the seams. But somehow, try as she might to appreciate the tribute, it seemed to Nathalie that she must be less familiar with English than she supposed, though she had spoken it all her life, for these glowing strains sounded almost like an unknown language in her ears.

The editor of the *Bohemian* was too wise a man to lose any time. On the very next day Nathalie signed various legal documents and a check for a goodly amount ; a share of that new lever of the world belonged to her, and her name would appear on the next issue as one of the editors.

Those first days were so full of occupation that Nathalie had little leisure for surprise or disappointment, though the moment she set eyes on the leaders of the clan, old Susanne expressed her opinion that if literary men wore such shabby trousers, for her part she would prefer those with less poetry and better clothes.

Nathalie had several articles to prepare for the *Bohemian*, and, as newspaper writing was new to her, of course they occupied a great deal of attention. Then her friends were much about her, and somehow, men and women, they always seemed to be eating—how it chanced Nathalie could not tell. She began to fear she had a mania for making people eat, and that those poetical natures yielded just to gratify her.

Why, there was Mrs. O'Moo, who gave lectures (in California) "On the Radicalism of Jesus Christ," who said that the fathers of women's children ought to be whatsoever men those women happened to have a spiritual affinity for at the time—even she ate, ethereal as her nature was—ate breakfast and dinner, often, and extra meals besides. And young Mr. Fustian, with his long hair in his eyes, and poetry upon his lips, whose soul had called Nathalie's soul across the vast deep, he ate ; and all the intermediates between these two extremes of the Bohemian clique did more eating during the first ten days after Nathalie's arrival than they had done in months.

It was a little blow to Nathalie when Miss Grun (who painted such lovely pre-Raphaelite pictures, which some man high in authority kept out of the exhibition from jealousy)—I say it was a blow to Nathalie, when the fair Miss Grun made a symposium at her studio in honor of the Queen, to be set down to cold beans and vinegar, and a huge pitcher of ale to moisten the repast.

But when Nathalie's hotel bill came in, she no longer wondered at cold beans and vinegar being the usual Bohemian ambrosia at supper. She was almost frightened to death, accustomed as she was to the moderate prices of the Continent, and Susanne gave her an inordinate scolding.

There were items in the bill which puzzled Nathalie exceedingly. The expense of the entertainment given by the Bohemians on her arrival was set down. This must have been forgetfulness on the part of the deputation—Nathalie felt that she could not bring herself to mention it. There were carriages at late hours of the night, and double prices for them in consequence. The only carriages ordered at such times had been those her guests had commanded ; but this was a matter also that she could not mention to her friends. Then followed items such as these : Three rum punches at bar ; four gin cocktails at bar ; six hot whiskies at bar. Nathalie did not even know what the bar was. Susanne was unable to comprehend the bill because the clerk had written it in English, but she sent for the hotel-keeper, and rated him fearfully. He listened with the composure only a French landlord can attain, then reminded Nathalie that the day after her arrival he had asked her if orders given by her guests were to be set down to her account. Nathalie recollected this—remembered, too, that she had replied in the affirmative, without stopping to think the question an odd one—her head had been full of her honors.

But Madame had not forgotten? Very well —all these extraordinary items were the result of this direction on Madame's part. Nathalie bethought herself that Bohemianism was fraternity, and held her peace.

Miss Grun happened to come in while Nathalie was still regarding the long row of figures, and Susanne upbraiding her loudly. Miss Grun soon understood the case. No doubt the bill was right enough (Nathalie could not bring herself to do more than show the total); she must expect horrible charges if she lived at a hotel.

"I do not know what your fortune may be," said Miss Grun, beautifully oblivious of the fact that nothing else had been talked of in Bohemia for months before Nathalie's arrival; "but it is only the very wealthiest persons who can afford to live at such places in New York."

"I did not know," returned Nathalie. "I wonder Mr. Counter did not tell me."

"Oh, Counter is always in the clouds," said Miss Grun, disdainfully.

"Or Mrs. O'Moo," continued Nathalie.

Miss Grun gave vent to a sharp, derisive laugh.

Even in Bohemia ladies sometimes quarreled, and a bitter enmity existed between the female lecturer and the maiden artist. The origin of the difficulty was quite obscure; but it appeared tolerably certain that a ruffled petticoat was at the bottom of the feud—a ruffled petticoat, and a man, of course.

In Bohemia it was by no means uncommon for people to borrow articles of attire. Nathalie had herself noticed a blue-crape shawl which belonged apparently to six different ladies, and was acquainted with a turquoise pin which made regularly the round of the younger gentlemen's shirt-fronts. So following this sweet rule of communism and fraternity, Miss Grun had once upon a time lent Mrs. O'Moo the ruffled petticoat—but she did not lend her lover. Mrs. O'Moo took him without leave; whether as a lawful perquisite on the ground of affinity, or a natural accompaniment to the petticoat, I am unable to say—she took him, however, and *hinc illæ lachrymæ.*

So now Miss Grun emitted a derisive laugh, and, as if the sound had been a magic spell which forced her into speech, she began the melancholy history. O'Moo did not, in reality, belong to the band over which Nathalie ruled. She was a New Light — had foisted herself upon Bohemia, and stuck there like a barnacle on a ship.

Miss Grun enveloped Nathalie in the petticoat—blinded her with the ruffle — produced a picture of the false lover—wept—moaned—had to be comforted with curaçoa and stayed with sweet-cake. At the end of all her eloquence, Nathalie's ideas were so vague that she could not tell whether the young man had tried to cut the border off O'Moo's under-garment as a present to his lady-love, or O'Moo had attempted to make a ruffle for her petticoat out of some article of the gentleman's attire.

Nathalie thought that Miss Grun ought to confine herself to telling stories with her brush.

But to return to the matter in hand, which they did, after Miss Grun grew composed. The artist advised Nathalie to take a furnished house, and the counsel met with the approbation of sev-eral of the male Bohemians who chanced to stray in at the moment.

These brethren took lunch, by the way. They found Miss Grun daintily nibbling her sweet-cake, and proposed joining her, "not to interrupt."

Nathalie did take a furnished house, and spent a good deal of money on what she called "trifles" for its further embellishment, and made it a very pretty abode indeed. Her expenses were lessened, but she had so many hangers-on that they were still heavier than she could afford. For instance, when Miss Grun confided to her with bitter tears that she was forced to sleep on a sofa in her studio, and cut her bread with a palette-knife, how could Nathalie avoid offering her a home? Then some poet would fling himself upon the floor in her drawing-room, and beg for a dagger wherewith to cut his throat — Nathalie would lend him fifty dollars instead. Somebody was always dining with her, more somebodies going to theatres or opera at her expense, and most of the band, male and female, soon appeared in entirely new wardrobes. But even this did not prevent articles of dress being frequently borrowed. However, old Susanne put a stop to that privilege. She and Mrs. O'Moo finally had a battle royal about the matter. Susanne caught O'Moo one evening rummaging among her mistress's trinkets and laces. O'Moo said she was searching for a pattern, Susanne swore that she was stealing a pocket-handkerchief. Between them they made such an outrageous racket that a stray policeman stopped before the house, and Nathalie and the rest of the Bohemians rushed upstairs in wild excitement.

Luckily Susanne could only tell her story in French, so scarcely any one besides Nathalie understood the charge she brought. But O'Moo was furious, and wanted the Queen to send the old woman adrift. Nathalie refused to do this, so O'Moo deserted the Bohemians in disgust, and went back to California in the society of a man who gave concerts to illustrate the "Music of the Future," and O'Moo explained his meaning in a lecture styled the "Probable Nebulistic State of Souls in the Inner Cosmos."

So the weeks went on to November. Nathalie's kingdom did not prove the golden land she had expected. What was the good of making pretty toilets for men who seldom combed their hair, and to sit in the room with women who pinned on their flounces, and wore stockings that needed darning?

Then one day there came a famous lady from another clique, and told Nathalie she had made a mistake—been swindled, in fact. The Bohemians were a low, impecunious set, possessing no influence whatever. Nathalie ought to join the Transcendentals — buy into their journal, which was the real lever that was to move the world. Then appeared somebody else belonging to another "ism" which was the only light to live by. Then a third set descended upon her, and the Bohemians fought all the intruders tooth and nail, and fairly set a guard in the royal abode to keep their Queen from being stolen. Between them all Nathalie felt terribly confused and at a loss, and was almost inclined to run away and subside into obscurity. Bohemianism in New York she found was very different from the upper world of Parisian Bohemia, glimpses of which had so dazzled her.

Then her ready money was almost exhausted. She had debts. The fortune from her new book did not pour in its golden tide. The editor of the *Bohemian* was constantly demanding material aid. Altogether, Nathalie began to find her crown a thorny one, and to be sorely perplexed and troubled whenever she had time to think. And a period came when she must take time, for her affairs were in a critical situation.

So it chanced that on the very evening of Darrell Vaughan's return she sat alone in her pretty salon. The whole Bohemian set had gone to a lecture for which Nathalie had been persuaded to buy a score or two of tickets, but she herself remained at home, and went down into the depths of despair.

Since her arrival in America, Nathalie's days had been so full of occupation that she had thought little of Vaughan. She was fond of indulging in a bit of sentiment over her girlish dream — fond of saying, writing, and believing that her heart had been crushed by a cruel tyranny which had separated her from the man she loved, and tied her fast in unholy wedlock; but it was a very pleasant misery. The Bohemians were not interested in politics, or in any thing or any body outside their circle, so it was only lately that mention of Vaughan had reached Nathalie. But she had learned something of the prominent position he occupied, and wondered occasionally how and when they should meet. She could not have accounted for the feeling which restrained her from making an effort to bring this meeting about. She liked to think of the possibility; yet mixed with the romantic pleasure there was a certain shrinking, almost a dread, which kept her passive.

Vaughan had lately read Nathalie's last book, though he had forgotten the name of the man she married, and did not connect this new author with the girl he had met at Clarens.

He recollected Nathalie herself very well, and often felt angered that he had not been able further to study the peculiar nature which had greatly impressed him. Girl and woman, Nathalie always showed for more than her mental gifts really warranted, and Vaughan had mistaken the glitter for gold. Often in his thoughts he compared her with Elizabeth, to the latter's disadvantage. There was a satisfaction in underrating his wife. The more he was obliged to make use of Elizabeth's talents, the fonder he became of doing this—probably to convince himself that she had no important part in his work.

When he dashed out of the house after the scene with his wife on the evening of his return, he went to his club to dine. A literary acquaintance whom he happened to meet told him over their wine—of which both drank a goodly share —the history of the woman whose novel he had just been reading, and Vaughan learned that destiny had again flung Nathalie L'Estrange within his reach.

So late that evening, as the Queen of the Bohemians sat alone, succeeding very tolerably in being miserable, because she hated solitude, the door opened suddenly, and Darrell Vaughan came once more, without warning, into her presence.

She had not looked up, supposing the intruder to be Susanne, armed with some sort of reproof or complaint.

"Nathalie!" he called; "Nathalie!"

She raised her eyes, and saw him standing before her—handsomer than ever, she thought. Dissipated habits — above all, the use of that poisonous drug which he craved more and more —had terribly sapped Vaughan's vigor, bodily and mentally; but as yet there were few outward physical signs. To-night the wine and spirits which he drank would have left many men helplessly intoxicated, but with him the only effect was to make his face deadly pale, kindle a fire in his beautiful eyes, and quicken fancy and tongue with the eloquence which grew daily more dependent upon such stimulus.

Nathalie started to her feet, and uttered his name, half in joy, half in terror—a terror for which she could not have accounted to herself had she sought to do so.

He was beside her, clasping her hands in his, raining kisses upon them, uttering wild words, the poetry of which rather than their full meaning struck Nathalie's fancy. But partly the spirit of coquetry so strong within her, partly that inexplicable dread which had sent a chill across her joy, enabled her quickly to regain an apparent composure.

"That will do," she said, laughing, "even as a tribute to an acquaintance so pleasant as ours was."

She drew her hands from his clasp, and sat down. He would have flung himself on his knees before her, but she held up a warning finger.

"I shall send for Susanne," she said. "Susanne outwitted us once—she will come down upon you like an ogress."

"And they married you—carried you off— and I was helpless!" cried Vaughan. "I only knew to-night that you were near; I have been away for several weeks. Oh, what a life it has been since I lost you! But I have found you, found you, my beautiful Nathalie!"

"I have seen your name frequently," she replied; "you have been growing famous, and I—I have not been idle."

"Idle? I should think not! Why, you are the most celebrated woman of the day. I have read every one of your books."

She believed his statement in regard to her fame, despite of the unpleasant fact that only to-day the editor of the *Bohemian* had been after more money to keep the journal in existence, and her publishers had hinted that if she decided to bring out a novel during the winter it would be well for her to advance the sum necessary to meet the expenses. But she forgot these trifles in the pleasure of listening to the exaggerated encomiums which he lavished upon her works and her success.

"And you are married too," Nathalie said, when her vanity was, for the moment, sufficiently gratified to be able to think of something else. "The only person I have met who knew you told me that—Mr. Peters."

Mr. Peters was the literary man who had informed Vaughan of Nathalie's whereabouts.

"Yes, I am married," returned he moodily.

"Tell me what your wife is like. Mr. Peters only knew the fact. Indeed, he did not pretend to be well acquainted with you."

"No; I just knew him from our belonging to the same club."

"Never mind him," broke in Nathalie; "I just know him too, and very heavy he is on hand." She uttered the bit of slang with a slight foreign accent that made it amusing. "Tell me about your wife. How does she look—is she handsome? Is—is she fond of you?"

"No, to both questions," replied Vaughan. "There is nothing to tell. I was married the spring after I saw you at Clarens. My wife is the dullest, most commonplace of women; she goes her way, and I go mine. The marriage was a family matter; considered a good thing for us both by our relations; and that's all there is about it."

"Ah," said Nathalie. His account was so perfectly in keeping with her French ideas of matrimony that it seemed natural. "And you have no sympathies, no tastes in common?"

"Bah! Does not marriage prevent such? Don't let's talk of her! I had lost you—nothing made any difference. Oh, Nathalie, those lovely days at Clarens!"

"But suffering develops the soul," she replied, with her grandest manner. "I should not have won the fame which is mine had I never suffered."

She looked so pretty, voice and gestures were so sweet and graceful, that Vaughan did not notice the absurdity of the speech.

"Then you did care, Nathalie?"

"Oh, don't talk of those days," she sighed. "We shall be good friends now; no one can hinder that—soul-friends!"

"All my heart and soul are yours!" he exclaimed. "I love you—I have always loved you."

She held up her finger, laughing, though her color changed and her eyes softened.

"I have forbidden such words in my hearing," she said. "You are my friend, my best friend—my only one, indeed. Ah, life is sad, sad—my way is very lonely."

She wanted poetry and sentiment, that was evident, so Vaughan prepared to do both to any extent. She talked freely about herself—few things pleased her more than to do this. She detailed her life in France, made a dramatic scene of her escape, the perils she had run, and brought up her narrative to the present. She told her plans, expounded her theories; and though Vaughan was perfectly able to perceive their absurdity, they did not seem absurd when uttered in her pretty words. He shuddered at the idea of the people by whom she was surrounded, but it would not be difficult to persuade her to give them their *congé*. He knew her well enough to be certain that she loved gayety and excitement better than any thing in the world, and the land of Bohemia had grown familiar enough to appear a little wearisome now.

There was nothing she concealed, even to the money anxieties, of which Darrell was delighted to hear.

"Oh, life shall be a different thing henceforth to us both!" he cried, and burst into excited blank verse, which sounded sweeter to Nathalie than any thing her most admired poets of the modern sensational school had ever sung.

Still, the interview convinced Vaughan that triumph would not be easy. The creature was an odd compound: tantalizing, bewitching. Darrell's head was in a whirl.

CHAPTER XXIX.

A REVELATION.

VAUGHAN had been at home about four weeks. When December came, Congress commenced its session. He went to Washington for a few days. The morning after his return, Elizabeth learned that he had resigned his seat in the House—had been offered, and had accepted, one of the principal city offices connected with the Port.

She read this in a newspaper—the first tidings that reached her in regard to the matter. She had scarcely seen her husband alone since the evening of his arrival. She understood perfectly that it was neither a feeling of shame nor guilt which caused him to avoid her—not even anger; but a sentiment of dislike, so strong that in his nature it might grow rapidly into positive hatred.

She was by no means satisfied with her own conduct—she knew that in her appeal to his conscience she nad meant for the best; but she might have erred — might only have rendered matters worse so far as their present life was concerned. Yet had it been to do over again, she felt that she could have adopted no other line of action.

But the subject still kept its hold upon her mind; discouraged as she was, helpless indeed, she could not relinquish the idea in some way of aiding that unknown woman. She was not dead— this conviction remained. But to find her, even to take the least step toward so doing, appeared utterly impossible. Yet to sit quiet, be passive, was terrible—it seemed like spurning a human soul that called for help.

Between herself and her husband no further conversation could be held in regard to the affair. He had not even asked how she discovered the child, or where it was—thrust every thing connected with the history aside, as he had done for years—perhaps did not even recognize it as specially the cause for the active animosity growing up in his soul toward herself.

Elizabeth was right in these conclusions. If he had put his feelings into words, she could not more accurately have understood them. The motives which had induced Vaughan to resign his seat in Congress and accept his present position were twofold. A question was coming up during the present session upon which he desired to avoid giving either speech or vote—he saw clearly that it would be full of complications for the future.

Vaughan comprehended that the two great political parties were on the eve of a crisis out of which would inevitably spring new platforms —possibly an entirely fresh party. He had no mind to involve himself just now in any important decision, and the city office gave an admirable pretext for a withdrawal. But there was another inducement at work—that insane greed for money which seemed only to increase with the growth of his fortune. The ramifications of the potent Ring extended to this office also. Vaughan knew that vast sums could be plundered— that they had been by his predecessor—without the slightest danger of incurring condemnation or even inquiry. So he found patriotic reasons for accepting the position, and made a brilliant speech, which was quoted in the journals from Maine to Georgia, and proceeded to plunge both hands into the public coffers without delay.

But occupied as he was, his passion for Nathalie La Tour became the ruling influence of his life—so absorbing that, in spite of his ability to reason, to regard the future, it would have led him into any reckless measure which she might have demanded.

But Nathalie did not ask or want this. She enjoyed the new excitement that his society brought, and she believed herself wildly in love with him; and, as usual, contented herself with dreams and theories, whatever the world might think.

Short as the time had been since Vaughan's finding her again, there was already plenty of gossip among his more intimate associates, and the Bohemians were greatly enraged by the change which his appearance effected in Nathalie's habits.

Vaughan absolutely refused to have any thing to do with the troop. He irreverently pronounced the men a set of cads, and the women worse. Nathalie was somewhat horrified at his openly expressed contempt for these high-souled creatures, but she would have given up a great deal more than their society for Darrell's sake.

Then, too, he brought a different set of people about her: men who dressed well, who could talk agreeable nonsense—had an odor of elegance, a glint of *jeunesse dorée* in every thing they said and did, which was delightful to one side of her capricious, excitement-craving nature, however much in theory she might believe herself attached to soul-intercourse, aims for human progress, and other matters equally grand and poetical.

She formed the acquaintance also of two or three French actresses; and it was delicious to talk *chiffons* and have perfectly dressed women by her side, and witty speeches and brilliant repartees flitting about, after so many weeks of aching eyes, caused by the ill-assorted colors with which the Bohemian sisters had vexed her spirit, and the constant strain upon her faculties from listening to long-winded poems that did not contain a line she could understand.

Her house was a convenience to Darrell: he could there indulge his love of high play without danger of discovery, and gather about him the brilliant, worthless men and women whose society he so thoroughly enjoyed. Therefore the Bohemians were furious, though wise enough not to ruin their cause by expostulations or complaints. They had the sense to comprehend that any interference would altogether deprive them of their Queen. And Nathalie was as ready as ever to give them money—to invite them to dainty suppers when Vaughan was not there. Still, they felt themselves injured, and were the first to give her intimacy with this man a coarse name, and assail her reputation in every way possible.

Probably in neither of the two opposite little circles between which Nathalie vibrated was there a human creature (save one) who believed her other than a bad woman—employing the word as people do where feminine sins are concerned; as if there were only one sort of evil-doing which can entitle a member of the sex to that name.

Yet Vaughan's passion had met with no other reward than tenderness and sympathy—sympathy for the dismal, thwarted life whose dreariness he had painted to her in such glowing colors. The people about them believed that he was her lover, and Darrell felt himself ridiculous in his own eyes at the position in which he was placed. Nathalie would talk sentimental nonsense to any extent; she would weep at the cruel destiny which had separated them—enjoy a melodramatic scene, and rave and rant like a second Juliet; but she stopped there.

It was not calculation; it was not that she doubted the strength of her love; it was not respect for any law human or divine—she gloried in believing herself above the reach of dull prejudices and senseless creeds. Still, neither Vaughan's passionate pleadings, her own weakness, nor the fear of losing him—and he sometimes threatened her with that penalty—were able to carry this woman, reckless and abandoned as the world believed her, one step beyond what society calls "flirtation," and permits its devotees to indulge without scruple.

Nathalie could not argue the matter in her mind—she was too inconsequent, too frivolous; but the fact was there. The more she became convinced of the power of her own affection, the more completely heart and fancy went out toward this man, the more did she retreat from a position which, theoretically, she boldly advanced in her books.

It was natural enough that no information should reach her whereby she could have connected Elizabeth Crauford with the tiresome, commonplace creature that she pictured Vaughan's wife to be. The Craufords were not a Knickerbocker family—Elizabeth had never lived in New York before her marriage; and among the men whom Darrell introduced to Nathalie there probably was not one acquainted with Mrs. Vaughan's maiden name. Of course there was no possibility of the two women meeting, unless it might be at the theatre or opera, and this season Elizabeth seldom went to places of amusement.

At the time Nathalie's book gained its brief notoriety, Elizabeth, attracted by the name of her former acquaintance, had tried to read the story; but its rehash of the Simonian doctrines was not even redeemed by the great genius which has given an unenviable celebrity to certain among the leading French writers, and Elizabeth flung it aside with a sigh, and a feeling of pity for the poor girl, whom she had always remembered with kindness and sympathy.

So, while Vaughan's infatuation became so well known that even Elizabeth's world caught up the story, she remained ignorant of Nathalie's presence in New York. She was not a person to whom her most intimate friends could bring a hint that might awaken any suspicion in her mind where her husband was concerned. Whatever her troubles, they were sacred. She would never, under any circumstances, be guilty of that most contemptible weakness a married man or woman can betray—the putting griefs into words,

and permitting those about to share the pain by so much as an expression or look of sympathy.

The winter dragged by; it could be of no service to any human being to detail its records. Day by day the path grew harder, the darkness more intense. Elizabeth tried to cling to her faith; tried to endure; tried to silence the bitter wail of her heart, which moaned ceaselessly —"How, long, O Lord, how long!"

There were such employments as she could find for herself: the round of visits and society duties; and that was all she had to fill up her life.

At last some unwise writer in a prominent literary journal gave vent to a long diatribe against certain bad books, thus attracting to them the very attention which he declared unworthy any clean-minded man or woman. Foremost in the bitter criticism stood Nathalie La Tour's works —a brief account of her life—the desertion of her husband—her present residence in New York— her absurd title of "Queen of the Bohemians." The whole thing was as injudicious and uncalled for as possible, but by this means Elizabeth learned that Nathalie was near. The fact could be of no importance to her—she could do the woman no good. It was terrible to think of the harm the creature was perpetrating, sad to recollect how many good qualities she possessed, and to what unworthy use she had devoted them—but nothing beyond this regret was possible.

A great crisis in any life is, oddly enough, nine times out of ten brought about by causes which seem the merest trifles.

Only the day after Elizabeth had been reading that review, and sorrowfully recalling the quiet weeks she and Nathalie had spent in the pretty Swiss valley, she received a letter from a friend in St. Louis, begging her to attend to some commissions at Madame Dirnier's, the famous *modiste* of the time. She was going out, so she drove at once to the establishment, as the business was connected with a wedding trousseau, and the articles must be sent immediately.

Madame Dirnier herself was condescending enough to attend to Mrs. Vaughan, and could not resist tempting the rich lady by the display of a marvelous dress of Point d'Alençon lace, which was just then driving half the society women of New York mad, not only by its loveliness, its costliness, but by the history connected therewith. The robe had been manufactured for a royal marriage which never took place; it was purchased by an English Duke for a famous Parisian actress—famous rather for her beauty and adventures than her talent. Mademoiselle P—— appeared once in the dress on the stage of the Gymnase. The next week she died suddenly— everybody must remember the story. Her creditors seized upon her effects, and this wonderful robe had been sent across the ocean as a matter of speculation, and the price set upon it was eighteen thousand dollars.

Elizabeth stood for a while examining the dress, full of the fancies which its history must have roused in any imaginative mind. ..Then she half smiled to perceive that she had gone leagues away from romance, and was simply wishing the thing could be converted into hard, prosaic cash.

One of the hospitals in which she was interested needed money sorely, and Darrell had absolutely refused to give her even a quarter of the sum she desired. He assured her that his available funds were at the time required in his affairs, and would listen neither to persuasion nor argument.

She finished her business, and went home. A week later she received a telegram from St. Louis; there was some mistake in regard to the purchase—a shawl or a scarf or other important trifle had been forgotten. Would Mrs. Vaughan have the goodness to attend to the matter at once? Of course she went immediately, wondering a little, as the most patient human being might have been excused for doing, that it had not occurred to the excited purchaser of wedding finery to telegraph directly to the *modiste*.

On her way out of the place she chanced to hear Madame informing certain customers, desirous of seeing the famous lace dress, that it had been sold that very morning; but Madame either could not or would not tell by whom it had been purchased.

She paid several necessary visits, which detained her so long that it was growing dusk when she returned. As she drove up to the house, Vaughan was just entering; they had not met for two days. He spoke politely enough in the presence of the footman who opened the door, and they passed on into the library together, talking of the first trifle which suggested itself—the weather, the dampness. Both had that consciousness of the eager eyes and ears watching every look and gesture which becomes habitual to all who attempt to keep a show of decency in their married lives when cruel secrets lie under the surface. Not that the eyes and ears ever are deceived, or that the pretenders believe them to be; but somehow playing the sorry farce is a kind of comfort—an absolute necessity, in fact, so long as people have a care to stretch the slightest shred of illusion across the loathsome reality.

Then another domestic Argus followed them into the room with such letters and cards as had arrived. Vaughan took his share, and, still under the control of the eyes, civilly handed Elizabeth's portion to her.

The man went out. Elizabeth sat down by the table, and read her notes—nothing of importance—then remained looking at Vaughan, as he stood by the fire-place busy with his letters.

"I shall not dine at home," he said, as he finished the perusal of his correspondence.

K

There was nothing surprising in this announcement; he seldom dined at home nowadays unless there were invited guests. Whether he took his meals at his club, whether he accepted invitations in which she had no share, Elizabeth never asked.

He was going out; she wanted to speak to him first. The managers of the hospital had written to her again—they were in great difficulty. She had been put to heavy expenses in various ways of late, and for the time had no further means in her possession. But it occurred to her that Vaughan might be willing—if he would give her nothing—to advance the sum she required upon dividends which would come to her in the course of a few months. She had the matter much at heart, and could not forbear this last effort.

"Will you wait a moment, please?" she said, nervously: she never could help being nervous when the necessity for any discussion in regard to money arose.

"What do you want?" he asked, coldly.

He had crossed the room before she spoke. He stood on the opposite side of the table, and looked at her. How rapidly his face was changing! what a worn, strange look it had! how bright and feverish the eyes were! She noticed this with a certain wonder. It was something more than the effects of dissipation: it was the expression of a man consumed by some strong, overmastering passion. This thought flitted rapidly through her mind even while answering his question.

"I wanted to speak to you again about that matter—"

"I told you I had no money to waste on such folly," he interrupted. "We live at the most expensive rate—forty thousand a year would not cover our expenses—I have got mixed up in those companies. I can't give, and I won't."

So gladly, long since, she would have reduced their princely establishment to a more reasonable footing, but this Vaughan would not permit; he was lavish and reckless where show and luxury were concerned.

"I did not mean to ask you to give it," she replied, quietly, with a certain chill disdain in her voice, for strive as she might against her faults she got nowhere near perfection. "I want to borrow it—I shall have funds enough in April. If you would get me the four thousand dollars upon some of my stocks—"

"Oh, if you could ever come down enough from poetry to be practical, and show a little common-sense!" he broke in. "Borrow?—and a miserable sum like that? What do you suppose people would think? I never heard any thing so ridiculous in my life—even from you!"

"You are right to call it a miserable sum," she replied, angry now, though her anger only betrayed itself in the cold scorn of her voice.

"It is ridiculous, too, that I should have any difficulty in procuring it. You are right there, also."

"Now you mean to talk about your accursed money, I suppose!" he exclaimed.

"I never have done so, I think," she said.

"But it is never out of your mind — never! A fine use you would make of it too, if it were in your power! You keep a set of harpies about, and let them plunder you. It's just your vanity, your desire for notoriety, which is at the bottom —that, and a wish to annoy me."

She might have known nothing but strife and harsh words would come of her attempt; she told herself this. An angry retort rose to her lips; she set them hard together, and kept silence.

"Now it is perfectly useless to speak of this again! Give—give—why, I am always giving! My name is on every list of charities and public schemes—"

"When there is any glory to be gained by it," she added, as he paused.

Repentance came as soon as the bitter speech found utterance; but it was too late—the words were spoken.

"I did not mean to say that," she continued, quickly, though it required a powerful effort to make the admission. "I beg your pardon — don't let us quarrel over the matter. If I can not have the money, there is an end."

"Always an end when you have done your best to irritate me by sneers and taunts. Quarrel? Bah! I'll not waste my time by talking to you—I can spend it more pleasantly."

He went quickly out of the room, and presently she was summoned to her solitary repast. She was a great deal alone this winter; they gave frequent dinners—Vaughan had insisted upon a couple of balls; but she accepted only such·invitations as it was impossible to refuse, and appeared in public just enough to avoid the reputation of singularity. Of late Vaughan had ceased to urge her to go out; he had grown fond of observing her peculiarities — of talking about them before others; and when he talked there was something in his face which fairly startled her. She had learned to know that Darrell Vaughan never did any thing without motive, but what his reason for this could be was beyond the reach of any supposition or fancy.

When she came back to the library, after dinner, one of the men was just entering with coals. He had expected to finish his task before she returned, but to-night she was too miserable even to go through the pretense of a meal.

"Is this of any consequence, ma'am?" she heard the man say, as he ended his string of excuses.

He had picked up a crumpled paper from the hearth, and was holding it toward her. She opened it mechanically, and turned to the table, where a reading-lamp stood.

"*Dear V.*,—I have bought the lace dress as you desired—sixteen thou. was the lowest figure; I have put it to your account, and I sent the robe at once to *la belle*. I am afraid, in spite of all our precautions, your part in the matter will leak out—"

That was what Elizabeth read on the scorched page—read so far without thinking. She did not look further; she crushed the paper in her hand, and·stood there till the servant had left the room. Then she went back, and thrust the sheet between the bars of the grate. She recollected seeing Vaughan fling the letter into the fire—it must have rolled off upon the hearth.

He had bought the dress; had commissioned some friend to make the purchase, in order that his own name might not appear; this was evident enough. Sixteen thousand dollars paid for that worthless thing, and he had refused her a quarter of the sum; had talked of embarrassments, of the cost at which they lived, as if her extravagance, her reckless tastes, were the cause! Oddly enough, she did not at the time view the matter from the side which would have been prominent in the thoughts of most wives. Her soul had gone so far from any possibility of contact with this man to whom her life was bound that jealousy had grown out of the question. As she sat by the fire, thinking, thinking, or walked up and down the room when some sort of physical exercise became a necessity—she was not dwelling upon the object her husband had in that purchase, not wondering for whom the robe had been bought—her reflections had gone back over the misery of her existence—its emptiness, its dreariness, its daily torture of pin-pricks, that deprived of all dignity even the current of dark tragedy which lay under.

The next day she did not see Vaughan. It chanced to be a night when they gave a dinner-party, and Elizabeth and her husband did not meet until their guests began to arrive. It proved a gay enough affair; Vaughan was in the highest spirits. It seemed odd to Elizabeth to sit there in the light and warmth—to talk, laugh, listen, and yet have a feeling of such unreality through it all; her heart shivering with a dreary chill.

Every body had engagements; coffee was served, and the people took leave directly after, Vaughan departing among the guests. There was no one left but an elderly gentleman with whom Elizabeth was a great favorite. He remained, perhaps because he understood something of the dreariness of her life, and pitied her; perhaps because he had no engagement, and the drawing-room was bright and comfortable—anyway, he stayed. Conversation was an effort: Elizabeth suddenly recollected that it was the first night of a new opera troupe; she might invite her visitor to go with her to listen to the last acts, and so escape the need of talk.

They did not reach the theatre until the interlude between the third and fourth acts. As they ascended the stairs into the upper lobby, a lady, accompanied by two gentlemen, brushed so close past Elizabeth that their dresses fairly touched. She had passed on before Mrs. Vaughan could catch a sight of her face, but the first glance at the costume would have been enough to make Elizabeth avoid doing so. The woman wore a moiré silk of a golden green, so vivid that it was as showy and *voyante* as scarlet could have been ; over this swept the folds of the lace robe she had seen the week before—the robe purchased by her husband.

Mr. Howland was speaking : she heard herself answer—walked steadily on.

The curtain had risen when they entered the box. Elizabeth had not been six times in the house during the whole winter. Music was often a positive pain to her at this period. More than once she had been obliged to leave the theatre. It was as if a voice of unutterable anguish called to her in every measure the orchestra played, in every note that was sung, while some voice away down in her soul moaned in answer. It was fanciful—absurd ; but she had grown full of fancies and absurdities, and could not struggle against them. It was the same to-night. She wondered why she had tried not to listen ; would have risen and gone away, only that she determined to yield no further to a folly of which she felt ashamed.

The curtain fell. Mr. Howland perceived some friend to whom he wished to speak, and left her for a few minutes. Elizabeth had kept in the shadow of the box draperies, and had asked her good-natured old friend to do so.

"I am stupid and dull," she said, "and I don't want any men to come and make me talk. You don't mind my stupidity, but I can't trust to other people's leniency."

And the elderly bachelor thought her smile the saddest he had seen in many a day, and, knowing Darrell Vaughan tolerably well, wondered why this beautiful creature should have met with so dismal a fate. For she was very beautiful, this weary Elizabeth. The great eyes were dark and soft as deep waters where the stars are shining. Her face had lost the first roundness and bloom of youth, young though she was, but hers had always been a countenance whose beauty depended more on expression and delicacy of feature than upon its coloring. She appeared older than her age—one would have said a woman of twenty six or seven. It was a countenance that possessed a language not easy to understand — untranslatable to many, who would have decided that it looked haughty, cold, and unsympathetic. But those were the fools and blind—it was all written on that melancholy face. The whole record of her disappointed youth was there ; the blighted hopes, the thwart-

ed dreams, the controlled passion and imperiousness, the effort at patience—aye, even to the earnest faith which alone supported her, and gave to eyes and brow the marvelous light which struck the dullest with a vague wonder as to what its signification might be.

After Mr. Howland had gone, she sat trying to occupy her mind with any trifle that she could call up. A passing excitement in a box nearly opposite attracted her attention—several men entering at once—laughter and conversation louder than one would have expected in such a place.

In the front of the *loge* sat a lady—the gleam of jewels on her neck and in her hair. She was fluttering a fan ; her hands moved in pretty gestures, which reminded Elizabeth of the women in Southern climes across the sea.

Something in the figure, the attitude, suddenly struck her with a strange sense of familiarity. Her opera-glass lay beside her on the cushion ; she took it up, and from the safe screen of the curtains looked out again ; then her hand dropped slowly into her lap.

She had seen Nathalie La Tour, talking, laughing, full of animation—prettier, more bewitching than of old. But this was not all : the rich lace dress she wore was the robe that had brushed against Elizabeth a little while before in the lobby—the dress purchased by Darrell Vaughan only the day previous.

The door of the box opened again. Elizabeth lifted the glass anew, and looked across the house.

Vaughan had entered the *loge*. The other men made way for him. Nathalie half rose from her seat, then sank back. She had grown singularly quiet ; the animation of her manner, the Southern gestures, all these had left her. But Elizabeth saw her face—saw the eyes that still had a sort of childish eagerness in their depths—saw the smile which brightened the features into positive beauty ; and she knew that Nathalie La Tour loved the man.

Elizabeth turned away ; she could not bear to look again. The first conscious feeling in her mind, the first tangible thought, was a sincere pity for this woman, whatever she might have become—pity.

There are many men, there may be women, though I think few, who will declare this unnatural ; but it was all that Elizabeth felt—pity. She was not even thinking of the sin, the shame —positively not remembering that she was Darrell Vaughan's wife—only recollecting what Darrell Vaughan was ; and she pitied this ill-brought-up, misdirected creature, whose evil destiny had brought her to so sad a pass.

Presently other reflections came as she leaned back in the shadow, hearing vaguely the pleasant murmur that rose about—a gayety and excitement in which she had no part—which only surged faintly to her ears as she sat there alone, just as the pleasant tumult of other lives, the lives of happy, ordinary people, made itself audible through the dreary stillness of her own; coming only like an echo—nothing real, nothing which she could grasp and hold fast—nothing she could claim in all the interests and enjoyments which were so freely granted to them.

Other reflections followed, harsh enough, angry enough, but this had been the first. Elizabeth could not close her eyes to facts so patent. Purity is not innocence; she was a woman and a wife, and there was only one interpretation to what she had seen. The paragraphs of that harsh review of Nathalie La Tour's works and life recurred to her. Elizabeth understood now the allusions they contained; she knew, too, that Darrell Vaughan was the man indicated in the record of the person "who had so bitterly disappointed the Bohemians by almost depriving them of the Queen they had selected."

She could scarcely feel shocked; first and last she had borne too much. Blow after blow had fallen with such rapidity that she seemed incapable of poignant sensations. Only cold and sick with a strange feeling of abasement and degradation—as if she had been unconsciously dragged down a flowery path into a noisome pit, and saw herself lying there bound hand and foot, her garments stained, impurity and loathsomeness all about her, and the noble face which had lured her on suddenly turned into the gibing countenance of a fiend that mocked at her.

What to do!—which way to turn! What was duty? How far did vows and promises bind the soul? What could be expected of her? Was there no mercy among men? not even in the God she had prayed to and believed in at the worst?

But the door opened, and Mr. Howland returned. The curtain had risen again without her knowing it; the tenor and soprano were singing one of the most beautiful duets of the whole opera—she had not heard a note.

The old bachelor stood quiet behind her chair, believing her absorbed by the music. The sound of his entrance brought her back to the present. She caught the crash of the instruments, the tones of the united voices; it was like heavenly music striking her ears from the impenetrable distance—flinging its echoes down into the black depth where she lay helpless.

It grew unbearable; she could not remain. She rose—caught up her cloak.

"I must go," she said; "take me home—please take me home."

The kind old man obeyed without a question, conscious that she suffered, wishing he had power to aid, but feeling that in the pass to which life had brought this woman not even the relief of human sympathy could be offered or received.

CHAPTER XXX.

HIS VICTIM.

It is deep in December. The snow lies thick in the streets of Moysterville; the mountains rise about it grand and awful, looking like gigantic icebergs towering above the white level of some frozen sea.

Out beyond the town stands a great pile of gloomy buildings, with walls almost as thick and strong as those of a mediæval fortress, with dreary courts, and dark passages, and grated windows. Every thing is stern and heavy and grim, as if the place itself had grown sullen under the burden of sin and crime which makes up the record of those who from the four corners of the earth have finally met here in dismal companionship.

In a long room on an upper floor—a bare, desolate place, though neither cold nor ill-lighted—sits a row of women, each bending silently over her appointed task. They are binding shoes. Not one of them appears to work slowly or unwillingly. The skilful fingers fly just as rapidly along the tedious seams even if the eyes of the taskmaster chance to be withdrawn for a little. Probably to each one of the ghost-like company the work is a solace. They all look ghost-like someway, even the strongest. There are a score of them—more than that; and though, perhaps, no two resemble each other, there is a dreadful general likeness running through the whole group, not arising entirely from the similarity of dress or occupation. One finds it difficult to tell in what the resemblance consists; but it is there—one feels it: it is a part of the shadow which affects the very walls themselves—that shadow of sin and crime.

Down at the farther end of the room sits a woman who seems, no matter how diligent the rest may be, to work twice as fast as they. She sits perfectly motionless, save for the swift movements of her fingers—sits so for hours together; and yet, paradoxical as it sounds, the apathetic stillness has no sense of quiet in it. You expect each instant to see her spring like a panther—rush out of that immobility into an insane fury. The guardians used to have this feeling in regard to her; the women, her fellow-prisoners, have it always—they catch themselves furtively watching her day after day. But the outbreak never comes. She is a model of orderly conduct, though she never receives praise for it. Nobody can help feeling there is something dangerous in the creature—no more sense of security in her stillness than there would be in that of the panther of which she reminds one.

These years of imprisonment have not aged her face. It is paler, thinner than it was the day it looked at Darrell Vaughan out of the prison dock, but it is the same face still. The eyes are a little deeper set, a little more sombre, as if the inner fire which lights them were slowly consuming the soul that feeds the flame. More hopeless than the countenance was that day it could not grow, but there is a certain strength and fixedness of purpose and will which it lacked then. This may come from the fact that for so long she has been unable to reach either narcotics or stimulants, but it does not seem as if that was wholly the reason. She looks as though some strong determination were keeping her alive—as if it would continue to do so through all failure of bodily power; some work to accomplish, some vengeance to take—who shall say?—and perhaps, after all, none of these.

She has never spoken a harsh word to one of her companions, and yet among the whole set there is not a woman but fears her. She seldom talks at all; that may be at the bottom of their dread. During the hours of recreation the others chatter among themselves—tell stories of their misdoings; scoff or are penitent according to their natures—but she never opens her lips in regard to herself. Several of them know about her, the old nickname clings to her still, but the boldest there has no inclination to question Milady, or rouse the nameless spirit they have sometimes seen in her eyes, though it finds no utterance. The rest have friendships and enmities, as their innocent sisters might in the ordinary walks of life; but Milady has, apparently, no more feeling for their memories or their pains than if she had been a ghost. The rest have found certain little interests which have a pathetic side to them. One woman pets a lame chicken that lives in the covered court where they go for exercise in the winter; one has a familiar in the shape of a spider that dwells in a chink of the window-sill near her seat in the work-room. Not a soul among them that does not yet show human capabilities and needs just in those trivialities—all except Milady. Nobody ever saw her moved but once—that was soon after her arrival. Those who were here when she came still relate the story to each new-comer who takes her place among the band of hopeless ones.

They were all out in the walled inclosure where they walked at certain hours during the pleasant weather. Milady was sitting as usual, dumb and apathetic, on a stone in the middle of the little misery of a garden the women were allowed to cultivate. Suddenly a child of one of the keepers—a sick baby, being carried up and down in the sunshine the other side of the wall—was heard to cry. The next thing the women saw was Milady on her feet—rushing to the wall—beating her head and hands against it in a mad frenzy — shrieking unintelligible words, as if she had lost even the power of human speech.

The keepers came and carried her away. Weeks, a good many of them, passed before she appeared among the women again. It was

known that she had been ill—raving in a brain fever, from which the doctors had no idea she could recover. But she lived and came back, more still and taciturn than before, and from that time until the present there has been no change.

Here she is in her place to-day, and, as usual, the other women find themselves, every now and then, watching her. There always seems to them something unfamiliar in her appearance; they never grow accustomed to it as they have done to each other.

Suddenly a door opens noiselessly—there is a horrible quiet about every thing that happens in this place. The warden enters, and he and the keeper of the room whisper together for a few seconds. Milady is the only creature there not interested, to a certain degree excited — the slightest event, if it be only a footstep at an unusual time, is a matter of importance to these poor souls. But Milady hears nothing — does not lift her head.

Then the keeper calls—"Number 37!"

Every woman starts except she who owns the number. Milady is "No. 37." She looks up slowly; the keeper speaks again. She lays her work on the bench in an orderly, methodical fashion, and walks the length of the room, neither interested nor excited, though her fellow-prisoners are ready to spring out of their seats and cry aloud from sheer nervous agitation.

She moves slowly down the chamber; the keeper motions her to follow the warden; the door closes. Milady has passed out of sight, and not one of those women who have been her companions so long will ever see her face again in this world.

She follows her conductor through a passage which her feet have not traversed since the day she entered the prison, down a flight of stairs, and into an apartment where several gentlemen are seated. She stands quite still near the door; not looking at any of the group, not conscious even that their eyes are fixed upon her. Somebody is speaking—she does not notice that he addresses her. The warden, who is near, nudges her elbow lightly, and she hears him whisper—"Why don't you listen?"

If she has had any thought at all since she left the work-room, it has been that she is to be removed to another prison—no possibility beyond this has crossed her mind.

But the gentleman is reading a paper aloud; he is reading a proclamation of pardon from the Governor of the State for the woman who has no name, even in the prison records, except "Milady."

They are all looking at her; the measured voice has ceased to read; there is an instant's silence. They see Milady sway to and fro and put her hands to her head. They think she is going to faint, and the doctor, who is among the group, comes toward her. But she only drops slowly into a chair which is behind her, and sits motionless, with her hands still pressed to her head. They bring some water, but she pushes the glass away. The chaplain feels it his duty to improve the occasion. Several times during the past years he has addressed words of exhortation to Milady, but he might as well have talked to the great door of the prison for any response he received, any sign that his warnings or counsels were heard.

He tells her now that she ought to be very grateful to God—and the Governor. He has not meant to put the two so close together in his speech, but Milady has glanced suddenly up, and her eyes have startled him so that he makes this blunder. The other men forget to smile—they are watching Milady too. So the chaplain begins again; he means to advise her to lead a different life, to employ the years which may be left in repentance for the past and endeavors to make her peace with her Creator. To his utter confusion, he hears himself, instead of saying a single word he intends, just repeating that unfortunate error. But he can not stop; once more he has advised her to be grateful to God —and the Governor.

He retreats, and whispers to the person nearest him—

"I think she's not right in her mind."

If he were to follow out his full thought, he would suggest a similar doubt in regard to himself. He has been a finger-post to heaven for a quarter of a century, and it is a horrible humiliation to have made such an utter failure when he has expected to be unusually impressive and eloquent.

There is a little further conversation among the gentlemen, then they all go out except one. Launce Cromlin is left alone with the woman whom he has at last succeeded in liberating from her unjust imprisonment. The case will not attract any especial attention. The pardon of a convict by a new Governor is too common for the newspapers to do more than make a brief paragraph in regard to it. The new Governor is popular, too. A few of the opposition journals may sneer, and observe that it would be satisfactory to the public mind to have some explanation of this extraordinary step; but in fact the public mind will be slightly exercised in regard to the matter. Events of a startling nature follow each other too rapidly in this age for any body, even among those present at Milady's trial, to remember much about it after this lapse of time.

So Cromlin is left alone with the woman. He is not laboring under the same difficulty as the parson; he has no desire to improve the occasion; his heart is full of pity and sympathy. He goes up to her as she sits leaning forward in the chair, her head drooped, her hands crossed over her knees.

"Do you remember me?" he asks.

She starts at his voice; stares wildly at him for an instant.

"You came to see me in the jail," she half whispers.

"Yes; I am Launce Cromlin—you would not believe it then."

She only looks stupefied—vacant.

"You hardly realize it yet," he says, "but you will presently. You are free—you can go away as soon as you like."

"Go away?" she repeats, with a sort of dull wonder in her voice.

"Yes; the formalities are all settled — the order is signed—you are just as free to go as I."

She gives him one glance, then drops her head again.

"Ten years," he hears her mutter; "ten years!"

She presses her hands to her forehead; he knows that she is conscious of the confusion in her faculties, and is struggling to right her brain. He perceives what might, perhaps, have escaped the chaplain, in spite of his wisdom: the creature is still so dazed that she can only think the ten years of her allotted imprisonment have expired. She knows it is not so, yet she can comprehend in no other way the fact that she is free.

"You have been pardoned," Launce says. "That was the meaning of the paper you heard read. It is more than four years since you came here."

"What do they let me out for now?" she asks suddenly. Then, before he can speak, a new thought comes, and finds utterance — so puerile, so unexpected, that if the chaplain were here he would have no doubt whatever of her helpless insanity—"I hadn't finished binding the shoes."

But she is not mad; it is only that her mind fixes instinctively on this petty, familiar thought, just to steady itself. You shall read in the records left by men who have spent half a life in prison that some similar slight recollection has been all they were capable of when the news of freedom came.

"You will find some other work to do," Launce says, gently. "You will be glad to work, will you not?—to have a home, and be taken care of, and helped on your way?"

Again she looks at him in dull surprise.

"Say that over," she half whispers; "say it slowly."

Launce repeats the words.

"I can't make it mean any thing," she mutters, in a still lower tone. "Sometimes I've heard the women say I was crazy—do you think I am?"

"No; it is only that the news has come upon you suddenly; you can not realize yet that you are free—completely free."

"I thought I dreamed it!"

She says this, and sits looking helplessly about. If he can find some strong impulse upon which to fasten her attention, the mist will pass, and her faculties begin to act.

"You had a child," he says; "you will want to find her."

A sudden spasm distorts her features—her face turns a deathly bluish white—she groans aloud, and falls back in her chair, pressing her hand to her bosom. Launce does not summon assistance; he brings some water, forces her to swallow a little, and gradually her breath returns. But Launce has medical knowledge enough to know what the attack means—the woman has heart disease.

Her wasted hands twist themselves together in her lap—a faint dew gathers in her eyes—the dull cloud lifts, and a strange gleam of the old beauty comes back to her face.

"The child, the child!" The words are almost a shriek. She presses her hands hard against her mouth, and struggles for composure.

"I sha'n't go to her," she says. "If the child's alive, it's with a good woman—I've no business near her."

"Some time you will go," Launce replies. "You are young yet; you will try all your life to redeem the past, and you will succeed."

Instantly her face becomes hopelessly sullen.

"I'll strike you if you say that again!" she cries, with a return of the old ferocious spirit.

"That is very silly," says Launce. "I shall think you are crazy if you talk in that way."

"Oh, yes," she sighs, with a sort of childish penitence. Absurd as the word sounds applied to a creature like her, it is the only one that answers. "I forgot. I almost thought I was in the court again. It seems a hundred years, and yet it is all like one day! Four years—did you say four years? Come here—come close—I want to whisper."

"What is it?" Launce asks, bending his head.

"Does he know?—did he let me out?"

"You had better not ask any questions to-day," he replies. "I am going to take you away from here now."

"Shall I be shut up again?" she demands, apathetically.

"No—try to understand. You are as free as I am. If you will let me, I will take you where you will be kindly treated—where you can rest, and when you are strong, and able to work, something will be found for you to do."

"Let me think—let me alone for a minute—my head turns!"

She sits for a few seconds with her hands clasped over her forehead. Presently she speaks again. "And you were Launce Cromlin all the time; I believed it after you'd gone."

"You had heard my name, then?"

"What do you want to help me for?" she continues, without noticing his question. "Do you know I'm the worst creature in the world? You've been in San Francisco—didn't you hear about Milady? That's me—I'm the woman."

"I know I am very sorry for you," Launce answers; "that is all you need care about now."

"Darrell Vaughan's cousin!" she mutters. "Darrell Vaughan's cousin! And he asks if I'd ever heard his name!"

She laughs, though she shivers from head to foot.

"Never mind about him," Launce says, and, noticing the shudder of fear, hastens, if possible, to strengthen her dread of the man, and thus keep her from taking any step toward exposing him, if such possibility be in her power. "I would advise you never even to mention his name to any human being—don't forget."

"I won't," she whispers. "He'd shut me up—he'd find ways and means—I'll be too wise for that."

An expression of such insane cunning brightens the dreary darkness of her eyes that Launce begins to think her faculties really disordered—perhaps hopelessly so.

"You must not keep me any longer," he observes; "I have a carriage waiting to take you away."

"He'll not find me?—he's not where we are going?"

"No; he is thousands of miles off. If you keep quiet, he will not even know you are out of prison."

"I will," she whispers; "I will. You are Launce Cromlin—you'll hide me safe."

"You will be perfectly safe. There is a good woman where we are going who will be very kind to you."

"Where is it?" she asks quickly.

"To the house my uncle lived in—"

He stops, more puzzled than ever, absolutely startled by the look of triumph, of savage joy, which kindles in her eyes.

"The house his uncle lived in!" she mutters. "Oh, yes, he's Launce Cromlin—I believed it after he was gone."

"When I went to see you that time, you would not tell me why you visited my uncle," Launce says. "You seemed to think that Darrell and I—"

She puts out her hand to interrupt him; draws a heavy breath; the cunning, frightened look comes over her face again.

"Who says I went to see the old man?" she returns, irritably. "He's dead, and can tell nothing. I don't know you—do you hear? I don't know any thing about you or him either!"

Launce can not decide whether she is in mortal terror of Darrell or half mad, but it is useless to question her further. Indeed, the old shrinking has come back to his mind: he does not want her to make revelations—they could avail nothing. He knows enough—more than enough! The past is dead—let its secrets lie; their exposure could only fling an added bitterness over his soul.

A faint groan from Milady rouses him out of his reverie. He sees that she has grown terribly pale, and presses her hand anew on her heart.

"You suffer," Launce says.

"I'm used to it. I never spoke about it; somehow it's worse to-day," she replies, brokenly.

A slight convulsion passes over her countenance; she groans again, and this time sinks back in her chair completely insensible.

Launce summons the doctor and the matron. It is a long while before they can restore Milady to consciousness. After that, they are obliged to put her to bed, and it is evening before she is able to leave the prison. At Launce's request, another gown is provided for her. He thinks that to find herself divested of the penitentiary uniform may help her to realize that what has happened is indeed real, for on waking from her swoon she seems more bewildered than ever.

She allows them to do what they please, asking no questions.

They get her into the carriage—the great gates open and close behind her, but she does not appear to heed. Her strength seems to have given way completely—she has not even vitality enough left to understand that she is free.

Launce takes her to the villa, as had been agreed upon, and places her under good Mrs. Simpson's care. Neither Launce nor Mr. Carstoe has stayed at the house since their return to Moysterville. They have lodgings in the town; to both of them it has seemed impossible to sleep under that roof.

Milady is ill for more than a week, and the fiery-haired Simpson nurses her as tenderly as if she were the purest and greatest lady in the land. It is enough for her to know that Launce and Mr. Carstoe are sorry for the woman. She asks no questions, and has no time. There is only one servant in the house, a new-comer, who does not even know who the sick woman is that has been brought there; so Moysterville has no idea that Milady is at hand, and, as I prophesied, Milady's pardon attracts slight attention in any way.

Mr. Carstoe has been very busy since his return, setting Vaughan's matters in complete order. He is ready now to resign the agency. He has lately received a letter from Darrell, expressing surprise at his hasty departure, dwelling lightly on Carstoe's desire that he would appoint a new agent, adding certain insinuations about ingratitude, and winding up by the offer of an increase of salary and percentage, as if he supposed that would settle the question.

So Mr. Carstoe has now to write that he has resigned his position, put Mr. Vaughan's affairs in the hands of a well-known lawyer, and proposes before long to leave California. It is difficult to frame this epistle. Poor Carstoe is so oppressed by the awful secret which he holds in regard to the man he once loved and honored that he has a positive sensation of guilt, from which, argue as he may, he can not free himself.

He is talking of these things with Launce as they sit in his room this evening—the tenth since Milady's liberation.

The woman is much better—able to sit up. They have been to the villa to-night, and seen her. She is taciturn, but not sullen. Launce thinks her mind quite restored, though he fears the effect of any excitement, and has been careful to talk of the most ordinary matters; indeed, he has ceased to think she could throw any light upon the forgery of the check. Her visits to his uncle might have had a merely personal motive—a desire to revenge herself on Darrell. Some terrible revelation she brought with her, that is certain. Some strong fear of her disturbed Darrell, that is equally sure, else he would never have devised the plan which he carried out with such unwavering cruelty. But she dreads him too much now to open her lips. The long confinement and this mortal disease, which the doctors are certain must end her life in a few years, have tamed the old savage spirit and broken the obstinate will. Launce has no fear for Vaughan where she is concerned.

To-morrow he is to leave Moysterville, but this fact has not been mentioned to Milady. He proposes to visit New Orleans for a while before returning to New York.

"I think every thing is arranged for the poor creature," he says to Carstoe. "Mrs. Simpson will take care of her until she is strong again, then she can go to the place we have found—she will be quite safe. She can earn large wages, and lay up all the money."

Milady embroiders in the most wonderful manner in silk and gold thread. Weak as she is, she has given them proofs of her skill, and Launce has already procured her an extensive order for the working of altar-cloth and robes needed by a Romish church in San Francisco.

"Later, I dare say, she will want to find her child, but I think there is no danger of her falling back into her old life."

"I don't agree with you about her being altogether right in her mind," Mr. Carstoe observes. "She's quiet enough, though; and, indeed, I think the poor thing can't last long any way."

"So much the better, certainly. It is the best wish one could make for her."

"Yes. They must have a plan up yonder for setting the errors of this world right," Mr. Carstoe replies, thoughtfully. "It's an odd muddle, Launce Cromlin, but it's good to hold fast to that belief."

"I should think so," returns Launce, with his pleasant smile. "Well, Carstoe, we've been able to set some part of a great wrong right also."

"Yes, thank God! I couldn't rest—I felt as if I should never sleep while there was a doubt. If there had been no other way, I must have spoken—let the whole out."

"I don't feel that we have any thing to do with his part now," Launce says. "The woman is free; after all, she is better off than she was before. But come, we've argued the whole question more than enough. We shall never be certain, either of us, whether we are doing right. But we can't expose Darrell; nothing but the sternest necessity, the impossibility of helping her without, would have made us. We may both be wrong; it has to rest so, any way."

Then they get round to the question of the business, and the letter which must be sent to Vaughan.

"I've written it over three times,"·sighs Mr. Carstoe. "I suppose it will do as well as any thing. I want you to hear it."

"I am listening," Launce says.

"First I wrote that I was not strong, was tired of California, and wanted to go East;" Mr. Carstoe interrupts himself in the reading to observe: "but I couldn't tell any untruths, or make any excuses; there's the fact, and he must be satisfied with it."

"You have decided to go, however?"

"Yes; I shall take what I have saved, and go to live in Albany again; it was home to me as a boy. I have a chance of employment—a bookkeeper's place. I shall do very well. Now let me read the rest of the letter."

"It is all that is necessary," Launce says, when he finishes.

"Do you suppose he will suspect that I have found out any thing?"

"If he happen to hear of this poor woman's release, he may; but he will hold his peace, of course; you will never be asked for reasons."

"I hope I shall never see him again," sighs Mr. Carstoe. "I don't think that he can persecute Milady any further."

"Of course not; he would not dare, if he felt inclined to try. The whole matter is at an end. We shall never even know why he invented that infernal plot for shutting her up."

"I did think she knew something—had some hold upon him; but there seems no chance of that."

"No. Perhaps it was only that he was afraid of her watching him—following him to Europe and preventing his marriage; that seems more probable than any thing else."

"You have never questioned her?"

"She is frightened at the mere mention of his name—at least it seems more fright than anger. But I don't want to know, Carstoe; it could do no good. Leave him and his secrets alone. God have mercy on him, is all I can say."

"God have mercy on him," repeats the other man. "But the judgment, the retribution, it must fall sooner or later; it never fails."

"That is in God's hands too," says Launce, "and we must leave it there."

"Only when I think of his wife. Ah, that's the strangest consequence of the law—that the innocent must suffer with the guilty."

Launce lifts his hand warningly; he has grown very pale, and his voice trembles as he answers—

"Don't, please; I have to put that part out of my mind."

He rises, and walks up and down the room for some time in silence. Mr. Carstoe comprehends what he suffers, and is conscience-stricken at having allowed his thought to find voice. There has scarcely been a mention of Elizabeth during all these anxious weeks; never a.syllable of confidence has passed between the two; but Carstoe, in his odd fashion, understands what a beautiful dream, what a golden hope, was stricken out of Launce Cromlin's life the day he read —oh, years since—the news of his cousin's marriage.

Presently Launce comes back to his seat, and the two talk of other matters—of a future meeting in New York—of Launce's long-deferred journey to Europe, which will take place in the spring. There is always a solace in work to a mind like his, and no pain would be insupportable to Launce as long as he feels that he is not wasting the precious weeks and months which grow so rapidly into years. There is so much he wants to accomplish—not just for Fame's sake, though he prizes that as any man ought; but to feel when the end comes, and the great portals open into another sphere, a new phase in the endless cycle of existence, that he has not played ill his part here, not neglected such gifts, such opportunities of usefulness, as this earthly career may have offered in its course.

It is late at night before they separate, and each goes to his bed-chamber; each, as he lays his head on his pillow, feeling a sense of relief in recollecting that the anxieties which were so incessant and so torturing during that long sea-voyage have been set at rest—Darrell Vaughan's victim is free. Not a night since Launce brought her forth from those dreary walls but this thankfulness has been the last waking thought in the minds of both these men; the last but one—always another comes after—a petition to God for mercy on a woman almost more to be pitied than this outcast—on her whose fate is indissolubly knit to Darrell Vaughan's.

Out in the villa, too, all is quiet and still. Mrs. Simpson sleeps heavily after so many days and nights of watching. Milady is quite herself again ; able to leave her chamber—to walk about ; she will soon be as strong as ever.

In her room only burns a light. The woman is standing by a window, and looking out into the star-lit sky. The face, wasted and worn, with a mere spectre of its wonderful beauty still clinging about it, has recovered a force and energy which it has not exhibited for years. She may be silent, she may shroud her features in Launce Cromlin's presence under a veil of passivity, which makes him doubt whether she feels or remembers any thing with keenness ; but this woman thinks clearly, consecutively ; and her brain is able to weave its plans—her will to carry them out.

She waits in her chamber till the little clock on the mantel strikes midnight. It would seem a signal she had given to her own soul. As the last chime dies she takes up the lamp, passes noiselessly down the stairs, and enters the library.

Of what is she thinking as she stands gazing straight before her into the shadows? Of the day she held her last meeting with old Mr. Vaughan in this room? Of a later meeting here with the nephew on the night that Mr. Vaughan died?

The face tells nothing ; the very eyes look dead and cold.

At one end of the apartment stands the cabinet which has been so many times diligently searched since Edgar Vaughan's death. She goes to it, and sets the lamp on the floor by its side. The cumbrous thing—almost as large as an organ—is a mass of wonderful carving and ornament. Four immense scroll-shaped legs support the ancient affair, which the strength of a dozen men would hardly suffice to lift.

Milady, on her knees, holds the light close to a panel near the bottom of the cabinet. She takes out of her pocket a long knitting-needle— the restless Simpson yesterday missed that needle from her work, and is dreaming about it at this moment. After several trials, Milady succeeds in pushing the slender steel far up under a mass of carved flowers. The panel flies out and discloses a drawer, in which lie folded papers. These Milady seizes and hides in her bosom, muttering—"I saw him open it. I thought afterward I was crazy to hide the papers here— but they have kept safe—they have kept safe."

Then, noiseless and ghost-like, she creeps back to her chamber, and the old house remains silent as a grave.

Two days elapse before she learns that Launce Cromlin is gone; but she asks few questions, though she looks troubled and disappointed at first. When she is alone again she presses her hand to her bosom, and the paper hidden there crackles under her touch.

"It doesn't matter," she whispers ; "they are safe."

She goes soon afterward to the home Launce has provided for her—a place where she will be perfectly secure should Darrell Vaughan make any attempts to discover her whereabouts.

Weeks go by—drift on to spring. Even Mr. Carstoe has left California. One day news comes to Mrs. Simpson that Milady has disappeared. She had taken the sum gained by her work—and never woman toiled as Milady did— and is gone.

Mrs. Simpson is troubled and anxious, but is obliged to wait, for Mr. Carstoe has not yet sent her his address, and she does not know where to send information either to him or Launce Cromlin.

CHAPTER XXXI.

THE GIANT'S CASTLE.

IT was a beautiful February day ; every trace of snow had disappeared ; the air was balmy and soft, with promises of spring — promises which the fickle goddess would be sure to forget by the time March arrived, as in the matter of pledges and vows she resembles the order of human beings who "protest too much."

But it was lovely weather, and useless to project one's soul into the future ; better to enjoy it, as we do the pleasant mood of some friend troubled by an uncertain temper, without questioning.

Mrs. Murray seldom got out of the house, except when obliged to go to the shop which gave her work. To-day, however, Meg persuaded her that it would be delightful to undertake a long-promised journey to the upper part of town, where lived an old Scotch woman whom they visited two or three times a year. The street-cars—that blessed modern invention which puts "a carriage-and-pair" at the service of the poor and ailing—set them down within a short distance of their destination.

But to Meg the ride was the chief pleasure, for she found slight entertainment in their hostess's room after she had exhausted the pictorial resources of an old Bible, and worn out her patience trying to persuade the misanthropic black cat who dwelt on the warmest corner of the hearth to play with her.

"Meg," said Mrs. Murray at last, noticing, with her usual thoughtfulness, that the child began to look weary of her efforts to amuse herself, "I'm thinkin' puss is like Mrs. MacLean and me, my woman—she's outlived her playin' days. But ye may walk in the square, if ye'll tak' good heed."

"And may I go over to the Reservoir?" asked Meg, ready, like any other human being, to demand an ell when an inch was granted.

"Yes, if ye'll be sure to mind the carriages at the crossings. Ye'll be back at the end o' the hour?"

Meg promised, and decided to leave the square for a future day, when the trees should be in leaf, and flowers in blossom that could be looked at, even if touching them must remain an unattainable bliss. To walk about under the shadow of the lofty walls that shut in the Reservoir was a pleasure which made these visits to Mrs. MacLean something to dream of in advance and long afterward, where Meg was concerned. The great mass of masonry might look prosaic enough to most people: it entranced Meg as much as ever a ruined castle on the Rhine did a poet. Jean Murray, unconscious as she was of possessing imaginative gifts, had a rare talent for story-telling. Meg never went to sleep without a wonderful story. She was familiar with all the fairy tales that have been sacred history to children for centuries, and believed them just as implicitly as those out of the Bible which were reserved for Sundays. Indeed, she somewhat confused matters, as many a small personage has done before, and often pictured one of her pet elfin kings in Joseph's gorgeous coat of many colors, and mixed up fairy-land and Eden in a fashion that would have horrified Aunt Jean's natural enemies—"the district visitors." And almost the next best thing to finding the road to the kingdom of the fairies—a feat Meg by no means despaired of if she could only get fairly out into the broad, green, tree-shadowed country of which she had caught occasional glimpses on bright summer days—were these expeditions to the Reservoir. Meg had no doubt whatever that these great walls hid a notable giant who figured in one of Aunt Jean's narratives—a giant who bore no family likeness to the generality of those wicked old fellows that infest the realm of Fable. This giant was as kind and gentle as he was strong, and helped princes to their rights, and screened beautiful princesses from their foes, showered costly gifts upon good children with a lavish hand, and was altogether the sort of giant one would be very glad to meet and propitiate.

So Meg gained the broad, quiet street—walked on past Sixth Avenue—past Broadway—and came in sight of the giant's castle. When she was tired of staring up at the frowning height, and fancying that she heard the sound of the giant's tread and the voice of the Princess Thelusia from within, there was a convenient deep doorway on the Fifth Avenue side where she could sit and watch the carriages and the horsemen dash past, and the beautifully dressed ladies saunter along the sidewalk, and find the real world about her nearly as marvelous as the fair Wonder-land familiar to her childish fancies.

She was to have a whole hour in the shadow of the giant's castle—and an hour is a lengthy period either for pleasure or pain at Meg's age. The great clock in the church-tower farther down the avenue had struck two as she neared the walls. Meg had so long to live before that hoarse voice would call again that it was not necessary to think about its warning. She was a conscientious little soul, however, and as soon as the first chime sounded would have set out on her return, even if the giant and the princess, the elf in Joseph's gorgeous coat, and the whole train of brilliant creatures had appeared in a body and tempted her to remain.

After Meg had been there a great while, and had begun to think she must listen for the bell (as if one of the seven sleepers himself could have failed to be roused by its brazen voice, that always sounds so angry and fiendish one is inclined to believe the unfortunate dissenting chapel where it lives possessed of a devil), a carriage drove up the avenue, and stopped in front of Meg's doorway.

A very pretty lady descended—almost as pretty, Meg thought, as the one who had been so kind the day Sally Baines's cat got her into difficulty, and who had several times since then visited the little rooms in Minetta Lane.

"You need not wait," Meg heard the lady say to the coachman; "I shall walk awhile before going home. Be at the house in time to take me to the theatre."

A very elegant lady, in a rich black dress Meg knew to be velvet, and with a bonnet so beautiful that the child immediately appropriated it for the benefit of the Princess Thelusia, and such clouds of golden hair under the bonnet that Meg decided them also worthy to decorate the head of her favorite heroine. Up and down the lady walked in a slow, meditative fashion, and Meg watched her, wondering if she knew the giant, and was waiting to have an interview with him. How Meg longed to run and ask, but even at her time of life one begins to be shackled by the proprieties, and Meg felt it was impossible to gratify her yearning. She watched her so attentively that at last the lady, passing several times close to the doorway, noticed the child. There was a look of admiration in Meg's face easy to read—especially to a woman as fond of such incense, from whatever quarter it might come, as this lady chanced to be. She glanced at Meg and smiled, and Meg thought the very sunshine grew brighter and warmer. The other lady had smiled at her too, but so sadly, so sorrowfully, that Meg had asked Aunt Jean if she were unhappy. Still, even as she compared the two, Meg was faithful to her allegiance, and decided that her first favorite was more beautiful: this one might be a princess, like Thelusia, but the other was a grand queen at the very least.

Presently the lady turned down the very street Meg must take, and not long after the bell chimed three. She started up at once, bade farewell to the giant's castle and her dreams, and descended to the actualities of life. Aunt Jean expects prudence on the part of a child considered fit to be trusted out alone, and Meg would not disappoint that confidence for the world.

Meg saw the lady in advance, walking slowly along. At length she stopped before a house which Meg had remarked on her way to the Reservoir, from the quantities of flowers in the windows. She lived there—she was going up the steps. Meg hurried on to get a last look before she disappeared. Just as the child reached the dwelling the door opened and closed behind the lady, and Meg was turning away disappointed at not having had another glimpse of the lovely face when she perceived something white lying on the lower step.

It was a handkerchief, as filmy and soft as a spider's web, Meg thought, and there was lace on it, such as she had seen in the windows when Aunt Jean took her into the region of shops away down Broadway, and an odor of violets that was like a breath of garden air.

Meg picked up the handkerchief, mounted the steps, and pulled the bell in great haste. An old woman appeared; she looked very cross, and began gesticulating and crying out in some unknown language, and was altogether so violent that Meg's first impulse was to fling the handkerchief down and run away, afraid that she had encountered some malevolent fairy—for, alas! there were evil-disposed natures even among fairies. But she stood her ground, and was trying to explain what had brought her, though the old fairy only scolded the harder, and refused even to notice the bit of lace Meg held up. Just then the pretty lady came back through the hall, and addressed the woman in that same unknown tongue, only it sounded sweet and musical from her lips. She perceived Meg, and said in English—

"What is it, little girl? What did you want?"

"Please, it's the handkerchief; I saw it on the steps," Meg stammered, not so much because she felt shy as from eagerness.

"Ah, thanks; you are a good child—I am much obliged. Let me see, what shall I give you?" returned the lady, regarding Meg. The child's dress was simple enough, but she did not somehow look as if one could offer her money.

The old woman was talking all the while; the lady put up her hand, as if annoyed by the buzzing, and sent her away. Meg knew that by the gesture which accompanied the words. The attendant clattered along the marble floor on a pair of preposterously high heels, chattering like an ill-natured magpie till she disappeared.

Meg could not help watching her, and the lady said—

"Were you frightened at my old Susanne? She is not so cross as she looks."

But Meg scarcely heard; she had caught sight of a flowering shrub in a great pot near the foot of the staircase—a marvel of dark glossy green leaves, and delicate pink blossoms hanging down like tiny bells. Meg clapped her hands in delight.

"Ah, I see—the flowers," said the lady, following the direction of her eyes. "You like flowers? Come in—there are some I shall give you—come."

Meg would have expostulated, remembering that the fatal hour had sounded, but there was no time, for the lady drew her into the vestibule and closed the door. Meg allowed herself to be led across the hall into a room hung with blue and some other color that Meg thought neither white nor gray, but like both, with silvery streaks through it. The bay-window was full of the plants she had seen from the street, and there were pictures, and a marble boy in the corner, and scores of marvels, which made Meg think fairy-land had opened at last.

"You shall have a bouquet to take home with you," the lady said, beginning to select flowers from the different plants, and talking pleasantly as she did so. "What is your name?—where do you live, little girl?"

"Meg; with Aunt Jean," returned the child, scarcely able to hear or answer at the moment.

"Ah, you think my room pretty, I see. What eyes the creature has!" And the lady stopped short, and gazed fixedly at her. "Why, they are like—what a goose I am!" she muttered to herself, then resumed her employment.

"Oh, I forgot—I mustn't stay!" exclaimed Meg, coming suddenly back to her senses. "It's past the hour, and Aunt Jean said I was to go as soon as it struck."

"Then you shall—why, what an honest little soul you are!" laughed the lady. "See—here is a pretty bouquet for you. Some time if you come back I shall give you more. I am much obliged to you—this is my pet handkerchief; I wouldn't have lost it for any thing!"

She put the handkerchief to her lips, and kissed it passionately several times, though laughing still, as if in mockery of her own childishness.

"Ah, little one," said she, "you don't know what my nonsense means; but you will understand if you remember it when you grow to be a woman—you will understand."

She had caught her dress in the *jardinière*. She tried in vain to extricate it, uttering impatient French exclamations, and rushing into a tremendous excitement at once.

"I see where it's fastened," Meg said. She laid her bouquet on a chair, and went upon her knees to pull out the fringe, which had twisted itself about some of the decorations of the stand.

The lady stood looking down at her. As Meg rose, the silver cross which she always wore swung out from her neck, and the lady saw it. She pulled the child up so suddenly that Meg was almost frightened; the face which bent over her had grown very pale.

"Take it off—let me see it," she said, pointing to the cross.

Meg obeyed; the lady turned away to examine the ornament, and stood for many moments with her back to the child. At last she seated herself in a chair, and motioned Meg to her side.

"Where did you get this?" she asked, almost in a whisper.

"I've always had it," Meg answered, ready to sob. "It was my mother's, Aunt Jean said."

"Your mother's? Hush—don't cry—don't be frightened! Oh, I—where do you live?"

"With Aunty Jean — down in Minetta Lane —number six," sobbed Meg, choking back her tears.

"*Mon Dieu! mon Dieu!*"

The lady was not noticing her; she was staring at the cross again. She had turned the other side, and seen the letter N that had been cut deep into the silver.

"May I go?" whispered Meg. "Aunt Jean will expect me—please, may I go?"

"What—did you speak? Oh, I know—you want to go; yes," the lady answered, controlling herself by a violent effort, though she looked very pale still, and there was a terror in her eyes far deeper than Meg's childish alarm. "Here is your cross—don't be afraid—it is only that I am not well."

"Aunt Jean takes drops," said Meg, practical, and ready to be of assistance, discomposed as she felt.

The lady laughed out again, but there was no mirth in the sound now. If Meg had been older, she would have known that the stranger was dangerously near hysterics.

"I shall be better soon — I don't want any drops," she said. "Tell me again where you live—wait, let me write it."

She hurried to the table, and scribbled the address which Meg repeated. Then she moved close to the child, and looked fixedly at her.

"I can not understand," she murmured. "Oh, I do think I must be mad! O mon Dieu!— maman, maman!"

She struggled with herself again, and tried to smile as she saw how her agitation confused and distressed the little girl.

"You want to go?" she said.

"Yes, ma'am, please. Aunty will be expecting me," faltered Meg.

"Good-bye. Ah, I must open the street-door for you. Stop, do not forget your flowers."

Meg recovered her precious nosegay, saying, "Thank you, ma'am, oh, so much."

She followed the lady across the hall into the vestibule.

"Perhaps I shall come to see you soon—be a good child."

"Yes, ma'am; thank you," returned Meg, trying hard to act up to her ideas of propriety and politeness.

The lady regarded the childish face wistfully for an instant, bent her head as if from an impulse to kiss the uplifted forehead, then drew back, and motioned her to go, repeating, "Good-bye, good-bye."

Meg hurried down the street, and reached Mrs. MacLean's dwelling just as Aunt Jean had begun to grow anxious, and was sallying forth in search of her. It was time to go home, so, after a hasty adieu to their hostess, they set off, Aunt Jean reserving questions till she found herself alone with Meg.

And the lady whom Meg had left went back to her drawing-room, and walked up and down for some time in troubled thought. At last she pulled from her bosom a cross which was the exact counterpart of that worn by Meg. Again she grew frightened and hysterical, moaning—

"*O maman, maman! O mon Dieu! mon Dieu!*"

Nina de Farolles had worn the cross up to the day of her death. She had given it to Nathalie when her dying terrors wrung from her that dismal confession, and caused her to burden Nathalie's soul with the promise which even her fickle nature could not forget.

CHAPTER XXXII.

THE PRESENTIMENT FULFILLED.

Two days later, Mrs. Murray, sitting in her cheerful room with her dolls, heard a knock at the door. Meg had gone to visit the violinist, who was not well, and had begged for the child's society. The musician was a crack-brained old fellow, with an odd gleam of genius, which enabled him to comprehend an imaginative little creature like Meg, just as it unfitted him for the ordinary duties of this hard world. Had he possessed less or more than this gleam, the case might have been different, but Meg was satisfied.

Mrs. Murray had reached a critical point in the embryo existence of the doll she was busy over, and did not feel best pleased at having to let the plump kid body and the waxen head fall apart on the table while she rose to see what ill-timed intruder might be at hand. She crossed the dark passage, and opened the outer door that led to the staircase. A lady was standing there. She did not raise her veil, but said quickly—

"I want to see Mrs. Murray—the woman who has a little girl called Meg living with her."

So Mrs. Murray knew that the visitor was the lady of whom Meg had spoken, and felt flattered and curious, naturally enough. But she only said—

"It's me, ma'am. Will you walk in?"

The lady followed her into the room, sat down in the chair Mrs. Murray offered civilly enough, and put her veil back. Aunt Jean looked hard at her—looked a second time; and then there was

neither curiosity nor civility in her face any longer. She had suddenly grown stiff and erect. If
she had borrowed the poker for a backbone she
could not have sat up straighter and more rigid.
By the merest chance in the world Aunt Jean
knew the stranger. She never forgot a face, and
she had seen this lady before—remembered, too,
the history related in connection therewith.

She had come out of M'Intyre's shop one day,
and was standing on the sidewalk, talking with
an acquaintance who worked in the establishment,
when Nathalie La Tour's carriage drove up, and
Nathalie herself descended.

"There's one with money to spend," whispered Aunt Jean's companion. "Just look at her;
and to see her smiling and happy, as if there was
no judgment and no hereafter!"

Aunt Jean's acquaintance was a vinegary-faced
old maid, who had never seen the bright side of
temptation, though she was as proud of her virtue as if she had fought scores of battles in its
defense. She loved gossip also, as so many virtuous people do, and knew all about the famous
Frenchwoman and her naughty books and her
naughtier life—her suppers, her *coterie* of bad
women, her lovers, and all the rest; and she told
the story so fast that Aunt Jean could not help
listening.

"She comes to the shop often," the old maid
said; "she's always ordering embroidery. If
you just saw the chemises of her! I've had to
take work to her house sometimes. Oh, its awful! with a naked boy in one of the rooms, and
she as bold as brass, and talking so sweet! I always feel like quoting Sodom and Gomorrah to
her, and Jezebel, and all the rest, but a body
doesn't dare. St. Paul says, 'Be instant in season and out of season;' but if he'd had to do embroidery for a living, and one's place lost if a
customer complained of impudence, maybe he'd
not have found it so easy to do his duty after
all."

Mrs. Murray had gone away, laughing quietly
to herself at the odd jumble virtuous Sarah Jenks
made of the matter, but the history remained in
her mind notwithstanding, and straightway at
sight of Nathalie's face she grew as rigid as Sarah herself.

"The little girl is not here?" Madame La
Tour was saying.

"No, ma'am," replied Aunt Jean.

"She was at my house the other day," pursued
Madame, with a smile which few people could
have resisted. "Perhaps she told you?"

Aunt Jean was sorely tempted to give utterance
to another "No, ma'am," but her worship of truth
compelled her to make the first word an assent
instead of a denial.

"Such a nice little girl," pursued Madame, trying to speak carelessly, though there was a trem-
or in her voice, and her features worked nervously, and her usually perfect English caught a slight

foreign intonation, as it did in moments of strong
agitation. "I was much interested in her, and
she said I might come to see her. I am very fond
of little girls."

"You're very good, ma'am," said Aunt Jean.
She was watching the visitor with her shrewd
gray eyes. She looked as upright and uncom-
promising as ever, and chopped off her words
with the same unresponsive coldness, but her
breath came quickly, and her eyes took a troubled, puzzled expression for all that.

She had pondered much over Meg's account
of the lady's odd manner—her examination of
the cross, her excited questions. She perceived
her agitation now, and a score of bewildering
thoughts rose in Mrs. Murray's mind. But one
determined reflection came quickly in the wake
of those perplexed fancies. This woman, whatever her motive might be, should neither see Meg
nor obtain a shred of information in regard to her.

"You are her aunt, she told me," Madame
continued. "Is her name Murray?"

The child was always so called. Aunt Jean
compounded with her conscience, and gave a
sign of assent.

"Then her father was your brother, I suppose?"
said Madame. She paused—Aunt Jean did not
speak. "Was he your brother?" demanded
Madame, a sudden impatience shaking the voice
she tried so hard to keep composed.

"No, ma'am," said Jean once more. She had
come too near a falsehood already for her peace
of mind—she would equivocate no further. But
she would tell nothing, even if she were forced to
take refuge in sullenness or incivility to avoid so
doing.

"Ah, her mother was your sister," returned
Madame, and there was a tone of relief in her
voice which did not escape her listener. "I am
sorry the little girl is not in," she continued; "I
would have liked to see her again. She does not
remember her parents, she told me."

"No, she does not," returned Aunt Jean, and
her voice likewise had a tone of relief in it. Something had changed the stranger's mood. She had
found wanting the clew that she had expected to
catch; her interest and agitation were both gone.

"Her parents dead! She is fortunate to have
a kind relative like you to take care of her."

"What's in my power, I do," replied Aunt
Jean.

If the lady would only go—go before further
question could bring back whatever doubt or
trouble had occasioned this visit. Mrs. Murray
had some wild idea of inventing an excuse to get
out of the room, but no reasonable pretext would
suggest itself.

"I saw—I want you to tell me—" began Madame.

Aunt Jean felt that her only hope lay in as-
suming the defensive. She said quickly—

"I'll ask your pardon, ma'am, but ye are

strange to me, I must just beg ye to mind. I'm a poor, plain body, but a' the same I dinna like to hae strangers come speerin' after me and mine this gait. I'm Scootch an' ye're Freench, if I may mak' boold to judge by your speech, an' that's the deeference betwixt us. I'm no meanin' to offend, but it's aye better to speak out what's in the mind, an' then each understands the ither."

And very "Scootch" Aunt Jean grew both in pronunciation and looks. She was frightened at the ideas her visitor's words and manner roused in her mind, and determined to guard her secret under a panoply of grimness and obstinacy.

No trouble or mental agitation, however great, could be strong enough to keep Nathalie's preposterous vanity in the background. Aunt Jean could not have stung her worse than she did by that unintentional thrust. To be told that she spoke English with an accent—she who prided herself on having "two native languages!" She colored sensitively, more hurt than angry, but of course Mrs. Murray ascribed the blush to the latter emotion.

"I've nae wish to be rude, ma'am," she continued, a little less stiffly, though she looked as grim and obstinate as ever. "It's on'y that you've made a mistake—my bairn an' me could na' hae ony interest for you whatever. I'm a plain body, as ye may see, and Megsie is all I hae, an' there's nae call for ony one to ask questions aboot her."

Nathalie would have liked to believe ; to depart and be done with the matter—put it out of her mind. She did not object to troubles of a certain sort—troubles which could assume a poetical coloring. But there was no romance in the business which had brought her here; it was a subject that, next to death, was always the most dismal for her to contemplate. Still she could not obey her first impulse—accept the obstinate old woman's assertion as proof that she had deceived herself. She recollected the cross—that initial scratched on the back. She would be glad to find that the woman knew nothing of its history—that it had come into her possession by accident—above all, that it had no connection with the child. The surroundings were so commonplace that Nathalie felt it would be a severe blow to be obliged to give the little girl a part in the fears and fancies which she had woven into a romantic background for the picture so long carried in her mind.

She would ask her questions, and go away; this blunt, stiff woman was an eyesore to her. If she had been a hag, like some creature of sensational romance, or the child in the depths of misery and danger, Nathalie could have found an excitement in trying to follow out the clew she had first believed found; but respectable poverty—poverty which toiled and was honest and content—possessed no interest whatever.

"I saw—she showed me a cross she wears," Nathalie said, trying to speak carelessly ; not so much from a desire to deceive the woman as to cheat herself, eager to believe that she expected some answer which would set her mind at rest—, be a proof that she had only excited herself over a chance likeness. "It was an odd little cross ; it is one you purchased for her, I suppose ?"

She stopped, and looked inquiringly at the old woman, who had picked up her work, and was sewing busily. If the creature would only say "Yes." But Mrs. Murray stitched on, and said nothing. "I have a reason for asking about it," continued Nathalie, her voice becoming tremulous again, for the silence troubled her. "A reason—nothing that has to do with you or the child — but I should like — You bought the cross, did you not ?"

It was full a minute before Mrs. Murray answered ; but she could not escape — she must speak.

"Nae ; I did na' buy it," she said.

She heard a heavy, gasping breath ; felt her arm seized in a quick, nervous grasp. Madame was leaning forward in her chair ; her face had lost its color again, and her eyes looked eager and frightened. "Where did you get it ?—tell me. How did you come by the cross ?" she exclaimed.

Speak ?—say a word which could in any way give this dreadful woman cause to think she had part or lot in that innocent child ? Never ! Aunt Jean would sooner have been trampled to death by wild horses.

"Ane gied it me, if ye maun ken," she said. "I hae naething in the world I did na' come by honestly."

"It's not that ; I don't doubt your honesty."

"Nae, nae, I should na' fear ye wad ; naebody e'er did that," retorted Jean, seizing at any pretense for anger, in the hope that her visitor might take offense and end the interview.

"Who gave it to you ?" cried Madame, more excitedly. "Can't you speak ?—don't you hear?"

Aunt Jean formed a sudden resolve.

"I'll tell ye," she said ; "I'll tell ye ; then maybe ye'll leave me an' mine to gae our lane."

"Who was it ? A woman, I know. Where is she ?—is she alive ?"

"Dead, most like ; I hae reason to think so," returned Jean, in a solemn voice, as she held up a warning finger. "Dead, nae doot. 'The wages o' sin is death.' If e'er ye read your Bible, ye ken that."

"She hae a conscience," Mrs. Murray thought. "I'll na' be baird as I was to the ither ; but if I could on'y speak the right word—if I on'y could !"

"Get me some water—I'm not well," sighed Madame La Tour, letting her hands drop into her lap, and leaning back in her chair with a frightened, helpless look which changed her whole face. Aunt Jean gave her a startled glance—a sudden resemblance to another face struck her for the first time; but, sorely as it dismayed her, it was only an added reason for hugging her secret fast. Speak? Never! She would save her child—her one treasure—her sweet Meg! That was her duty in this world. God would require at her hands the precious soul His mysterious workings had intrusted to her guardianship.

She was thinking this as she hurried to fetch the water. She came back to Madame La Tour —put the tumbler into her shaking hand. Madame drank eagerly; her color and strength began to return.

Aunt Jean felt a pity for the woman rise in her heart. It was not only that she wanted to say some word which should strike to her soul, but something that should bring comfort too.

"Ma'am," she said softly, "there's ither things in the Bible too: there's loving promises, an' there's a hope, if on'y a body will turn from the evil—it's ne'er too late. He raised the dead to life—He pardoned the Magdalen—Oh, He's just as kind an' pitiful this day."

"You're mad!" cried Nathalie. "You're a hopeless, raving lunatic! How dare you talk to me like that! What idea have you got in your head?—for whom do you mistake me? Why, you crazy thing! What dreadful words!—what a horrible old woman in every way! I don't want to hear your ignorant fancies, your antiquated superstitions," Madame cried, desperately. "You are rude and impertinent; you're a bad-hearted creature, too."

Nathalie had all her mother's horror of death. The very word was enough to give her a nervous spasm in her calmest moments, and now, when half beside herself with excitement, it was torture of the most horrible description to hear this cruel creature complacently naming it, and talking as her mother used to talk in her dark moods of pain and remorse. That death-scene before her—the moans, the prayers, the imprecations; but through them all came the words which had been reiterated over and over—the words she could never forget, which had a hold upon her mind such as no other memory ever did or could possess. "You have promised, Nathalie!—you have promised! I shall watch you—I shall be near: take care that you don't forget!"

Why, many a time she had awakened from sleep with those words ringing in her ear; had run to Susanne's room for refuge, almost expecting to see her mother's ghost appear and demand if she had forgotten. Here, in the broad daylight, with the sun shining through the window, and in the midst of these commonplace surroundings, the same dreadful terror came over her. She hid her face in her hands, and shivered piteously.

What could Jean think but that her warning had struck home—awakened some gleam of remorse in the heart of this woman, whose depraved life was too well known for harsh judgments to be a slander?

"You ought to feel as if a queen had honored you by coming! You might see my name the first time you go out; you can read, can't you? I saw the placards with my books and my name at the corner even; why, I am Madame La Tour!"

That the very stones in the street would have recognized this title was a solemn faith to Nathalie's positively sublime vanity. The Empress of all the Russias could not have revealed her identity with a more perfect confidence of her name being a familiar sound through the length and breadth of Christendom.

That appalling old woman! She only shook her head sadly, and, as firm in her conviction that she was following out the line of duty as ever one set of Christians were when they put to death those who presumed to reject their creeds, said, with a mingling of firmness and pity—

"It's because I do know your name that I speak—just for that; an' oh, if ye wad listen! I'm poor an' plain an' ignorant maybe, but it's all written there—ye can na' mistake it." She put her hand on the great old-fashioned Bible that lay upon the table. "Nae money, nae youth, nae beauty can escape; the time o' reckonin' comes—'The wages o' sin is death!' Oh, dinna reject the warnin': it's ne'er too late—never!"

"Go away from me!—let me get out of your house!" exclaimed Nathalie, really convinced now that the woman was mad.

"It's nae use, it's nae use!" sighed Aunt Jean, and sat drearily down in a chair opposite, and gazed with tears in her eyes at this brand which refused to be plucked from the burning.

Pathetic and solemn as the scene was, I think had there been a saint in the room who understood the characters and motives of both, he must have laughed in spite of himself.

The old woman's restored composure brought back Nathalie's courage. She was a lunatic no doubt, but not a dangerous one. Aunt Jean sat resting her elbow on the table, supporting her head with her hand.

She was thinking of that lost creature who had crossed her path years ago—of the time she saw her in the fullness of youth and beauty—before her sin had found her out. She was thinking of that last interview; of the desolate, desperate, homeless wretch whom she had rescued from the night and the storm, and taken under her roof; who had drifted away to new misery—new sin.

Ah, if she could only tell the tale in fitting words; if she could only bring the history close to the heart and conscience of this pretty, arrogant creature, who was treading the same downward road—treading among flowers still, but beyond loomed the night and the storm, and worse —worse! Strive as she might, believe in God's goodness as she did, Aunt Jean's mind was so troubled by dark, Calvinistic creeds that all hope, all promise, ended with this life.

The silence and the woman's quietness of manner had given Nathalie time to recover her wits. She shook out her ruffled plumage, smiled, and said sweetly—

"Now please tell me all you can about the cross, there's a good soul; it is time I was gone."

"The crucifeex?" cried Aunt Jean. "Did na' ye hear me say ane gied it me?"

"Yes, yes; but who—who?"

"It's na' a story about me or mine, remember that; but I'll tell it ye—yes, I'll tell it; mayhap it'll bring the warnin' hame."

"O mon Dieu!" groaned Nathalie. "There she goes again with her warnings and every sort of horror! My good creature, don't excite yourself—just give me a plain answer."

"I'll gie ye ane; I will!" said Aunt Jean. "It's to ken how I haed the crucifeex? A wicked, papistical emblem, that's been a sair trouble to me mony a time, but I could na' bring mysel' to put it awa' for by—but that's na' the question."

"No, no; I only want to know who gave it to you," Nathalie said, growing anxious and eager again.

Aunt Jean leaned forward, speaking slowly, with her lean forefinger extended to point her words.

"She was nane o' me or mine, do ye mind that? A poor, lost creature that I saw ance in the midst o' her wealth an' her luxury—goin' down a flowery path; but it led straight to hell—dinna' forget that! Ye may cover up the sin wi' gauds and treenkets—ye may ba' the voice o' hairps an' the soonds o' revelry, but it wins straight to hell a' the same."

"The cross—I only want to hear about the cross," shivered Nathalie.

She would have got up and run away, just from a vague, nervous terror, but Aunt Jean's solemn eyes and Aunt Jean's warning finger held her fast.

"It's just a pairt o' it," the old woman answered. "That was the way I see her first—in broidered raiment an' jewels an' a' the rest, an' it's on my soul that I was na' merciful eneugh—for she was young—oh, younger than you, my leddy, an' just as fair—"

"I'll not have you talk about me," broke in Nathalie, passionately. "I'll not stay; you shall be made to speak—I'll send those who will force you to; but I'll not stay."

Yet Aunt Jean's eyes held her fast—she could no more have stirred than if she had been bound in her chair.

"An' I left her in the midst o' her sin, for she'd hear nae warnin'—mind that!" continued Jean, in a deeper voice, with an added trouble in her keen gray eyes. "An' where did I find her next? In the street, wi' ne'er a shelter left—lovers an' freends far aloof, an' she speerin' at the black river an' dazin' her poor brain wi' its roar, an' the worst sin o' all temptin' her like a fiend."

L

"O mon Dieu! mon Dieu!" moaned Nathalie.

"I gie her shelter—I'd hae saved her if I could, but she wad na' bide. She went her lane—stole off while I slept, an' journeyed on down the fearsome road—down, down; an' I hae reason to think the end cam' at last—the awfu' end, an' she lies in a nameless grave, awa' by the great Paceefic shore, an' ne'er a sign o' her left but the bit cross I let my childie wear to comfort me auld heart a bit by thinkin' that though I was haird at first, I softened—little eno' I did, but I had the wull—I'm aye glad an' thankfu' for that."

She put her hand before her eyes, and sat silent.

Dead! That was the one thought in Nathalie's mind. She could not tell if she were shocked or grieved that the dread which had haunted her so long was lightened. Dead! There need be no further remembrance of her promise—there was nothing to do.

Then every other reflection vanished in a desire to get beyond the woman's reach—out of the sound of her voice. She rose quickly, and hurried toward the door. She was weak and shaken; she could bear nothing further—not a word—a syllable; she should faint or go into hysterics if those dull, grating tones struck her ear again.

Aunt Jean heard her rise, but she did not move. She watched her depart in silence, with a keen feeling of relief. She had uttered her warning—she was powerless to do more. And Meg was safe—God had cared for the nameless little one. No further danger would beset the child; she might grow up humble, honest. The Lord would spare her—He would spare her! For when it became a matter that touched her beloved, Aunt Jean could forget, as the sternest do, the mysterious sentence in regard to the transmission of punishment for sin from father to child, though ordinarily she held fast to it in all the horror of its full meaning—accepted it literally, forgetting that though "the letter killeth, the spirit maketh alive."

She watched the graceful creature float out of the room with her golden hair and her silken robes, and all the radiance that to most eyes would have brightened the shadowy haunt; and when the door closed Aunt Jean went down upon her knees, and while she thanked God for having been allowed to keep her darling safe, she prayed for the beautiful woman, compassionating the sinner even while she shuddered at the sin.

As Nathalie La Tour reached the lower hall she encountered a lady who had just entered the house. They both looked up simultaneously—their eyes met; once more she and Elizabeth Cranford were standing face to face.

"Elizabeth!" exclaimed Madame La Tour, forgetting her recent agitation—forgetting what she had always remembered when thinking of her former friend, that Elizabeth's judgments upon her books and her doctrines would be too condemnatory for any chance of future companionship to be possible—forgetting every thing except that she saw before her the one member of her own sex for whom she had ever really cared — "Elizabeth! How glad I am—how odd to meet you — after so long! Aren't you glad — won't you speak to me — don't you know me, Elizabeth?"

She had begun eagerly—the broken exclamations came more and more slowly, as she looked at her former friend standing there silent, unresponsive, not noticing her extended hand, and saw, too, the mingled emotions which stirred the pale, proud features — aversion — horror. Nathalie was too quick in her perceptions not to read the whole.

Her voice died in a sort of sob; her lips quivered, her eyes filled with a sudden trouble, which gave her face the childish look Elizabeth recollected so well — the look which in the old days had never failed to soften her heart, however much Nathalie might have annoyed or shocked her by the utterance of her absurd theories or wicked transcendentalism.

But she was not softened now. One could not say that it was anger which filled her heart. This woman had stolen no treasure that was hers; the law bound her to Darrell Vaughan; but in listening to his love Nathalie brought to her no appreciable personal wrong. Horror and aversion were in her face—Nathalie read its language aright; but neither jealousy nor pain had any part therein. It was only as if a spirit of evil had started up before her under a semblance of beauty, and were trying to cheat her, in spite of all her knowledge of the truth, into a belief of its purity.

After an instant she spoke; courteously, quietly — except that she uttered the name just as she might have addressed a stranger.

"Will Madame La Tour allow me to pass?" she said.

"Oh, Elizabeth!" exclaimed Nathalie again. There were positively tears in her eyes. Tears did not mean much with her: she could weep over touching poetry, a pathetic novel, a sorrowful play. It was the same sort of sentiment that moved her now; still to her it was real — light, transitory feelings were all that her facile nature could hold. But to Elizabeth the mournful voice, the pretty, pleading gestures, the misty eyes, were only a paltry bit of acting, that had not even the excuse of a motive.

She moved a step forward, impatient of the scene, but Nathalie did not stir—she was standing on the lower stair, and kept her place.

"I have thought so much about you—I wanted so to see you again! I wondered how and where we should meet—and now you'll not speak to me even. Oh, Elizabeth, Elizabeth!" she cried anew.

"I must again ask you to let me pass," was all Elizabeth said.

"Oh, you hard-hearted thing!" exclaimed Nathalie, a hot anger drying her tears and flushing her face. "I couldn't treat any creature so that I had ever called my friend, no matter what had happened."

"The difference between Nathalie L'Estrange and Madame La Tour is too great for me to feel that they are one and the same," Elizabeth replied. "If you will not let me pass, I must go away again."

She turned; Nathalie caught her dress, and said, in a voice which was only pleading and earnest—

"Don't leave me like that—don't!"

"I must," Elizabeth answered. "Madame La Tour ought to feel the impossibility of our meeting even—standing face to face—exchanging so much as a word."

A vivid scarlet rushed into Nathalie's cheeks. Proud of her daring creeds, at the same time, in odd contradiction, proud of the personal purity of her life, she felt a certain shame in listening to Elizabeth's rebuke—shame so strong that she could not even be angry. Naturally Elizabeth ascribed that confusion to a very different cause from its real one. She could but recollect that she was Darrell Vaughan's wife, and this woman one for whose sake he was periling reputation, honor, setting at naught the common decencies of life.

"I don't see why you should be so hard on me," said Nathalie, with another sob in her voice. "You may not like my books, you may not think as I do; but I have won fame—I have proved that I am not an ordinary, frivolous woman; and you used to talk so much about worshiping genius, and all that."

"Madame La Tour remembers my opinions so accurately that she ought to recollect there were things I prized more highly," was the response.

"Oh, you always had all sorts of old-fashioned ideas!" retorted Nathalie, impatiently. "But you can't say I'm not famous and admired! Did you ever read one of my books?"

"You know I never have."

Nathalie was vexed. She could have borne coldness, would not have minded rebuke or harsh language; but to have any human creature deny that she was pretty, or speak scornfully of her literary labors, was too much for her patience.

"Ah!" said she, with a shrug of her shoulders; "I'd have said there was one woman in the world incapable of envy, but I see you are not different from the rest."

That speech was so thoroughly Nathalie, Elizabeth could almost have smiled — almost have believed that these weary years since they parted were only a dream; that she and this absurd, contradictory, impossible creature were back in the pleasant Swiss valley, and no sin on the woman's soul worse than that of holding borrowed theories, whose wickedness she seemed too frivolous to comprehend.

She moved aside a little, and Elizabeth took advantage of this to pass her. Again Nathalie put out her hand and caught Elizabeth's dress.

"So you mean to go?" she asked. "You think because I have a soul broad enough to hold new, true creeds, that I must necessarily be what you call bad. Go, then. I would not be you with all your virtue and your pride. Narrow, petty, and so cold! Go; we shall not see one another again. Oh—"

She broke off suddenly. A new thought struck her.

"Why, what are you doing here?" she asked.

"There is a woman I come sometimes to visit," Elizabeth said. "Please to let go my dress, Madame La Tour."

"A Scotch woman, with a little girl—a niece?"

"Yes."

"Great heavens!" cried Nathalie. "You don't know about the cross?" She struck her hands hard together; her anger at Elizabeth's scorn of her books gave her a new idea. "Why shouldn't you bear part of the burden?" cried she. "I wouldn't have told you; I'd have died to keep the knowledge from you, for I loved you —yes, I did. I never cared half so much for any girl; but you hate me, you brush me out of your path, and I'll tell!"

Was she about to boast of her empire over Vaughan? Had she sunk so low that, to gratify her malice, she would be capable of this baseness?

"Tell me nothing," Elizabeth said. "Whatever you may have become, you would regret it some day, if there is a trace of the old Nathalie left. Go your way, and let me go mine. Our paths need not cross."

"There is a fate links your way with mine," cried Nathalie, in her theatrical fashion; "the threads were woven before you or I was born. Aye, that was what my warning meant when I first met you—that was the trouble I must bring you. Maybe I shall be sorry, but I'll tell all the same. I've borne it alone long enough; take your share."

She was holding Elizabeth fast again. Without an absolute physical struggle Mrs. Vaughan could not have freed herself.

"Speak, then," said Elizabeth. "I, too, have borne so much that my heart is callous. I can bear even this."

Still she misinterpreted Nathalie's meaning, still gave it the only significance it could have to her mind.

"You don't know, you don't know—"

"Hush!" interrupted Elizabeth. "I have

seen with my own eyes. Nathalie, I know every thing."

"And did you ever try to find her—to help? I thought I had a clew, and it has failed, only I know she is dead."

"Dead! Who?" asked Elizabeth, wondering if the woman had gone out of her senses.

"Marguerite—my sister and yours—the child of your father and my mother, Nina de Favolles!" exclaimed Nathalie.

Elizabeth clutched blindly at the banisters, and would have fallen had not Nathalie held her up.

"Oh, Elizabeth!" she cried, struck with a sudden remorse. "I am so sorry, indeed I am. You didn't know, you—"

"Hush!" interrupted Elizabeth again, sitting down on the stairs. "It is not true! it is not true!"

"It is true. I have old letters of your father's that would prove it. Mamma gave the child away. She was brought to America. When mamma was dying she told me—begged me to find her, if I could. She wore a cross—like this."

Nathalie drew from her bosom a cross exactly like the one Elizabeth had been shown by Mrs. Murray. She was stunned and faint. The last prop seemed forced from under her feet by this tale of her father's sin.

"She is dead," pursued Nathalie; "dead. I saw the cross on that child's neck. But these people were nothing to Marguerite; the old woman was kind to her once, and Marguerite gave her that."

Elizabeth found strength to get upon her feet, and turned her white face on Madame La Tour.

"I don't believe the story you have told me," she said; "I don't believe it."

Again anger overcame all other emotions in Nathalie's mind, even her sudden remorse. She took two letters from her pocket, and held them toward Elizabeth.

"Then read these, and you will believe it," she cried. "I brought them thinking that if the child proved to be Marguerite's I might need them. They weren't wanted; but look at them, you—"

She unfolded one, and held it before Elizabeth. She read almost in spite of herself—read enough to know that doubt was impossible. She closed her eyes for an instant, and clung to the banisters again.

"Oh dear, oh dear, I wish I had not!" moaned Nathalie, thrusting the letters into her pocket, with a return of terror and remorse. "Elizabeth—Elizabeth!"

Mrs. Vaughan let her hands drop to her sides —bent her death-like face upon Nathalie.

"If you are satisfied—go," she said.

This time Nathalie shrank away without a word.

"I am sorry I told her," she muttered, as her carriage rolled off. "But she vexed me so! Well, we shall not meet again—and I did not even ask if she were married! Oh, I was very fond of her, my beautiful Elizabeth! *Ah, mon Dieu! mon Dieu!* But I don't want to think about her—thank goodness I know nobody who will ever mention her name. And it's all so odd! Poor Marguerite—oh, mamma, mamma!"

She began to shiver and sob, and was so exhausted by the time she reached home that she could only creep into bed and let Susanne dose her with sedatives. But when evening came she was quite restored, able to receive Vaughan and other guests, and charm them all by her brilliancy and high spirits.

CHAPTER XXXIII.

SO NEAR DEATH.

It was very late the next morning when Elizabeth left her chamber and went down into the breakfast-room. She was ill; suffering bodily as well as mental pain. In all the dismal watches which had become so familiar to her during these years of trouble, perhaps no vigil had been so sad as that of the past night.

Even without the testimony of the letter, it would have been useless to try for comfort by any attempt to disbelieve the tale Madame La Tour had revealed in her reckless anger. Motive for a falsehood, there could have been none; besides, there was the stamp of truth in Nathalie's face—in every word she uttered. Circumstances long forgotten came back, and added their proof to the record. Even the name Nathalie had spoken—Nina de Favolles; it struck Elizabeth with a sense of familiarity when she heard it: the time and place recurred to her before her vigil ended. Years and years ago, in Europe, when she was a tiny child. It was one of the rare occasions on which Elizabeth could recollect seeing her mother roused to anger. Now and then Mr. Crauford would persevere in teasing and annoying her until he excited a storm before which he quailed. There had been contention between the parents, and they quarreled, unconscious that the little daughter had stolen into the room. Nina de Favolles! It was Mrs. Crauford who had uttered the name in the midst of angry and disdainful reproaches. Elizabeth remembered how white her mother was—how her great eyes flashed as she spoke; remembered her father's growing humble and penitent at once.

Then there returned the recollections of Mr. Crauford's anger and nervous dread when he discovered the identity of their neighbor at La Maladèyre — the odd, rude words Nathalie's

mother had several times spoken to her. There was no memory, however slight, which would not have brought its evidence, even without the letter.

If she could only have got away from all thought—could have put the matter out of her mind as a history which perished with those dead and gone—a tale which could in no way concern her. But this was impossible. The name by which Nathalie had mentioned their sister—yes, great God, their sister—Nathalie's as well as hers! And Nathalie believed her dead; but there was no actual proof of that. Elizabeth had found strength after Madame La Tour left her to go on up to Jean Murray's room—had heard the story of the interview; Jean's belief of some relationship between this wicked woman and Meg's mother; her thankfulness that she had been able to keep from betraying any thing.

Meg's mother! Oh, it was too horrible—for the whole loathsome truth struck Elizabeth at length. Milady—Marguerite—this was Meg's mother; the girl Darrell Vaughan had deserted—left to find a grave for her shame as best she could. And that unknown sister, hers and Nathalie's—this was Marguerite too, the same Marguerite.

It was as if Fate had taken a horrible pleasure in weaving the most unlikely events into one web; working out a drama the most improbable, with a pitiless persistence which rendered the slightest unity complete.

So the night had gone by. To be quiet, to lie in bed, was out of the question. Elizabeth set the doors open that connected her suite of chambers, opened the door even into the corridor, to afford herself a longer march, and paced up and down their length for hours. A window-shutter in the hall had been left ajar; the moonlight streamed in and trembled across the floor like a ghostly presence. Up and down, up and down, Elizabeth passed; thinking, thinking, watching, her whole thwarted life spread before her. She was too crushed and broken for active rebellion; worn and weakened in mind as well as body, yet no more able to drive thought away than she was to seek physical repose.

Ah, no wonder the shock of the first discovery she had made, the connection between Meg and Darrell Vaughan, had held a horror deeper even than the knowledge of his sin. No wonder the idea of the lost girl fastened with such persistency on her soul, and the feeling that she must find, must help her, had been like a command from some higher power.

Her sister—hers! Not a blow spared—not a love of her life allowed to keep its reverence and purity! Sin—treachery—wretchedness—wherever she turned. And what could it avail that all this knowledge should fall upon her? What could she do—what work was there for her in the atoning for these crimes? If Marguerite were alive, how find, how aid her? And she was; Elizabeth could neither content herself with Mrs. Murray's conviction nor believe Vaughan's tale. The wretched outcast had not been freed from her misery and shame—she was alive. These revelations had a force and meaning; they came thus into her life because she was expected to act. But how—which way turn—what step take even to learn if Marguerite were living or dead?

So the night dragged on. Toward morning Elizabeth heard a sound below stairs—a key turning in the street-door. Vaughan had returned; she knew that it was not unusual for him to enter at this hour. She slipped back into her room, and partially closed the door. She never watched him—shrank always from seeing him at such seasons; but to-night somehow she could not stir—she must stand there and look.

Presently he came up the stairs, wearily, heavily; passed along the corridor, carrying a taper in his hand. He was pale as a ghost—his eyes gleamed with an unnatural fire—his step steady enough, though slow. But Elizabeth was no longer blind—a doleful experience had rendered that impossible. She knew the night had been spent in some wild carouse. To make him look as he did now—like a coarse spirit of evil showing through the face she could remember so fine, so noble—was the only effect of potations which would have reduced another man to brutal intoxication.

He walked on, and entered his chamber. She closed her door, crept into her bedroom, put out the light, and sat there shivering in the silence till at last the dawn peeped through the curtains, and warned her that another day had begun. Then she undressed and went to bed; and there followed the heavy, unrefreshing sleep which morning often brings one after a wakeful night of suffering.

So it was very late when she went down-stairs. A pile of letters and newspapers lay by Vaughan's plate. Soon he came into the room; the servant was present, so there were quiet salutations, and the idle attempts at conversation which decorum demanded. When the man went out, Darrell began opening his letters. One of the epistles was in the handwriting of Mr. Carstoe, Elizabeth saw. The contents irritated Vaughan evidently. He read, crushed the sheet in his hand, and muttered an oath—he had long since ceased to pay his wife the compliment of guarding against such brutality in her presence. Formerly it was her habit to rise and leave the room when he outraged her in that manner; but she had ceased to do this. She could not escape from the coarse horrors of her life, why vex him, and perhaps bring on a disgraceful scene by noticing an insult not directed her way?

He took up his newspapers; among these she noticed a California journal, which he had sent to him regularly each week. He had given the order as long ago as when he was in the Pacific State, and the paper still continued to come—not that he cared particularly for it, but he had grown accustomed to its arrival, and so had never withdrawn his subscription.

Elizabeth, seeing him occupied, rose from the table to leave the room. For days past he had been in one of his moods of not speaking to her; he would pass her on the stairs, or in the hall, without a word—sit at meals speechless, except when the servants were about. His sullen fits had ceased to irritate her, though there are few things more vexatious than such conduct, even on the part of a person to whom one is perfectly indifferent, if forced to live in the same house.

She stopped on her way out to look at some hyacinths in one of the windows—delicate purple-and-white blossoms, heavy with a delicious fragrance, which brought memories of her happy childhood—of a summer she had once spent at her Aunt Cranford's place off in the heart of Pennsylvania.

Then she heard Vaughan give the table a push which made the cups and plates rattle. She glanced instinctively round. If Mr. Carstoe's letter had vexed him, there was something in the journal which roused him to a more fiery anger. The wildest malediction, the most atrocious blasphemy she had ever heard from his lips, caused her to hurry on, eager to escape. He did not notice her; he was absolutely tearing the newspaper with fingers and teeth, as a wolf might worry its prey.

She knew that dissipation and evil courses had left him more and more incapable of self-control, but there was something inexpressibly painful in this exhibition. He was so fierce in look and gesture that it took away from the pettiness of the act. The show of emotion was absolutely terrible from the possibilities it suggested for the future—the danger that his very reason had begun to be troubled by the reckless degradation of his life.

It might have been an hour after that he entered her morning-room, where she sat making a pretense of work—to read was out of the question. Somehow, in the quiet in which she was forced to sit down, agitated, feverish with a wild desire in her soul to rush forth—to do she knew not what—attempt some effort at the task which Fate seemed to call upon her to perform, and yet toward which it opened no possible way—she found a sensation of comfort in letting her fingers plod along the weary hems. No pretty fancy task, no delicate crochet or ladylike embroidery: just a thick, warm dress she was making for a pensioner; one of the few acts of usefulness left in her power—to her who had dreamed of being a strength, an aid in her day and generation!

"Didn't I give you some papers to keep

a while ago—it may have been last autumn?" he asked.

"Yes; just before you went to Virginia," she replied.

"I want them," he said; "they are the deeds of those lots I bought in Albany—there's a good chance to sell." Then he could not resist saying something ill-natured. "Sorry to disturb your *dolce far niente*," he sneered. "I am aware you don't like me to intrude into this *sanctum;* but I happened to remember the papers as I was passing your door, and so ventured to enter."

Last night's dissipation had left him pale and haggard, but there was a disturbance in his face beyond those signs—a strange trouble and anxiety. Elizabeth was thinking this; conscious of pity for the man so obstinately bent on self-destruction. In spite of what she knew him to be, she could not help remembering there had been capabilities in his nature of results so different—the possibility of making a real good, a true use, of the life he wasted, growing daily less careful to cover its baseness with the veil of fine pretense under which he had once shrouded its reality.

Thinking these things even as she rose to seek the papers, trying at the same time to recollect where they had been put. She sank into an arm-chair, and sat watching her. Had she glanced at him again, she would have seen other revelations in his face—a frown of irritation and dislike so black that it was fairly like hatred. He did hate her sometimes. She looked so pure, so noble this morning—with a strange patience in her sad eyes. He was feeling how far off she was from him; how something—that religion he sneered at, that faith he held to be a weak delusion—put her soul beyond his reach. And she was so beautiful! Even with a mad passion in his heart for another woman, her beauty at this moment had its influence. Faithfulness was out of the question in his nature—he would have bartered his soul for Nathalie; yet that love, absorbing as it was, would not have hindered his plunging into the first disgraceful amour that chanced to offer itself.

But though he felt the spell of her beauty as he gazed, he was hating her; no matter what occurred to irritate him, however distant the thing might be from any connection with her, he was always bitter toward her at such moments; longed to do her a mischief; found a vent for his ill-humor by torturing her; felt always as if she in some way must be to blame.

Elizabeth remembered where she had put the papers. She had kept the desk which had been old Mr. Vaughan's; it was strong, and the lock peculiar—a safe receptacle for small articles that needed to be secure. Besides, she liked having this memento of the dead man toward whom her fancy always turned so tenderly. She took the desk out of a cabinet, set it on a table, sought her keys to open it. Darrell, idly watching her, noticed the desk—recollected it.

"Where did you get that?" he called. "Have you been rummaging among my things? What the devil do you mean by such a performance?"

She glanced at him over her shoulder with one of those looks of icy disdain with which she always met such attacks.

"You wrote me to look for some deeds that were in a trunk of yours," she said. "I found this desk; it was empty. I took a fancy to have it—that is all."

"Oh, don't be tragic!" retorted he. "Come, get me my papers; I can't wait all day; I hate this room anyhow."

In removing the contents of the desk to find the deeds, Elizabeth came upon the box of jewels, placed there the day she showed them to Launce Cromlin; she had never recollected to speak to Vaughan of their discovery. The box was lying on the documents she wanted; she took them both out together. Vaughan had risen in one of his sudden fits of impatience—he reached her just as she turned from the table.

"At last!" said he, rudely taking the papers out of her hand. The box fell upon the table, the lid dropped off. The ring, the stud, the unset jewels, lay in a little glittering heap upon the cloth.

There was a sound from Darrell Vaughan's white lips—something at once a groan and a curse. The next instant Elizabeth felt herself seized in an iron grasp—was flung forward upon her knees. In her utter bewilderment and confusion she saw her husband's face bending over her, convulsed and awful almost beyond any semblance of humanity.

He could not articulate; he was trying to speak—nothing but gasps escaped him. Specks of foam flew from his lips, his eyes glared like a wild beast's. He shook her to and fro as she knelt. It was death at last! He would kill her! This was to be the end. She was not frightened; she did not even know that his clutch hurt; only conscious that his face meant murder, and that there was a strange comfort in feeling death near, for death meant freedom — escape.

"I don't mind!" she whispered, gazing always into his mad eyes, not aware that she spoke. "Kill me—I don't mind!"

He pulled her up from the floor, and flung her into a chair. He must have realized then how near he had come to murder—the devilish temptation must have been strong in his soul still. He retreated, made a spring toward her, forced himself back, got the table between them, griped it with both hands, and held himself quiet.

"Say something!" he groaned. "Quick! Call somebody — get out of my reach! I shall kill you this time — I can't help it — I shall kill you!"

"Oh, do it!" she cried, in a voice scarcely less wild than his own. There was no patience, no fortitude, no thought of right or wrong, no recollection of any thing for the moment but the untold horror of her life—the insane longing that it should end—no matter how—only end!

He staggered down the chamber, opened the door, crossed the corridor into one of his rooms directly opposite. He left that door open too. From her seat Elizabeth could see him. He went to a closet, unlocked it, took out a decanter of brandy, more than half filled a goblet, and swallowed the contents at a draught. If she had wished, she lacked force to stir — to lock herself in from danger; but she did not think of it. If she had any distinct thought in her mind, it was a feeling of disappointment that after all death had not come when it was so near—so near.

He stood still in the middle of the room; she sat and watched him in the same blind, uncomprehending fashion. He came back into her chamber, closed the door behind him, and sat down, still keeping the table between them. His face was livid yet, his eyes kept their sombre fire; but the spasm so like insanity was over — the brandy had given his nerves a temporary strength.

"How did you come by those things—I mean, where did you steal them?" he asked. "You're a thief—do you know that?—a thief!"

"Oh," she said, with slow, concentrated bitterness, "I might have known you were too cowardly to murder me—you haven't courage to go beyond insult and outrage."

"Those things — those jewels — how did you come by them?" he repeated.

Her first impulse was to remain silent, but her power to reflect, her better feelings, returned. The whirl and confusion left her brain. She was calm enough; could recollect that to tantalize him would perhaps be a wickedness beyond his: he might be mad—she had sometimes feared such a fate for him; it might have come at last.

"There is no secret, no mystery," she said. "I found them in one of the trunks I opened. I supposed you had forgotten them—I took them out, and did not remember to tell you."

He had forgotten them. Another of those strange lapses of memory which had grown more and more frequent during the past years, torturing him with a dread which he would not study nor face. He leaned his elbows upon the table, and rested his head on his hands, pressing them hard across it. His brain reeled; the diamonds danced like specks of fire before his eyes. These mute but potent proofs of his guilt, these evidences of that awful episode which he had put aside as easily as other men would the recollection of a trifling fault, here they appeared again.

He could have sworn that he had destroyed them — had flung the box into the ocean one night during his voyage back from California. Then he remembered. He had mistaken one box for another in packing his things. He found when too late that he had reserved a box containing a watch — the jewels he had put into a trunk which was down in the depths of the hold, and could not be reached.

When he changed steamers at Panama he would open the trunk and get the jewels. He had stayed two days on the isthmus before the Atlantic steamer was ready to sail. The dullness, and a desire to convince himself that the painful effects of the last doze of hasheesh were only caused by some peculiar physical state, caused him again to indulge in its use.

Lying on his bed under the influence of the drug, he had in fancy enacted the work he meant to do. He was on the steamer, he opened the trunk, took the jewels out, and flung them into the sea. It was all real — every link perfect — even to the excuse he had given for wishing that particular trunk placed in his state-room. He had gone to the stern; the moon was shining; the foam looked to his eyes as if the gems he had cast down were rising and flashing in countless multitudes. As he walked back he had met the captain — they had talked — he could recall the conversation.

From that day to this he had not thought of the affair. Now here the diamonds appeared again, and the hasheesh dream separated itself from the reality. He saw the dream and the fact side by side; yet, though he realized it was a vision, it looked real as ever.

And he had betrayed himself—he could recollect this too. Impossible that Elizabeth should not feel there was an awful secret connected with the jewels after the insane scene he had made. He must find some excuse, offer some reason; and his brain was so dull—his invention failed so!

"I'm sorry," he said, with a kind of sudden hesitation. "I'm not well this morning. You couldn't know—but those jewels had something to do with my uncle's history." (The tale seemed to frame itself as he went on. Elizabeth did not even deign him a glance.) "I thought he had sold them—got rid of them; he meant to. I can't explain—the matter can't be talked of even between us; it was my uncle's secret, and that fellow's, Launce Cromlin."

He had not thought of his cousin a second before he spoke; the name came to his lips, and he uttered it.

"I don't wish any explanation," Elizabeth said, quickly.

He looked at her; she had raised her eyes. She was perfectly calm and self-possessed; he knew that she did not believe a word he had spoken. Once more he felt his fingers quiver with the hot thrill — the murderous instinct which had animated him when he held her in that stern grasp. He clasped his hands together, and pressed them hard down on the table.

"Yes—Launce Cromlin's secret; more of his misdoing," he went on slowly. "If it had not been for his conduct, my uncle might be alive this day."

It was on Elizabeth's lips to defend Launce—to tell the man what she knew of his treachery, his falsehoods; but what possible good could come of such an avowal? She sat silent; turned her eyes away from his face, certain that they told the tale almost as plainly as words could have done.

"Be good enough to give me no explanation," she said, wearily. "Take the diamonds; don't let me have to see them—be obliged to remember this day."

"You are very chary of hearing any thing against our cousin," sneered Vaughan, with a sudden look of suspicion.

"Yes," she replied, coldly; "I believe him to be a good man: we need not talk about him."

He only answered by that same evil look. He began collecting the jewels and putting them into the box.

"This matter must rest between you and me," he said; "forget it if you can. No one has seen the diamonds?"

"Your cousin saw them, and Mr. Carstoe too," she answered.

This time, had he reached her, she would have been a dead woman before he could have got his senses back. She saw him coming—saw the murder in his blind, staring eyes. She was out of her chair—across the room—her hand on the bell-pull. She was not frightened—even the desperate feeling which before had kept her unstruggling in his grasp was gone.

"If you come any nearer," she said, "I shall ring: it's an electric bell, remember, and sounds from garret to cellar."

He stopped short—her perfect calmness acted like a dash of ice-water on his frenzy. He could think too; rather, he could listen to what some power, which seemed extraneous to his faculties, whispered like an audible voice. Useless to kill her—no harm done after all; that is, no harm could come to him. Carstoe could prove nothing. Milady even, free, pardoned, as the California journal had this morning told him, could prove nothing, if she wanted revenge. And Carstoe would take no step—this was why he had resigned the agency; but that would be the end. Nothing would come of the matter. Launce Cromlin himself could not hurt him. Bah! plenty of traders could be found, if necessary, to swear they sold him the jewels—swear they bought them in California. He had been a fool to be frightened—overcome. And there that woman stood defying him—knowledge of his vileness, his cowardice, written in every line of her marble-like face! How he hated her! How he longed to expose her to some awful torture, some unutterable degradation, which should strike body and soul—leave her incapable to cleanse either from the stain, and then let her live and be forced to bear it!

"So, so!" he cried. "I understand a few things that were not clear before. You and master Launce hoped to hatch some plot. I know what he has been at—all a failure! But you—I comprehend your little game now: you the pattern of modesty and purity—you so religious and virtuous! You're an infamous woman, and Launce Cromlin is your lover: I know the truth at last."

She still kept her hand on the bell-pull—she neither stirred nor spoke. He went back to the table, and thrust the box of jewels into his pocket.

"When you write to your paramour," he said, "tell him I have discovered it all; tell him if he takes another step, opens his lips, I will commence a divorce suit against you for adultery, and I'll find proofs at any cost. You know what money will do!"

She did not speak—did not move.

"There sha'n't be any more attempts at decorum and decency between you and me," he went on; "we look at each other just as we are, without disguise. Remember—a word, a single step, and you shall go into court, and come out of it a woman so infamous that you'll find no shelter short of that heaven you're fond of talking poetry about."

He spoke partly because a devil of jealousy really had seized his depraved mind, partly from an idea that he might frighten her into begging Cromlin to be silent, if there had been any idea of exposure—most of all, because he was so insane with passion that to hurl the coarse threat at her was a positive delight.

Then he passed out of the room, and Elizabeth was alone.

CHAPTER XXXIV.

"THEN I'LL TELL."

Two weeks went by, weeks without incident—without a break to the dull monotony in which Elizabeth sat dumbly waiting for the next blow to fall. Fate had not done with her yet—there was more beyond; it would come soon.

Lent had arrived. There were decorously sober festivities to which she was invited: she went. There was the ordinary round of duties: she fulfilled them. She and Vaughan met—never alone. If he entered a room and saw her sitting there in solitude, he retreated. On—on—drifted the days. She could do nothing—nothing. She was not heeding that last disgraceful scene. She was not especially hopeless from this new degradation which had been cast upon her; it was not that. Marguerite—Milady—her sister—hers and Nathalie's—a bond between herself and this woman whom she seemed now every time she left her house to meet with Vaughan.

It was always as if some voice urged her on to help that unknown sister—as if the peace of departed souls depended upon her doing it—but how? Could Nathalie have aided, she would have gone to her. In spite of the bar between them, the shame and disgrace which separated their lives, she would have acted hand in hand with her as if no Darrell Vaughan existed, or had been personally a stranger to her own life; but Nathalie was powerless as herself.

She had written to Mr. Carstoe—that was all she could do—simply asking him to find out any thing concerning a woman called Milady, or Marguerite, who had at such a time lived in San Francisco. She put the date which had been on the last check sent to Mrs. Murray—gave the name of the bankers from whence it was issued. Having done this, she could only wait, and she had little to hope. It was long since Mrs. Murray had heard of her there. Whither since then the desperate creature might have drifted, God only knew. She felt no horror, no disgust, at the thought of this unfortunate woman. Even the fact itself—separate from the poor girl—the sin, the shame, coming into her life, did not horrify her as it would once have done. In thinking of it she could fancy what such an idea—the bare possibility—would have been to her in her early youth. She wondered if she had become hardened, her nature coarse, that she had no such shrinkings now.

Pity—that was her only sensation: pity for the wretched, nameless outcast; a readiness to help her; a will to aid, to raise her up. At least she was not to be blamed. However the sins of others might look, there were pleas for this creature which Elizabeth knew the angels themselves must heed.

She went one day to visit an old lame man and his paralytic sister, who had lately fallen under her notice. There is nothing picturesque, nothing romantic, to offer in the way of description. A couple of bare rooms; an old man bending over a shoemaker's bench, his poor limbs distorted by the tortures of rheumatism, toiling composedly, as if each breath were not an effort, each movement a pain. A woman, almost as old, lying on a bed where she had lain for fourteen years, where she must continue to lie till the strange vitality which supported the half-dead frame wore out. The paralysis left the upper part of her body untouched; she could talk, use her hands, manage bits of sewing. As she lay propped among the pillows, her lean fingers moved deftly along the seam, and she was humming a hymn in her weak voice, which had a touch of youthful sweetness in it, just as certain flowers will retain a breath of perfume even after they have grown withered and sere.

This was the picture that met Mrs. Vaughan's eyes as she entered. Nothing to make a dramatic scene of or write poetry about, as men do in regard to the old-time martyrdoms, which lasted for a few hours only—but God knows! There shall be others than Peter and Paul, others than Catherine and Agnes, and all the shining throng whose history the world has kept, whom we shall see wearing the martyr's palm up yonder in the light; men and women among whom we moved daily in our blindness here, and caught no gleam of the saint's halo which encircled their patient brows.

"It's nothing but good news to-day, ma'am," old Richard said, with a smile that lighted up his wrinkles like sunshine, as he hobbled after Elizabeth toward the bed.

"Nothing but good news," repeated old Miriam, looking up at her visitor with eyes that were sweet and solemn as a prayer. They had received a letter from a nephew long supposed to be dead. The patient couple had taken care of him during his childhood and early youth; he proved a wayward, disobedient fellow, and finally disappeared shortly before Miriam's paralytic stroke. But whatever errors lay in the past he desired to redeem. His wanderings had ended in California; his business was thoroughly established, and he promised that, if it continued to prosper, they should have a visit from him in the course of the ensuing year, and gave the assurance that tangible proofs of his gratitude and affection would not henceforth be wanting.

"I never could believe he was dead," Miriam added, wiping away her happy tears. "He had a good heart always, if he was a bit wild."—"Always a good heart," echoed Richard. They had a habit of repeating each other's statements, as if there were only one will and opinion between them.

Mrs. Vaughan must read his letter—such a beautiful letter; it had only come two days before—a bank-check with it; but welcome as that was, the affection and tenderness were still more to the foolish old pair.

"And a newspaper, with a notice of his business—quite grand," Richard said. "Where is the paper, Miriam? Show it to Madam; she'll like to see it, I know."

"Of course I shall," Elizabeth said, smiling. The sight of the two old bodies' happiness came like a ray of light to the desolate woman. She was groping in a darkness so profound, life had reached a pass so dismal, so positively loathsome, that to watch their faces and listen to their thankful words was like having a new prop suddenly steady her tottering faith.

Miriam drew the journal from under her pillow, and pointed with pride to her nephew's name among the advertising columns. Elizabeth sat absently turning the paper in her hands while the pair talked. Its pompous title, *The Cali-*

fornia Clarion, sent her thoughts back to the dreary round in which during the past days they had circled aimlessly like frightened birds.

A paragraph upon the first page caught her eye—just the heading and the opening lines. She dared not look again. She could only gripe the sides of her chair with both hands, and struggle with all her might not to shriek. She heard the two voices still; they seemed to come from a great distance. A gray mist gathered before her; she could see nothing distinctly save the half-open journal which had fluttered into her lap.

Presently she found strength to rise, to speak a few words—bid the brother and sister a kindly farewell.

"I'm afraid the room is close," Miriam said; "the Madam looks very pale, Dick, old man."

"Only a headache," Elizabeth heard herself reply. "I would like to take the paper, if you have read it; there is an article I want to look at."

She was out of the room—going down the stairs—so dizzy that it was like descending a precipice. Her carriage waited at the door; she had taken her seat.

"Where to, ma'am?" the footman was asking.

"Home." Oh, the awful mockery of that word!

The journal was in her hand still; she thrust it out of sight among the folds of her dress; she could not trust herself yet to examine it. The carriage reached her house; it seemed to her she had been making an interminable journey. She was up-stairs in her own room, the door fastened, the dizziness and confusion gone, a chill like that of death locking her senses in an apathy which deprived her of the power to feel acutely—only a dull horror and fright struggling up through the arctic coldness that froze her soul.

It was all clear at last—not a link wanting in the dreadful chain of evidence. She read an account of the pardon which had been granted to the woman called Milady.

Another specimen of the manner in which justice was administered in our land, said the journal. What motive the Governor could have had in his decision was beyond the journalist's conception. But it was the same old story. The law condemned a guilty woman, and a mistaken sympathy, a morbid sentimentalism, set her free to begin a new course of crime. A recapitulation of Milady's trial followed: the charge against her, a description of the jewels, Mr. Carstoe's name, Darrell Vaughan's evidence.

The whole was briefly told, but when Elizabeth finished the paragraph there remained no secret. She understood every thing, from Mr. Carstoe's resignation of the agency to Vaughan's mad passion of the morning.

An hour passed; some one knocked. Elizabeth hid the journal, rose, and unbolted the door. There are blows so terrible that they leave us outwardly calm; they deaden the soul as a mortal wound does the body. She felt as if walking in her sleep—found herself wondering if she should soon awake.

Prudence Anderson entered the room. She had come to the town mansion this winter as housekeeper.

"I'm right sorry to trouble you," she said; "but I want to ask for a little laudanum. Joanna's been bad all night with cholera morbus, and still has so much pain she can't sleep."

Joanna was a chambermaid, as good as she was ugly, with a fatal propensity for devouring things that agonized her interior. This time she had overdone the business with stale lobster-salad, to which she had been treated on the previous evening while visiting a friend with cormorantish propensities like her own.

"Had she not better have a doctor?" asked Elizabeth, able even in this moment to be thoughtful and sympathizing.

"No, ma'am; there ain't a bit of need—the laudanum will set her all right. I'm sorry for her; but the way she will make a cupboard of her stomach to turn every thing into she can lay hands on is too much for a body's patience," Prudence averred. "I expect every day I'll find her eating a brass door-knob, just out of curiosity."

"I will go and see her presently," Elizabeth said.

"Yes, ma'am," returned Prudence; but she still lingered. She looked so anxious and troubled that Mrs. Vaughan added—

"Is there any thing else the matter?"

Prudence shifted one foot, then the other; turned red and pale, and finally said—

"Excuse me, do excuse me, Miss Elizabeth." (She often used the old familiar name when excited). "Don't take it for a liberty; I ought to tell you. We've been deceived in Mary Liscom; she ought to leave the house."

For the last three weeks Elizabeth had given employment to this young girl as seamstress. It is no matter about the story. She was friendless—overworked to support an invalid mother and a brutal step-father, until she fell under the notice of the lady who had recommended her to Mrs. Vaughan. A pretty creature; educated beyond the station in which they found her; looking positively elegant in her simple dress. A marvel of delicate contours and wonderful coloring, such as only an American girl can be; with graceful ways, a merry laugh in spite of her hard fate, and sly, mischievous black eyes that brightened her whole face.

Mrs. Vaughan and Prudence invented a quantity of needs in the matter of bed-linen and the like to give the girl occupation. Elizabeth would not even allow her to take a room in the servants' quarter. She had quite a luxurious little retreat assigned her, with books and a pleasant view from the windows. Elizabeth could not sufficiently sympathize with the girl's pathetic tale. During her father's life she had been comfortably off, petted and loved. The vicious habits of her mother's second husband had dragged them rapidly down, lost a school she had been teaching in Tarrytown, and ruined any hope of her obtaining more congenial employment than that of a needlewoman. Elizabeth trusted later to find her a position as companion to some solitary lady who would be kind to the unfortunate creature.

Within the last week an odd change had come over the girl. She had answered Mrs. Vaughan petulantly, and was more than insolent to good Prudence, and overbearing with the servants.

Just as Mrs. Anderson had begun this complaint, Margot appeared. There were two gentlemen down-stairs who wished to see Madam. No; not gentlemen Margot had ever before seen at the house; there was the card.

"Dr. Street," read Elizabeth aloud; then another name written in pencil. As Prudence Anderson heard the name, she turned very pale, and went unceremoniously out of the room. All the while Margot was continuing her voluble explanations. The gentlemen were sorry to intrude, but they came on business important to themselves; they ventured to trespass upon Mrs. Vaughan's well-known kindness.

Elizabeth left Margot still talking and descended the stairs, glad to escape reflection a little longer. As she entered the reception-room the two visitors rose—one an elderly gentleman with white hair, who introduced himself as Dr. Street; the other, less pleasing, less gentlemanly in appearance.

"You wished to see me," Mrs. Vaughan said, too cold and apathetic still to wonder what their business might be. "Pray be seated."

She sat down in an easy-chair; they placed themselves near her. She was conscious that they both watched her very intently, but could not give much thought. The doctor began a long, rather rambling explanation. He was the medical adviser of a private hospital on Long Island; his companion was the manager. Mrs. Vaughan's goodness was so well known; Mr. Vaughan's philanthropy a virtue so widely admired, that they had ventured to come, hoping to interest the lady in their undertakings. The doctor talked as volubly as Margot herself. He asked questions too—a great many—managing with much tact to bring them in somehow, even while going on with his account of the hospital, and always Elizabeth was aware that the silent man watched her furtively but keenly from under his bushy eyebrows.

And still the doctor talked; he contrived (it seemed to Elizabeth, still thinking in the same dull, uncomprehending fashion) to mingle every imaginable subject in his fervid periods—and yet the hospital was the basis always. He told amusing stories. It would have been difficult for a human creature to be more fascinating in conversation. Elizabeth found herself listening with interest, chill and numb as she felt. Mrs. Vaughan's fondness for music, Mrs. Vaughan's love of painting—no trifle in the room which could bear evidence as to her tastes escaped the physician. Then some words in regard to her health—a remark that she looked pale—lack of exercise, perhaps. The doctor regretted that his countrymen so often failed in that duty; no hope of keeping mind and nerves in proper order without due attention to it. Then, before one could think him impertinent, or remember that he asked odd questions, he was back at the hospital again—a hospital for nervous patients. Mrs. Vaughan would be interested, he knew, if only he could persuade her to visit it.

Always the bushy-eyebrowed man watched her furtively, and had little to say. The doctor now and then brought him into the conversation, but talked too fast for the silent man to take advantage of the opportunity if he wished.

After all, what was the motive for the visit? Elizabeth began to ask herself this as the doctor talked on. He had darted off on a little excursion to Italy, and was waving his plump white hands over the ruins of the Roman Forum, when Elizabeth got to that inquiry in her mind. Did he want money? The affairs of the hospital appeared to be in a wonderfully flourishing condition; but all this eloquence, this circumlocution, this effort to please, must mean money. The doctor returned from Italy, stopping at Westminster Abbey on the road. But what was he saying now, for still it was an effort to keep her thoughts fixed any length of time upon his words? Her father, the late Mr. Cranford—nervousness—peculiar habits—what could he mean?

"Did you know my father?" she asked.

The doctor had never enjoyed that pleasure—that great pleasure; he regretted it deeply! He was fond of studious men! More compliments, more pretty speeches, and yet, as well as she could understand, he seemed somehow to be building up a theory which connected her pallor and her father's nervousness—the transmission of mental ills; then leagues off in generalities—and the silent man watching!

She had had enough of it, agreeable as the doctor was; one could not think of calling him impertinent, and yet his conversation would have been an intolerable presumption in another. If he would not in his delicacy come to the pecuniary matter, which must be his real errand, she would broach the subject and be done. She had uses enough for more money than she could control; a new duty had just opened—Marguerite. Then a quick impatience came over her. Would he never go—never leave her free to try for a ray of light, some means, some way to set about the solemn task which had devolved upon her?

Before she could speak, Vaughan's name was on the doctor's lips again. He knew her husband! He got away from the fact with the speed of lightning; it had been an accidental admission—the doctor's one blunder; she felt instinctively that he had blundered.

"You are acquainted with Mr. Vaughan," she said—the words were a statement, not a question.

The doctor with another wave of his white hands put Mr. Vaughan away off—almost beyond acquaintanceship; but he had seen him, he was forced to admit that. Elizabeth saw the glimmer of a smile upon the silent man's lips—gone instantly; but she was in the dark no longer. So far as personal peril was concerned, she knew that never in her whole life had she stood in so black a strait as this present crisis—not even on that morning when her husband's murderous gripe seized her, and his eyes, threatening death, looked into her own. She felt that her face did not change nor her eyes betray, even to the doctor's keen gaze, a glimpse of the discovery which had struck her.

Now he was back at the hospital; his plans, his arrangements, the beautiful grounds; this, that, and the other—no matter what—it afforded Elizabeth an opportunity to say—

"You interest me very much; I should like to visit the place exceedingly."

While the doctor burst into eloquent thanks—rushed at the clinching of the business by asking her to set a day—Elizabeth, smiling at him, was able with a woman's quickness to study the silent man. She saw a gleam of satisfaction just as she had seen the passing smile.

Elizabeth Vaughan was physically a brave woman. Her health had always been so perfect that even the suffering of the past years had failed to shake her nerves. Once in her girlhood she had been on a Mediterranean steamer when a fire burst out in the middle of the night. She had been firm and composed as the strongest man on board — had given aid and counsel when most of the passengers and sailors alike were mad with fear.

Just as she had felt at that moment she felt now, and she knew the danger she had run then was less terrible than the present peril. She did not try any more to hurry the doctor. She talked—asked questions too—was cheerful and affable to the last. Very soon she hoped to be able to gratify herself by a visit to the hospital. Name a day? Well, yes; it would be a disappointment if she should miss the doctor. This was Tuesday—say toward the close of the next week. Would the Friday but one be a convenient time for Dr. Street? All days and hours of the doctor's life were at Mrs. Vaughan's disposal. Next week, Friday. Mrs. Vaughan would take the rail at Brooklyn—no journey to speak of. At Longwood the doctor would meet her himself with a carriage—only half-an-hour's drive to the Retreat. Pretty name, was it not? Suggestive of quiet—rest—all that sort of thing, so pleasant to contemplate by us of the busy nineteenth century, with our high-strung, over-tried, nervous organizations!

"I have no doubt Mr. Vaughan will accompany me," Elizabeth said, after she had duly admired the fitness of the title, looking full in the doctor's face with a smile.

This was positively blissful to hear—a reward to the doctor for the earnest labors of a whole life. He should dream like a poet, prosaic as work had rendered him, of the day which would bring Mr. and Mrs. Vaughan to the scene of his duties. Next week, Friday?

"Next week, Friday," said Elizabeth, still smiling.

The physician went out of the room a perfect *feu de joie* of pretty speeches, and the silent man followed, dull and dark as the smoke in the train of fireworks.

Elizabeth hurried into the next room, which gave a view of the street; she wanted to look out of the window and obtain another glance at her visitors. A door that opened into the hall was ajar—the two men were passing it—she distinctly heard the silent man whisper, "Who'd have thought it would be so easy to manage!" and the doctor's whispered response, "A clear case, a perfectly clear case. Worn-out nerves at the bottom. Sad, very sad. But Mr. Vaughan is right; repose—guidance—all she needs. Yes, yes."

A short laugh from the other—they were gone.

As Elizabeth stood there motionless the partially open door was swung to; from behind came Prudence Anderson, pale and trembling.

"I have been in this room all the while," she said, in a choked, frightened voice; "I've been listening. Do you know who that man was?"

Dr. Street! Elizabeth had recalled her association with the name before the interview ended. The scene of the doctor's labors was a private mad-house on Long Island. Darrell Vaughan did not wish to murder his hated wife, he only meant to confine her to the physician's parental care amid the retired haunts of the Retreat.

"Do you know?" repeated Prudence.

"Yes," Elizabeth answered.

"But you can't understand what his coming means; you couldn't be so quiet!" cried Prudence. "Didn't you hear what they whispered as they went out?"

She caught Elizabeth's dress, as if to protect her.

"I know—I heard," her mistress replied.

"I remembered him the minute I heard his name," continued Prudence. "I knew what it meant—I listened. He couldn't take you off, but I was scared all the same. Oh, Miss Elizabeth, get away—send for help—do something! Oh, don't you understand what is afore you?"

"I understand," Elizabeth returned, calmly as before.

"And you promised to go to the place!"

"That gives me time, at least. I must think—I don't know what to do."

"You must speak out at last!" exclaimed Prudence, with a flash in her old eyes. "You have borne enough; you must save yourself! Oh, don't be angry; I can't keep quiet; I don't mean to be impudent. Oh, Miss Elizabeth, Miss Elizabeth, no woman ever stood in a blacker danger than you do now."

She began to cry and wring her hands.

"Hush, Prudence, it is useless to be frightened; I am not."

"You will go away—you will?"

"I should be no safer; he could follow me," she said.

Prudence was past remembering the difference in their positions; she could only recollect that they were both women; that this unfortunate creature must be made to save herself.

"You've got to speak out!" she exclaimed. "You've got to appeal to your friends—to the law. I tell you there's a worse danger than murder close by—there's a mad-house waiting for you! Oh, Miss Elizabeth, my deary, my best, don't wait—don't waste a minute!"

In the agony of her appeal she fell on her knees before her mistress, still holding fast by her dress.

"Let me sit down," Elizabeth said. "Get up, Prudence. Hush, there's no danger yet! I can't, I can't! I have said there is only one cause that can give me a right to free myself—not suspicion either, not circumstantial evidence—proofs."

She had sunk into a chair. Prudence, still on her knees, held her fast and looked up at her.

"I can not tell the world—it is bad enough to have even you know, dear soul," pursued Elizabeth.

"You won't go—you won't save yourself?" cried Prudence, in an altered voice.

"I shall tell him that I know—that I am on my guard."

"What good will that be? You'll be carried off—shut up in a mad-house—do you hear, a mad-house!"

"I think not; I shall do my best."

"There's only one way—the law, Miss Elizabeth—the law!"

"Man's law, Prudence!" she groaned. "The Bible only holds one permission; other causes do not give it."

Prudence sprang to her feet.

"Then I'll tell!" she cried. "I've held my peace for a week, but I've known!"

At this instant Mary Liscom's voice sounded

at the farther end of the hall; she was calling Margot to ask Mrs. Vaughan if she might go out for a while. Prudence stopped speaking at the tones; when they died she drew closer to her mistress, and added in a choked whisper—

"Hark! You heard her! Ma'am, ma'am, I've known for a week—even the Bible won't support you in clinging to that man any longer."

CHAPTER XXXV.

OUT OF HIS REACH.

THE iron gates opened with a discontented murmur, as if loth to admit visitors; the carriage passed on up the winding road, and stopped before the house—a fine old mansion, surrounded by spacious grounds, but so solitary, so neglected, that one would have needed to be either very happy or very miserable to tolerate existence there any length of time.

It was toward sunset when Elizabeth arrived. She had left town by an early train, and traveled all day—for many hours amid the gloom of mountain scenery, round dizzying curves, close to the edge of precipices, through black tunnels, up grades so steep that it seemed wonderful the ingenuity of man could have contrived the track, amid the shadow of pine forests odorous with the scents of early spring, musical with the voice of birds and waterfalls—on and on, the way growing more tortuous, the engine groaning like some living thing tasked beyond its strength. At last the summit was reached, and the road plunged down the descent toward the beautiful valley which lay sunny and bright among the lofty hills, with the Susquehanna winding slowly through its midst, in the very heart of the great Pennsylvanian mountains.

The train stopped at the village station. On the previous day Elizabeth had announced her arrival, so the carriage was waiting. She drove through the bustling streets, across the bridge, and on toward the shadow of the hills where the old house stood. This was Tanglewood—Miss Janet Cranford's place. In her loneliness and desolation Elizabeth had come hither to seek refuge, at least for a time. Miss Janet was the only relative she possessed in the world, and her home seemed the most fitting haven.

Three days had elapsed since into the misery of Elizabeth Cranford's life came the crowning degradation which caused her to fling down her burden—throw off the weight of the galling chains she had worn so long.

She could fix her mind on but one thought—that determination to get away, to flee and cleanse her soul from the impurity about her; as a wretch suffocated by the stench of a noisome pit might employ the last remnant of his strength to struggle out. To get away—that was the one thought. She could not even pray. For the time, though she did not realize it, she was almost as far from the possibility of Divine help as if she had given voice to anathemas and cursed God and man. To go—to flee! She had reached the point where even the Bible admits that duty ends.

Perhaps the hardest thing of all was the necessity of confiding to human ears the hitherto jealously guarded secret of her married life. Even in that hour of supreme suffering it was a terrible humiliation to her great pride; but there was no possibility of avoiding it now. She sent for Mr. Howland—she told what was necessary to tell in Darrell Vaughan's presence. It was the first intimation the bad man had received of her full knowledge of his guilt. The case was perfectly clear—if Vaughan offered the least opposition, the law could be called in to protect her. Utter disgrace to him would follow upon exposure, and the circumstantial evidence there was of his having contemplated carrying out that most awful treachery against her with the assistance of the mad-house doctor would, he knew well, in the hands of an eloquent counsel, make a tale that must blast him forever.

The scene was quiet enough. I do not describe it—I see no good purpose that such description could serve. Vaughan was sullen, but he could refuse nothing that was demanded, and Mr. Howland's claim went beyond what Elizabeth would have asked, though perfectly just. Mrs. Vaughan's fortune must be restored to the last penny. This was a hard thing to Darrell. During these past years he had become very rich, as we know; his dealings with the Ring had absolutely thrown millions into his coffers; but it was as hard to give up what belonged to his wife as if it left him poor, though in reality he would scarcely miss the amount from his dishonestly won treasures.

Elizabeth left the two men together, and the matter was arranged before they separated. Mr. Howland remained perfectly cool; but he would hear of neither compromise nor delay. Vaughan had his choice between restoring the money at once, signing a confession which would render him powerless in any way to trouble his wife for the future, or to stand a trial by law.

"She'd never do that," he said; "she's too cursedly proud. Come, come, Howland, you're going beyond your instructions."

"She will do it if there is no other way to gain her liberty," the other replied. "And I may as well tell you honestly that if she faltered, I should send for Miss Janet Crauford, and she would commence a suit as Mrs. Vaughan's nearest relative. You know enough of that old lady to be certain she would not hesitate."

So the man yielded, signed the necessary papers, and Mr. Howland went out of the room to find Elizabeth, carrying the warrant of her freedom in his hand. There would be no exposure, no gossip even. Mrs. Vaughan would go to her aunt—nothing more natural than that she should be required, considering Miss Crauford's age and feeble health. Later she could visit Europe; Mr. Vaughan's business and political duties would serve as an excuse in the eyes of the world for his remaining behind. If gossip and hints did at last arise, at least there would be no scandal. Vaughan need fear nothing so long as he left his wife unmolested; but that he must do. Not even so much as a word or an insinuation could he permit himself. The instant that should happen, Mr. Howland assured him every detail would be made public; and Vaughan knew the man with whom he had to deal.

He hated to give her up; love of power was as strong as his greed for wealth. He hated to see her slip from his hands—to know that he could never torture her again, never visit disappointment or ill-temper upon her. With it all he was faithful, like the rest of humanity, to his inconsistency. Even with a mad passion for another woman burning in his soul, this pale, worn beauty of Elizabeth's looked suddenly precious again, now that she had passed out of his reach forever.

So the end had come. Darrell himself spoke of the visit, and Society thought the proceeding natural and wise. Miss Crauford was old and ailing, and very rich, he said; of course a person to be cared for and cherished, even at the expense of a temporary separation between husband and wife.

Prudence Anderson was going away too; she had no mind to remain in the house, and long years of service had given her a competency which enabled her to seek repose.

Neither she nor Elizabeth forgot the weak, miserable girl who had fluttered to ruin like a moth toward a candle. They did the best possible for her, hoping, or trying to hope, that her anguish and promises were the result of contrition, not merely the effect of shame at discovery.

The end had come! Elizabeth said that over and over to herself during the days of hurried preparation. Liberty was not precious to her—she had no use to make of it. The future could hold nothing — not even a hope. There would be a round of little duties, years of quiet without rest. Life was so long, and she was young yet! She had often pitied the old for having to sit passive and see others live — no interest, no strong inducement left; and this fate had come upon her, and she was in the fullness of youth and strength.

Oh, it was hard, hard! God was cruel to her — existence a curse! She knew at length that faith itself was slipping from her, and she could not hold it fast, she was too frozen and apathetic even to pray.

All over—the journey accomplished—she had

done with the past. The sound of the carriage-wheels brought old Thomas and Jane Flint, her aunt's chief adherents, upon the veranda. Elizabeth had paid a yearly visit to Tanglewood since her return from Europe, so her arrival excited no surprise in their minds, though she had never before come so early in the season.

It was March now. The sheltered valley was already beautiful with promises of spring. The trees were in leaf, the young grass green upon the lawn, the crocuses and hyacinths brightened the garden walks. Elizabeth paused for a few seconds on the veranda and looked about. The house stood upon an eminence; she could see for miles down the narrow vale. There was a sweep of pasture-lands, groves, and cultivated farms. Pleasant homesteads peeped out here and there. Tiny villages nestled along the valley's length, the river wound like a silver mist through its heart, the blue hills shut in the far distance on every side, and the soft spring sky bent toward them, bright with sunshine and white fleecy clouds. The whole formed a picture of tranquil loveliness, which struck on the confusion and coldness of her soul like an added pain. Thomas and Jane Flint were busy superintending the removal of her luggage into the house—nobody had time to notice her. She had come quite alone—she could not bear, for the present, to see a single face that had been about her in the desecrated home from which she had fled, so even her maid was left behind. The sun was setting; the amber and pink clouds billowed up in the west; the breeze brought the voice of the river and the murmur of the pines; a thrush, perched in the topmost boughs of an acacia, sang his evening hymn; from the distant farm-yard came the lowing of cattle, the bleating of sheep—all the pleasant sounds of country life which had once been so sweet and full of poetry to her.

It was inexpressibly sad and dreary now, the whole scene. She felt a vague surprise at the beauty and freshness about; the new life and growth of spring. It seemed wonderful that the earth could remain so fair under its burden of human wretchedness. She passed into the entrance-hall, and walked on through the solitary apartments toward a room where her aunt always sat, opened the door, and entered.

Every thing looked as she expected—certainly there was no brightness here to vex her weary eyes. The windows gave a view of the shrubberies, which grew neglected and wild; rosebushes and woodbines trailed over the casements, and helped to shut out the light. For years Miss Crauford had suffered greatly with her eyes, and had chosen this gloomy nook for her special haunt, just because it was shadowy and dark. Nothing in the cold rigidity of the place had altered, from the old-fashioned chairs ranged in a solemn row against the wall, to the figure that sat in the centre of the room knitting mechanically, yet as assiduously as if a human fate were being woven into the web. Upright and stiff she sat—a tall, gaunt, pale woman, dressed in dull gray, without a speck of color to relieve its sombreness, hair of the same hue as her dress, a face which looked taciturn and cold, almost grim. There were traces of pain and suffering in every feature, but suffering borne in silence, and with a fortitude which came as much from obstinacy as patience. This was Elizabeth's aunt, old Miss Janet Crauford, who had lived here alone among the shadows for more than thirty years. "Is that you, Elizabeth?" she called as the door opened and the visitor paused upon the threshold. "I heard the carriage, so I supposed you had come. I can't get up—it's one of my blind days."

The voice was not even fretful; there would have been a humanity somewhat refreshing in that—just cold and emotionless, as if a stone or something entirely beyond the reach of sympathy with this world had spoken.

"Yes, Aunt Janet, I have come," answered Elizabeth, going toward her. "How do you do? Will you kiss me?"

"How do you do, Elizabeth? But I shan't kiss you—you know I never do kiss any body. You are at home now—you know what to do with yourself. Jane Flint has got rooms ready for you—here is mine when you want to see me. Make yourself comfortable in your own way. Don't expect me to listen to any complaints. From first to last you have chosen for yourself. You married—I suppose to please yourself. Now you have left your husband, to please yourself too; so there's an end of it. George Howland wrote me all that was necessary for me to know, and there's never any use in talking over what's inevitable."

She spoke without the slightest change of tone or emphasis, her fingers never pausing in their task.

"No use whatever," Elizabeth answered; "I am not likely to trouble you with complaints."

"No; that wouldn't be your way; you're a real Crauford. More than one could say for your father, who liked nothing so much as to get hurt and cry over it," resumed the passionless tones. "I dare say your husband was as bad as possible; he wouldn't be a man if he hadn't been."

"I told you I did not mean to complain, Aunt Janet."

"It's possible you were not perfection, though you would hardly be a woman if you did not think you had been. Just fancy we have droned on for the past few years as we shall do till you are tired of staying, and we shall do well enough; there's no good in looking back."

"Do well enough!" repeated Elizabeth, mechanically.

"Oh, there's worse in life than that, dull as it sounds," said Miss Janet.

"Yes, there's worse than that," replied Elizabeth. "I will go up-stairs now."

"Jane Flint will have dinner for you. I dine early, you know."

"I only want some tea," Elizabeth said; "I am afraid I have kept you waiting for that."

"If my hour had come I shouldn't have waited," returned Miss Janet; "it's not half-past six yet."

Elizabeth went close to the upright woman and kissed her forehead; Miss Janet permitted the caress, but did not return it. As her niece was moving away, however, she touched her arm with one of her lean, cold fingers.

"I dare say you endured more and longer than most women would have done," she said, in a voice that had softened slightly. "You were never a coward, and you were never weak. But knowing you were right won't make you happy, and my sympathy won't; so things must just stay as they are."

A stranger would have thought her utterly unfeeling, but Elizabeth knew her better. For thirty long years Miss Janet had been an invalid and a misanthrope, but she was not a stony-hearted woman. She believed in few people—professed to doubt all. She simply could not allow herself the luxury of being sympathetic and demonstrative. If she had given way in the least she would have suffered a whole night's physical agony, and she had learned to breathe, eat, move, and sleep by rule, as the only means of avoiding or rendering less frequent the terrible paroxysms of nervous pain to which she was subject. Almost her first words, "It's one of my blind days," possessed full significance to Elizabeth. She understood that the reading of Mr. Howland's letter—the brief explanation necessary—had shaken Aunt Janet out of her enforced composure, and brought on the usual result of agitation.

"When the old place gets unbearable you'll have to go away," Miss Janet added, picking up her work again. "There's little company to be had in the neighborhood, and if there were I can't bear noises. I'm a nuisance, of course, but as long as this old machinery insists upon working, out of order as it is, I can't help that. You must endure it while you can, and then go away."

"I have no doubt it will do very well, Aunt Janet," said Elizabeth. "There'll be peace at least."

"Hum!" returned the old maid. "There'll be quiet enough and dullness enough. Well, well! Now go and see what Jane Flint has done for you in the way of chambers, and come back for some tea."

Elizabeth met that important personage, Jane Flint, in the hall, and Jane told her of the dreadful day and night Miss Crauford had passed.

"The least thing upsets her! The very idea of expecting you, I dare say, was enough. But she's been better since yesterday. I'm glad you've come, ma'am, and I hope you can stay a good while; she oughtn't to be so much alone, it's my opinion."

So even in the first hour of her arrival Elizabeth was able to see that a duty had opened before her, neither dignified nor heroic, but one that needed to be fulfilled—petty, wearisome, as it might sometimes appear, just as important as the framing of monarchies or freeing of peoples; the plan of the universe holds no trifle.

Elizabeth's days settled at once into an unvarying monotony. She rose early, walked in the grounds or rode on horseback, breakfasted with Miss Janet, and devoted as great a portion of the time to her as the spinster would permit.

"I'm not used to being coddled, and too much of it would give me an indigestion," she said, and by that Elizabeth knew she liked her companionship, found pleasure in her ministrations. Life seemed ended, so far as personal hopes and aims were concerned, but there was still something to do for others—not always a pleasure, not always easy, but she did what she could. She would not sit weakly down and lament. She must struggle through the night and find daylight beyond. At least she might gain such reliefs as come to age—resignation and faith; patience to wait till her existence, so blighted, so dwarfed, should find its resurrection in the sphere beyond this.

Not long after her arrival at Tanglewood she sent for Jean Murray and little Meg. There was a pretty cottage on Miss Crauford's estate which the old lady placed at her disposal, and here she installed the two. The child must be henceforth her care; and without revealing the truth to the Scotchwoman, she put the matter in a light which showed Aunt Jean she had no right to oppose a determination that would offer the girl a future so different from any thing her love or care could hope to effect.

Elizabeth waited with great anxiety to receive news from Mr. Carstoe, but no letter came. She knew he would not neglect her mission; it could only be that he failed so far to find any trace of Marguerite, and was postponing his answer until he had some certain information to give.

She had been a month at Tanglewood; it was the close of an April day. Elizabeth had been far up the river in a little boat which she rowed herself, drifting along among the mountain shadows, trying to forget mental weariness and pain in physical fatigue. Lame Dick was not in sight when she rowed her boat to the landing near a gate which gave admittance to her aunt's grounds. Some one was standing on the shore—a gentleman. He approached as a sweep of her oars sent the light bark up on the sand—it was Launce Cromlin.

He had spoken her name, uttered common-place salutations, and helped her out of the boat before she could decide whether the meeting were a pleasure or a pain.

"You are surprised to see me," he said; "but I hope not too much so to be glad."

"I supposed you away in Germany or Italy," she answered. "When did you come back from Europe?"

"I did not go, Mrs. Vaughan," returned he. "I have been in California."

"Then you have seen Mr. Carstoe," she said, quickly; "you can tell me—"

He interrupted her by a smile and a gesture of his hand. She looked in the direction he indicated, and saw Mr. Carstoe coming toward them round a point of the shore. Elizabeth hurried forward to meet the old man with both hands extended. She had not believed any thing could give her a sensation of such pleasure as did the sight of his ugly, honest face lighted up with emotion. The three stood there and talked for a few moments. There were no questions asked her—no astonishment was manifested. She comprehended that in some way both men had become acquainted with the change which had taken place in her life. She shrank from the idea of publicity, but at least their knowledge would spare her interrogatories difficult to answer. Though both avoided any remark which could trouble her, they talked freely enough of themselves and the affairs which had brought them into her neighborhood.

A distant relative of Cromlin's, on his father's side, had died a few months previous, and left Launce a valuable mining property near the village.

"As I am not a business man," Cromlin said, "I persuaded Mr. Carstoe to leave California, and come East with me."

"Which means," Mr. Carstoe explained, "that he has offered me a partnership, and a chance to realize a competency in my old days."

Cromlin had accompanied his friend into the valley to see him fairly established in the business, and later in the spring meant to start upon his long-deferred journey to Europe. They were living at a house which belonged to Launce, not far from Tanglewood. The place would continue to be Carstoe's home, and it was pleasant to Elizabeth to think she should have the kind old man's companionship. It was dusk before she remembered that Miss Janet would be waiting for her tea. The two gentlemen walked with her through the grounds, and she invited them to enter the house. She left them in the drawing-room, and went to tell her aunt what she had done, though scarcely expecting that she would see the visitors. But during their conversations Elizabeth had often spoken of Mr. Carstoe, and the old lady chose to break over her rule of seclusion and receive him.

M

"Who's the other?" she asked. "Oh, yes—Launce Cromlin—Vaughan's cousin; not much in his favor that. But he can come—they can both come if they like; I sha'n't go to the drawing-room. Ring for lights first, unless you want them to break their necks."

So Elizabeth conducted them to the apartment, and Miss Crauford received Carstoe with a nearer approach to cordiality than she often vouchsafed any one. Then Elizabeth presented Cromlin.

"Hum!" said Miss Janet. "How do you do, sir? If you choose to shake hands with a half-blind old woman, you can. I knew your father long before you were born; he was an honest man, and that's saying a great deal. I don't suppose you can be like him, for two honest men would be too much to expect in one family."

Launce laughed at the odd speech, took the cold hand she extended, and said—

"I hope you will try to believe a little good of me for my father's sake."

"I never believe any thing," returned Miss Janet. "Just now I want my tea, and so do you, I dare say."

"Yes," Cromlin answered; "I have been sketching all day, and ate a cold dinner, so I lay claim to a very unromantic appetite."

"So much the better; I hate romance. Why didn't you turn peddler instead of artist?"

"On account of the difference in the pack I should have had to carry," he replied, laughing again.

"How old are you?" demanded the unscrupulous spinster, suddenly.

"I am thirty," he said, quietly, as if the question had been the most ordinary one in the world.

"Thirty, and you can laugh like that! So could your father. Well, it would be odd if you turned out a decent man too."

"At least you will like my laugh?"

"Yes; I have forgotten how, and Elizabeth's—"

"Oh, never mind me, aunt," she interrupted.

"But I do mind!" retorted Miss Janet. "Elizabeth's laugh sounds like thorns crackling under a pot; the only consolation is, I don't hear it often."

"Shall I ring for the tea, aunt?" asked her niece.

"No; Jane Flint has been punctual for fifteen years; we'll see if she fails at the end."

But, faithful to the moment, Jane just then appeared with the tray.

As a rule, Miss Janet hated to be helped in any manner, doing every thing for herself that her glazed sight would permit; but Cromlin managed to pull the table toward her, and make her comfortable in a variety of little ways, without calling forth the reproof which Elizabeth momentarily expected.

He talked pleasantly and well, and made Elizabeth and Carstoe talk also. If Miss Janet did not speak much, she at least refrained from any of the frosty sarcasms wherewith it was her habit to congeal the blood of such luckless visitors as she admitted to her presence.

After a time, Mr. Carstoe found an opportunity to speak alone with Elizabeth.

"I received your letter," he said. "I should have answered it, only I knew that I should reach New York as soon as my reply."

"And have you any news for me?"

He had not yet heard from Mrs. Simpson of Milady's disappearance.

He told Elizabeth that Marguerite had a comfortable home; was overlooked by a trusty woman. He thought it better to leave her where she was, at least for the present.

"God bless you!" whispered Elizabeth. "You do not know what a weight you have lifted from my mind."

He looked at her with a great pity in his face, stretched out his hand, drew it back, and lapsed quickly into one of his shy, awkward moods. Elizabeth knew the signs.

"You have something else to tell me," she said.

"Yes—I think I ought; we shall all go on easier it seems to me," he said, hesitatingly.

"Tell me."

"Only that Cromlin saw his cousin in New York. Mr. Vaughan chose to explain to him that—that your absence was likely to be a long one; in fact, that—"

"I saw you both knew," Elizabeth hastened to add. "Yes, it is better."

"You—you feel—how sorry I am—how I would give my right hand if it could serve you—"

"I know," she said, as he broke down again. "You are a good, good man—I thank you. But do not be troubled or unhappy about me; at least I have peace and quiet here. Life looks dark and confused. I seem to be of no use, to have no place; but I try to be patient."

"And there's all the life beyond," he said, softly; "it must come right there—it must."

Then they went back to Miss Janet and Cromlin; the subject was at an end.

At last Jane Flint appeared to conduct the old lady to her chamber. The clock was on the stroke of ten, and nothing short of an earthquake would have prevented military punctuality on Jane's part.

Mr. Carstoe was horrified when he discovered how long a visit they had made, but Miss Janet put his excuses unceremoniously aside.

"If I'd wished you to go, I should have told you," said she. "You'll always find our tea-table laid at the same hour, and you'll be welcome at it just as often or as seldom as you choose to come. That invitation is for Mark Cromlin's son too. Good-night, every body. Jane Flint, give me my stick and your arm, and take up the line of march."

Elizabeth walked to the door with the two visitors, and stood absently looking out into the moonlight as they passed down the road to the gates. Once they turned to look at her, but she did not see them. They spoke very little of her, confidential as they were on most subjects. Neither had expected to find her here—neither had known where Miss Crauford's home was. This new glance into her desolate life, this sight of her pale, beautiful face, with such unrealizable capacities for happiness still visible through its pain, tore both their souls with pity and grief, which it seemed a desecration to mock with words.

The next evening but one Launce called at the house again; Mr. Carstoe was occupied, and could not come. Cromlin understood that the one kindness possible was to rouse Elizabeth out of herself. He talked on every subject which could touch her old enthusiasm for beauty and art, and appealed so frankly for sympathy in his own pursuits that she could not fail to listen. Miss Janet let him converse as unreprovedly as she had done before, and even asked a question now and then, which showed that she was interested.

"Have you no piano here, Mrs. Vaughan?" Launce asked.

"Yes," Miss Janet answered for her; "there's one in the drawing-room that she sent a couple of years ago."

"It must be sadly out of tune," added Elizabeth. "I have not opened it since I came here."

"There's a tuning-key in that table-drawer, if Mr. Cromlin knows how to use it," said Miss Janet. "Only, if you drum, don't do it loud enough for me to hear."

Launce promised not to disturb her, found the key, and insisted on being shown the piano at once; so Thomas was ordered to take lights into the drawing-room.

"I am starved for music," Launce said. "I have not played for weeks, and bits of the 'Songs without Words' have been haunting me all day."

Elizabeth led the way to the drawing-room—in perfect order, thanks to Jane Flint's care, though seldom used, and a degree more old-fashioned in its decorations than Miss Janet's apartment.

"Now go away, please," said Launce. "I don't wish to torture your ears by the tuning process."

Elizabeth left the room, and wandered out of the house, walking for a long time in sight of the moonlit river. As she approached the dwelling, a delicious melody made her pause. Cromlin was playing a strain of Beethoven's—a wild, spiritual movement from one of the sonatas, which sounds as if some spirit newly freed, and still oppressed by the shadows of this world's troubles, were questioning and receiving consolation from a mighty angel.

The chord was struck. Elizabeth sat down in the shadow of the veranda and wept; blessed drops, which refreshed her as tears had not done for months, flowed from her eyes. When she grew calm again, she entered the drawing-room. Cromlin had turned down the lamps and opened the windows wide. The moonlight flooded the apartment, and in that heavenly radiance he awakened the hidden life in the cold, white keys till Elizabeth's pulses throbbed in new harmony.

For a while he neither noticed nor addressed her. At last he turned round from the instrument, saying gently—

"Has it done you good?"

"Thanks," she answered.

"And to-morrow will you try for yourself?" he continued. "Will you sing for me then?"

She bowed her head.

"I must go now," he said. "I hope I have not disturbed Miss Crauford."

"Miss Crauford is here," replied a voice from the door.

There she stood, upright and grim, leaning on her stick. Jane Flint appeared in the background, with the moonbeams weaving a silvery tracery across her black gown.

"You must be the devil," observed Miss Janet. "I haven't listened to any body's music in twenty years."

With those words she turned about, took Jane Flint's arm, and marched away.

CHAPTER XXXVI.

"WHAT GOD HATH JOINED TOGETHER."

SIX weeks passed; spring was deepening into summer. There are no words to paint the loveliness of those charmed days, the glory of those azure nights, the weird melodies the river sang as it hurried away beneath the shadow of the cliffs, the marvelous beauty which wrapped the mountain valley in its glow.

Launce Cromlin still lingered, though the time he had set for his departure had come and gone. Mr. Carstoe was greatly occupied, full of interest and enthusiasm for his new business—delighted to keep Launce's society as long as he might.

Cromlin's daily presence at Tanglewood had become a matter of habit. Miss Janet herself seemed to think it the most natural thing in the world to see him there. He wandered with Elizabeth among the hills; he talked to her while he sketched; read sweet poets when they paused to rest; and evening after evening made the piano talk inspiringly to her tired spirit. He persuaded her to sing in her rich contralto voice till her own pain was hushed under the harmony, and his soul floated, all unaware, further and further into a charmed realm.

No tidings from the world without came to rouse them; there was nothing to break the quiet. Even in the man's mind there was not a breath of consciousness; the sympathy which bound them had no sex. It was the free communion of two kindred souls, who had put earth aside—as may happen by a vague restlessness which was not pain—and met without restraint in the beautiful land whither their feet had unwittingly strayed.

So time went on.

One evening he did not appear at the usual hour. Elizabeth walked up and down the long veranda, sat for a brief space at the piano, playing snatches of the melodies she had caught from him, oppressed by a vague restlessness which was not pain—oh, as unlike the Elizabeth of these later years as if her soul had gained its resurrection, and stood, too bewildered and entranced to think, upon the shore of the Infinite.

A step aroused her. Old Miss Janet stood by the piano, peering into her face with those dim yet watchful eyes.

"I am going to bed," were her first words. "My back aches. It will rain in just two days. I shall keep my room till it is over."

"Can I do any thing for you, aunt?" Elizabeth asked.

"Nothing but let me alone. My back is mine, and I'm my back's; if it wants to ache, it must and shall."

Elizabeth's white hands strayed idly over the keys.

"Humph!" said Miss Janet, suddenly. "Elizabeth Crauford!"

"Well, aunt?"

"Have you made up your mind to do what another woman would have done long ago?"

"I don't understand," Elizabeth said, puzzled, yet startled by the odd speech.

"Have you decided to get a divorce?"

"What do you mean? How dare you?" she exclaimed.

"I neither say I would nor wouldn't," pursued Miss Janet; "the law permits, and other people do it. I only asked if that was what you meant."

Elizabeth's hands dropped in her lap; a ghastly pallor spread over her face.

"Aunt Janet! oh, Aunt Janet!" she moaned.

Reproach, sudden consciousness, an awful terror—all these emotions were in her voice.

"If you don't," continued the spinster, "play no more Beethoven, and show your painter the way out of the valley. Now my back and I will go to bed."

She left the room, closing the door behind her.

Elizabeth slid slowly forward in her seat till her head rested upon the keys. These words had been a lightning flash which showed her soul where it stood.

A voice called—"Elizabeth!"

She looked up. In the open window stood Launce Cromlin. One glance at his face was enough. He too had heard.

"Elizabeth!" he repeated. The tone was nearly a whisper now, trembling with emotion akin to the terror which shook her, but a great joy quivered through it.

He came slowly toward her. She could not move; could only look into his face with dumb perplexity and fright.

"God is my witness that I never thought," he went on, "never once—not a feeling in my heart that you could blame; and I thank Him for it."

He stood leaning heavily on the piano, and looked down at her.

"I seem to have lived a whole life since she spoke," he went on; "a whole life. It all looks so different. I was so used to seeing you bound, shackled, helpless in the purgatory where you had been dragged, that I forgot you were free—free!"

The wild joy lighted his face anew, and made a heaven in his eyes that gazed straight into her own.

Then through her confusion and blindness she heard his voice still. He was telling the story of their first meeting, when she had not seen his face—telling the story of the treachery which had separated them so long. After the first instants of pain and fright there was a season—she could never tell whether it lasted minutes or hours—during which the whole material world passed out of sight, and no sound or thought save that man's voice and his glowing words could reach her.

"In the sight of God you are already free; man's law will make you equally so before the world. Oh, Elizabeth! you do care—you know it now! Ah, let us be happy. Have pity on yourself as well as me. Think of all you have suffered. Do not reject the happiness which opens before us at last."

The solemn words of the marriage service rushed to her lips, not from any direct volition, but as if some unseen influence had uttered them through her—

"'What God hath joined, let not man put asunder.'"

"It is not you who have done it, Elizabeth. That man has wrought all the sin; but his acts leave you as free as though he had never cast his shadow across your path. The sin would have been in continuing his wife after he had broken every vow, and made marriage void and null. But his wrong-doing can not wreck your whole life: that would be bearing punishment for him. You are more widely separated than if death had parted you—free to choose your own path, free to claim the happiness which every human being has a right to expect."

"I can not think," she moaned. "All the old landmarks are swept away. God help me, I have no guide, nowhere to cling!"

"Take my hand, Elizabeth—trust yourself to me. My great love could not misguide; believe in it, cling to it, and it shall be a light to show us across these mists into a new world."

It had come upon her so suddenly—it was as if she had been lifted bodily into a new sphere; she could not think. He was telling her of the future that lay before them—he was opening his heart, and revealing the treasures of love hidden there. He employed every argument which his eloquence could furnish to prove to her that in the sight of God and man she was free.

Verily there was reason, there was a show of right under it all.

Heaven itself could not demand the sacrifice of a whole life to a bond which sin had deprived of sacredness. It was only a broken shackle which galled her heart and held her a prisoner by her own weakness, since with a single effort she might wrench it away, sweep every trace of the past aside, and enter a future as completely separated from it as if she had indeed reached a new cycle of existence.

It was not these arguments which moved her most. She listened, and tried to believe when he told her that God gives every human being a right to happiness; that the blind superstition which could make her still cling to the wreck from which every hope, every living thing had gone down, was madder, more fanatical, than the frenzy which induces the Indian woman to cast herself upon the funeral pyre of her husband—it was none of these things that touched and swayed her.

But when he talked of her as his wife, painted their future as it should pass, honored by the world's sanction, and rendered so beautiful by their love, it seemed as if heaven opened to her sight, and she had but to extend her hand to be raised forever into its glory.

And she loved him—she realized this too. Not the affection a young girl gives, which is half from the necessity of loving that belongs to extreme youth, half made up of dreams and ideal imaginings; but the love of a soul matured by suffering. The love of a heart gentle and womanly in spite of all thwarting influences, which recognized its likeness in the man beloved, and sprang up eager to grasp its long-delayed bliss.

What wonder if her first impulse was to snatch at this promise of peace, crying out with him that she had a right—a right to claim it. Think what her life had been. Remember how the dream of her girlhood was torn away—not dispelled slowly, but rudely crushed—without warning—every heart-chord strained, every good feeling shocked; vice and sin bared to her shrinking gaze, forced ruthlessly upon it, till the last trust in humanity died out, and she flung herself down among the ashes of her ruined offerings, and called upon the desecrated altars to crush her.

Remember the horrible years—and now their contrast! A contrast offered so suddenly, so utterly without warning, that she had no time to steel her soul by a thought of former creeds, of doctrines held sacred, even by a prayer—God help her!

The old life, with its clouds from spent tempests, its ruins, its pale corpses, its charnel-house odors—not alone securely shut out, but hurled resolutely into the tomb of the past, as far beyond any possibility of contact with her future as that existence which we sometimes fancy was ours before this sphere claimed us.

Was it strange that she faltered?—was it unnatural? Was it to be wondered at if she caught at the theories which possess much reason and weight, in regard to the carrying out of which we have no right to judge where individual instances are concerned, however we may disapprove of them in the abstract?

And he was saying—

"Let me think for you—trust yourself to me; put your hands in mine, and let me lead the way."

Many women in this strait would have done so blindly, and perhaps have reproached the man afterward. Elizabeth could not act thus. As in the future, if she accepted this new destiny, she would take courageously a full share of the blame, if blame there were, so in the contemplation of that act she must exercise her own judgment, and walk side by side with him, supported, not led. She could remember this, confused as her brain was.

"The acts necessary to free you from your trammels are no more in reality than a law process to enable you to procure any other property withheld from you; and what you claim is your freedom, your life!"

It was strange, but his very arguments brought up with new force the beliefs which had always been hers.

"'What God hath joined, let not man put asunder,'" she repeated.

"But the bond is broken—you are free. You do not consider that man your husband?"

"No, no!"

"You would not, under any circumstances—no matter if he repented, if he tried to atone—believe it right to return, and live with him after his sin has annulled your marriage?"

"No, never!"

"Then you are free! The scruples which would make you hesitate are dead, without power in the mind of any liberal man. The very warning pronounced by Christ against the offending husband or wife—the injunction that he or she put away for sin is forbidden to marry—proves that the innocent one is free in every respect."

Then he ceased to argue. He was telling her again of the life that should be theirs—the sweet haven of rest—the new day! There was his stronghold; more potent far than all his arguments.

"We would travel, Elizabeth—not among the ruins of the old world—we are sick of men and their follies. Such journeys into the far West—out on the boundless prairies, and farther on, the healing wind of the mountains! And the tropical scenery you love so much. Oh, we will find that out first! Don't you remember that description we were reading the other day of the old Chilian city? We shall have one of those picturesque houses at the foot of the hills, with the sea in front—just we two in the world alone."

It was no longer as a possibility that he spoke of these things—it was the present time in his excitement.

"Think of the long golden days—the nights with such moonlight as they saw in Eden—sharing every pleasure, every task—our lives growing always more closely into one, till even death could not separate us, but needing either, must claim both."

Could she think?—was reflection possible? She only looked into his face, and in all the world there was no sight but the glory of his eyes, no sound but the music of his voice.

"You will go, Elizabeth! Think—every day wasted is so much happiness lost! Eternity itself can never give back an hour of neglected bliss—you will go!"

The scent of the tropical wind seemed to dizzy her brain; she heard the waving palm-trees whisper of peace and rest. The low rush of the sea bade her follow him.

"Come, Elizabeth, come!"

The very words the blessed palms and the silver sea had uttered—"Come, come!"

And her whole soul was lost in a wild longing to float away over the molten billows into the new world, the fadeless Eden! Only one thought, one feeling: that overwhelming wish to be gone—at once; not to have time for fear or doubt—away into the shadow of the palm-trees, and within reach of the siren voice of the silver sea.

It had grown very late. The house was so still that it seemed as if they were solitary in the world. The full radiance of the moon lay about them like a promise of peace, and still Launce Cromlin talked with the force and power a man possesses when heart and conviction inspire his words.

And it was so; for the time every argument was truth to him.

Elizabeth was torn and weak from emotion; a thousand diverse thoughts tugged at her soul and left her powerless.

"Only go away to-night," she pleaded. "Give me time—only a little time."

He saw how pale and worn she was, and took

pity on her. He did not even offer to touch her hand.

"Good-night," he said, softly, and was gone.

She did not know how she reached her chamber—could not tell whether the hours that intervened had brought sleep or insensibility; but when the early summer dawn flashed into the sky she was lying on her bed, gazing straight before her; every sense stupefied, every limb rigid, as if she had just awakened from a cataleptic trance.

Then a dull, cold pain stirred at her heart, like a benumbed snake warming into vitality and slowly uncoiling itself—grew sharper and hotter, till every fibre of her frame responded with physical agony to the suffering in her soul.

Through the closed curtains brighter gleams of daylight shot in, and troubled her by their curious glances. She shrouded her face in the counterpane, and tried to sleep, but there was no Eastern drug which could have lulled her to repose.

At last Jane Flint's niece Hannah knocked at the door, as she had been bidden to do each morning. Elizabeth had just sense and strength enough to answer that she was unwell, and should not leave her room that day. Then she was left to herself once more.

Without sleep to bring forgetfulness, without a tangible thought on which to steady her mind, the morning dragged away. Later, she heard steps on the veranda. Her room was at the front of the house, and every nerve had become so overstrung that her hearing was painfully acute. She knew that Launce had come; she heard his voice in parley with old Thomas, then his retreating steps.

More hours of mad restlessness. At last her soul fastened upon one word Launce had spoken, and clung to it as if it had been an anchor. His wife—his wife! Only that; but the words were a spell which deadened pain and raised a magic barrier against thought.

At length the nervous tension gave way, and she sank slowly to sleep with those blessed words upon her lips.

The sun was setting when she awoke. Hannah had entered the room, and stood near the bed; she and Jane Flint had grown alarmed.

"Are you better, ma'am?" the girl asked.

Elizabeth looked at her wonderingly. She could not recall her dreams, but it seemed as if her soul had been absent from her body, and that it was with a struggle it returned.

Hannah opened the curtains and shutters, and the dull red of evening, precursor of a storm, streamed across the chamber.

Elizabeth arose and began to dress—slowly, wearily—like a person recovering from a long illness.

"I shall bring you some tea and something to eat," Hannah said. "Miss Cranford's in bed too; she won't get up, though there ain't much the matter."

By the time Elizabeth was dressed the girl returned with the tea and such edibles as Jane Flint thought might please her.

It was growing twilight when she descended to the drawing-room. Thomas had only lighted the lamps in the hall, and they cast just radiance enough into the apartment to make a pleasant gloom. Elizabeth lay down on a sofa, and remained listening to the rising swell of the wind and the angry murmurs of the river.

For a long time there were no other sounds, but the outer door opened at length. The rush and whirl began anew in her mind, and the physical pain responded to it as before.

Launce Cromlin entered, and stood for a moment looking about among the shadows. He saw her, and hurried toward the couch. She put up her hands, as if in sudden fear.

"You are not afraid of me?" he said, sadly. "You are ill; how wrong I have been! Let me sit here; I'll not distress you by word or look; at least accept my companionship in your loneliness."

He drew a chair close to the sofa, and sat down, talking kindly and gently, till gradually a sensation of delicious rest stole over her tired soul. It was not until he rose to go that he made even an allusion which could disturb her. Then he said, "We will not think; we will not question. For a few days let us be quiet here, away in this charmed land where the world can not reach us."

She accepted his verdict for the time; rest and sleep came that night.

She only saw her aunt for a few moments during the next day. Miss Janet still kept her bed, though the storm had passed, and she confessed that her back was no worse than usual.

"I'll get up to-morrow," she said. "Let me alone, else I shall turn rusty and cross."

Toward sunset Launce came to the house and persuaded Elizabeth to walk a little way. They stood by the river, and watched the gorgeous lights pale on the mountains. The twilight floated down: that glory which is neither of night nor day rested on all things; and amid its quiet they returned to the old house, standing up under the gloom of the cedars.

Launce talked; he played her favorite melodies; and distinctly through both, so blending with his words and music that each seemed to grow out of the other, she heard the soft whispers of the palms, the tender murmurs of the Southern sea.

"Elizabeth!" he said, suddenly.

There was a tone of inquiry in his voice that brought her wholly back to the present. The question which rose in her mind was the impulse of the moment—she had not been thinking, had not meant to ask it, but it was on her lips.

"Have you always believed in divorce?" were the words.

Cromlin grew a little pale.

"I have always believed that, under certain circumstances, it became a sin for a woman to remain in bondage—for a man to hold to the unfaithful wife," he replied.

"Have you always believed it right for the injured husband or wife to marry again?"

"I had never thought it clearly out," he said, tremulously; "nothing had ever brought the matter home to me."

"One creed or the other you must have held," she replied, slowly, and her voice was low and firm. "You never did believe it right; you have answered me."

"But I do!" he cried. "I have no doubt. The Romish Church has again and again granted divorce—our own Church permits it. Ask the best friends you have—Mr. Carstoe, your aunt. They—"

She interrupted him by rising from her seat. Her face was like that of a dead woman. He could scarcely believe it her voice which answered.

"I must ask my God," she said. "I had forgotten—oh, I had forgotten!"

She was gone before he could speak or move.

Elizabeth was alone in her chamber. The moon had been shut out—the lamp lighted. The commonplace aspect of the spot seemed to bring her back from the world whither she had wandered down into the finite again.

She was on her knees by the table. The open Bible lay before her. As if some unseen agency guided her hand, she turned the very pages that held such counsels as might befit the strait wherein she found herself.

It was an altered face now which bent above the sacred volume; out of it looked a soul that the angels must have pitied and pleaded for.

Up through the stillness went a low sob, which bore a breaking heart on its tone, and Elizabeth, groveling on the floor, tugged at her breast in blind agony, as if to tear out the crushed heart which murmured so.

The spasm passed. Tears came—prayers; but the angels must have guarded her still, or she could not have escaped with both life and reason from that awful night.

It was almost daylight when Elizabeth sat at her table with the letter to Launce complete under her hand. There were no tears now, no struggles—they belonged to the life that had died this night.

I have told you all briefly. You will ask me what helped her? what gave strength for the sacrifice? Neither human reason nor a conviction of right or wrong; only faith in God and help from the Saviour, whom every one of us, at some crisis of existence, has been tempted "to crucify anew."

This was the close of her letter:

"If I obtained my freedom only to marry one I love, how would my sin be less than that man's? I should only be trying to give to my acts a lawful covering which might show fair to the world and hide my guilt.

"I have said that I can not argue upon this point. I do not even say that, to those who can believe, divorce may not be pardonable in the sight of God as it is in the eyes of many good, just men and women. For myself, I can only cling to the one way open to me. Life is forever, the suspense here a brief one. I can not cloud the happiness which may be ours in some existence our spirits shall reach at length. I think to save your soul I could give my own—oh, I know I could! I can not lose my soul and yours. I must go.

"I am calm, calmer than I have been in years. Another man would upbraid—think harshly of me—not you. Oh, Launce, you know it is right —the one way! Somewhere in eternity Christ himself will tell us why it had to be."

In the gray of the early morning Janet Crauford was awakened by a cold hand laid upon her arm, and a voice like that of the dead crying— "Wake up, wake up!"

There Elizabeth stood, prepared for a journey. It needed but a few words to tell her story.

"I am going away at once. He will obey me—he will not stay here. When he is gone, I shall come back. Try to love me a little. Help me to reach toward the light. Aunt Janet, Aunt Janet! Oh, my God, my God!"

Then a brief silence, then her voice again—

"'Out of the deep have I called unto thee, Lord! O Lord, hear my voice.'"

It was the cry of her breaking heart going up to God out of the darkness.

Then Aunt Janet was alone.

CHAPTER XXXVII.

NO HOPE.

It was Mr. Carstoe who received the letter Elizabeth had written to Launce. The old gentleman had breakfasted alone this morning —Cromlin did not appear. Mr. Carstoe was standing on the porch, smoking a matutinal pipe before setting out for the mine. His horse had come up—Cromlin insisted on life being made easy and comfortable in every way to the good man.

But these last days had been full of unrest to Mr. Carstoe. Like most reticent people, he was observant of the persons dear to him; and old Miss Crauford, with all her shrewdness, had been less quick than he to discern the secret which so long remained unsuspected by Launce and Elizabeth themselves.

Like many of our generation, even among the good and wise, Mr. Carstoe believed in the justice of divorce on the grounds permitted in the Bible; believed, too, that the sentence pronounced upon the guilty husband or wife implied a permission to the offended one to form new ties.

He had known persons who had done this—men and women whom he liked and honored; and had never disapproved or even thought much about the matter. Yet when his mind suggested the possibility that Elizabeth Crauford might thus act, he was filled with pain and regret. In his estimation she ranked so far above ordinary humanity that a freedom of action which he would have considered justifiable in another seemed unworthy her. But it was hard—he said this over and over to himself, with a tender pity for both Launce and her. It seemed a horrible thing that the sin of a bad man should wreck two lives still in the freshness of youth and vigor. Vaughan's crime had so completely cast him out of all possibility of contact with Elizabeth's existence, as if the gulf that yawned between them were the black eternal sweep beyond purgatory and heaven. If he were to repent—to atone so far as in him lay—Elizabeth could never be his wife again. Even if his cruelty had not tired her heart out before that crowning guilt separated them, the guilt would remain the same impassable barrier. If she had loved him still, she could not have gone back, as she valued her soul's safety, as she believed in the teachings of her religious faith, save as a sister, to guide him, help him, hold him up.

But the man had not repented. There was no hope, humanly speaking, that he ever would wish to turn from the slough and the mire; and she did not love him. In her girlish purity, ignorance even, she had been attracted by an ideal to which she gave this man's semblance—nothing more. Mr. Carstoe understood the whole history as well as if it had been put in words. Had Darrell Vaughan not broken the bond which bound them, Elizabeth would have struggled on to the end of life with patience and resignation, her heart so crushed and shut in under its heavy load that the possibility of happiness with another would never have crossed her soul. A thought, a dream, which would then have been wrong, would never for an instant have shadowed the whiteness of her spirit. She was incapable even of feeling the temptation which—God help them!—has come close to more than one wretched husband or wife, sunk in the most horrible solitude—that of a marriage which possesses neither affection nor sympathy.

But she was free—free in the eyes of God and man, Mr. Carstoe considered. She had no husband. He was gone, lost—swallowed up in a hell black as ever Calvinistic doctrine devised for the world beyond this. She had a right to call upon the law to cancel the shattered bond.

Had physical death overtaken Vaughan, the law would have commanded her to let it certify thereto before his burial. She had a right now to command the law to give witness to his moral death. She was a widow; no more doubt of her privilege to marry again, if she so willed, than in the case of any other widow.

Yet, after Mr. Carstoe had gone over and over the whole round of argument—acknowledging its justice, perfectly convinced of its utility—the pain at his heart remained when he thought of Elizabeth thus acting. She was like a haloed martyr, a saint—something fairly superhuman in his eyes. He could not bear to have the spiritual height whereon she stood troubled by a single earthly shadow.

So, as he lingered this morning, absently watching the beautiful landscape, and musing upon these matters, old Thomas came up the garden walk, and gave him a letter.

Carstoe asked after Miss Crauford and her niece. He never uttered the other name which still clung to her if he could avoid it.

Miss Janet was well, Thomas said. Miss Elizabeth had set off on her journey by the early train. Thomas hoped she would not stay long with her old governess, whom she had gone to visit, for the household needed her sorely, and Miss Janet most of all.

Not a question did Mr. Carstoe ask; in no way did he betray that this departure was a surprise. His heart gave one mighty bound as he turned in-doors. He comprehended what her going meant. In another instant he could feel only pity for her and Launce. He understood Cromlin's restlessness during these past days. Every thing was clear. He knew that Elizabeth had made her decision—had won her martyr's palm. " 'Whoso loseth his life for my sake shall find it again."

Still the old man could have wept from sympathy and tenderness. It was so hard—so hard! They were both young still, and they deserved happiness. Then, inconsistent as humanity always is, his loving heart cried out that it could not be right; God could not desire such sacrifice. But Elizabeth's face rose before him in its patient beauty, and the yearning and rebellion died.

He opened the envelope. It contained a sealed letter, and a few lines addressed to himself.

"Give him this," Elizabeth wrote, "and oh, comfort him, dear friend; he will need it. I have no necessity to explain to you; but you will help him, I know you will."

If ever a human being sent his whole soul out in prayer for those dear, it was Sheldon Carstoe, as he stood in the darkened parlor holding those papers in his hand.

He bade a servant take the letter to Cromlin's room, and went away. His innate delicacy taught him that this was no time to intrude—

the first agony must be borne without mortal aid.

It was dusk when he returned to the house. Mrs. Clement, his housekeeper, informed him that Mr. Cromlin had just come in and was up in his room. He had been out all day, she said. She was afraid he had walked too much, for he looked very pale and tired.

Mr. Carstoe mounted the stairs, knocked softly at Cromlin's door, and was bidden to enter.

Launce sat by a table, his face buried in his hands. He raised his head as Mr. Carstoe appeared, and said, with a ghost of his pleasant smile—

"She has told you—she says you will help me, and I must let you try, for it is all I can do to prove that her every wish is my law."

A very foolish old man was Sheldon Carstoe, when one remembers that he had lived fifty-five years in this most realistic of centuries. He went up to Launce, laid both hands on his friend's shoulders, and the great tears streamed down his withered cheeks.

"I can't feel it, I can't be satisfied!" Launce exclaimed. "But I don't blame her now. I have been fighting all day with a legion of devils, but I don't blame her now."

Mr. Carstoe patted his arm, and fondled his cold hands as if he had been a child, this white, stern-faced man, with the impress of an unutterable agony on every lineament.

"I know she is right," he continued, "but I can't feel it. I think if I live to be a hundred I shall never feel it; but all the same she is right. You must tell her to come back—she will not find me here; we shall never meet again in this world—oh, Carstoe, Carstoe!"

———◆———

CHAPTER XXXVIII.

TOGETHER.

TEN days had passed. It was a lovely June afternoon.

Little Meg sat on the grass beneath the walnut-trees in front of the pretty cottage where she and Aunt Jean lived.

Below the house the tall chimneys of Tanglewood rose among the trees; beyond spread the sweep of the valley. Above the dwelling the road curved suddenly down toward the river; great cliffs towered frowning and dark, crowding themselves almost to the water's edge.

It was a fair, peaceful spot, and in her childish fashion Meg fully appreciated its beauty. The country air had already done her much good; she looked fresher, her color was brighter, and she was growing tall.

She had seated her dolls on moss thrones at the root of one of the great walnuts, put their table and tea-things before them, and they were supposed to be enjoying a ceremonious feast; and Meg was certain they understood the whole matter just as well as herself. She talked to them, and confided her small secrets, and they talked—yes, indeed, and laughed too! Commonplace grown-up mortals might perhaps have watched the waxen ladies carefully and caught no word or smile; but Meg was not so stupid: she understood their language without difficulty.

The birds sang; the butterflies flitted past; the rabbits scuttled away through the grass; the bees hummed by; the white clouds cast long shadows over the lawn; the river murmured softly—the whole made up an enchanted scene of whose marvels Meg never wearied.

She left the queens at their tea, and wandered off down the winding path, to watch a troop of little yellow butterflies that were circling about in the sun, looking like flecks of sunlight themselves. Meg, with her head full of a fairy story Elizabeth had told her, was inclined to believe the winged creatures the very knot of elves which, according to Elizabeth's legend, transformed themselves into the bright-hued insects during the hours when mortals are awake and watchful.

But the butterflies floated away on a sudden breeze that sighed down from the mountains, fragrant with the odor of pine-trees and wood-flowers, and Meg was next attracted by a great sweet-briar which grew close to the gate, and had burst into full blossom since the previous day.

While she stood there, looking out from the thicket of flowers, a woman came along the road which led from the village, past Tanglewood and the cottage, and curved here toward the river, following the course of the stream for miles and miles above the valley.

Meg made a lovely little picture framed among the shining green leaves and pink blossoms. She was singing, in her clear, childish voice, just from sheer happiness, a melody that had no rule or words, yet was musical and sweet—a chant such as one often hears from childish lips, making one marvel if it be not a memory of the strains the angels used to sing to them in some brighter world than this to which their tiny feet have strayed.

The woman caught sight of Meg standing there, and paused. She was thin, wasted, and worn, but there were traces of wonderful beauty in her face still. She stood and watched the child, and a great eagerness and longing brightened the sullen gloom of her eyes. A kind of awe, almost a fear, struck her too, one would have said; for she made a movement forward, then checked herself, and sat down upon the grass, hiding her face in her hands—not weeping, though her whole frame shook with the convulsive sobs that heaved her bosom.

Meg looked out, and saw her sitting there

among the daisies. She had been too kindly treated always to know any thing about shyness. She pushed open the gate, which happened to be unlatched, and went close to the woman, who had not noticed her approach. "Don't cry," she said, softly; "don't cry."

The woman raised her head—the eager, yearning expression swept over her face again—the look of awe, of dread, appeared too. She pressed her breath against her heart. Her breath came and went in gasps. Her pallor took a livid, bluish tint, and she leaned heavily against the trunk of a sycamore by which she had seated herself.

"Don't be frightened," she managed to say. "I'll be better in a minute."

She was better before Meg had time really to become alarmed.

"Don't you want something?" the child asked, with the practical common-sense which was already one of her strong characteristics. "I could call Aunt Jean, or fetch you some water."

The woman caught her dress, and held it fast. "Don't call any body," she said; "I'm better now."

"You might go into the house and rest," Meg suggested.

"No; I like to sit here. Will you sit down too?" Her voice had grown very soft and sweet. As Meg looked at her again she wondered why at first she was a little startled by the stranger's eyes; they did not flash and burn now—they were misty and sad.

Meg sat by her, quite ready to be communicative, and entertain the lady to the best of her ability. She was dressed in black, Meg's quick glance noticed—Aunt Jean had told her that was a sign people had lost friends.

"Maybe you had a little girl once," said Meg, putting her thought into words at once, and pointing to the stranger's gown. The child could not have explained her fancy to herself; but she comprehended, without understanding, that the eager, yearning expression of the pale face bent upon her spoke the language of pain and regret.

The woman turned away her head for an instant.

"Yes, I had," she answered.

"And you've lost her?"

"Yes—I've lost her; yes."

"I'm so sorry," said Meg; "so sorry."

She put out her little hand, and slipped it into the stranger's. The woman let the dainty fingers lie on her palm, looking down at them with a sort of wistful wonder.

"You're sorry," she muttered; "you're sorry!" Then aloud—"Will you tell me your name?"

"Oh, I'm little Meg, and I live with Aunt Jean in the cottage, and Elizabeth lives in the great house yonder."

"Who is Elizabeth?" asked the woman.

"Oh, she's so beautiful—I love her so!" cried

Meg. "She's got another name—I can't think —she said I might call her Elizabeth. It was she brought us here to this place to live—it's a nice place, isn't it?"

"Yes, very nice," the woman answered, absently. "And—and you haven't any mother?"

"No," said Meg; "but I've always had Aunt Jean. Don't you think you'd better go into the house, and see Aunt Jean?"

"No; I like to sit here. I am going away presently."

"Do you live near?" Meg asked.

The stranger shook her head.

"That's why I've never seen you," said Meg. "But I really think you'd better go and see Aunt Jean—you don't look well. She's got all sorts of things to take. I help her gather the roots, and she always knows just what to do for people."

"She couldn't do any thing for me," sighed the woman; "I'm past help—past help."

Meg looked at her, troubled more by the tone than the words.

"I'm so sorry," she said again, with her beautiful childish eyes full of pity. "Are you going back to your home—is it far?"

"My home?" said the woman. "Oh, yes— very far; I'm going toward it, though, fast enough," she added, with a bitter laugh.

"I'm afraid you ain't happy," sighed Meg. "I wish Elizabeth was here."

"I don't want to see any one but you," replied the woman.

"I wish I had my white frock on; I've a beautiful one Elizabeth gave me for Sundays," said Meg; "but it's only Wednesday now."

"You're very fond of that Elizabeth," returned the woman, with a kind of irritation in her voice.

"Oh my, yes; and so is Aunt Jean; she's so good. But she's not home now; she's gone away for a while, and there's nobody but Miss Crauford. I'm afraid of her."

"Who—what was that name?" asked the woman, quickly. "Is Elizabeth's name Crauford?"

"Yes, but something more; she's married, only I don't know where her husband is."

The stranger pressed her hand hard upon her heart again, and fought against the new spasm which seized her.

"You'd better come and see Aunt Jean. How pale you look again!" Meg said, watching her.

The woman shook her head. She could speak presently.

"I can't, child; I can't. I am going away. I want to take the next train, and it leaves soon."

"Yes, I know; it's the six o'clock—oh, what is the word?—Express!" cried Meg, with pride. "Mr. Carstoe told me the name."

"Great God!" exclaimed the woman. "Is Mr. Carstoe here too?"

"Oh, to be sure," said Meg; "and Mr. Launce was here, but he's gone. I like him, but I like Mr. Carstoe too; he took me up to the mine in his wagon."

"They're all good to you, and you love them all?" returned the woman. "You'll not miss me."

"Oh, I'd like to have you stay, and so would Aunt Jean, I know," said Meg. "But perhaps you'll come back again soon?"

"I don't know; I've something to do; I must go and do it," said the woman, looking away from Meg, while the sombre fire blazed in her eyes again. "I must do it, and I will."

Meg did not hear the words; but the voice was so fierce, low as she spoke, that the child shrank back.

"Oh, don't be afraid of me—don't!" cried the woman, passionately, sinking on her knees.

"No, I won't; I'm not," faltered the little girl.

"It's no use to stay; I've seen her. I wanted to see her," said the woman, under her breath, with her great eyes intently studying Meg's features. "There's no curse on her; maybe it'll not fall if I keep away. I'd like to come back and die here—just here."

She sat down on the ground, and buried her head in her hands, rocking herself to and fro. Meg touched her shoulder.

"You'd better let me call Aunt Jean," she said.

The woman lifted her white face.

"I wish sometimes you'd think of me, and say 'Poor Marguerite'—will you?" she asked.

"Every night when I say my prayers," said Meg.

The woman shuddered, and rose slowly from the ground.

"Good-bye, now," she said. "I'd like to kiss you; it couldn't do you any hurt."

"Oh, kiss me, please," sobbed Meg; "I'm so sorry for you!"

"Don't be sorry; don't mind."

She stooped, pressed the child to her in a passionate embrace, then hurried away, looking back once as she went down the road. On she walked, round the curve, past the cottage, the woodlands, and close to the gates of Tanglewood.

Elizabeth, who had this morning returned, came out of the grounds, and took the road toward the cottage. The woman looked hard after her, half paused, and then hastened on.

"Who is that lady?" she asked a man who had stopped his cart to light a pipe.

"That's Mrs. Vaughan," said he.

"Who?"

"Mrs. Darrell Vaughan; old Miss Crauford's niece."

The woman groaned aloud, and hurried on. The man puffed meditatively at his pipe, and glanced after her.

"Wrong in the head; that's what ails her," he said to himself: chirruped to his horse, and went his way also.

Elizabeth and Aunt Jean found Meg still seated near the gate; she was weeping softly, and saying—

"Poor Marguerite! poor Marguerite!"

A few days after, Mr. Carstoe came to Tanglewood late one evening with a telegram he had just received from Launce Cromlin:

"*Bring Mrs. Vaughan to town. Must be here to-morrow. Darrell needs her.*"

CHAPTER XXXIX.

NINA'S GHOST.

IT was twilight. Nathalie La Tour stood at the window and watched Darrell Vaughan drive away from her house. He was obliged to go to Albany—would return the next day. Early in the following week Nathalie was to sail for Europe—he would join her there.

It was a warm evening, and the window was open. Nathalie still stood there after the carriage disappeared. A woman who had been walking up and down the pavement during the whole time of Vaughan's visit stopped suddenly under the casement—put up her veil, and looked full at Nathalie.

Nathalie saw her, and shrank back in a terror that had no name. In spite of the difference in years, it was her mother's face—the same deadly pallor, the same hard, reckless mouth, the same sombre fire in the great eyes.

"Open the door," said the woman; "open the door, Madame La Tour; I want to speak with you, and I will!"

Nathalie could no more refuse than if her mother's ghost had halted there demanding admittance. She dragged herself across the hall, opened the outer door—the woman was on the steps. She entered quickly, closed the door behind her, and motioned Nathalie back into the parlor.

They stood there face to face—the woman wrapped in her black garments, Nathalie dressed in white, flowers in her hair, pearls on her neck and arms. She could not speak—the eyes that looked into hers seemed turning her to stone.

"Young and handsome," said the woman slowly; "covered with jewels and flowers; but you're going the same road. Look at me! I'm the ghost of what such women as you become—look at me!"

"Who are you? what do you want?" moaned Nathalie, struggling against the conviction which smote at her heart.

"I want to see Darrell Vaughan's mistress—his last love: I'm looking at her now."

"It is false!" exclaimed Nathalie, in sudden anger.

"Hush!" said the woman. "I know all about you; I know how you have paltered with your soul. But you're going to Europe to meet him; you have yielded at last."

Nathalie sank into a chair, putting up her hands, trying to close her eyes; she could only stare in a fascinated horror at the face before her.

"Will you tell me your name?" she asked, in a frightened voice.

"I told you I was a ghost—ghosts don't have names," returned the woman.

"*Mon Dieu! mon Dieu!*" moaned Nathalie.

"Oh, Lord, you're French," exclaimed the other. "What can one expect of you? French! That's what my mother was who sent me off—sold me—got rid of me."

"Who was she?— what was her name?" demanded Nathalie.

"Oh, let her alone," cried the woman, impatiently. "I don't remember her."

"You must tell me. Was it Nina?"

The woman nodded.

"Nina de Favolles," she said. "How did you know?"

"She was my mother too! Marguerite—Marguerite—I am your sister!" shrieked Nathalie.

She fell on her knees, shivering and sobbing. The woman showed no emotion—not even surprise.

"Two days ago," she said, "I saw another sister of mine; I'm rich in relations all of a sudden."

"Do you mean Elizabeth?" groaned Nathalie.

"Yes, Elizabeth. Stop crying—get up; I hate such a noise."

Nathalie managed to rise and get to a sofa near.

"You saw Elizabeth?" she asked.

"Didn't I say so? My sister—Cranford's daughter—Darrell Vaughan's wife," returned the other.

Nathalie shrieked again.

"What did you say—what?"

"Darrell Vaughan's wife. What do you make a racket about that for?"

"Who said so?—who told you?"

"Lord!" exclaimed her sister, impatiently, paying no attention to Nathalie's face and voice of horror, "what a row you do make about every thing—you're so French."

"Elizabeth—Vaughan's wife!" repeated Nathalie, in a strangled tone.

"Any body would suppose you had made a discovery," retorted the other.

"I never knew—never—*O mon Dieu! O mon Dieu!* It can't be—I don't believe it. Who said so?"

"Here's a case!" said the woman, with a little laugh. "Never knew?"

"No. no! I tell you it can't be.

"Darrell Vaughan's wife, I say," repeated she. "They told me out there where she lives; no mistake whatever—Cranford's daughter, Darrell's wife."

"*O mon Dieu! mon Dieu!*" groaned Nathalie again.

She fell back half fainting; hysterics followed; but her companion stood looking on with a certain cold wonder in her face, not offering the least assistance.

"You needn't cry now," she said at length, as Nathalie's sobs began to lessen; "it's rather late for that."

"I tell you I never knew!" moaned Nathalie. "Years ago she was my friend, and I loved her so—oh, Elizabeth!"

"Oh, Nina de Favolles' daughter—Nina's daughter!" exclaimed the woman, with another low, dreadful laugh.

"Don't!—stop!" cried Nathalie. "Bring me some water. I'm choking—I shall die!"

"Not a bit of it—dying's not so easy," was the answer. "I'll find you some water though, for I want you to get your senses back. Oh, here's some wine on the table; drink this."

Vaughan had asked for wine, and it had been brought. The glass held to her lips was the one from which he had drank. Nathalie pushed it away, a sudden wrath springing up under her terror and confusion at the thought of him.

"Never waste good drink," said Marguerite, as the wine splashed over the floor. "I can't touch it myself—ten drops bring on the spasms: they're not like hysterics, I can tell you."

"Water—give me some water!" cried Nathalie.

She drank a little, had a recurrence of the hysterical sobs and suffocation, Marguerite standing by as unmoved as before.

"Sister Elizabeth," she said at last, "Darrell Vaughan's wife! I do think that completes the thing—and you didn't know!"

These words brought a hotter flash of anger into Nathalie's heart, and restored her strength.

"No; he deceived me, lied to me. Oh, the base wretch!"

"Why, of course he did," came the contemptuous reply; "what else would he do?"

"Oh, Marguerite, Marguerite!"

"Don't you call me that—I'm Milady; he gave me the name."

"Oh, she must be crazy, she must be!" moaned Nathalie, unconsciously thinking aloud.

"No," said Milady, perfectly unmoved. "Somehow even my devils seem to let me alone. I came to see what you were like, and you're my sister. Now I've my work to do; you can help, if you want to."

"Help in what? Oh, I never hated any body before. I want my revenge, my revenge!" gasped Nathalie through her set teeth.

"Do you? Oh, yes—you love him! I neither love nor hate—I'm a ghost. I have my work to do, and I must do it."

"Oh, I can't believe—I can't! Elizabeth his wife—oh, my presentiment that she laughed at. No, I don't believe it!"

"Well," said Milady, indifferently, "I don't see that it matters to me whether you believe it or not. I suppose I may as well go. I don't know why I wanted to show you where your road ends by the sight of such as me; but I did. It won't do any good—you'll keep on."

She made a movement to leave the room—Nathalie caught her dress.

"Don't go—I'll not let you go!" she cried. "I promised our mother—she was sorry; when she came to die, she told me—"

"Oh, I don't mind about her," interrupted Milady. "Hell must be a largish place—Nina and I sha'n't interfere."

"She repented—she was sorry, I tell you; don't say such awful things!" returned Nathalie.

The expression of dull surprise came back to Milady's face.

"Why, you're afraid of it," she said. "Are you hoping to get out of the business by a death-bed repentance too?"

"I'm not a bad woman!" exclaimed Nathalie, stamping her foot. "I never had a lover; oh, I was going away with him—I own that."

Milady broke in with another laugh.

"You'll go yet," she said. "I'll wager what you like he'll make you believe black's white; you'll go."

"I'd have given up every thing for him!" cried Nathalie. "But he has deceived me: he knew how I loved Elizabeth."

"I suppose his setting me on the road to hell doesn't count," said Milady, calmly.

"You didn't say—you didn't tell me—he—"

"It's such an old story now. I was the girl he fooled and ruined; I'm the woman he shut up in prison; and I've just been to see my child—mine and his."

"Oh, I shall go crazy, I shall!"

But Milady checked the hysterical outburst at once.

"If you keep that up, I'm off," she said, "and you'll not see me again. I can't bear a noise; it hurts me here," and she laid her hand on her heart.

"I won't, I won't," whimpered Nathalie, making, in this terrible crisis, the strongest effort at self-control that she had ever done in her whole life. "I hate him; oh, how I do hate him!" she exclaimed, rushing from grief and horror into a passion which seemed childish and weak beside Milady's stern composure. "What did you mean about work and my helping? He shut you up in prison. Oh, he shall suffer—"

"Stuff!" interrupted Milady. "What could I do, or you either, against this rich, respectable gentleman? If we had nothing better than that to go upon, you might whistle for your revenge, as you call it." Then she stopped to laugh—that dull, cold laugh, which still had something so savage in it that Nathalie trembled. "You wanting revenge! It sounds so droll! You're only a miserable, weak little butterfly, if you are Nina's daughter and Milady's sister."

Neither grief nor anger nor horror, though Nathalie was shaken to the very soul as nothing but her mother's death had ever moved her, could prevent her feeling the sting to her vanity which those words gave.

"You know nothing about me," she said, proudly; "I am a very famous woman. I have written books—"

"Oh, yes," interrupted Milady, "I know. When I first saw you, the night before last, with Darrell Vaughan, I asked about you. So you had to show your relationship to Nina and me by some sort of wickedness, though you're too childish to half understand."

"I don't know what you mean! Don't talk to me like that, Marguerite."

"Don't you call me Marguerite again," said her sister, with a look in her eyes which made Nathalie's blood run cold. "Mean? Nina ruined all the men she could, and I once kept a gambling-house! But, bad as we were, I don't suppose we did the harm you have by your wicked books; and never knew they were wicked—you ridiculous moth!"

"Oh, that's what Monsieur La Tour said, and Elizabeth," shuddered Nathalie. "I don't believe it!—I don't believe it!"

"Well, well," returned Milady, wearily. "It's of no consequence—a little wickedness more or less in the world; and probably nobody ever read your trash after all."

Nathalie would have expostulated further, but Milady held up her hand. She had seated herself, and was gazing straight before her, thinking deeply. She looked so like a representation of some merciless, passionless Fate, that Nathalie was more afraid of her than ever, and shrank into a corner of the sofa. Her eye was caught by a photograph of Vaughan that lay on the table. First she sobbed and moaned a little over her broken heart, then she snatched up the picture and tore it into fragments, with a passion which for an instant gave her childish face a painful resemblance to her mother's, and the stern, fixed countenance of Milady, who paid no attention to her outburst.

"Don't sit there like that—don't look so; you frighten me," cried Nathalie. "What are you thinking about?"

"Do you know Launce Cromlin, his cousin?" asked Milady.

"Yes—no," returned Nathalie, coloring. She

had met Launce once at a private exhibition of pictures in the Academy, and he had declined an introduction to her. "He's a brute," she added. "He was very rude to me."

"Wasn't anxious to know the famous book-writer and Darrell's friend," sneered Milady. "Well, it is he who must help in the work too." Then her voice changed. "A good man!—a good man! And the other, Carstoe; why, seeing them almost made me think there might be a heaven, and a God in it; I can believe in the other place easily enough. They took me out of prison. Launce Cromlin shall have his rights; yes, he shall. When is the other man coming back?"

"To-morrow night." She began to cry again, but very quietly; Milady's eyes kept her from giving way further. "Oh, I was to have sailed on Saturday—he was to follow; and to think of you and Elizabeth! It's too dreadful—too dreadful!"

"It is rather a mixing up of family affairs," said Milady. "You needn't snivel though. From your own account, you've escaped."

"I've told you the truth—indeed I have," pleaded Nathalie, humbly.

"I don't doubt it—you've no blood in your veins. Maybe you'd be a better woman if you were worse."

"Oh, how hard you are!" moaned Nathalie.

"Hard?" repeated Milady. "I've drank gall and fed on stones for a good many years now, my pretty authoress! Oh well, when one has been—loved by a man, and had a mother who repented—"

"She did repent," broke in Nathalie. "Oh, let me tell you—I promised her to tell if I ever found you. She said she'd haunt me unless I did."

"She won't come while I'm here," replied Milady, grimly.

"You were with rich people. She was poor just then—"

"You don't tell it right," said Milady, as Nathalie paused. "Nina sent me to a foundling hospital. Mrs. Rivers had a baby born dead. She'd lost so many, they knew she would die if she was disappointed then. Mr. Rivers went to the hospital and got me—Nina's cast-off child. Till I was seventeen I never knew I was not their own—never knew."

"Yes, yes," Nathalie said, eagerly. "Mamma kept track of you—she was so content to know you were happy, rich. Then, after all those years, she heard Mr. Rivers was dead, and you had quarreled with his wife, and were gone. Oh, she never had a moment's peace after that."

"They had a daughter born to them less than two years after they took me," said Milady. "But he loved me—yes, he did; loved me better than all his silly wife's children, for she had three. How she hated me! I wondered why

she was so different from other mothers; but I had him—I didn't care."

"She knew you weren't her child?"

"Yes; she found it out—hunted up every clew—got letters that fool Nina wrote Mr. Rivers about me. She held her peace, waiting for him to die; she knew he couldn't live many years. She had the whole story—Nina, Cranford's name. So I was seventeen, and he died. He never knew how she hated me; she was always artful as the devil, and I didn't complain."

"Ah mon Dieu!" sighed Nathalie.

"Then I had my part in his will—his daughter Marguerite. She flew at me before he was in his grave; told me who I was—that I should not have a penny; told the whole story out to any body that would listen. That's what came to me when I was seventeen."

Nathalie could only shiver and weep, motioning her to go on.

"Oh, the rest doesn't need words," said Milady. "Darrell Vaughan was their friend: I loved him. He took me when madame turned me out to starve. Every door was shut in my face—not a soul to help! He took me—he took me—I loved him."

There was something appalling in the coldness and unconcern of her speech; it frightened Nathalie past the relief of tears.

"A year of heaven—how a body sticks to that word!" laughed Milady. "Another year of being let gradually down into hell. He struck me once; that was just before the baby was born—we were in New Orleans. The night she was born he left me—left me without money even, for he'd been gambling, and had sold the jewels he had given me. He went away with another woman—that's all. Can you understand, you butterfly?"

"O mon Dieu! mon Dieu!"

"Deafer than a stone, my dear, even if He's any where about—deafer than a stone," said Milady.

"Ah, don't, don't! And where did you go? What did you do?"

"She's interested!" sneered Milady. "It's like a novel to her; she'd put it in a book, if only she had the power. You must drink fire and live among devils before your dainty pen can write my history, pretty dear."

"You frighten me so! Let me call Susanne! Don't you want to lie down?" sobbed Nathalie.

"No, my poppet," replied Milady, with another smile of woful derision. "I must be up and about my work."

"What are you going to do?"

"Only to tell," said Milady, drawing a paper from her bosom, and replacing it before Nathalie could move. "I want Launce Cromlin; I've found where he lives."

"Don't go; let me send for him; you're not fit."

Milady had risen, but a spasm seized her. She sank back on the sofa, her face livid, her eyes closed.

Nathalie thought she was dead, and shrieked till she brought in Susanne. The old woman caught sight of the figure lying on the couch—the room was dim with shadows, but a last ray of light flashed through the window, and fell upon the death-like countenance. Susanne shrieked louder than Nathalie had done, and dropped upon her knees.

"Madame's ghost! Madame's ghost!"

Nathalie started up in wilder alarm, glanced about, half expecting to see some phantom shape arise. Then she saw that Susanne's eyes were fixed on the prostrate form, and understood what had caused the exclamation.

"It's Marguerite. I've found her," she cried.

Susanne knew the history; had heard of Nathalie's promise, and understood the whole.

"Is she dead?" the old woman asked, in an awe-stricken tone, as she struggled up from her knees.

At the same instant Milady roused herself—the cramped hands relaxed, the features lost their convulsive rigidity.

"Who ever dies?" said she, answering Susanne in French. "Get me some water—some opium too. What a pair of fools you are, always expecting Nina's ghost; you must wait till I'm gone to see that. Nina de Favolles—Nina!" She began to laugh, to mutter more broken words. She seemed to realize that her mind was wandering. "Get the opium, you idiots!" she exclaimed.

The voice was so like the voice of her mother, the face tortured by pain so like Nina's face as they had seen it time and again in her paroxysms, that even Susanne was nearly out of her senses with fright, and Nathalie cowered down into her chair, and hid her eyes, utterly helpless. But Susanne recollected there was opium in the house—Darrell Vaughan had sent her for it one night with a physician's prescription that he always carried about him. Susanne had put the bottle away in case he should some time ask for it again. She ran up-stairs to fetch it—the necessity for action made her helpful once more.

She came back with the drug, and began to measure a spoonful into a tumbler in which she had put some water, but Milady snatched the *flacon* as Susanne stood by the sofa, and drained nearly the whole contents.

"*Sacré nom d'un chien!*" howled Susanne; "she's poisoned herself;" and started for the door, with a half-defined intention of seeking doctors and stomach-pumps. Nathalie dared not even look up; she only slipped out of her chair at Susanne's exclamation, and lay huddled on the floor. But a stern command from Milady stopped the old woman in her flight. It

was Nina's voice again—just the words Nina would have employed.

"Stay where you are, *fille d'un serpent !*"

"Won't it hurt you?" asked Susanne, creeping timidly back—she who had never feared any body till now.

"Hurt me? I shall need another such dose before morning," said Milady. "Where's that moth—that Nathalie?"

"Here I am—here," replied Nathalie, sitting up on the floor, fairly stunned by her varying emotions.

"I want Launce Cromlin—I can't go out—send for him," said Milady.

"Susanne will go. Where does he live?"

Milady gave the name of his hotel.

"Tell him Milady wants him," said she; "and be quick about it, old woman, for the opium may make me sleep. *Entends-tu, vieille sorcière ? Ne me regardes pas avec tes yeux hébétés — ça m'ennuie.*"

"She speaks French as well as we," muttered Susanne.

"Of course I do," returned Milady, still speaking in that language. "I was brought up to be a *grande dame* — more than you can say for Nina or your Nathalie either."

Then she reiterated her commands, and Susanne hastened away.

Milady lay back on the sofa, and spoke no more. Nathalie dared not stir nor address her. The room was quite dark, but she was near enough the sofa to catch the glare of Milady's eyes as she stared into the gloom. Nathalie recollected that she was absolutely alone in the house with the woman. She had intended to dine out, and the servants had taken a holiday. She pressed her hand hard against her mouth to repress a scream; she was afraid to anger Milady by a sound.

The room grew darker — the muslin window-curtains rustled in the breeze — the sound was like phantom footsteps in Nathalie's ears. If her mother's ghost should appear! She could see that face always on the sofa — such a terrible likeness to Nina's! She could not bear it, she should go mad!

"Marguerite!" she whispered. "Marguerite!"

There was no response, no sign that her call had been heard; she could see the great eyes staring always. If she only dared light the gas; but her fear of her companion, a horrible sensation that something supernatural was in the room with them, coming closer, closer, deprived her of all power to move. She heard the clock strike, then a silence and waiting that seemed endless, and still Susanne did not come. The clock beat the half-hour, and the slow stroke was like a heavy weight falling on her brain. The moon came up over the opposite houses, cast a long ray through the curtains, and lighted up the sofa and the motionless figure thereon, leaving the rest of the room in deeper darkness.

The window draperies rustled more like ghostly footsteps than before; the sigh of the low wind was like a ghostly voice whispering some terrible menace in an unknown tongue. If she could get away—only out on the steps, and sit there till Susanne appeared. But she could not move. She must cry out—no matter what Marguerite might do, her anger could not be so terrible as this stillness. She tried to shriek—her voice was gone; even in her own ears there sounded only a hoarse murmur which seemed no effort of hers.

And now memory after memory came up, stunned as she was. Her mother's death-bed—her husband's warnings. Oh, was she dying? was this hell already—the hell in whose existence she had hitherto been certain she had no belief? Terrible, denunciatory sermons her mother had made her read drifted through her mind—the awful papistical warnings to heretics and reprobates—and she was both. Elizabeth's face, like that of an accusing angel, rose. Her own mad theories, the absurd creeds which she had believed in and helped to promulgate, haunted her. Passages from her own books, that she had admired as brave and fearless to fling in the face of the world's prejudices, rang in her ears like a knell of doom.

She was dying, dying, and the warning her husband had uttered was being fulfilled!

"Darrell Vaughan! Darrell Vaughan!"

It was Milady's voice that broke the stillness. She had not moved; the lids had dropped partially over the dull glare of her eyes; the powerful narcotic had begun its effects.

"Marguerite! Marguerite!" called Nathalie, but it was only a strangled whisper still—no answer came.

Was Marguerite dead?—had she died with that name on her lips? Oh, would Susanne never come back? If she could only shriek for help; she heard some one passing along the street, singing as he went. With one last mighty effort she got upon her feet, and staggered toward the door, but the momentary strength gave way, and she fell senseless.

Half an hour later, old Susanne, entering the drawing-room, followed by Launce Cromlin, stumbled over Nathalie's prostrate form.

They lighted the gas, and looked about. Milady lay on the sofa in a deep lethargic slumber, from which no efforts could rouse her; and when Nathalie was brought back to consciousness, she was only capable of hysterical bursts of anguish, fright, and rage, by which Launce gathered enough to know that retribution was guiding two merciless women on Darrell Vaughan's track, and that he must act quickly if he would save the man from utter ruin and disgrace.

CHAPTER XL.

THE MILL OF THE GODS.

THE night has passed—another day gone—the twilight has come again.

Darrell Vaughan rings at the door of Nathalie's house—is admitted, and hastens into the drawing-room. He has sent word of his arrival—he has come to dine. Nathalie is waiting for him, beautifully dressed; her neck and arms bare; the plume of jewels that he gave her shining among her yellow curls.

"My beautiful—my star!" he cries, and hurries forward, bending on one knee to kiss her white hands, knowing how she likes effective scenes and exaggerated gallantry. "Why, you are superb; one would think you were dressed for a royal ball!" he adds, laughingly.

"Hasn't the king come again?" returns she, with easy playfulness, leaving her hands in his clasp.

"And you are glad to see me—you missed me?"

"I never missed you so much," she replies. "I never was so glad to see you—never!"

He wants to take her in his arms—to kiss the lips for whose sweetness his passionate soul is hungry. But Nathalie has never permitted this, so her repulse neither surprises nor angers him, only increases the wild tumult in his heart. He pours forth anew the story of his love, and Nathalie listens. She makes him vow and swear; she is teasing and capricious, tender and coquettish, all at once; and Vaughan declares that even if he had to relinquish his whole future, it would be well lost for her sake. He has forgotten the weary numbness which has oppressed him for days—making pleasure an impossibility, business a maze. Wine and opium have failed in their effects, but he has had recourse to hasheesh, and is full of life and nervous vitality to his very finger-tips.

Desperate, shaken as Nathalie is, sick and frightened by remorse, the details she has this day heard of Marguerite's life—shuddering at the very sight of this man—she finds a certain pleasure in acting the scene. She is waiting for Launce Cromlin—she knows he will come. Launce has been too wise to oppose the implacable women—careful not to awaken their suspicions, lest they should expose Vaughan before he can bring Elizabeth—he has no hope save in her.

But Launce does not appear. The dinner-hour has arrived—Vaughan will wonder; besides, her anger rushes up again, and she longs to begin the work.

"Do you like surprises?" she asks.

"Any you could give me would be pleasant," he replies.

She laughs; he sees her eyes glitter oddly.

"You are not well, I do believe," he says. "You are nervous; not like yourself, somehow."

and her laugh fairly
)ut Darrell Vaughan
About my surprise,"

inner. I have eaten

onger time than that,
ntirely deserted him.
on stimulants for a
thought of food does
nd abhorrence he has
vants champagne too.
he goes on his knees
Nathalie, laying her
—
rprise first," lifts her
!"
nt at the back of the
man dressed in black
as a ghost close to
:o his feet with an in-

this is Milady!" he
nd then Milady's an-

ll Vaughan."

his reeling faculties,

up that mad woman,
ory has she been tell-

es are so near giving
s put upon herself to
ux that she can only
ight against hysterical
sure adds to her ex-

) the other, Vaughan's
would come to most
[e does not think of the
ng some actual proof
the world—does not
ce. He only realizes
his patience, Milady
g creature, for whom
ice so much. One of
his impulse is to spring
n to the floor.
eyes," says Milady,
)arrell Vaughan; you

iently upon her.
she is a mad woman
m in California; you
may tell. Send for
y."
haps," says Milady.
he same game twice;
cal in my name now."
ten to me!" he ex-
k of her—of his love,

of his wild passion, which has never had its first fever slaked.

"I don't want to look at you, to hear your voice," sobs Nathalie, unable to be either heroic or dramatic. "I hate you!—I hate you! The whole world shall know—liar—forger—thief!"

The coarse instincts inherited from Nina de Favolles break out in Nathalie as they have never done in her whole life. She finds pleasure in screaming these denunciations in his ear. Compared to her, Milady's frozen impassibility is dignified and feminine.

But Vaughan does not half take in the sense of the added imprecations which Nathalie pours out in Nina's voice and with Nina's very gestures. She looks diabolically beautiful in her fury; he can only think of that—that and his desire to murder Milady and stifle Nathalie in his arms with hot kisses.

He makes a step toward her. Nathalie shrinks back, crying—

"I'll kill you if you touch me; I'll call the police."

"Nathalie!" he groans. "I love you!—I love you! I never loved any other woman—I care for nothing else in the world. Don't mind her—I tell you she's mad; I'll not give you up, I'll not!"

Furious as she is—in spite of her horror, of the newly awakened remorse for the errors of her life which have this day beset her—Nathalie is touched by the plea. He looks so handsome too—like a god, she thinks. No man can talk like him, no man's love be worth the having —and he is lost to her; a gulf, black as the horrors of the eternity in which she has suddenly begun to believe, looms between them. She loves him—she loves him: no, she hates him; but the excitement has gone from her life—the drama is played out; she is afraid of him—herself; the very fame of which she has been so absurdly vain has grown loathsome and abhorrent.

So Nathalie can find nothing better to do than to go into strong hysterics, struggling, fighting, striking at Vaughan as he tries to get to her, with some mad intention of carrying her off before she can get sense to resist; and Milady's icy voice rises again, making itself audible alike to Nathalie in her spasm and Vaughan in his insane whirl of resolve.

"What a family party!" she repeats. "Be quiet, both of you; I've had enough of this."

That cold, passionless voice—it has a power which stills them both, even at this instant. She looks so like a ghost, the voice is so dead. Had she indeed come back from the grave, they could not regard her with deeper horror.

Before either of the three can stir or speak again, the door opens. A carriage has driven to the house unheard by them; now the drawing-room door opens, and Elizabeth enters, followed by Mr. Carstoe and Launce Cromlin.

"I am not too late—oh, I thank God for it!" are the words that fall from Elizabeth's lips.

She walks directly up to Milady, who stands dumbly staring. Nathalie has retreated to a sofa. Darrell Vaughan's eyes wander from Carstoe to Launce with a look of murderous hate, then remain fixed by a kind of fascination upon the face of the woman who was once his wife.

"Marguerite," says Elizabeth, softly, "do you know who I am?"

"Yes, I know," replies Milady, in her defiant voice. "Crauford's daughter! There's Nina's girl yonder! Here's Milady, with the blood of both in her veins!"

"Marguerite—my sister!"

Elizabeth's tone is low, but it does not falter; it strikes with unearthly sweetness on the ear of every listener there, and her pale face is lighted with a look of tenderness and patience which renders its loveliness more than mortal.

"Marguerite—sister!"

Milady's defiant head droops; she sways back and forth, drops on her knees, and stares up in Elizabeth's face as a lost soul in purgatory might stare at an angel suddenly descended into the midst of the darkness with words of heavenly comfort.

"Don't!" she gasps, in an awful whisper. "Pretty soon you will make me believe in God Almighty."

None of the others utter a sound—even Nathalie is dumb. As for Darrell Vaughan, the numbness in his brain, the ringing in his ears, has returned. He can only support himself against the table, and wonder vaguely what is to come next.

"You will believe," Elizabeth answers; "it is for that He has brought us to this hour."

Milady gazes from one to another, pointing at Elizabeth with her wasted hand. Her face has lost its icy coldness: it is troubled, shaken. She looks as she used in the prison, when wondering if she were indeed mad.

"Crauford's daughter," she says, in a difficult, broken tone.

"And your sister," adds Elizabeth.

Milady struggles up from her knees, and looks round the group—then her eyes go back to Elizabeth.

"Would you take me home? would you not be ashamed—you that are grand and respectable—not like her, she's nothing to lose" (pointing to Nathalie)—"would you?"

"Yes."

Again Milady's eyes wander to the faces about her, with the same expression of troubled wonder—come back once more to Elizabeth with a wistful eagerness that makes her whole countenance look younger.

"I wouldn't go," she says, abruptly. "I'm not human, but I seem to have a touch of humanity about me—I wouldn't go."

She tries to shrink away; Elizabeth takes her hand, and holds it fast.

"Marguerite," she says, "you have a paper that I want you to give me."

Milady wrenches her hand free, the dull fire kindles anew in her eyes, the look of dogged resolution hardens her features.

"I had forgotten every thing," she mutters. Then she points to Darrell Vaughan, and adds, in a louder tone—"Yes, a paper; he and all of you shall hear."

The strange numbness is growing stronger through Vaughan's whole frame; only something in his temples seems to beat and turn like the roll of a noisy wheel. He feels about for a chair, and sits down.

"So this is a plot!" he exclaims, "and you're all in it; much good may it do you."

"Marguerite," continues Elizabeth, regardless as the others that he has spoken, "give me the paper—we don't want to hear it."

Milady looks confused and troubled; her eyes wander toward Cromlin, and her face grows determined again.

"I must tell," she says. "I don't want vengeance! I'm a ghost, but I must tell."

"How much longer is this little scene with that mad woman to go on?" Vaughan breaks in. "Carstoe, you used not to be quite a fool; you must know this is nonsense! As for my precious cousin there, of course I understand his little game."

Neither of the men appears to hear. Vaughan clenches his hands over the arms of his chair to hold himself still. He can not even venture to go on speaking; he feels his utterance become thick, and that remorseless wheel turn faster and faster in his brain.

"You're fond of calling people mad, Darrell Vaughan," cries Nathalie, with a hysterical laugh and sob. "You were going to shut your wife up! He was, Elizabeth! He told me his wife was a monomaniac, and needed to be confined. Oh, I didn't know it was you—I didn't know it was you!"

"Hush, Nathalie," returns Elizabeth.

The wretched creature cowers back into her place, and weeps silently. For the first time in her life a sense of shame oppresses her—she is positively afraid to meet Elizabeth's eyes.

"She's only a silly little moth," says Milady; "she's not even what they call wicked, you know."

"I know," replies Elizabeth.

"She believes me—she believes me!" shrieks Nathalie. "Oh, I can die contented now."

Vaughan laughs. Nathalie's sobs redouble, and she moans incoherent words of grief and passion.

"Be still!" orders Milady, sternly, and the weak, half-made creature buries her head in the sofa pillows, and presses her handkerchief against her mouth, frightened into a fresh effort at self-control.

"Give me the paper, Marguerite," repeats Elizabeth, in the same low, gentle voice, which has such a ring of command in spite of its persuasiveness.

"No!" answers Milady. "It must go to the lawyers — I can't give it up — I must do my work; it has been set for me—I must do it."

"There is no need now, Marguerite."

"Yes, there is; you don't know! It is the will—the will Darrell Vaughan thought he had burned: it gives all the fortune to him" (pointing to Launce); "he must have his rights."

"You set of infernal liars!" exclaims Vaughan, starting out of his chair. "Pretty instruments you choose, Madame Elizabeth—a street-walker, a convict — to help you and Launce to my money. Launce, who is your—"

Cromlin strides forward—Mr. Carstoe pushes him back, and himself stands over Vaughan.

"One word more, and I'll call in the officers myself," he says. "That angel yonder is trying to save you—one word, and I will take your punishment into my own hands. I tell you it is of no use to struggle—all is exposed."

The old man positively looks grand in his stern indignation. Vaughan falls back in his chair—not from fear—he can stand no longer; the beat, beat of that wheel leaves him half deaf to Carstoe's words.

"I'm just what he says," pursues Milady, looking at Elizabeth; "he made me so. I've been a convict — he shut me up — he stole the jewels—he came to my room—drugged me—"

"We know, Marguerite," breaks in Launce.

"But you must have your rights," she goes on, in the same passionless tone. "The fortune is yours—"

"I have had moral proof of that for years," Launce interrupts again; "it does not matter."

Elizabeth has not once glanced toward her former husband. Now she turns—it is with a great effort, as one can see—and walks toward him. Even the horror and dread leave her face as she looks into his, altered greatly in these weeks, and comprehends as none of the others do the possible effects of this scene upon his broken frame. There is nothing save pity in her eyes now. He tries to meet her glance, but when he sees that look his eyes sink.

"Mr. Vaughan," she says. "Marguerite is right. You must make over to your cousin the fortune left by your uncle; it is his."

"I don't want it; let him keep the whole," cries Launce.

Elizabeth silences him with a gesture.

"Will you do this, Mr. Vaughan?" she asks.

He gathers up the remnants of his failing strength in a mad passion, that for a moment overcomes the weakness, the intolerable physical agony.

"No!" he fairly shouts. "Oh, you devil; if I had only murdered you long ago!"

Nathalie shrieks aloud at his face and voice, but the others are unmoved.

"Madam," says Mr. Carstoe, addressing Elizabeth, "you must allow Marguerite to tell her story; nothing else will convince that wretched man of his madness in hesitating."

"Tell it, then, Marguerite," rejoins Elizabeth, wearily, and she moves away from Vaughan's side.

Even in the excitement of this moment, Mr. Carstoe and Launce are both conscious of thinking it is like seeing a good angel turn from a sinner's presence, warned that intercession is no longer possible.

"I knew he forged Launce Cromlin's name," says Milady, slowly. "It was before he took me to New Orleans. He was tired of me; he struck me once, but I couldn't tell of him. I have the papers where he used to practice writing the name. Long afterwards, in California, Jem Davis, the man that helped, confessed when he was dying; it's all written down."

She speaks in a chill, mechanical fashion, without the slightest trace of emotion.

Vaughan has to make a great effort to listen and understand. The numbness increases—the wheel turns faster in his brain.

"You fools!" he calls, hoarsely. "That thing's chatter is no evidence; you can't make a witness of her."

"But the written documents in her possession, with signatures which can be sworn to, are evidence—you know that," replies Mr. Carstoe.

"She has none!" cries Vaughan.

"Davis's confession is in my hands," returns the lawyer. "She gave it to your cousin last night. He tried to get the will, tried in every way to save you, but she would not consent. You intercepted the check your uncle sent to Cromlin; you altered it to fifteen thousand dollars—forged Cromlin's name. Davis presented it at the bank; the teller was your accomplice. Davis had three thousand dollars for his share; he was in difficulty, and wanted to get off to Mexico. He swore to all this on his death-bed. You see we know every thing."

"You are an old villain! you are their tool!" thunders Vaughan.

"As a last resource," pursues Mr. Carstoe, "that much-injured lady, who was once your wife, has come to plead for you and with you. For God's sake, don't render her interposition useless—don't force the rest of us to act."

"I don't want any preaching!" cries Vaughan, shaking his fist aimlessly in the air. "I'll fight it out!—I'll fight it out! It is a plot—a trick; the woman is hired by my wife and my wife's lover."

But even Launce can not be roused beyond pity now.

"'Marguerite," says Mr. Carstoe, "let me look at the signatures to that will."

She hesitates.

"You can keep it in your hands; I only want to assure this man of the folly of more words."

Milady draws the paper from her bosom — three fragments rather.

"He tore it," she explains.

Mr. Carstoe examines the pieces; fits them together; Milady not trying to prevent his taking them.

"I can swear to the signatures," he says. "I can bring twenty men in Moysterville to swear to that of Mr. Vaughan. The witnesses, Mrs. Simpson and Anthony Turner, will swear to their own. Mrs. Simpson always assured me that she signed three documents; one was the codicil made out to go with the other will."

"The other will!" repeats Vaughan, with a laugh. "You're a fool after all, Carstoe; how many could there have been? I don't suppose you, at least, will attempt to deny that the will we found in my uncle's desk, giving me the fortune, was a genuine one?"

The sudden loophole which has suggested itself clears Vaughan's brain enough for him to speak collectedly. It is a tremendous effort, and in spite of himself his head sinks back against his chair as he ends.

"It was a genuine document," Mr. Carstoe replies; "it was a will made long before his death; the codicil, I suppose, was added when he learned that Cromlin was innocent in the forgery matter."

"There," mutters Vaughan, "you have upset the plot yourself."

"The codicil was drawn up," continues Mr. Carstoe, "when Mr. Vaughan's lawyer discovered that Launce Cromlin could not have forged the check, because proof had come that, for six weeks before its date and six weeks after, he was unable to use his hand. He had had a compound fracture of the right arm; that came out in a chance conversation with the physician who attended him: you all know that as well as I. Now I had supposed that Mr. Vaughan then made a will dividing the fortune equally between his two nephews; but I found the codicil attached to the will drawn up long before, when he first believed Cromlin guilty — the will by which you, Darrell Vaughan, inherited the property."

Vaughan is too dizzy to speak, but his face lights with triumph. His head is so confused that every thing still seems secure to him.

"I can tell," says Milady; "do you want me to?"

"Yes—every thing," returns Mr. Carstoe.

"When Jem Davis made his confession," she begins again, in the same slow, methodical fashion, "I took the paper he had signed in the presence of a clergyman, and went to Moyster-

ville. I was alive then, and I wanted my revenge"—she looked at Elizabeth as she said this—"but I'm a ghost now: I don't hate him; but I have to tell."

"Yes, Marguerite," Elizabeth whispers.

"I went to old Mr. Vaughan," pursues Milady. "He was ill, but he was in his library. I gave him Jem's confession; then I told him all about myself. He was very good to me—"

Her voice falters slightly, and she breaks off for an instant, then continues as quietly as ever—

"It was a dreadful blow to know about Darrell; but he didn't forget to be good to me. When he could talk, he showed a will he had made a few days before, giving the property equally to those two there, and he read me the codicil about Elizabeth; it was written to go with that will."

Even Mr. Carstoe looks perplexed now, and watches her narrowly, to see if there is the least sign of mental aberration, and Vaughan laughs again.

"The codicil was fastened to the will by three seals," says Milady. "Mr. Vaughan broke them off, then he destroyed the will—I put it in the fire for him myself."

The room has been still enough before; it grows strangely silent now—even Vaughan does not stir.

"He told me to come back to him the next day—he meant to. help me.—help *me!* So I went; he was in his library again, but very weak. He had had Mr. Smith there; he showed me the new will, leaving every thing to Launce Cromlin —this will," and she holds it up.

"And therein he tells the reasons," adds Mr. Carstoe. "What more, Marguerite?"

"He put this will, giving the money to Cromlin, back in his cabinet," says Milady. "He saved the codicil because he said he had not decided how to alter it, but it must apply to Launce alone. He showed me the letter he had that morning written to Elizabeth—he called her my sister; that letter was for Launce to give her. He said that he had put the first will of all—the one by which Darrell inherited—away where he could not find it. His head was bad, and he could not remember—he should hunt for it later; but it was no matter, because the last one would hold good."

She has been standing all the while—she looks about now wearily—Elizabeth draws a chair forward, and seats her in it.

Darrell is trying to speak, to collect his thoughts to find some hope of escape. But he can only lean back, faint under the dull thud in his brain, which Milady's voice pierces like a cold wind.

"Then, just as he had begun to talk again about me," she goes on, "he fell on the floor in a fit. I ran to call help, and met Mrs. Simpson. Then I went away—I had no right to stay."

"I wonder if she has almost finished?" they

hear Vaughan mutter—not in defiance or scorn. But no one comprehends that it is just bodily pain which wrings out the words—her voice hurts.

"The next day Darrell Vaughan came," says Milady. "I stayed in Moysterville—something kept me. I watched the house—I watched him. I learned how to get into it day or night by a back door—down through the cellar, and up into a closet where they kept the wood for the library fire; the closet had a door into the library."

"Oh, that woman!" mutters Vaughan. "I always wondered how she got there—why, I thought it was her ghost at first!"

"The night Mr. Vaughan died I went to my hiding-place. I'd seen Darrell at the papers before—I knew he would destroy the will now; I thought I could call some one in time. I saw Darrell at the cabinet; I stood behind him without his knowing I was there. He had found both wills, and the copy of Jem's confession—Mr. Vaughan had told me to keep the original myself for the present; he meant to confront me with Darrell—was expecting him every day."

She stops to rest for an instant—nobody moves.

"Darrell fastened the codicil to the old will—I don't know why."

"Because I had read it—had told him so," says Mr. Carstoe.

"He tore the new will, got up, threw it on the fire. I was going to stop him; but there was a noise overhead—he ran out of the room. I picked the will off the coals—the fire was almost out. I hid that and Jem's confession in the secret drawer of the cabinet—old Mr. Vaughan had opened it when he was hunting for the first will—he said nobody knew the secret or could discover it. Then I threw another paper on the fire."

"Why did you hide them?" asks Mr. Carstoe.

"Because I wanted to stay and see Darrell, and I was afraid he might suspect, and get the will away."

"Yes; go on."

"He came back—he saw me—he did choke me, and drag me about the room; but he noticed the ashes on the hearth, and thought the will was burned."

There is a sound from Vaughan, more like the growl of a wild animal than a moan, yet it is a sound of suffering. Every body except Milady starts forward; he waves them off—struggles fiercely for strength, and sits upright.

"Go on, you devil!" he says.

"I told him it was I who had come to his uncle—I who had done the work; that I would defeat him yet. He beat me—he tried to bargain with me; finally, he told me to do my worst, and he opened the glass door that led onto the veranda, and pushed me out."

"There she was in my hands, and I didn't kill her!" mutters Vaughan's voice again.

"I was ill for several days—he had hurt me; and besides it was raining that night, and I caught cold. I knew the funeral was over, and the will read, and Darrell had the fortune. The first day I could get out I went to the pawnbroker's to get some money on a ring, for I had none left. I saw Darrell and Mr. Carstoe in the bank door. I meant to tell Mr. Carstoe; but I dared not then—I wanted to get the will first. Then towards sundown Darrell came to my room—I had gone to bed again. He talked softly—pretended he was willing to help me, and I acted as if I believed, for I wanted to fool him till I got the will. Then he gave me the hasheesh—he had taught me to crave it—and I was in great pain. Then I went off—off—oh, I don't know where; and when I woke up the officers were in the room—and that's all."

She stops abruptly, and sits quite still.

Elizabeth looks at Mr. Carstoe; he comprehends that she wishes him to finish as quickly as possible what remains to do. He seats himself at the table near Vaughan, and writes rapidly for a few minutes—Vaughan watching him with his insane eyes.

"This is what you have to sign," says Mr. Carstoe; "then, for the sake of others—not for yours—this secret remains among us here." He reads aloud:

"MR. CARSTOE,—A will of my uncle's, the late Edgar Vaughan, has been discovered, which gives the whole of his fortune to my cousin, Launce Cromlin, not even excepting the sum named in the codicil. I am ready at once to restore to my cousin the whole property, including interest for the time that I have held it in my possession."

"I wish—" begins Launce, but Mr. Carstoe checks him.

"I can compound with my conscience no further than this," says the lawyer, firmly. "Darrell Vaughan, will you sign this paper, or will you have the whole matter made public from this night?"

Again that sound from his lips, half moan, half snarl, like a wild beast at bay. His glazed eyes wander to Elizabeth, on to Cromlin. Mr. Carstoe holds the pen toward him—he pushes it away. A look is exchanged between them, defiant on his part, stern and determined on the lawyer's. He snatches the pen, and writes his name.

"Curse you!" he cries, starting up. "Curse you all. Oh, if I—"

The words die in a fresh groan; he totters back, slips from the chair before Mr. Carstoe can catch him, and falls upon the floor, still and white, with his glazed, senseless eyes staring blindly upward.

Before Elizabeth and Launce can reach Mr. Carstoe's side, Milady springs forward, pushes him off, and drops on her knees by the prostrate form, moaning—

"I loved him; nobody else ever did; I loved him!"

She believes that the soul has gone out from that motionless shape. Feeling, womanly instincts come back in this awful moment, and the wild love of her girlhood comes too. Rooted out as it has so long seemed — murdered, forgotten—back it comes now.

"I loved him—I always loved him! Nobody else ever did—nobody! Oh, my Darrell, my Darrell!"

She sways forward till her head rests on his breast; one convulsive quiver shakes her limbs, then all is still.

The first thought in the minds of the horrified watchers is that the betrayer and the betrayed lie there dead together.

CHAPTER XLI.

FIVE YEARS.

MANY weeks passed before Marguerite was released, but there were kind friends about her to the last. She died holding Elizabeth's hand in hers, able to trust that He who had pardoned the Magdalene could forgive her.

"When you called me sister, I believed in Him," she said to Elizabeth; and Elizabeth felt with tears of thankfulness that she could never again call her life utterly barren of fruit.

Of course, Nathalie took to her bed at the first, and was as helpless as possible; but she grew rather ashamed of that, and though a good deal afraid of Elizabeth and Mr. Carstoe, and much in awe of Marguerite herself, she did make an effort; and the lessons of those days had an effect even upon her frivolous nature.

While Elizabeth was occupied with Milady, remaining most of the time in Nathalie's house, Launce Cromlin assumed the care of Darrell Vaughan. He had been carried to his own home, senseless, mindless, unable to move. He would remain so, perhaps, to the end.

So Milady was buried, and the new duty of Elizabeth's life began.

She did not see Launce again. He sailed for Europe and the East on the day before her return to that dwelling whose threshold she had thought never to cross again.

All the business arrangements had been settled by Mr. Carstoe so quietly that the world had slight opportunity even to weave a romance in regard to the newly discovered will. The vast fortune which Vaughan had accumulated during these years of course fell under Elizabeth's management. She could not dispose of the principal, but the whole income went toward charities—it seemed to her that she thus offered a little atonement for him.

Nathalie was going back to France—back to Monsieur La Tour. A spasm of repentance had seized her. She rushed into it in the same headlong fashion which had always characterized her proceedings.

"I'll buy up every book I have written, and burn the whole," she said to Elizabeth, and she was encouraged to do so.

Perhaps it proved a shock to her vanity, crushed as she was, to find this "buying up" a less expensive matter than she expected. The editions of her works had been small, and the publishers did not place any exorbitant value upon the stereotyped plates in their possession.

As the autumn came on there was a change in Darrell Vaughan. He was able to sit up—to be wheeled into the air; but he would never walk, and his mind was hopelessly wrecked. The physicians decided that the quiet of the country would be best for him; so during the golden October days Elizabeth took him away to Tanglewood.

"You used to talk a great deal about finding your real home," said Aunt Janet; "have you found it now?"

"It was too plainly shown for me to doubt," Elizabeth answered.

For many a day there was a cold wonder in Aunt Janet's eyes as she watched her niece, but she softened gradually under the influence of Elizabeth's example.

So the months passed—grew into years. I shall not tell you that Elizabeth was happy in her sacrifice—that she was even content. Often the struggle was almost as hard as in the old days—but peace came.

She had Mr. Carstoe's companionship, and Meg was like a little sunbeam to her. She had constant occupation too, for Vaughan could not bear her out of his sight. During the later time occasional gleams of memory came back, but none that were dark or unpleasant. The doctors thought it probable that he would live to old age; and it was the feeling that she had found the work which might last her whole life that helped Elizabeth to grow patient and settled—to feel at last a mournful but serene quiet in the thought that great changes, whether of joy or sorrow, were over for her.

So three whole years went by; and when she least expected it, Elizabeth's long watch ended. Darrell Vaughan roused suddenly out of the stupor which usually oppressed him. For a day or two memory and bodily strength seemed returning; then as suddenly he failed, and the flickering gleam of intelligence faded. Mr. Carstoe and Elizabeth were with him. He died as a child might, vacantly repeating the prayer Elizabeth whispered; and she could remember that "Our Father," on whom he called at her bidding, is infinite in His mercy.

Now five whole years have gone, and in the bright autumn weather Elizabeth has once more sought the beautiful Swiss valley, and for a time taken up her abode in the quaint old dwelling where she had spent some of the pleasantest weeks of her girlhood.

Miss Janet was urgent that she should have at least a twelvemonth's change and relaxation, so Elizabeth has come away. Meg is with her, growing a tall, handsome girl, loving, gentle, and affectionate—a constant source of comfort to Elizabeth.

Darrell Vaughan had few relatives; they were men upright and just as Launce Cromlin. When Vaughan died, the whole of his great fortune was still devoted to the uses to which Elizabeth consecrated it during the past years; the heirs signified to her through Mr. Curstoe their desire for this.

Launce Cromlin has won great fame during these years. Elizabeth hears of his success, and is glad; but even since her freedom no communication has passed between them.

Elizabeth hears of Nathalie too. Poor Nathalie! she can not help smiling when she thinks of her. Excitement Nathalie must have. While Monsieur La Tour lived, she found it by worrying him with her penitence and remorse. Three scenes each day and two in the night were the least Nathalie could consent to make; and Susanne grew so weary of so much repentance and goodness that she took her money and went to live in Brittany.

Nathalie has gone through many phases of religious belief since she was a widow. For a while she remained a fervent Papist—on one occasion undertook a pilgrimage in the dress of a Dominican nun, with sandals on her feet, and looked in the newspapers to be horrified by a glowing account of her adventures, and wept bitterly when she found none. She wearied of Papacy after that, gave up all idea of entering a convent, fell in with some new sects, and for a season was a prophet and at the head of a society where all the members worked with their hands, and fed on vegetables, and saw visions, and were generally very uncomfortable. Finally, Nathalie had a vision which warned her to set out for Jerusalem to convert Jews and Moslems. On the road she encountered some dignitaries of the Greek Church, and became a proselyte at once, and, not venturing longer to believe in visions, relinquished her work of conversion. After that, she thought of becoming a missionary to some Cannibal island, but recollected the long sea-voyage necessary to reach such a spot, and decided she was not really "called."

About the time of Darrell Vaughan's death Elizabeth heard from her in Geneva; she was living in that dull town, and had become a Calvinist. She sent Elizabeth several brimstone tracts and threatening Sunday-school books of her own composition. She added warning letters, in which she urged Elizabeth to renounce her errors of faith, and follow in Calvin's footsteps, if she would save her soul alive.

Elizabeth has lately seen her—she stopped at Geneva on her way to Clarens. Nathalie has married a Geneva preacher, one Monsieur Fantal—a little, bony man, the ugliest of his race, but an earnest and sincere one. Nathalie wears striped dresses of coarse worsted, has cut her hair short, is prematurely thin and old. She hates the change, and cries over the loss of her beauty, and is terrified at her own regret. Her faith is as full of brimstone as her tracts, and she hates that too, yet is afraid that, in spite of her efforts, her hard work, she is among the luckless wretches "fore-ordained to damnation," and sometimes has hysterics in the midst of the prayer-meetings. But Monsieur Fantal is very patient with her, and she has great influence as the minister's wife in her little circle. She is always trying to drag sinners into the fold—upon one occasion absolutely attacking the Roman Catholic bishop on the steps of his own chapel. Poor Nathalie! Elizabeth smiles and sighs as she thinks of her, but hopes the restless soul may at last reach the dawn—at least she wants to do right.

So in the twilight of an October evening Elizabeth sits under the great willow by the lake shore, and looks out at the mountains, still glorious with heavenly light. Meg, seated in a window of the villa, sings softly as she dreams the dreams of budding girlhood, and her voice reaches Elizabeth, and mingles pleasantly with her meditations.

She is thinking of the past, as she may do now—thinking a little, too, of the future, but trying to avoid fancies and hopes—content to leave it all in God's hands.

The twilight deepens; the last glow fades from the mountain-tops. The waters ripple past, shadowy and dark, till on a sudden the moon comes up, and tinges their sweep with her yellow splendor. Meg has ceased to sing; the low breeze has died; the very waves are still. Elizabeth thinks the whole scene a type of the great silence and repose which have come into her life; but she will not be saddened or impatient. A step sounds on the greensward—a voice calls her name. She looks up—Launce Cromlin is beside her.

THE END.

www.ingramcontent.com/pod-product-compliance
Lightning Source LLC
Chambersburg PA
CBHW030552040726
47497CB00008B/2696